CAGED

The new Detective Sam Becket novel

Life is good in the Becket household. Sam is planning a surprise for Grace's birthday, Cathy's back from California and Grace is seeing patients again. And then the killings begin. A newly-wed couple is found horribly slain in Miami Beach. As Detective Sam Becket's investigation gets into stride, a second couple is abducted. Soon, couples all over Miami-Dade are fearing for their lives, and Sam and the squad are battling an unseen enemy, against whom no one is safe...

CAGED

Hilary Norman

Severn House Large Print
Lonodn & New York

This first large print edition published 2012
in Great Britain and the USA by
SEVERN HOUSE PUBLISHERS LTD of
9-15 High Street, Sutton, Surrey, SM1 1DF.
First world regular print edition published 2010 by
Severn House Publishers Ltd., London and New York.

British Library Cataloguing in Publication Data

Norman, Hilary.
  Caged. -- (Sam Becket mysteries)
  1. Becket, Sam (Fictitious character)--Fiction.
  2. Police--Florida--Miami--Fiction. 3. Detective and
  mystery stories. 4. Large type books.
  I. Title II. Series
  823.9'14-dc23

  ISBN-13: 978-0-7278-7996-7

Severn House Publishers support The Forest Stewardship Council
[FSC], the leading international forest certification organisation. All
our titles that are printed on Greenpeace-approved FSC-certified paper
carry the FSC logo.

MIX
Paper from
responsible sources
FSC® C018575

Printed and bound in Great Britain by the
MPG Books Group, Bodmin, Cornwall.

For Helen and Neal

ACKNOWLEDGMENTS

My grateful thanks to the following: Howard Barmad; Jennifer Bloch; Batya Brykman; Isaac and Evelyne Hasson; Jonathan Kern (for everything, as always); Christian LeVan, BVM&S, MRCVS; massive thanks again to Special Agent Paul Marcus and to Julie Marcus (couldn't do it without the 'real' Sam and Grace); Wolfgang Neuhaus; James Nightingale; Helmut Pesch; Sebastian Ritscher; Helen Rose; Rainer Schumacher; Jeanne Skipper; Amanda Stewart; Dr Jonathan Tarlow; Euan Thorneycroft; Ruth Wilson.

They lay on the ground, limbs entwined, joined together.

Like a couple in the midst of sex.

Pale, though. Not quite alabaster, yet almost sculpted looking.

A work of beauty only a little spoiled

By terror.

And by violent death.

They lay together much as they used to.

Before.

ONE

February 6

The keeper was down on the floor just outside the plastic walled cage.

Best place to be, spending quiet time with them.

Isabella the Seventh was out of the cage, nestling on the keeper's stomach.

All rats had their own characteristics, but this Isabella liked snuggling close, had grown to enjoy human touch and skin.

Soon, the keeper knew, the doe would be in oestrus, and then, like her female predecessors, she would become quite wonderful to watch, all squeaking, urgent vibration. And then, at the slightest touch by Romeo the Fifth, her ardent buck, Isabella's tail would lift and her whole furry little backside would rise, exposing that secret, tiny part of her as it changed colour, turned sweet violet, and opened to him.

Her keeper found this beautiful.

Her buck liked it too. Though Romeo, like any number of healthy, horny males, would probably willingly have mounted a whole row of females if they'd displayed their little primed fannies to him.

There being nothing else of significance to

report today, the keeper picked up Isabella, grasped her firmly around her small body, took her temperature, measured her heart rate and, finding all fine and dandy, made basic notations on the observation chart and put her back down.

The doe nestled back down on the warm human flesh, and the keeper stroked her head.

Rats were nice creatures, misunderstood by many. The keeper had studied and cared for them for a while now, liked them, was both touched and impressed by them because they were as individual as dogs and cats. And humans.

They liked to eat, play, fight and fuck.

And some liked to kill.

They had their limitations, mind, needed careful control. And after a while, when there was nothing new left to observe about them, the keeper grew bored and replaced them. One Isabella giving way to another, ditto Romeo.

Not a long life, even by rat standards, but a comfortable, perhaps even a happy one in a home complete with cedar shavings, cans for hiding, boxes for nesting and good, nutritious food.

A cut-price miniature, in fact, of Rat Park, the Eden built in the 1970s by a Canadian shrink named Alexander, who'd conducted drug-addiction experiments on rats and found that the creatures didn't like being high, preferred plain water to morphine and sugar-laced stuff.

Rats weren't dumb.

No way.

Isabella the Seventh stirred and began to tread

a path south.

'Not today,' the keeper told her, lifting her gently again and stroking her cute little nose.

This Isabella had always been special.

When her time came, the keeper would end her life kindly.

Not yet, though.

Romeo hadn't finished with her yet.

TWO

Life was good in the Becket household.

Everyone safe, healthy and content in the small white Bay Harbor Island house that Grace Lucca Becket had lived in for some years before she'd met and married her husband, Sam.

It was the kind of ease that made Grace just a little nervous.

She hadn't been superstitious in the past, but over time it had crept up on her, and sometimes she even knocked on wood, surreptitiously, so no one else would notice, except Sam, of course, who noticed everything.

That's what you got, being married to a police detective.

You got a lot of other things, too, when the detective was Sam Becket. Like all kinds of love and caring and kindness, and not just directed at you and your baby son and grown-up daughter, but also at the other people who mattered in your world.

You also got tension.

Every time he stepped out of the door to head for work.

Because even in a jurisdiction as civilized as Miami Beach, a Violent Crimes detective all too often had to deal with madness and evil, so you just never knew.

But for now, right now, life was good, the dark times behind them.

Knock on wood.

Joshua was seventeen months old, a walking, clambering, blessedly easy-going, endlessly inquisitive little boy who was finding potty-training entertaining and had more than twenty clearly comprehensible words in his vocabulary. Grace had begun seeing patients again in her role as a child and adolescent psychologist; and Cathy, their twenty-two-year-old adopted daughter, had come home in time for Christmas after nine months away in California, so the whole family had been together for once for the holidays – even Grace's sister Claudia, with husband Daniel and their boys, who'd seemed good too, healing from their shaky spell.

And then no sooner had Cathy come home, than she'd packed up all her belongings and moved out again, this time perhaps for keeps. And neither Grace nor Sam had ever imagined feeling happy about that, but Cathy's return had coincided with Sam's younger brother Saul finding his own apartment in Sunny Isles Beach, and asking Cathy if she'd like to share. And Saul was doing well enough with his furniture-making to be able to afford the rent, and the legacies that Judy Becket had left him and Sam three years ago – startling them both – had given him a solid base, and the deal had been that as soon as Cathy had a job she'd contribute, but until then, Saul was content with the status quo.

Uncle and niece on paper, but with only a year between them, he and Cathy were more like brother and sister or, better yet, best friends. When Dr David Becket and his late wife Judy had adopted Sam, an orphaned eight-year-old African-American, they could never have imagined what a fine family custom they were initiating. All those different heritages stitched together like the best kind of American quilt, Cathy as integral a part of that as Joshua.

The question, after her time away, was what Cathy was going to do.

Not go back to university to resume her social work studies.

'It's not just the bad memories,' she'd told them right after her return. 'I think I'd feel like I was going backward.'

'So are you going to focus on athletics?' Sam had asked, because running had always been Cathy's great passion, and she'd written them about how much she'd loved her time as a track coach's aide in Sacramento.

'I'm not good enough to compete,' Cathy said. 'And teaching would mean going back to college, too.'

She'd suggested soon after New Year's that

15

she might come and work for her mother, and for a moment Grace's heart had leapt, but she'd suppressed that, because even if she hadn't already had a fine helper in her office, Grace felt that Cathy, having established her freedom, might find it restrictive, even smothering.

'I doubt that,' Cathy had said. 'But anyway, if you ever need more help...'

'I'd ask you in a heartbeat,' Grace had told her.

And then she'd asked if Cathy had anything else in mind, any ambitions, even just a stirring of something.

'As a matter of fact,' Cathy had said, slowly, 'there is something. Though you guys might think it's a little out of left field.'

'We won't think anything,' Grace had said, 'unless you tell us.'

THREE

February 7

Just after eight fifteen on Saturday morning, Detectives Sam Becket and Alejandro Martinez and a team of Crime Scene technicians were standing in a large backyard behind Collins Avenue.

Not so much a backyard, really, as a rather once-handsome garden, its lawn a little overgrown, its topiary bushes looking in need of a barber's care and its jardinières empty.

The three-storey mansion to which it belonged had formerly been an art gallery. The plaque on the wall beside the entrance still declared it to be the Oates Gallery of Fine Arts, but the old grey stone house was locked up, shutters covering the windows, no signs of life or light from within, the mailbox on the sidewalk sealed.

It might have looked peaceful but for the police presence and the ribbons of crime scene tape cordoning off the house, the land to the side and rear and the sidewalk out front.

There were no signs of a break-in, though on both sides of a tall iron gate to the east side of the mansion, the paved pathway and lawn appeared to have been recently disturbed, a double row of narrow wheel tracks visible as indentations on the grass and intermittent rubbings along the paving stones – every inch of disturbance already marked out.

The mansion stood on Collins opposite the North Shore Open Space Park near 81st Street. Not far, as the gulls flew, from where a murdered man had been found on the beach about eighteen months back, sparking a horrific case for Becket and Martinez.

No link to this crime, for sure, the perpetrator of that killing long dead.

Besides which, this was very different.

It might yet turn out not to be unique, for all they knew, but neither of the Miami Beach Police Department Violent Crimes detectives had ever seen anything like it.

'It's not the ugliest,' Elliot Sanders, the on-call ME, already on the scene, said to Sam, 'but it's certainly damned nasty, not to mention down-right weird.'

There were two naked bodies, one male, one female. Both Caucasian, perhaps mid-twenties, the male dark-haired, the female blonde, her hair long and tousled, a tiny tattoo of a willow tree near the base of her spine.

From a distance, they might have appeared to have died in the act of intercourse, still united, faces contorted. But closing in, the detectives saw the edges of two gashing, bloodless wounds across both their necks.

'Cause of death probably asphyxiation or haemorrhage or both,' Sanders said.

'But not here,' Sam said.

Looking again at the arrangement of the bodies, he thought first of sculpture, a grotesque parody, perhaps, of a Rodin pair – though then again they might almost, his mind swam on, be a pair of cruelly conjoined twins, attached at the loins.

Yet that was not the strangest thing about the scene.

They were lying in the middle of the lawn beneath a large plastic dome-shaped cover measuring approximately eight feet in diameter and less than five feet high at the centre.

'The doc's right,' Martinez said. 'It's a weird one, man.'

'They look like exhibits,' Sam said, pulling out his notebook and starting a sketch of the crime scene. 'Maybe specimens.'

It was customary for Crime Scene, where possible, to complete the preliminaries before the

ME's arrival, but though the technicians had been here a while, they were still working, measuring the location and collecting and zipping into plastic bags anything that might hint of evidence: a piece of tissue, maybe, a thread or cigarette butt, or – nothing so providential here – the murder weapon itself. Their photographer still taking her pictures of every aspect, anything to help record it all before the dome was raised to allow access and before wind or rain or other elements might alter the scene forever.

Sam looked back toward the mansion, including it in his sketch.

Whatever might or might not have gone on in there would have to wait for a search warrant, unless the owner could be located first. Though even if consent was given, they'd probably choose to wait. Time-wasting as the procedure was – Sam and Martinez had known it to take anything from two to ten hours – that was still nowhere near as frustrating as seeing potential hard evidence rendered inadmissible in court.

They did not, at least, need a warrant to look at the tracks in the grass. Wheel marks, no more than two inches wide, leading from the gate – closed, but not locked – to the centre of the lawn.

'Some kind of dolly, maybe,' Sam mused, while Martinez went across to speak to the patrol officers who'd been first on the scene. 'Maybe a gurney.' He made some notes. 'What else do you have, Doc?'

'Nothing yet that isn't plain as day.'

On the other side of the garden, Martinez was

19

using his cell phone.

'The gardener who found them had himself a heart attack,' Sanders went on. 'The paramedics were still working on him when I got here, had him pretty much stabilized.'

Martinez, still on the phone, was already on his way back, moving carefully around the garden perimeter, eyes on the ground as he walked and ended his call.

'Doc tell you about the gardener?' he said.

'Poor guy,' Sam said.

'Mr Joseph Mulhoon,' Martinez said. 'Comes here once a month, he told the EMT treating him.' He made a note. 'We'll check him out.'

The Becket-Martinez partnership was informal but well established in the unit, the men taking their turn, same as the other Violent Crime detectives, as to who got appointed lead investigator on each case by Mike Alvarez, their sergeant. This one had gone to Sam, meaning he'd be the guy working the extra hours keeping up with the report-writing and the load of paperwork that came with any investigation. Other than that, he and Martinez divided the labours, pooled thought processes and tasks. Bottom line, though Sam had pulled through more than one bout of disciplinary problems created by his tendency to act on instinct rather than by the rulebook, and though Alejandro Martinez had been criticized for a lack of ambition, together they made a fine investigative team, and Sergeant Alvarez and Tom Kennedy, their captain, recognized that.

'Mr Mulhoon is seventy-one years old,'

Sanders said now, 'and I'd be surprised as hell if he knew a damned thing about this before he happened on it.'

'Do we know who pays him?' Sam asked Martinez.

'Company called Beatty Management in North Beach takes care of the property. Their office is closed, but a woman picked up as I was leaving a message, and I told her we'd appreciate having the owner's consent to search, and I don't know how much luck we're gonna have with that, but she said she'll see to it that we get the keys soon as.' He glanced at his wristwatch. 'If we're real lucky, the warrant might get here first.'

The go-ahead having been given for the domed plastic cover to be raised, the ME blew into a new pair of latex gloves, put them on, then donned coveralls, shoe covers and a mask. One investigator at a time being the general rule in order to minimize damage to the scene, Sanders approached the bodies alone.

Sam, watching the doc crouch to begin his examination, was in no hurry to don his own booties and move in.

The dead, newly slain, had always been difficult for him, his stomach still having an aversion to ugly death, not to mention his soul.

As it should be, he supposed.

He thought, now and then, about transferring to another unit or even of leaving the police department altogether, but he knew he'd probably never do that, at least not out of choice. The victims and those left behind needed all the help

21

they could get, and though Sam knew there were plenty of detectives waiting to take his place, many of them smarter or sharper, certainly younger and fresher than him, he also knew that there was no greater asset in the job than experience. Every single victim of violence he'd dealt with over the years was logged someplace in his mind, as were the significant steps of each investigation, the changing methods over time, the eureka moments that soared suddenly out of the grind, the more solid leads that came from doggedness, and the interrogation breakthroughs. Most depressing of all, the cases that had eluded them, the victims they'd let down.

Leaving would be a simple waste of the resource that his mind had become. It would also, as Sam saw it, be a betrayal of his colleagues and those people he might have been able to help.

It would be giving up.

Anyway, however tough it got, he loved the goddamned job.

He sneezed on it, twice.

'*Gesundheit*,' Sanders said, finished for now, pushing down his mask and taking a deep breath of unusually chilly Florida morning air. 'You got a head cold, keep it to yourself.'

'Doing my best,' Sam said.

Sanders pulled off his gloves, which would be discarded to avoid cross-contamination, as every item of protective clothing was discarded each time they left any crime scene.

Martinez took two steps closer to the victims. 'They really look like they were doing it when...'

22

His round face and dark brown eyes showed distaste for the crime. Several inches shorter than Sam, the forty-five-year-old Cuban-American had been known to be tough as a charging bull when roused.

'They weren't,' the ME said flatly.

'You do have something,' Sam said.

'Rigor still present,' Sanders said, 'but you know I can't tell you more on that till later.' He paused. 'Definitely washed post-mortem, probably positioned before rigor mortis, then moved. The marks on both ring fingers aren't very distinct, so they may have been married, but perhaps not for long, and possibly, though obviously not definitely, to each other.'

Sam waited. 'And?'

'I won't know this for sure till I get them back to the office.'

'Goes without saying,' Sam said.

'Glue,' Sanders said grimly. 'I think some sick bastard stuck their genitalia together with some kind of goddamned superglue.'

Now Sam and Martinez both felt sick.

FOUR

Saturday was one of Mildred's days for helping Grace out in the office.

Sam said that no one who'd ever seen her in the old days would recognize her now. Grace had never met Mildred back then, but Sam had spoken about her often, had said it was clear to him that what lay beneath the layers was remarkable.

Up until mid-June of last year, Mildred Bleeker had been a bag lady who slept on a bench in South Beach. Now, she was living in a Golden Beach house with Dr David Becket, a semi-retired paediatrician, though if you were to ask her, Mildred would probably have insisted that she was 'just staying awhile'. And maybe that was true, but all the Becket family hoped that it was not.

For one thing, although David was only sixty-four years old and in good physical and excellent mental health, Grace was sure that Saul would never have felt entirely easy about moving into his own home if it hadn't been for Mildred moving in.

It seemed to Grace that some things were just meant to be.

None of the Beckets knew Mildred's true age

because she wasn't telling, and if she'd had a birthday any time in the last seven months, she hadn't divulged that either, and as with most personal things relating to this lady, they'd all come to understand that they would just have to wait for Mildred to be ready to share.

Sam had first become acquainted with her because, as a homeless citizen, she had by definition been *out* there on the streets, eyes and ears open. And Mildred, having particular cause to wish the truly wicked – most especially those who profited from illegal drugs – off those streets, had few misgivings about assisting the police, if she happened to be in a position to do so.

Sam and Mildred (who insisted on calling him Samuel, his given name *and* from the Good Book, as she pointed out) had developed a mutual respect and, over time, something more than that, a real friendship. And then a killer calling himself Cal the Hater, fearing that Mildred might identify him, had struck late one night, and against all the odds she had survived, but after that Sam had hated the idea of her going back to the streets.

His father, having taken to visiting her in Miami General Hospital and having come to relish those encounters because of the lady's courage and wit, felt the same way, and felt too that Mildred Bleeker harbored a secret wish to be needed again. So David had dropped in regular mentions of how big his house was for one old man, and how much he was coming to value their conversations, and finally he'd told

25

her that if she would not agree to spend her convalescence at his place, then he'd be forced to find a lodger, since otherwise his younger son, Saul, would never grab hold of the freedom he badly needed.

'A lodger sounds just the ticket,' Mildred had said.

'I don't want some stranger,' David said.

'They wouldn't be a stranger for long,' Mildred pointed out. 'And they'd pay you, which I could not, as you know.'

'I'm fortunate enough not to need the money,' David said.

'Most folk seem happy enough to get more.'

'I'd rather have your company,' David had persisted. 'Besides, like you, I'm fond of an occasional drop of Manischewitz.'

'If Samuel has been casting aspersions on my good character,' Mildred said, 'I'll be wanting a little talk with him.'

'Samuel thinks you're the bee's knees,' David said.

It was the first and only time he'd seen her blush.

Much more to Mildred than met the eye, though she was a striking-looking woman, her eyes blue, her face lined, but less weather-beaten since she'd come off the streets, and with a new haircut that accentuated her fine bone structure. And Mildred Bleeker had believed her own vanity long dead, yet now she secretly relished the flattery her new appearance had brought her, reminding her a little of the way Donny, her late

26

fiancé, had paid her compliments in the old days.

Her new friends had changed everything.

Dr Becket, a wise, rumpled, craggy-faced, kindly warhorse of a man. Grace, Samuel's beautiful, golden-haired psychologist wife, who seemed to grasp more than most that Mildred needed time and space and, above all, privacy.

Samuel, though, was her hero. The six-foot-three African-American cop, who'd always shown her true respect. Who'd gone to the trouble and expense of buying her a cellular telephone of her own so that she'd be safe from a stranger who'd alarmed her. A man with a precious family, good friends and a job that made a real difference to the citizens of Miami Beach. A man who faced danger and worked too many hours most days, but who'd still made time for her.

Who had made space in his own *family* for her.

Not that she'd found that altogether easy. Having people who cared brought responsibility. Having a room that David insisted was her own, yet had never entirely *felt* like hers, and walls still bothered her, and there had been – still were – some sleepless nights when she almost longed to be out there again with the ocean and the whole night sky to gaze at.

Though then she'd be alone again.

'If I'm going to visit with you for any longer,' she'd told David last fall, 'I have to do something to earn my keep.'

'You help babysit Joshua,' he'd told her.

27

They'd been washing dishes after dinner in the kitchen that was as old-fashioned and well-worn as every other room in the house that he'd inhabited for over thirty-five years.

'That's a privilege,' Mildred had said, 'not a job.'

'You don't need to get a job.'

'I don't need to be told what I need,' Mildred answered crisply.

David had asked what she had in mind.

'Seems to me,' she said, 'you could use a housekeeper.'

He was shocked. 'I thought we were friends.'

'I hope we are,' she said. 'Though I can't see what that has to do with it.'

'But we're fine as we are,' David said. 'We take care of each other, muddle along. You, me, and Saul, of course, until he goes.'

'You're a doctor,' Mildred said. 'A busy man.'

'I'm less and less of a doctor,' David pointed out. 'And you're no housekeeper.'

'You don't know what I am,' Mildred said. 'Or what I have been.'

'How could I know,' he said, 'when you won't tell me?'

'In time,' she said, 'perhaps I will.'

'So setting the past aside, as always,' David said, 'what would you like to do now? *Other* than cooking and cleaning for an old man.'

'Not so old,' Mildred said.

'Thank you,' David said.

'I do have one other idea.' Mildred paused. 'Your office is a mess.'

'Perpetually,' David said.

'I don't want to clean it,' Mildred said. 'But it does strike me that your filing systems could use some organizing.' She paused again. 'If you're concerned about confidentiality, I know how to keep my nose out of other people's stuff.'

'I don't doubt it,' David said.

She'd asked him to think it over, and he had, because the running of his office had, until her final illness three years before, been Judy Becket's domain, and so David had felt he'd needed a silent word with her just then because it seemed to him that this smacked, a little, of infidelity.

Judy had sent down no thunderbolts, and Saul, when consulted, had said he thought it a fine idea.

So Mildred had gone to work.

'The woman is a wonder,' David had told Sam a week later. 'She has energy like you wouldn't believe, but most of all she has the greatest intelligence.'

'Doesn't surprise me,' Sam said.

And after that, adding Grace's office to Mildred's schedule had seemed a natural progression.

The necessity of finding someone to help her keep order once she'd returned to practice after having Joshua had become a bit of a bugbear for Grace, her experiences with her last administrative assistant having turned into a nightmare.

David had made the suggestion.

'It would solve all your problems,' he'd told her. 'Aside from her excellent organizational skills, Mildred could babysit Joshua on the

29

premises while you see patients.'

'Do you think she'd consider it?'

'She's had her eye on the job ever since I mentioned you could use some assistance.' David paused. 'Though I think she's concerned that your patients' parents or guardians might not be keen on your employing a former vagrant.'

'Mildred wasn't a criminal,' Grace said crisply. 'Seems to me they couldn't ask for a more exemplary person.'

'Sounds to me like she has the job,' David said.

'I think we'd better meet,' Grace said. 'Maybe agree a trial period, for both our sakes. And a salary, of course.'

'I'm not sure she'll be keen on taking money from you,' David said.

'If Mildred works for me,' Grace had said, 'she will most definitely be paid.'

'She did mention to me once that she has a social security number.'

'And knows it by heart, I'll be bound,' Grace had said.

FIVE

Two representatives from Beatty Management, dug out of their respective Saturday activities, drew up in a Lexus outside the Oates Gallery just after noon, almost an hour after the unusually speedy arrival of the search warrant.

Larry Beatty, CEO of the company, thirty-something, tall, nattily turned out in a well-cut navy blazer, blue jeans and an open-necked blue and white striped shirt, was sober-faced as he emerged from the driver's side, identified himself to an officer, then stooped to duck beneath the tape and finally introduced himself to Becket and Martinez on the front pathway.

'Terrible thing,' he said. 'Whatever I can do to help.'

Beatty was handsome, fair-haired, hazel-eyed and even-featured, but there was, Sam thought, a blandness about the man that made him less attractive than he might have been.

'We appreciate it, sir,' he said.

The door on the passenger side of the Lexus slammed belatedly, and a harassed-looking young red-haired woman in a dark pants suit and sneakers, carrying a battered briefcase, came hurrying around the car and followed Beatty's route under the cordon.

31

'Ally Moore,' she said breathlessly, quickly amending: 'Allison.' Her eyes were grey and anxious. 'I've brought keys.'

'And I'm here primarily to give the owner's consent,' Beatty said. 'Her name is Mrs Marilyn Myerson, and I have her full Power of Attorney.'

'I have certified copies of those papers, too,' Ally Moore said, edgily pushing strands of curly hair off her freckled, lightly made-up face.

'Ms Moore is responsible for regular checks on the property,' Beatty said.

'Though I imagine, sir,' Sam said, 'that as CEO of Beatty Management and as Mrs Myerson's legal representative, you have overall responsibility.'

'For using our firm's best endeavours to care for the property, of course,' Beatty accepted. 'Though the security levels here have been somewhat limited by Mrs Myerson's budget.'

'There is an alarm system,' Ally Moore explained. 'But the power's turned off most of the time, so security's been down to locks and regular checking.'

'Mostly to guard against trespassers or squatters,' Beatty said, 'since there's nothing left to steal.'

'So no alarm,' said Martinez. 'But they pay for a gardener.'

'Poor Mr Mulhoon,' Ally Moore said. 'That's right.'

She rummaged in her case, withdrew some papers and a bunch of tagged keys and, although the mansion had been entered within minutes of the securing of the search warrant, Martinez took them from her anyway.

'Does Mr Mulhoon usually work weekends?' Sam asked.

'Sometimes,' Moore said. 'He comes on the most convenient day – to him, I mean – closest to the fifth of each month. A cleaning firm comes in too, around the twentieth.'

'The aim has been to keep up basic maintenance,' Beatty said. 'As I said, fixtures aside, there's nothing the average burglar would be interested in.'

'Maybe the fireplaces,' Ally Moore said. 'You hear of things like that being dismantled and taken away.'

'The side gate to the garden was unlocked,' Sam said.

'It's always kept locked,' Moore said quickly. 'But I guess Mr Mulhoon would have unlocked it when he arrived.'

'Did the Oates Gallery belong to Mrs Myerson?' Sam asked Beatty.

'She was the landlord,' the other man said. 'The place was run by a manager and staff, and my firm took care of the property requirements. If you need our files, I can send them over Monday.'

'Today or tomorrow would be better,' Martinez said. 'We could come to you.'

'Thank you,' Larry Beatty said. 'I'll do my best, though it might not be easy to locate them over the weekend.'

'When did the gallery close down?' asked Sam.

'Just over a year ago,' Beatty said.

They were still on the front path, and the part of the backyard in which the deceased lay was entirely obscured from view, but Ally Moore's eyes kept veering toward the gate leading to the garden and its new, apparently appalling contents.

'Two people?' she said softly. 'Is that true?'

'I'm afraid so,' Sam said.

'Do you know who they are?'

'Not yet.' Sam turned to Beatty. 'We'll need to speak with Mrs Myerson, sir.'

'I'm afraid that won't be possible,' Beatty said. 'She has advanced Alzheimer's disease.'

'I'm sorry to hear that,' Sam said.

'Does she have close relatives?' Martinez asked.

'None I'm aware of,' Beatty said.

The structure having been pronounced clear of danger, the power back on and Crime Scene having given them the OK, the detectives finally escorted Beatty and Moore into the mansion.

'So all you need,' Moore asked nervously, 'is for us to say if anything seems out of place, right?'

'Main thing,' Martinez told them, 'is you need to be careful not to touch anything.'

'We'll be very careful,' Beatty said.

Their footsteps echoed in the silent house, even the padding of Moore's rubber soles audible. Picture lights and unevenly sized pale spaces on walls attested to paintings that had once hung there, and an absence of dust or cobwebs on the rather ugly chandeliers indicated a decent job carried out by the cleaning firm.

Its barrenness notwithstanding, Sam found the mansion unattractive, an architectural mishmash of Doric-style columns, ornate covings and fireplaces plucked from different periods and styles. Though as a showplace for paintings and sculptures it had probably served well enough, offering no competition to the art, and maybe it was just his head-cold making him so unappreciative.

Not to mention the bodies in the backyard.

They moved carefully and methodically through the house.

'Everything looks the same,' Ally Moore said, partway up the broad central staircase. 'Though I guess I've never looked at it quite this closely before, you know?'

'Sure,' Sam said, easily.

'When were you last here, sir?' Martinez asked Beatty.

'About three months ago,' Beatty said. 'For a formal check.'

'I come in the middle and at the end of every month,' Moore volunteered.

'And how does it *feel* to you?' Sam asked her.

She stood at the top of the stairs. 'It feels OK.' She took another moment. 'The same as before, I guess.' She gave a small grimace. 'No offence to Mrs Myerson, but it's always felt a little spooky to me.'

'Some old houses do seem that way,' Sam said.

'But you do always check over the whole place?' Martinez asked.

They moved into a large room, its walls

35

similarly patchy, but though the shutters had been opened, the chandeliers were switched off and the light was poor.

'Always,' Moore said.

'Do you think you might know if someone else had been in here?' Sam asked.

'You mean *sense* it?'

'People sometimes get a feel for such things,' Sam said. 'If they know a house really well, as you must do this one.'

'I guess, maybe if it's your own home.' Moore shook her head. 'Not me – not here, anyway.' She glanced at Larry Beatty. 'But I'm no clairvoyant.'

'We'll need a list of keyholders,' Sam said.

'I have that with me,' Moore said. 'I should have given it to you right away.'

'You've been very efficient,' Sam told her and thought he saw a faint flush, guessed that praise from her boss might be hard to come by.

'It isn't a long list,' she said.

'What should I tell the insurers?' Beatty asked. 'I presume you'd prefer them to wait until your people are through.'

'Have you seen any damage?' Martinez asked.

'Only to the area around the gate,' Beatty said.

'Really?' Martinez was dry. 'I didn't notice.'

'Still,' Beatty said, 'this whole thing could harm the property's potential.'

'Dead people'll do that every time,' Martinez said.

Sam waited until they were back outside before he asked if they'd mind looking at some photo-

36

graphs of the deceased for identification purposes.

'Oh.' Ally Moore grew pale.

'Just their faces,' Sam reassured her. 'It could be helpful.'

She nodded. 'OK.'

'Mr Beatty?'

'Sure.'

They looked at the Polaroid headshots together.

'I've never seen either of them before,' Beatty said without hesitation.

'Ms Moore?' Sam asked.

She was still looking, taking her time, her eyes troubled, though no more so than was reasonable, Sam figured, considering what she was looking at.

'You doing all right, ma'am?' Martinez asked.

'I'm OK,' she said. 'And no, I don't recognize them either. It's just...'

They waited.

'Nothing,' she said. 'Except it's just so horrible, so sad.'

'That it is,' Martinez said.

'One more thing,' Sam said. 'We'd appreciate it if you'd consent to being fingerprinted.'

'Really?' Beatty looked shocked.

'For elimination purposes,' Sam said.

'Is that really necessary?' the other man asked.

'All persons with legitimate access to a crime scene should be fingerprinted,' Martinez told him. 'In case your latent prints are found.'

'In your own interests, sir,' Sam said. 'But if you have an objection...'

'Of course not,' Beatty said.

'Me neither,' Allison Moore agreed. 'It makes sense.'

'What about the cleaners?' Beatty asked.

'We'll be in touch with them,' Sam said.

'They're on the keyholder list,' Moore said.

The Lexus having driven away, and the Crime Scene truck en route to remove the plastic dome from the lawn – from where it would be transported to the ME's office – Sam and Martinez stood in the garden exchanging first thoughts.

'He's a cold fish,' Martinez said.

'Nice woman, though,' Sam said.

'A little nervy,' Martinez said.

'Hardly surprising,' Sam said. 'But we'll check them both out.'

'Better make sure Mrs Myerson's Alzheimer's is for real,' Martinez said.

Nothing and no one taken at face value in the early stages of a homicide investigation, not even an absentee sick old woman.

'If it weren't for the glue and the dome, or whatever the hell that thing really is,' Sam said, 'I guess I could buy them having been dumped on vacant land for no special reason. But this being a former art gallery...'

'We should take a look at their old exhibitions,' Martinez said. 'See if they've ever had any weird kind of sculptures, like couples lying under plastic covers.' His lips compressed for a moment. 'The glue ring any bells with you?'

Sam shook his head. 'We'll see what the computer throws up.'

'I wonder what shape the gardener's in,' Martinez said. 'Better make sure he keeps this thing under wraps.' He made a note. 'I know what the doc said, but I'll check him out anyway.'

Sam looked across the lawn, past the numbered flags marking places where the techs had spotted items of possible interest, over toward where a tent covered the dome and bodies.

'You know anything about performance art, Al?'

'Uh-uh.'

'Me neither,' Sam said. 'Except I think the performers are usually alive.' He pulled a handkerchief from his pocket and sneezed twice, then blew his nose. 'I'm sorry.'

'God bless you,' Martinez said.

'Thanks.' Sam took a moment. 'Two victims, moved from one location to another, so we're either looking for one highly organized ... I guess it's not impossible that this could be one physically strong individual acting alone.' He shrugged. 'Though it could just as easily be two, or more.'

'Great.' Martinez stifled a yawn. 'Excuse me.'

Said out of courtesy to the dead, more than to his partner.

'Good evening?' Sam asked.

'There's no other kind with Jessie,' Martinez said.

'How's she doing? I haven't seen her in a week or so.'

'She's great,' Martinez said. 'Really great.'

Sam smiled.

SIX

Alejandro Martinez was in love.

Seriously, head-over-heels in love, for the first time since Sam had known him. The closest he'd come before was when Mary Cutter had first joined the unit, and Martinez had been distracted for a while back then before he'd plunged into a relationship from which they'd both, luckily, emerged with mutual respect, able to continue as colleagues.

This was a whole different ball game. Jessica Kowalski worked as a secretary in the Personnel Resources Unit on the second floor, one down from Violent Crimes, and she was not only good to look at, delicately featured, blue-eyed, with shoulder-length wavy blonde hair and a petite figure, but she was also the type of person it was impossible not to like. Kind, considerate and willing to put herself out for people, like the colleague who'd fallen on the staircase at the station and busted her ankle, and Jess had accompanied her to the hospital and taken care of her when she'd gone home, had shopped and cooked for her and made sure she was kept up to speed with work in her absence.

'Everyone goes to her, you know,' Martinez had told Sam after they'd started dating last

November. 'Little problems or big, they take them to Jess because she makes them feel better. And she doesn't talk about that at all, she doesn't even seem to realize what a good person she is – but I get people who know we're seeing each other telling me I'm a lucky bastard, except I don't need them telling me because I know it.'

He'd brought Jess to Thanksgiving dinner at the Becket house, because her parents lived in Cleveland, Ohio, and though most years their daughter headed home for the holiday, this time she'd chosen to tell her family she was having to work through.

'I have to say,' Sam had told Grace, 'I'm kind of glad she lied to her parents, or I might be worrying about her being too good to be real.'

'More of a fib than a lie,' Grace had said. 'And just to spare their feelings.'

They'd both taken an immediate liking to Jess. She'd brought a Polish honey cake that she'd baked herself, a gingerbread house for Joshua and some turkey-shaped Thanksgiving dog cookies for Woody – the dachshund-miniature schnauzer cross they'd rescued some years back – and the dog had loved her even before she'd taken the cookies out of her bag.

'She's so easy to be around,' Saul had said later. 'It feels like she's been with Al forever.'

Which had made Sam deeply happy for his friend. Martinez had always claimed that there was a lot to be said for confirmed bachelorhood – no one to worry about, no one to fret about him – and though he loved Grace, he'd never shown so much as a trace of envy of his partner's

41

happiness, but Sam knew that Martinez had been lonely for a long while.

Jessica Kowalski was a keeper, no two ways about it.

SEVEN

Cathy loved her job.

Sam had found it for her, which she might have been a dope about, let her pride get in the way, but given that it was exactly the kind of on-the-job training she'd have chosen for herself, she knew she'd have been a horse's ass not to have jumped at it.

Home aside, the Opera Café on Arthur Godfrey Road near Sheridan Avenue had for some time been one of Sam's favourite places to drop into for anything from breakfast en route to the station – in South Beach on Washington and 11th – to a late night bowl of soup or a sandwich when he and Martinez were pulling an all-nighter. Since Matt Dooley and Simone Regan had taken over the café about six months back, they'd turned it from a so-so eatery to a comfortable, friendly little café-bistro-restaurant serving top-notch food.

The first time Sam had ventured inside, hungry as a horse after a long evening's stakeout, too tired to cook for himself and with no intention of waking Grace, they'd been about to close the place, and Sam would have settled for a takeout, but the waitress he'd since come to know as Simone had said they didn't do takeout, but she'd made him welcome anyway. She showed him to one of their banquettes because their cushions were comfy and he looked so weary, and then Dooley had come out of the kitchen and asked if it was early breakfast or late dinner Sam was after, and if it was the latter, then their minestrone was a good starter.

More than good, in the event, on top of which the choice of music playing at just the right, gentle level – Leontyne Price singing 'Summertime' – happened to be one of Sam's all-time favourites and balm to his tired soul. Opera, in general, being Sam Becket's big *thing*, possessing as he did a rich baritone that had earned him a number of leading roles with local amateur company S-BOP, but which, these days, was mostly appreciated by his son when his daddy crooned to him.

'You got yourselves a regular customer,' he told them, and he'd been true to his word, and Martinez liked it too, though his drop-in cafés of choice tended to be Cuban, and anyway, he lived over on Alton Road these days, so the place was not on his regular route.

Whatever Matt Dooley cooked turned out great. He said it was because he knew his limitations and respected the boundaries past which a decent, 'average' cook had no business straying.

'I'm no chef,' he told Sam once. 'Just a whole lot better than some short-order cooks.' And Simone Regan – a slim, attractive brunette in her

43

forties with soft green eyes – was the perfect partner for him, knew exactly how to look after their customers, and Sam had witnessed her dealing with difficult diners, had seen her expression sharpen in a way that most people seemed disinclined to challenge, especially with Dooley there to back her up.

He was a big guy, tough looking but with gentle brown eyes, and tender as a mother cat with Simone on the rare occasions when she was flagging or getting a migraine; and Sam had witnessed the sudden onslaught of one of those attacks, had seen the capable, energetic woman suddenly fumbling and slow, and he'd started to move to try to help her once, but Dooley had been there ahead of him, had emerged from the kitchen as if he'd picked up her frailty by sonar, and Sam had liked the way he'd taken over, taken care of her.

All of which was why the Opera Café had flown straight into his mind after Cathy had told Grace about the career change she was contemplating.

She'd been thinking a lot lately, she'd said, about her late stepfather, Arnold Robbins – a man she'd dearly loved, and the first to have adopted Cathy in her horribly disrupted young life. Robbins had run a small, successful chain of restaurants called Arnie's until he and Cathy's mother, Marie, had been brutally murdered. Now, as she sought new direction more than eight years later, Arnie's had been returning to Cathy's mind with what felt like a haunting, nagging sweetness.

44

'It's almost like he's trying to help me, you know,' Cathy had told Grace. 'Except Arnie used to make yummy food that probably jammed up people's arteries just by being on the menu, and what I'd like to do is make yummy, healthy food instead.'

Like an incalculable number of others in the greater Miami area, Grace had thought but managed not to say, their daughter's enthusiasm being something she and Sam hated the idea of trampling on.

'I know,' Cathy had said. 'Like ten zillion other people around here.'

'It's certainly a competitive business,' Grace said.

'I'd want to learn, of course, maybe do a kind of apprenticeship,' Cathy said. 'I waited tables in Sacramento.'

'You never mentioned that.' Grace was surprised.

'The woman I worked for said I had a gift for it.' Cathy smiled. 'Not so much for waiting tables, but for understanding what the customers wanted. It was only meant to be part-time, but I got promoted to manager the nights my boss took off.'

'I'm impressed,' Grace had said.

'I didn't tell you guys because if you'd known how well I was doing, you might have worried I was never going to come home.'

Grace couldn't argue with that.

'I agree it's a tough world for her to choose,' Sam had said, later, 'but it's probably a picnic compared to athletics.'

'Competitive athletics, perhaps,' Grace said. 'Not so much teaching.'

'But she doesn't want to teach,' Sam said. 'And everything's tough when you look at it long enough.'

And since he'd heard Matt Dooley say that he might be looking for help at the café because Simone's mother was sick...

Dooley had seemed a little hesitant when Sam had made his suggestion, as if he had something on his mind, and then abruptly he'd come right out with it.

'I have a record.' He'd paused. 'Though you might already know that.'

'I didn't,' Sam said. 'I'm not in the habit of checking up on friends.'

'Anyway,' Dooley had gone on, 'I figure if your daughter does try out here, you're bound to be the protective kind of father. Which is what I hope I'd have been if I'd had a daughter.' He'd paused again. 'I stole some stuff when I was young. I did it with friends, and I didn't have a good reason, I wasn't hungry and I didn't need the things I stole, and I'm heartily ashamed of it.'

'Hey,' Sam had said. 'We've all done things we're ashamed of.'

'I just thought I should tell you,' Dooley said.

'I appreciate that,' Sam said. 'Though it really wasn't necessary.'

'I guess we don't even know if Cathy's going to want the job.'

'Or if you're going to want her,' Sam had said.

'I have a pretty good feeling about it,' Dooley had said.

He was right.

Cathy had started work in the first week of January, and a little over a month later her enthusiasm for the Opera Café and everything connected to it was still going strong. And though living with Saul, she was still forever dropping by the house to play with Joshua and chatter with her parents about Dooley's recipes and Simone's patience and the nice things Dooley did for people.

'He doesn't often get mad,' she'd said last Sunday after she'd dropped by for supper. 'And when he does, it's usually at himself because a dish isn't perfect or he's dropped something or a gadget's let him down, but usually all he does is grit his teeth and jam a dollar bill into this huge cookie jar they keep on the counter.'

'Like a swear box.' Sam had smiled. 'I've seen him do it.'

'And Simone jumps in,' Cathy had turned to Grace, 'grabs the moment to tell anyone in the café that the charity *du jour* is whatever it happens to be. But she's never pushy about it, so no one minds.'

'How's the work going?' Grace asked.

'It's pretty tough, because I'm kind of like their busboy, but you know I like hard work, and they're both cool about showing me stuff, so I'm learning a lot.'

'That's good,' Grace said.

Cathy played with her hair for a moment. It

was straight and so close to Grace's shade of blonde that people often assumed they were biological mother and daughter. In the past she'd worn it long, tying it back when she ran, but she'd had it cut to a jaw-length bob in California, and guys were frequently complimenting her on it. Not that Cathy was ready for dating even now, more than a year since her last serious relationship had ended in tragedy. Too much confusion in her still, too much uncertainty about her own judgement skills, let alone the true nature of her sexuality...

'I know you've both been worried I'm turning out to be a flake,' she'd said.

'I'm sure you've never heard us say anything like that,' Sam said.

'You wouldn't say it,' Cathy said. 'Doesn't mean you mightn't think it.'

'We don't,' he said. 'No way.'

'I'd like to think you know we're always honest with you,' Grace said.

'Sure you are,' Cathy said. 'But you're also kind, and you hate hurting me.'

'That's true enough,' Sam said.

'So in case you're stressing because I might just be filling time at the café...'

'If it does turn out that way,' Grace said, 'then that'll be because it wasn't right for you, and then it'll have been another step on your journey.'

'It isn't always easy finding your path, sweetheart,' Sam said.

'I know,' Cathy had said. 'And I know it's early days, but I am beginning to feel that this really might be it.'

'Then that's all we could possibly hope for,' Grace had said.

EIGHT

The identification of a homicide victim found without clothing or personal effects was often difficult, unless there was a clear resemblance to a known missing person or some other link with such a report, or where a DNA sample from the victim provided a match with someone on the FBI's CODIS – Combined DNA Index System – database.

Having two victims, Sam and Martinez knew, was either going to make it easier or a whole lot harder.

Easier, in this case.

A couple named Suzy and Michael Easterman had been reported missing on Friday evening by their parents. Mr Easterman, an architect aged twenty-six, tall, dark-haired, his face with boy-ish, sweet features. His wife an illustrator, two years younger than her husband, with long blonde hair, pretty, even features and a tiny willow tree tattoo on her lower back designed, according to her mother, by herself.

Leaving little room for doubt.

The report stated that the couple had married at Christmas and moved into their house on La

Gorce Drive – less than three miles from the Oates Gallery – just three weeks ago. Suzy spoke to her mother, Audrey Stein, most days and had been due to meet her Friday lunchtime at Bal Harbour. When her daughter had failed to appear and after repeated calls to her cell and home phones had proven useless, Mrs Stein had attempted to contact her son-in-law and learned that the reliable young architect had also been a no-show without explanation at his office yesterday.

Following a series of increasingly frantic calls to family members and friends of the couple, Mrs Stein had raised the alarm.

Newly-weds.

Sometimes, Sam and Martinez both hated their work.

NINE

These days, Miami's morgue was known either as the Joseph H. Davis Center for Forensic Pathology, or as the Miami-Dade County Medical Examiner's Office. But though it was an attractive, comfortable enough place to visit, the grim fact was it took in over three thousand corpses a year.

Its address was 1 Bob Hope Road, but there was little laughter there.

Still a morgue.

The ME investigator who'd brought the identification photographs to the two sets of parents waiting in the Family Grieving Room off the lobby, had never grown used to watching people's worlds crashing.

'I'm so very sorry,' he told Suzy and Michael Easterman's parents, after he'd helped snuff out any lingering trace of hope.

William Stein voiced one of the questions on all their minds. 'Did our children suffer?'

The investigator wished he could have flat-out lied to the man, but all he could do was offer kindness and courtesy and ask them to wait for the medical examiner's report. He knew, looking at the wreckage of these poor people's faces, that their suffering was only just beginning.

'I want to see my son,' Ben Easterman said.

Which was not yet possible.

To the parents, that seemed like cruelty being piled on savagery.

Like the detectives, the ME investigator did not always like his job.

In his office on the second floor, away from the grieving families, Elliot Sanders was sharing grim findings with Sam and Martinez.

'Glue, for sure,' he said. 'Inside as well as out. In Mrs Easterman's vulva and vagina and her husband's urethra.' He shook his head. 'I'm still putting this together, but I'd guess that whoever did this washed and dried them after death, and then went to work with anything from a turkey baster to a syringe pump.'

The two detectives looked at each other wordlessly.

'Three more things, by the by,' Sanders said. 'Plain-edged blade on the weapon that killed them. Sliced, not slashed. No serration, no distinctive markings, but you're probably looking for a blade an inch or more wide.'

'How many million of those in this fucking city?' Martinez said.

'I did find some marks on Mr Easterman's left ankle and on his wife's right leg that could have been made by shackles of some kind.'

'This just gets sicker by the minute,' Martinez said.

'Or more evil,' Sam said, and for a moment he felt a terrifying awareness of their helplessness in the face of true wickedness.

And then his head-cold came to save him with another big sneeze.

Brought him back to a kind of normality.

'You said three more things,' he reminded Sanders.

'Crime Scene found a little blood in the old art gallery, and some traces of cocaine,' the ME said. 'I'll keep you posted.'

TEN

With the rest of the team working the neighbourhood around the former Oates Gallery, Sam and Martinez had come to the Easterman house on La Gorce Drive, a beautiful creamy two-storey home set back off the exclusive road near 59th Street, its palm-shielded front garden making it potentially more vulnerable to crime.

A warrant had been applied for, though not yet obtained, but consent for a search had been given by next-of-kin, both sets of grieving parents frantic to assist in any way possible, and the detectives knew that the relatives would in due course have a torrent of questions for them – too many unanswerable – but for now they had their early crushing shock to deal with, and Sam and Martinez planned to wait until tomorrow to speak to them.

For now, they had a possible witness to interview, though if anything at the house appeared likely to provide evidence of the crime, they would halt and wait for the warrant before continuing.

Mayumi Santos, the couple's Filipino housekeeper, had returned early Friday evening after staying with a cousin during her weekly twenty-four hours off, to find Suzy's anxious mother

53

waiting.

Now, seated in her employers' kitchen, Mayumi appeared distraught.

'Mrs Stein tell me she phoned Mrs Easterman many times when she did not come to Bal Harbour–' her English was stilted but rapid – 'and then she came here and we went to the bedroom and I see they have not slept here because when Mrs Suzy – my employers tell me to call them Suzy and Mike, but I don't like...' She broke off and began weeping.

The kitchen was a palace of granite and sleek stainless steel, and before long the detectives would be ushering Santos from the house in order to preserve any possible evidence; but since she'd been here since yesterday evening, had slept here and presumably bathed, cooked, eaten and washed dishes, Sam and Martinez saw little to be gained by rushing the shocked young woman out of the home she might never have the opportunity of living in again.

Kinder and perhaps more productive to speak to her here.

'Have you noticed anything missing in here, Ms Santos?' Sam asked.

His eyes passed over a knife rack on the wall above a granite counter, registered six gleaming knives of different sizes all present and correct, and they'd come to those later, ensure that any with plain blades an inch or more wide were examined for evidence that might, feasibly, have been missed by a killer during washing.

The young woman's eyes followed his gaze and widened in alarm. 'Nothing, sir.'

ELEVEN

February 8

No one in the unit liked working Sundays, especially when they were working a homicide, but it was hard for Sam and Martinez to picture anything much lousier than having to pay their respects to the shattered families of two horribly slain young people.

Having to start prying into their too-short lives.

People all took homicide investigations in different ways, some with their responses dulled, some raging against every step. Some relatives were unable to face anything more than the fact of the death, or not even that – especially not that. Others wanted to be *doing* something to help nail the evil that had stolen their loved ones, and whichever way they leaned, buffeted by their agony, it could be pretty hard on the cops too.

Nice people here, open with their pain, wanting to help and be helped.

'I was so anxious not to seem to be poking my nose into their marriage,' Audrey Stein told Sam and Martinez just after eleven in the elegant grey living room of their tenth-storey apartment overlooking Bal Harbour. 'Suzy called me most days, but if she didn't I held back, made myself wait to hear from her. If I hadn't done that on Friday morning...'

She had to stop to press her sodden white handkerchief to her eyes as her shoulders shook and her hands trembled.

William Stein, his own eyes red, put an arm around her and gazed helplessly at the detectives. 'Some of the friends Audrey called thought that Suzy and Mike might have decided to go somewhere overnight because it was Mayumi's day off—'

'But I knew that was nonsense,' Audrey Stein broke in, the handkerchief back in her lap, being twisted back and forth by agitated fingers, 'because even though they really liked May, Suzy and Mike both loved having the house all to themselves for a little while.'

There was no clutter in the room, everything perfectly maintained, with a handsome cabinet housing a Lalique glass collection. Photographs everywhere in polished silver frames, many of their daughter, alone or with her husband.

'Anyway,' William Stein added, 'there was simply no way that Suzy would leave town without calling her mom.'

'Is there anything you can tell us about Ms Santos, ma'am?' Martinez asked.

'May's a good girl,' Mrs Stein said, quickly and emphatically. 'She used to work for friends of ours, but they moved into a smaller apartment in Boca and had to let her go.'

'I know that Mike had all her papers and references,' William Stein said. 'They'll be in the filing cabinet in his home office.'

'Who could have done this?' Audrey Stein said, and began sobbing. 'Why would anyone do such a wicked thing to two decent, beautiful young people?'

The detectives had no answer to give her.

Their first interview with Ben and Sissy Easterman was just as sad, though whereas Suzy had been the Steins' only child, at least this living room was brimming with Michael's siblings and other family who, it seemed to Sam and Martinez, just kept pouring into the apartment.

A West Country Club Drive residence with gorgeous views over the Turnberry golf course. Another beautiful, affluent home.

Nothing enviable here today, most people in black or sombre clothing, yet still managing friendliness, introducing themselves to Sam and Martinez, all desperate to help: Michael's older brother, Anthony, with his wife Trish, and younger sister Debbie with fiancé Richard, and Ben's sister, Rose Graber.

'It doesn't seem real,' Mrs Graber told them. 'One minute Sissy's sitting having her hair coloured at Danny Mizrachi, and then Michael – that's her hairdresser, not our Mikey – says there's a call for her, and it's the beginning of the end.' She took hold of Sam's right forearm, her fingers gripping his sleeve tightly, tears brimming in her eyes. 'And when people tell you how special these kids were, please believe them, detective, because it's true. My nephew and Suzy were a delight.'

'That's good to hear,' Sam told her gently. 'And it's kind of you to share it with us.' He made no attempt to free himself, and anyway, he could see that Rose Graber hadn't finished.

'I'm not just talking about talent,' she went on. 'They were both clever and very gifted, but they were also kind young people, and not just to each other or even their parents, but to *everyone*.'

Finally, she released Sam's sleeve, turned and hurried from the room, sobbing, and Anthony Easterman went after her.

Good, close-knit family would help them get through in time, Sam knew.

Circles of hell to pass through first.

'Mike and Suzy were just so crazy about each other,' Debbie – dark and sweet-faced, like her late brother – told them. 'They were always cuddling up, they were just so much in love.'

'At least they...' Richard, her fiancé, sandy-haired and tall, stopped.

'What?' Debbie asked.

He shook his head. 'It's going to sound nuts,' he said, 'but just because they did love each other so much, I was going to say at least they were together.'

'I know what you mean,' Debbie said very softly, and began to cry.

Circles of hell.

TWELVE

Isabella the Seventh was in oestrus.

Which had made her keeper happy.

Or would have, if Romeo the Fifth hadn't started acting so aggressively.

He'd bitten poor Isabella on the neck the last time he'd mounted her, bitten her so hard she'd squealed.

The sound of rat pain was terrible. It pierced the keeper's skull, seemed to reverberate for hours, stayed in the memory long after.

There was no doubting now that this Romeo would have to go soon.

Meantime, the keeper planned to separate the couple and calm the little guy down with one milligram of diazepam, then tend to the doe's wounds, complete a few notations and withdraw.

All three of them in need of a little rest.

It was becoming increasingly hard to contemplate losing this Isabella, but that time was coming inexorably closer. Isabella the Seventh was overdue for subrogation, would have to be replaced, perhaps by one of her own offspring, perhaps not.

So after the litter was weaned, the keeper

would just have to toughen up.

Like Pharaoh in the Bible, hardening his heart.

Power came at a price.

THIRTEEN

February 11

Out in the Miami Beach that most residents and visitors occupied, the first two days of this particular February week had been about the end of the cold weather and forecasts of sunshine, but for the homicide cops, Monday and Tuesday had been all about grim routine and discovery.

All too little to discover about a young couple without apparent enemies.

Without much of a past and no future at all.

On Wednesday morning in the conference room, the squad – comprising Sergeant Alvarez, Sam Becket, Al Martinez and Detectives Beth Riley and Mary Cutter – met to go over what they'd assembled so far, much of it a rehashing process. They would do this again repeatedly, especially in the absence of a real lead, since early findings often remained important even when superseded by new facts.

All the significant findings to date had come out of the medical examiner's office early Monday. Neither victim had been raped or sodomized, nor had any injuries been found commensurate with any sexual assault, and, aside from the fatal knife wounds to their throats and some minor abrasions and contusions, Elliot Sanders had found no other injuries.

The blood found on the floor in the mansion matched neither victim, nor had the lab discovered any match on the CODIS database. Same deal so far on the usable fingerprints lifted from any number of surfaces in the old gallery, though Allison Moore's prints had, as expected, been found in several locations as, in just one place, had Larry Beatty's.

Michael Easterman's last meal had consisted of beef with cream and paprika – so possibly goulash or beef stroganoff, the detectives had hypothesized – and Suzy Easterman had eaten white fish. They'd both had potatoes and one more added ingredient: a hefty dose of temazepam, which Sanders thought might have taken effect quite quickly because they'd both drunk alcohol.

'So if the drugs were in the potatoes,' Sam reprised at the meeting, 'maybe someone cooked for them at home and did a major clean-up, or maybe they went to a restaurant where someone didn't like them.'

'They might have ordered takeout,' Martinez said.

'Or maybe someone invited them to dinner at their home,' Beth Riley said.

'Nothing new on the restaurant front?' Alvarez asked.

'Nothing,' Sam said.

They'd already conducted a scan of restaurant

menus in the area, had found two serving stroganoff and salmon, but no white fish, one place
further away in Coral Gables serving both goulash and a variety of fish dishes, and, a more
probable geographic candidate, a swanky Indian
Creek restaurant also serving both; and Sam and
Martinez had visited and come away with
reservation sheets and a shared instinct that it
was a non-starter.

'Though at this point, we're ruling nothing
out,' Sam said.

'Nothing more from the neighbours,' Mary
Cutter said.

No one had reported seeing anyone delivering
or leaving with any kind of food containers,
though even if some residents were nosier than
they might be admitting, with so many trees
blocking the views from front windows, it would
have been hard to see the victims' pathway or
front door.

'Nothing from Easterman's office,' Martinez
reported.

'Nothing from anyplace.' Riley raked her short
red hair.

Everyone they'd spoken to had seemed
shocked: colleagues, friends, locals.

No one with even the tiniest shred of a clue as
to the young couple's whereabouts prior to their
abduction.

'OK,' Sam said, trying to lift the energy. 'Let's
check the list of people we still need to interview.'

'Or re-interview,' Alvarez said.

All the neighbours, again.

Colleagues, again.

Mayumi Santos again *and* the cousin she'd gone to stay with during those key twenty-four hours.

'Maybe her friends, too,' Sam said.

'For sure,' Cutter said.

'You feeling OK?' Sam asked Martinez back in the office, his own cold having dried up, wondering if he'd maybe passed it on to his partner.

'I'm good,' Martinez said.

'You seem on edge.'

'Maybe a little.' Martinez paused. 'You got time to talk before we get moving?'

'I can make time,' Sam said.

'This is personal stuff.'

'I assumed.' Sam's heart sank a little. 'Problem with Jess?'

Martinez looked around the open-plan squad room to see who was in earshot.

No one except Riley and two of the guys at the far end.

Three too many sets of ears.

'Can we get out of here, man?' he said. 'Go get a cup of coffee?'

They walked fast along Washington, both mindful of the clock ticking in the case, and went into Markie's, one of their regular haunts, going to sit right at the back with an Americano for Martinez and a cup of English breakfast tea for Sam – who had in the past been a coffee aficionado, until a cup had almost killed him.

Last cup ever so far as he was concerned.

'So what's up?' Sam asked after several moments of silence. 'Restful though this is.'

The coffee shop was almost empty, just two women in the front and Markie herself working at her laptop on the counter.

'Maybe a lot,' Martinez said.

'You going to elaborate?'

'Give me a chance, man.' Martinez took a gulp of coffee, scalded his mouth and swore.

'You OK, Al?' Markie called out. 'Need some water?'

'I'm good, thanks,' Martinez called back, then waited another second before he said: 'I'm going to ask Jessie to marry me.'

'You're kidding me,' Sam said. 'Al, that's great.'

'If she says yes, it's great.'

'Why wouldn't she say yes?'

'Why would she, more like?' Martinez sagged back in his seat. 'I'm no oil painting, in case you didn't notice, and I got lousy prospects.' He shook his head. 'Women date cops, but they don't want to marry them, it's a known fact.'

'Grace married me.'

'You're a handsome black guy, man. I'm a short, middle-aged Cuban.'

'Give me a break,' Sam said, laughing.

'Jessie's a beautiful young woman – she could have anyone.'

'But she wants you,' Sam said.

'Maybe,' Martinez said. 'Maybe not.'

'When are you planning to ask her?'

'Tonight,' Martinez said. 'If we finish early enough.'

'Done deal,' Sam told him.

'I gotta heap of paperwork besides the new case.'

'Dump it on my desk before you go.'

'Grace is gonna hate me if you work late again because of me.'

'Grace is going to be cheering you on,' Sam said.

FOURTEEN

On Wednesday evening, Elizabeth Price and André Duprez were working late.

They were almost always working, together or separately, were always either in meetings at Tiller, Valdez, Weinman, the law firm where they both worked, or dealing with clients, or in court, or in their own offices or in the library at TVW ploughing through law tomes.

Sometimes they stopped to eat or do chores or to have sex, which they both enjoyed a *lot*, though their mutual ambition as divorce lawyers frequently drove them even harder than their physical urges.

Both in their early thirties, they were doing pretty well. André, from Quebec City, drove a second-hand BMW and lived in a condo in Miami Shores. Elizabeth lived in a small town-house near Maule Lake in North Miami Beach. When one of them made partner, they'd agreed to move in together, but they intended to wait until they were both earning higher salaries before they considered marrying, because they believed in stability and equality.

For the most part, their conversations centred on the law, but they talked endlessly, never tired of hearing the other speak, sharing points of view and new experiences, learning together, respecting each other's minds.

It was already after ten, and they'd worked through dinner at André's apartment, and now they were too bushed, but Elizabeth had already said that she had to go back to her place for the night because she hadn't done any laundry for a week, and she didn't have a single white blouse left for the Thursday morning meeting at the office.

'But we haven't finished,' André said in the Québécois accent that Elizabeth had come to adore, 'and you're already tired.'

'I'm OK,' she said.

André stifled a yawn and frowned. 'I'm sleepy, too, matter of fact.'

Elizabeth regarded the work on the table. 'Let's just see if we can get a little more done,' she said, 'and then I'll go.'

FIFTEEN

Sometimes, Martinez hated himself.

All that talk, all that focus on wanting to get things right, and he'd got *nothing* right, and then he hadn't even managed to get the damned words out during dinner the way he'd planned.

He'd taken her to the Bleu Moon, one of the restaurants in the Doubletree Grand Hotel on North Bayshore Drive, because a guy he'd gotten talking to in a bar two weeks back had told him about the great romantic evening he'd had there with his girlfriend. He'd seemed like a nice enough guy and there was no one else Martinez had wanted to ask; he'd felt a little embarrassed about asking even Sam, because a middle-aged police detective ought to damned well know where to take his girlfriend for an important dinner. So he'd taken the stranger's advice and had reserved a table overlooking the bay.

Trouble was, he'd hated the place before they even found the restaurant, because the hotel was massive, jammed with tourists, and to reach the Bleu Moon they'd had to take an escalator, which made it feel like a goddamned shopping mall or a train station, and all he could think of as his beautiful girlfriend clung to his clammy paw was that she hated it too, and so she had to be thinking that if this was his idea of romance, then maybe she'd be better off looking else-where...

The restaurant itself was nice, in fact, and the table, too, overlooking the marina, but it was *modern*, which was all wrong for Jessica Kowalski, who was an old-fashioned girl – but then, right after they'd sat down and he'd ordered her Chardonnay and his beer, she'd looked around and said:

'Al, this is so beautiful.'

God, he loved her.

'I wanted something special,' he'd said, and her smile had just lit up her blue eyes, and he'd thought for a moment that he was going to do the deed right then, but then their drinks had arrived, and suddenly it seemed to Martinez that he'd messed up again, because he ought to have ordered champagne. Except then Jess might have guessed what was coming, and that would have made him even more nervous, so there he was, feeling wrong-footed, and then they'd started looking at the menu and after that it had all been about food.

Things had gotten a little easier during the starters. He'd had calamari and she'd had seared scallops and she'd said they were delicious and asked what she'd done to deserve this whole treat, and he'd told her she deserved the best, but then he'd gotten all tensed up again.

Jess had asked him, during the entrées, if he was OK.

'I'm great,' he'd answered. 'My steak is fine.'

'It's just you seem a little strained,' she'd said.

70

'I'm just tired, I guess,' Martinez had said, wanting to kick himself for losing another opportunity, telling himself he'd put things right during dessert, except then Jess had said that she couldn't eat another thing.

'Al, something isn't right,' she'd said, seeing the look on his face.

'Only that I don't deserve you.'

'What do you mean?' Jess had asked.

Real concern in her eyes.

'Later,' Martinez had said.

'Now I'm scared,' Jess had said.

'Oh, God, Jessie, don't be.'

'Easy for you to say–' she'd tried to smile – 'because you can't see your face.'

'You know what?' he'd said. 'This place is making me nervous.'

'So let's get out of here,' Jess had said.

'Now why didn't I think of that?' he'd said.

So now, at half-past ten, they were in his Chevy in the parking lot on the corner near the hotel, and suddenly Martinez knew, as he was about to start the engine, that if he waited even one more second to try to get the scene just right, it might all go wrong again.

'So here's the thing, Jessie,' he said.

She'd opened her window, and the breeze blew her hair, and the moon was sending glints of silver through the gold.

Often, when Martinez looked at this woman, he got the kind of fanciful thoughts about love that he'd never really allowed himself before, though if someone had pressed him to explain

71

why, he didn't think he'd have been able to. Until now, it had simply felt easier for him to be alone.

'You're everything I want in this world,' he told her.

Getting there at last.

Jess turned to face him fully.

Her eyes were shining now.

He knew it was going to be OK.

So he asked her.

Dug the fingertips of his left hand into his seat, and popped the goddamned question.

Finally.

'Jessie, will you marry me?'

The answer was already there in her face, nakedly clear, but she whispered it anyway.

'Yes.' A tiny pause. 'Thank you, Alejandro.'

Martinez sent up a prayer of thanks.

He thought about Sam, who might still be in the office, working.

His good friend would be happy for him.

Right now, Martinez felt happy enough for all mankind.

Two young guys, laughing as they passed the car, stooped to stare into the Chevy, but he didn't give a damn, just started the engine, moved the car toward the exit, put out his right hand and laid it on Jess's knee, felt warmed through as she covered it with her own hand.

'You know what?' she said. 'I think I need to go home.'

'Sure,' Martinez said. 'We can stay at your place, if that's what you want.'

The fact was, they almost never stayed at

Jess's place up in North Miami Beach because his house was a whole lot more comfortable and more convenient for them both for work, but tonight he could care *less* where they stayed, so long as they were together.

'No,' Jess said. 'I mean, I think I need to go home alone tonight.'

'Why?' Martinez felt a pang of dismay.

She saw his expression. 'Don't look like that, Al.'

He'd stopped his car, just inside the exit. 'You've changed your mind.'

'Never,' she said. 'It's the exact opposite.'

'So why don't you want to be with me, tonight of all nights?'

She took a moment, wanting to get the words right.

'I guess this may be hard for you to understand,' she said. 'Because you're a guy, and you're a little older, and we both know you're much more experienced.'

'I never asked anyone to marry me before,' Martinez said.

'And I never had a proposal,' Jess said.

'Honest to God?'

'I wouldn't lie about it,' she said earnestly. 'I feel this is the most important thing that's ever happened to me in my entire life, and I don't know why, but it's made me feel kind of ... old-fashioned, I guess.'

A horn honked behind them, and checking in his mirror, Martinez saw it was the kids who'd gawped at them earlier, but now he felt less benevolent about them, and if they did that one

73

more time...

'That's why I want to go home alone,' Jess went on. 'Because I want to drink in the fact that the man I'm crazy about has asked me to be his wife. I want to go to bed on my own and think about you and how it's going to be.'

The car horn sounded again, but Martinez's aggression had melted away again, and he lifted a hand in apology and drove out on to the street.

'OK,' he said to Jess, and knew that it really was, that he hadn't blown it after all, that it was all going to be better than wonderful.

'Does that make any sense to you, Al?' Jess asked.

He glanced sideways at her, saw her looking at him, saw the love in her eyes.

'All the sense in the world,' he said.

SIXTEEN

'You're much too tired to drive,' André told Elizabeth as she was piling her files into her attaché case before leaving. He stifled another big yawn. 'Me, too, it seems.'

'I'll be fine,' Elizabeth insisted, 'so long as I go right now.'

'Or we could just go to sleep and set the alarm early so you can go home then and iron a blouse.'

'Except I don't have anything clean *to* iron.'

74

André knew when there was no point arguing with Elizabeth, and it was an easy drive to her place, which was in a safe neighbourhood, besides which he had no strength left *to* argue tonight, felt he was almost drooping with fatigue, so instead he saw her down to her Honda in the parking garage. They had no significant crime issues in this area either, but André liked to think he was a gentleman and anyway, Elizabeth was the most precious person in the world to him.

'No one like you,' he told her after a last kiss, leaning against the car.

It was something he said often, and always meant.

'Nor you,' she said back to him.

Meaning it too, with all her heart, or at least all of that segment of her heart that was not devoted to her career.

She knew she'd never find anyone like André again.

Knew they truly were a perfect match.

SEVENTEEN

When Martinez had found his neat little foreclosure one-storey house on Alton Road near 47th about eight months back, he'd had some qualms about taking on a piece of serious freehold property as a confirmed bachelor, not to mention as a police detective with few hopes, or

75

even ambitions, of serious promotion. The odd lonely moment aside, he'd always liked his life pretty much the way it was, so in the midst of negotiations he'd wondered exactly why he was taking such a step at forty-five. A roof to maintain, his own windows to hurricane-proof; most of all, a mortgage which, even though he could afford it, having spent a lot less in his life to date than most guys he knew, was still going to be a stretch.

Within a week of meeting Jessica Kowalski, the house had suddenly begun making sense. *Everything* had begun making greater sense.

Coming home tonight, he thought he could even begin to understand what Jessie had meant about going back to her place alone to let it all sink in.

His house looked different to him tonight.

His whole life felt different.

She'd said she was crazy about him.

Those words felt *fat* inside him, were filling him with warmth and goodness.

Because Jess was exactly those two things to him.

He considered phoning Sam, but like his fiancée – and that was a word he'd been known to mock in the past, but never again – he thought he'd just be quiet with it for a while, maybe grab himself a beer and do what Jessie was doing, go to bed by himself and think about her and their future...

Together.

EIGHTEEN

The road where Elizabeth lived, a gated cul-de-sac where every vehicle entering or leaving was recorded, was quiet.

It was usually quiet here, with a sense of tranquillity and understated affluence.

Elizabeth had felt safe ever since she'd moved into her town house.

This evening no exception.

She passed under the raised security barrier, vaguely aware of another vehicle passing through behind her, its lights disappearing before she touched her remote to open her garage door and automatically switch on the lights, and then she slowly drove the Honda inside, closed the up-and-over door behind her and turned off her engine.

The garage light went out.

'Shit,' she said, though she was too sleepy to care, and there was enough light coming through the high glass panel in the door for her to be able to see to pick up her purse and attaché case.

She got out of the car, dropped the keys on the floor and stooped, feeling abruptly woozy, fumbled to find the keys, then straightened up and turned to the door that connected the garage to the rest of the house, barely managing to fit the

77

right key in the lock.

'What is wrong with you, girl?' she murmured.

Unwashed laundry flitted back into her mind, but she knew she was too damned out of it now to contemplate washing anything, and she could have stayed over at André's...

She got the door open – but suddenly she felt a weird, alarming sense that someone else was in the garage with her, and she started to turn, but her reflexes were off-kilter, and there *was* someone...

'Hey,' she said, fear rising.

Something landed on her mouth, a *hand*, and instinctively she tried to scream and bite it, tasted and smelled latex, but another hand was pushing at her back, propelling her inside, into her house, and she wanted to fight, but she didn't have any strength...

'That's it, Elizabeth,' a voice said right against her ear. 'No more talking now. You just sleep tight.'

NINETEEN

Sam climbed carefully into bed, trying not to wake Grace, but she rolled over toward him, slid one arm under his shoulders, the other over his chest, and wrapped her legs around his.

Full body hug, just the way they both loved it.

She was naked.

'I was going to say I'm sorry I woke you,' Sam said. 'But that would be a lie.'

'I've been waiting for you.' Grace's voice was a little husky.

'Oh, my,' Sam said. 'You're horny.'

If anyone had asked him, as he'd climbed the staircase after greeting Woody and locking up, if there was a chance in hell he might be up to any kind of sex tonight, he'd have laughed his bone-weariest laugh.

But first he'd looked in on Joshua, and the sweet curves of their little boy's cheeks and lips and lashes had affected him as they always did, making love swell in him till he was fit to burst. And now his beautiful naked wife was wrapped right around him, and it seemed there might be just a little life left in this old dog yet...

'It doesn't matter,' Grace said. 'If you're too tired...'

He knew she meant it, but his body was waking up.

Was it *ever*.

'Oh,' she said, as she felt him. 'How lovely.'

Sam thought, for just a moment, about Martinez and Jess, thought that if they were destined to have one-tenth of what he and Grace still had after more than ten years together, they'd be blessed.

And then he stopped thinking about them.

'Hi, Gracie,' he said. 'I'm home.'

And rolled over to face her.

TWENTY

February 12

'André,' Elizabeth said.

It was the third time she'd said his name.

He did not answer.

She had come to a few minutes ago and, almost immediately, had wished with all her soul that she had not.

This had to be a nightmare, the worst ever.

She was lying on a cold stone floor, felt the chill and the hardness over the full length of her body.

Knew that she was naked.

There was something around her right ankle, something even colder than the stone beneath her.

Steel.

She opened her eyes and saw that it was a cuff, like a shackle, and that a chain led from it to a thick, vertical metal bar.

One of many bars.

Because Elizabeth was in a cage.

A cage within a padded room.

There were only two runs of bars, one along the wall behind her, the other straight ahead, a gate with a lock in the centre of that run. A pool of dim light wanly illuminated her and the area around her, the light coming from a single overhead bulb screwed into the ceiling.

She couldn't see what lay beyond the bars ahead of her.

Only darkness.

And within the cage, she was not alone.

André was there, too, which was a mystery to her, because she'd been alone when she'd been taken – and his presence ought to have been some comfort to her, but was not, because he was lying on the ground several feet away from her.

Naked and shackled, like her, and almost certainly unconscious.

If not worse.

Elizabeth had tried repeatedly to rouse him, had called his name softly, warily, then more loudly, even though she was deeply afraid that whoever had brought them both here would hear her voice and come.

But André had not responded, and because he was lying with his back to her, and because the light was so poor, she couldn't tell if he was breathing or not – she couldn't *hear* any sounds of breath.

So she was terrified that he might be dying or already dead.

This had to be a nightmare.

Had to be.

Elizabeth thought about her father in Sarasota, how proud of her he'd always been. She thought about her mother, long dead to cancer. About her younger sister, Margie, in law school and all set to follow in big sis's footsteps. Thought about what this would do to them.

Whatever *it* turned out to be.

She and André were here for a purpose. Someone's purpose.

The one who'd been waiting for her in her garage.

She thought about that voice now, about how hushed it had sounded so close against her ear, and she didn't even know if it had belonged to a man or woman, did not know anything for sure.

'André,' she called again.

Nothing.

She'd already moved as close to him as her chain would allow, but now she tried again, felt the pressure of the steel shackle on her ankle.

She began to cry, and thoughts began to clamour in her head.

About why they were here, about what it meant.

She thought about rape. She thought about being left here forever, in this cage, with her unconscious, maybe dead, lover. About being left to starve and, over time, to rot away. She thought about torture.

She considered the wisdom or folly of screaming for help.

Her nakedness had stripped away more than clothes or warmth or even dignity. It seemed to have removed almost everything that had made Elizabeth Price special.

Everything except her mind. And even that – especially that – felt alien to her now, too filled with terrors.

Of the worst thing of all.

The unknown.

TWENTY-ONE

Martinez reached for the baseball bat he kept under his bed.

A coiled spring he was *not*, he registered even as he was straining to get to it in time.

If this was an intruder and if he survived, he vowed to do something about his fitness.

He made it over to the door just as it started to open.

Raised the bat high over his head...

Jess crept into the room, barefoot.

'Jesus, Jessie!' Martinez put down the bat and turned on the light. 'You almost got your head smashed in.'

Not just barefoot. She was wearing a matching brassiere and panties in the sheerest imaginable black and scarlet. Martinez had never seen her in anything like it, but she looked like heaven on a plate.

'I wanted to surprise you,' she said, breathless from the shock of his reaction.

'There's surprise,' he said, 'and there's a god-damned heart attack.'

'I'm sorry,' she said. 'I should have thought.'

'It's OK,' he said, and put his arms around her, delighting instantly in how she felt against him. 'I'm getting over it already.'

'You gave me a key, remember?'

'Sure,' Martinez said. 'But you never used it before.'

'Do you mind that I did?'

He could feel tension in her now, didn't know how to make up for ruining her surprise, so he did what came naturally, kissed her and cupped her breasts in his hands, drawing away from her mouth to say: 'That's how much I mind.'

'I bought these for you a while ago.' Jess fingered her tiny panties. 'But I never felt right wearing them until tonight. I figured they were perfect for celebrating.'

'You figured good,' he said, drawing her to the bed. 'What happened to going to bed alone and thinking about us?'

'I tried it.' She sank down beside him. 'But it felt lousy.'

'I'm glad,' Martinez said.

After they'd made love, Martinez got out of bed to turn out the light, but neither of them could sleep.

'Do you mind,' Jess asked, 'if we talk for a while?'

'Talking is good,' Martinez said. 'I wanted to ask you anyway about how you want to play this? Is it OK with you if we tell people?'

'I guess,' Jess said. 'Except, I know we're in different units, but what if the department doesn't want engaged people working in the same building?'

'I don't think that's gonna be a problem,' Martinez said. 'But anyway, it's just Sam I'm thinking about telling, for now.'

She took a moment. 'OK,' she said. 'He's a good guy.'

'He's the best,' Martinez said. 'He'll want to tell Grace, too, because they tell each other everything, but they won't spread it around if we ask them not to.'

'I guess that's all right then.' She smiled into the dark. 'It's going to make you happy telling Sam, isn't it?'

'He's my friend,' Martinez said. 'They're both going to be happy for us.'

'Then you go right ahead and tell them.'

'Who are you going to tell? Your mom and dad?'

'I don't know,' Jess said, 'because if I do, they'll want to fly over, and Mom hasn't been doing too good.'

'You didn't tell me that,' Martinez said, concerned.

'You've been busy.'

'I'm never too busy to hear your troubles, Jessie.'

'She's had some women's stuff, you know? And I think travelling might be a little much for her right now.'

'Then maybe you should wait till we can get to Cleveland.'

'You wouldn't mind doing that?' Jess asked.

'You kidding me?' Martinez said. 'I can't wait to meet the people who made you.' He hesitated. 'Though maybe they might think you could do better for yourself.'

'They won't think that, because it isn't true,'

Jess said. 'And even if they did, it wouldn't make me change my mind. But they never would.'

Martinez shifted position, but that took him away from Jess, so he moved back again, and he'd thought he'd never be comfortable sharing a bed with anyone long-term, but with Jessie even that was different.

'I was thinking I wanted to get you a ring,' he said. 'But if you don't want to tell people at the station...'

'You can still get me a ring, Al,' she said. 'I might just not wear it to work.'

'That's good,' he said.

'So this is real?' Jess asked softly.

'As real as this.' Martinez kissed her again, her smooth forehead first, then her lips. 'You feel that?'

She made a murmur of assent.

'Any time you get a doubt in your head,' he said, 'you shut your gorgeous eyes and remember how that feels.'

'It feels real beautiful,' Jess said.

'Like you,' he said.

TWENTY-TWO

Sam got to the Opera Café at seven ten Thursday morning, with plenty of time before the meeting he'd arranged at Beatty Management at eight thirty, and in the mood to treat himself to a decent breakfast with the added bonus of knowing that Cathy was on early shift.

She was waiting on customers at a window table, so he held back on a hug and sat at a vacant table halfway back. From the kitchen, Dooley saw him through the glass partition and waved, and about three seconds later, Simone came through the street door and planted a kiss on his daughter's cheek, which delighted Sam.

He felt good about this for Cathy.

Dooley was starting the day, audio-wise, with the duet from the first act of *Marriage of Figaro*, and that was fine, too. Sam watched as Simone took over from Cathy, who grinned at him and transferred into the kitchen to help Dooley, and within moments she was hard at work back there, and her movements looked deft and calm, and there was something about her bearing and expression that looked just right to Sam, as if Cathy really might have found her métier.

Which made him just so happy for her, made him want to call Grace and share the feeling with her.

His cell phone vibrated in his pocket and he drew it out, took the call.

'Hey, man,' Martinez said.

He sounded good, too.

'So?' Sam hoped there was no need to hold back. 'How was your evening?'

'Pretty good.'

'If you don't want to talk on the phone,' Sam said, 'I can wait.'

'Yeah,' Martinez said. 'Let's wait.'

'Works for me.' Sam called his bluff. 'Collins and 73rd, twenty after, OK?'

Martinez couldn't stand it.

'She said yes, man.' His voice sounded almost like it was bubbling.

'That's so great,' Sam told him. 'I'm so happy for you both.'

'Me too, man,' Martinez said. 'Never been happier in my whole life.'

Larry Beatty was out of the office when they arrived at Beatty Management, but Allison Moore was ready and waiting for them, having assembled everything the detectives had asked for.

'All the gallery's records from their last five years.'

She'd provided an office at the rear for as long they needed it, had laid out everything on the teak desk together with a pot of coffee and some small bottles of Evian water. 'Exhibitions, artists, items sold, clients.' She paused. 'A bunch of photographs, too, of exhibits, sculptures, that kind of thing – anything I thought might be useful.'

'If only everyone was as helpful,' Sam told her, 'our lives would be a whole lot easier.'

'I just hope it does help,' Ally Moore said. 'Those poor people.'

'If it doesn't give us anything directly,' Martinez said, 'it'll help by elimination.'

'I guess that's something.' She hesitated. 'I was taking a look through the old catalogues – I mean, I didn't really know what to be looking for, except for what I heard about the weird plastic thing – but there was an acrylic sculpture exhibit two years ago.'

'Where did you hear that?' Sam asked.

'It's there,' she said, 'in one of the catalogues.'

'Detective Becket means where did you hear about the "weird plastic thing"?' Martinez's antennae were up too, because there had been no moment on Saturday when the scene in the backyard could have been visible to her or her boss.

'I don't remember,' the young woman said. 'I think it was one of the people milling around – Crime Scene people, I guess.'

There was a moment's silence.

'If there's anything you want to tell us, Ms Moore,' Sam said, 'now would be the best time.'

'There's nothing,' she said.

Sam watched her, saw something that might have been evasiveness or plain old-fashioned nervousness because she was being quizzed by detectives in a grim double homicide.

'Something you saw, maybe?' Martinez said.

'You never know what's going to make a difference.' Sam was gentle.

'I guess not,' she said. 'If there were anything.'

'But there isn't?' Martinez said.

'Of course not,' she said. 'Or I'd tell you.'

'And you can't remember exactly who mentioned the "weird plastic thing",' Sam said.

'No,' she said. 'I'm sorry.'

'Maybe it'll come back to you,' Martinez said.

Moore shook her head in a helpless gesture, her red hair bouncing a little. 'I was just hoping I could help.'

'You already have.' Sam gestured at the paperwork on the table. 'Though there is one more thing, if you don't mind.'

'Anything,' she said.

'A little blood was found in the house,' Sam told her. 'Not much, and almost certainly unconnected to the crime, but same as with the fingerprints, it would make sense to ask you to provide a voluntary sample for DNA purposes.'

Now Moore looked downright edgy.

'Just a simple swab,' Sam said. 'Not blood.'

'Do you remember cutting yourself at any time in the gallery?' Martinez asked her.

'No,' she said. 'Never.'

'It could have been no more than a scratch,' Sam said. 'Something you hardly noticed at the time.'

'That's why it's better to be sure,' Martinez said.

'Only if you give your consent,' Sam said. 'Nothing for you to be worried about.'

'Sure,' she said.

'Thank you,' Sam said.

'Did you find my fingerprints in the house?' she asked.

'Sure did,' Sam said.

'So if you hadn't had my prints to compare, you'd have been looking for some unknown person,' Moore said.

'You got it,' Martinez said.

Sam and Martinez returned to that *moment* later, after they'd finished trawling through the material Moore had set out for them, finding, at first sift, nothing of apparent use, the acrylic exhibit having been of animal sculptures that Sam thought looked like poor imitations of Steuben Glass.

'So where'd she get that from,' Martinez said, 'about the plastic?'

They were sitting in the Chevy out on Collins, tourists and locals flowing by, enjoying the sunny late morning, checking out places for lunch before some of them headed back to the beach.

'Beats me,' Sam said.

Neither of them buying her story about a Crime Scene tech having blabbed in earshot.

'Think she might have been listening at key-holes?' Martinez said. 'So to speak.'

'Uh-uh,' Sam said.

'Me neither.'

'Maybe the gardener called her first?'

'Why wouldn't she tell us that?' Martinez said.

No way of getting that from Joseph Mulhoon, at least not yet, the gardener – who'd checked out as a regular old guy – still on a ventilator at Miami General.

'Maybe Moore was nosing around before Mulhoon,' Martinez said, 'and she's too embarrassed to tell us.'

'Doesn't ring true to me,' Sam said.

'Think she's been spending time there?'

'Or maybe letting someone else do that?' Sam said.

The blood and cocaine on both their minds again.

'Maybe she was meeting her lover,' Martinez said. 'Not exactly a love nest, but it takes all kinds.'

'She said she thought the place was spooky.'

'You thinkin' she's a suspect?'

'Uh-uh.' Sam shrugged. 'Nothing's impossible, as we know.'

'I'd buy Beatty over Moore,' Martinez said.

'That's just because you didn't like him,' Sam said.

Both of them had checked out, too.

'Bet he doesn't consent to a swab,' Martinez said.

His cell phone rang.

'Hey, Jessie,' he said. 'What's up?'

'I'm so sorry, Al.' She sounded upset.

'What's wrong?' He felt his heart rate speed up.

'Nothing except I have to work late,' Jess said. 'One of the girls lost a bunch of files on her PC, and I offered to help her after hours, but then I suddenly thought maybe I shouldn't have offered without checking–' she lowered her voice almost to a whisper – 'with my fiancé first.'

Sam, glancing across, couldn't help but see the smile on his friend's face.

The kind of smile that made everyone feel good.

TWENTY-THREE

Elliot Sanders called, back in the office, to say that the glue analysis was going to take time, that they might never discover which brand had been used on the victims.

'One thing, though,' the ME said. 'Unless it came from some big industrial-size container, it would be reasonable to say that the quantities needed for the job might have seemed unusual to a salesperson if someone purchased it from a store.'

'If it was bought online,' Sam said, 'that's going to be a whole lot harder to track down.'

'Can't help you there,' Sanders said.

Tracing the origins of the plastic dome-shaped cover was proving no easier.

'I'm still thinking,' Martinez said, 'it was something made for display, like maybe at exhibitions.'

'It could be a theatre prop,' Beth Riley said. 'Even a movie prop.'

'Maybe it's a component in some bigger scientific *thing* we can't even begin to picture,' Mary Cutter suggested.

'Jeez,' Martinez said. 'Now all we gotta do is identify "thing".'

They'd drawn up chairs around Sam's desk in the corner, Riley sitting below his old Florida Grand Opera poster for *Aida*.

'Maybe it's from a sci-fi movie,' she said.

'Turn it upside down–' Sergeant Alvarez, just arriving, glanced again at the photos on the cork board beside the poster – 'and it could be a giant salad bowl.'

'It would have no base,' Sam said dryly. 'It would rock.'

'It kind of reminds me of something they might keep weird insects in at a zoo, or maybe in a lab,' Riley mused. 'It could get real hot and humid under there.'

'Sam said right off the victims looked like specimens,' Mike Alvarez said.

'Or exhibits,' Sam said. 'So I guess "display" seems to be the link.'

'I like the movie props idea too,' Martinez said.

'Let's get on all that then.' Sam got to his feet, feeling the need to energize again. 'Movie sets, zoos, labs, exhibition companies – anyone who might have sold off our "thing", or might be missing it.'

'On it.' Riley was up too.

'Could just as well have come off a dump.' Martinez saw Sam's face, held up his hands. 'I know, we gotta look anyway.'

* * *

94

They were no closer to finding the actual crime scene. The Easterman house had yielded even less than the former gallery, and though their interviews with relatives, friends and colleagues were still at an early stage, with two such apparently genuinely popular young victims, there seemed little likelihood of some enemy lurking in the shadows.

Suzy Easterman had illustrated mainly children's books. Michael Easterman had been an architect specializing in commercial property, with no adverse publicity linked to his name or any history of litigation against him or even his firm.

Random selection likely then. Scary as hell and even harder to solve.

Highly organized killings. Boastful too.

And one of the spectres creeping Sam out was that unless there was some *specific* reason for the Eastermans having become the victims of a crime as vile and brazen as this, the mind or minds behind it might be planning to do it again.

Nothing had shown up yet on the computer to indicate that they had done it before, either in South Florida or anyplace else in the US.

But every killer had to start somewhere.

TWENTY-FOUR

Elizabeth had slept for a while, a tiny time-out, a fragment of escape.

She was awake again now, and she was cold, and André had still not shifted, but at least she was finally certain that he was *alive*, thank God, because a moment or two ago his shoulder blades had moved just a little, and she could hear his breathing...

Something distracted her.

Something *else*.

Movement. Not in the cage with them, not exactly, but...

Shapes were moving on the wall to her left, galvanizing her now.

Monochrome figures in a black-and-white movie.

A silent movie.

With a cast of two.

Herself and André.

TWENTY-FIVE

Sam and Martinez were at the Milton Zuckerman Home, a high-priced nursing home on Biscayne Boulevard a few blocks north of the Aventura Mall, where they'd come to meet with Mrs Marilyn Myerson.

They'd seen Larry Beatty's documents, including a psychiatric geriatrician's report confirming the Alzheimer's diagnosis, but they needed to see for themselves.

Beatty had said that her dementia was advanced, and he had spoken the truth.

No hope of even a few lucid words from this poor woman.

'I know we're on duty,' Martinez said as they emerged from the home into the warm sunshine, 'but I could use a goddamned drink.'

'Know just what you mean,' Sam said, because though they had both, for their own emotional health, developed a degree of immunity to suffering, the plight of complete strangers could sometimes still hit hard.

'So how about you tell me now,' he said as they got back in the Chevy, 'about last night?'

'I told you. She said yes.'

'Did it go the way you planned it?'

'I screwed that up,' Martinez said. 'I figured

I'd blown it for sure.'

'Clearly not,' Sam said.

'I ended up asking her in the goddamned car. She was sitting right where you are, can you believe it?'

'Sure I can. Nice view of the bay?'

'We were in the parking lot,' Martinez said wryly.

'And she still said yes?' Sam smiled. 'She must really love you.'

'She really does seem to,' Martinez said with a kind of awe.

He started the engine, the sad plight of the old lady who'd once owned the big mansion and art gallery on Collins already fading away, though Sam found himself wondering if anyone ever came to visit Mrs Myerson these days and if the lady was ever sufficiently aware to notice if they did.

'Why the parking lot?' he asked, belatedly.

'Any port in a storm,' Martinez said. 'If I'd waited till we got home, I knew I might have lost my nerve again.' He grinned. 'I'm gonna love that parking lot till I die, man.'

TWENTY-SIX

There was some kind of fine mesh screening right across the wall to the left of the cage that Elizabeth hadn't noticed until the 'movie' started, though she guessed it had to have been there all the time.

She wondered what the time was, had no way of knowing, thought that perhaps it was better that way, and oh, dear God, she was so *cold*, and she needed André to wake up, she needed him to hold her...

The movie was still silent, though she could hear a low electronic hum.

If this were a real movie, no one would pay to see it, for sure, but Elizabeth found she could not look away.

It was all footage of her and André sitting somewhere, talking.

Talking, talking, endlessly.

It was impossible to see where they'd been when it was filmed – when they'd been *spied* on – because the shots were all in close-up, and as Elizabeth went on staring at it she realized it was a series of short sequences edited together. Their clothes – what she could see of them – were of no help in identifying the date or location, because she was wearing the white cotton blouses

99

she put on most work days with her suits, and she often still wore the same clothes when they went out for drinks or dinner directly from the office; and André, too, wore one of his favourite Brooks Brothers slim-fit one hundred per cent cotton shirts most days...

Her shoulder-length dark brown hair was different in each sequence, once tied back, once loose, once held partially back with one of the tortoiseshell clips she sometimes used, but Elizabeth's mind was much too confused now to even begin to try to recall what hairstyle she'd worn on different occasions.

It was dizzying to watch, because despite its jerky editing, it was still one piece, playing repeatedly like a loop, and sometimes she and André were speaking earnestly, sometimes it was one talking and the other listening intently, then they seemed in the midst of one of their rapid fire exchanges, but that was *all* there was to see – *talking*.

And then, at the end of the final clip, the end of the loop, the camera had zoomed in on their faces, close up to their lips, so that their mouths appeared ever larger, which made Elizabeth feel violently ill each time she saw it, and she wanted to look away, but she had a terrible, almost superstitious sense that if she did that, her life, *their* lives, might end along with the sick movie.

As to what it might mean, she was too afraid to know that, too terrified to think about who was playing this tape, to wonder if they were doing it remotely or if they were here now, if they were watching her watching *it*. And so she switched off those questions, shut down the inquisitorial part of her mind that had always been a significant part of being Elizabeth Price, and just went on staring up at the screen as the compilation rolled over and over again.

She wanted to scream.

In time, if this kept on for long enough, she knew she might do just that.

Except that might make the *director* of this movie do more than watch her.

It might make him or her come back.

'Please,' she said, very softly, then repeated it. 'Please, please, please.'

She took another look at André, at the man she loved, torn suddenly between gladness for his lack of suffering, and rage at his *absence* from her, because he was useless to her like this, and of course she loved him, but...

'Please,' she said again.

And turned back to the people on the wall.

Who seemed, increasingly, to her tortured brain, like strangers.

TWENTY-SEVEN

Thursday afternoon, Grace had been out shopping with Joshua.

She'd seen two patients this morning, but now she was free until tomorrow and feeling energized by the sunshine, and they'd been to Laurenzo's on West Dixie for pumpkin ravioli and to Fresh Market for fish and fruit and to Publix for everything else, and though she'd already dropped in several bags of shopping at David's house, the trunk of the Toyota was still loaded.

She was at Saul's place now, had changed Joshua's diaper and was sitting on the peaceful terrace that overlooked the Intracoastal Waterway, sipping a glass of iced tea; and Cathy had just come in from the café and said that she was going to be heading out for a run on the beach just as soon as she'd gotten over the big plate of penne that Dooley had made for her after her shift. Saul had been around the corner when Grace had arrived, busy in his small rented workshop off North Bay Road, fulfilling an order for a beech table and chairs, and the furniture looked so handsome that Grace had felt a rush of pride in her young brother-in-law – and now she felt the same way about Cathy, who looked so happy, seemed so positive.

'Unky Saw,' Joshua shouted suddenly, and Saul, in cut-off T-shirt and shorts, gave a whoop and scooped up his nephew, joined after a second by Cathy, tickling her little brother's tummy.

'Caffee!' Joshua screamed with joy.

'Joshi!' Cathy responded in kind.

'Mommy!' Joshua urged Grace to join in, but she just sat, enjoying the moments, reflecting yet again that baby laughter surely had to be one of the most beautiful sounds in life.

Sam had told her last night, soon after they'd finished making love, that Martinez was going to propose to Jess, and a sense of warmth enveloped her at the thought of that good man finally getting a taste of *this*.

Good times.

The best.

TWENTY-EIGHT

Early this Thursday evening, the rats were alone, their food all eaten.

In her section of the cage, the doe named Isabella the Seventh was quiet, but Romeo the buck, separated from her, was hungry and becoming increasingly agitated, and need had sent him a while ago to one of the cage's ventilation holes, to a small gap on the outer edge that the keeper had not yet noticed.

Gnawing brought some satisfaction.

Freedom would bring food.

This young buck was not a fancy rat, had not been bred as a pet. Romeo the Fifth was a common-as-shit roof rat, *rattus rattus*, a sleek, graceful critter with a slate grey back and a paler grey belly, as happy in a hollow wall munching on insulation or wiring or pipework, as most of his kind.

If Isabella or any other female had been immediately accessible, Romeo might have thought twice about leaving right away, would at least have jumped her one more time before

103

hitting the road. But she wasn't available.

So he kept right on gnawing.

Urinating and dropping faeces as he went.

Same as any other self-respecting roof rat.

TWENTY-NINE

Elizabeth could hear new sounds.

'André,' she hissed, beyond desperate for him to wake at last, for him to be here for her *now*.

But the man who had always been so animated, so young and lean and clever, who had made love to her with the same kind of verve that he'd brought to his work – that man just went on lying there, all his strength and vitality stolen along with his dignity by whatever they had done to him.

The movie was still playing, but Elizabeth had quit looking at it, had burrowed back down into sleep for a while, waking to fresh realization and terror, which was when her bladder had finally let go, making her weep with humiliation. Nothing more she could do about it than shift closer to the wall, out of her own mess, taking her even further away from André.

Lonelier than ever.

The new sounds came closer.

Something rattling, creaking, *rolling*.

Wheels, perhaps.

And now she heard jangling.

A key in a lock.

Elizabeth's eyes, wide in new terror, darted toward the sound, trying in vain to penetrate the darkness beyond the front of the cage.

But the key was turning, and now an unseen door was opening, and with it came a sliver of light that expanded to a triangle and was instantly muddied – by *someone* entering – and then the triangle shrank and vanished as the door closed and the blackness was complete again.

Elizabeth felt the most abject dread crawl through her.

'André,' she whispered one last time.

She thought again of her father and sister, and of her dead mother.

Her heart felt strange and painful.

Breaking, perhaps.

THIRTY

Sam's mind kept veering off the case to his surprise plans for Grace's birthday.

She wouldn't be expecting anything, this being her thirty-ninth, but he hadn't wanted to wait a whole year until the 'big' one because Grace deserved something special *now*, and when it came to her fortieth, he'd do something else, something even bigger, if their reserves held out; and his mom's legacy had made a substantial difference to their security, and Judy would have approved of his putting some of it into spoiling Grace, because she'd grown to adore her daughter-in-law in the five years they'd spent together.

So this year, for her birthday on March first, it was going to be a cruise – departure three days earlier from Fort Lauderdale.

One of Sam's concerns was that the surprise was a bit of a long shot, because cruising was something they'd never considered before, and for all he knew, they might both hate the whole thing, and Lord knew their previous experiences with boats had been small and anything *but* soothing ... Still, First International's *Stardust* was certainly not small, and he wanted to whisk Grace away from it all, but he couldn't take more than a few days, and this way there'd be no need to negotiate airports and long flights, and if by chance they hit bad weather or got seasick or hated vacationing with so many other people, then heck, it was only four nights and, bottom line, they'd still be away and together...

And the notion of sweeping his Gracie right off her gorgeous feet and on to a beautiful cruise ship, when she was expecting nothing grander than a family dinner, warmed him right down to his toes.

Hardly anyone knew about the plan to date – just his dad, Martinez, Sergeant Alvarez and Captain Kennedy, all of whom he'd had to inform before he'd handed over his Amex details to First International – but he was going to have to involve Saul and Cathy soon, because they'd have to help him play this little game, and he couldn't wait much longer.

Except, before they left, there was a double homicide to solve, and no signs of an imminent breakthrough, so Sam needed to keep *all* of his mind on the job and off the cruise.

THIRTY-ONE

February 13
On Friday morning, when Karen Christou first opened her bedroom blinds and looked out on to her backyard, her first reaction was to laugh out loud, because the joke was *so* on her sonofabitch husband.

And then she took a closer look.

Stopped laughing.

Started screaming instead.

Loud enough to wake the neighbours.

But not the dead.

Neither the scores of exotic fish and shrimp spilled over their lawn.

Nor the two wretched human souls who had displaced them in their three hundred gallon acrylic home.

Elliot Sanders – given a heads-up by the on-call medical examiner, Mike Dietrich – notified Sam at ten twenty-two.

'You and Al need to get over here,' he said.

To a one-storey house on Prairie Avenue.

'We got another one,' Sanders told him. 'That

107

is, another two.'

Sam felt his insides clench. 'Same MO?'

'Not exactly,' the ME said. 'But close enough.'

'Throats cut?' asked Sam.

'Yes. Sliced across, not slashed.'

'Glue?'

'Yes, indeed,' Sanders said.

The lady of the house was still in shock when the Miami Beach detectives arrived.

Handsome house, gleaming white with a red-tiled roof, beautifully planted front yard and Spanish-style front door.

Crime scene now.

Neal Peterson, one of the patrol officers who'd been first on the scene and who knew Sam and Martinez of old, told them that Mrs Christou's husband, a restaurateur, was on the way down from his place in Boca Raton.

'Separated, not divorced,' he said. 'Not too amicably, by the sounds of it.'

'Think she recognized the victims?' Sam asked-ed.

'I don't think she got close enough,' Peterson said. 'Can't say I blame her.'

Sam and Martinez headed straight through to the back.

The stink of the dead fish already warming in the sun caught them right off.

'Nice.' Elliot Sanders nodded at them. 'Real nice.'

'Jesus,' Sam said under his breath.

The victims lay inside a huge fish tank. One male, one female, both Caucasian, both mid- to late-twenties, the female lying on top of the male.

Face to face.

Outside, on the lawn, fish and shrimp were spread all over the grass.

The tank in which the human dead lay measured ninety-six inches in length, but only twenty-four inches deep, and though even on its stone plinth the whole thing stood just forty-five inches high, there was no space for anyone else to get inside.

'They're about ready to cut out the front of the tank,' Sanders told Sam, 'but the dust's going to fly, however careful they are, so I asked them to wait so you could take a look first, get the picture.'

'Appreciate it,' Sam said, his mind recoiling along with his gut.

Martinez had his notebook out, was already making a sketch, his face stony.

The ME waited as Sam took it all in, then nodded to two men in coveralls, booties and masks, waiting over by one of the white stone walls with sheeting and a powerful-looking saw.

'Took some time to get what they needed from the lawn and the outside of the tank,' Sanders said. 'They'll bring the whole damned thing over on the flatbed later, but Mike Dietrich and I got a good first look.'

The guys were efficient as lumberjacks and painstaking as surgeons, carving out the huge slab of solid acrylic in one piece and contriving to keep most of the dust and debris outside the tank.

The ME went in first, moving fastidiously, treading the same path as the techs, then taking his time over his examination and returning to the detectives.

'Rigor still present,' Sanders said. 'Washed and moved after death again. Blade used might be the same. No wedding ring marks this time. More later. You guys go ahead.'

The victims were both attractive, as the Eastermans had been, but this woman had shoulder-length dark hair and the man's buzz cut hair was fair. Partially obscured as their faces were, there was more visible suffering in the woman's expression than the man's, who, Sam thought, looked almost peaceful.

'If you hunker down right there,' Sanders said from a few feet back, 'you can see the glue. I suspect there's more that's not visible from here, but that much is clear enough.'

'Holy shit,' said Martinez.

Sam quietly exhaled.

'Lips this time.' Sanders's voice held pure disgust. 'We won't be able to say if it's filling their oral cavities or not till they're back at our place.' He watched the detectives scanning the bodies. 'I can't see any traces around their genitalia.'

'We got ourselves a monster,' Martinez said grimly.

'Or more than one,' Sam said.

'Lot of work for one perp,' Martinez said.

'Could be one mastermind,' Sam said, 'running a team.'

They straightened up, took another look

110

around. Whoever had done this had first scooped out the fish in a wholesale massacre, dumped them on the grass and drained out the water before placing the human bodies in the tank.

'I'd say they were lowered in very carefully,' Sanders said. 'So as not to ruin the gluing handiwork or the positioning.'

Sam turned, then crouched again, eyes narrow, looking at a section of grass that had been cordoned off and flagged.

A double row of wheel tracks of similar appearance to those at the mansion.

'I'm guessing a gurney,' he said. 'Maybe the kind where you can adjust height. That would make it easier for a solo perp.'

'Something else to add to our shopping list,' Martinez said. 'Pricey.'

'Not if they stole it from a hospital,' Sanders said. 'Maybe with a hoist, too, to help with the lowering.'

'Lot of equipment to move around discreetly,' Sam said, then looked up and around. 'No cameras.' He glanced back at the house. 'Mrs Christou must be one hell of a sound sleeper to have missed all this.'

'Her neighbours, too,' Martinez said, making notes.

'I guess it could have been done pretty quietly,' Sam said. 'Well-oiled wheels on the gurney, mostly over grass. Draining the tank.'

'And fish don't scream,' Elliot Sanders said.

THIRTY-TWO

Anthony Christou arrived less than an hour later, went out to the backyard with Sam and Martinez to take a look, and then, visibly shaken and close to tears, followed them back inside, into the living room, where his wife sat huddled on the sofa, smoking a cigarette.

The drapes were drawn, blotting out the horrors, and the air-con was blowing cold air, but the room was still unpleasantly smoky, five lipstick-tipped butts resting in a chunky glass ashtray on the marble-topped coffee table.

'You got what you wanted then,' Christou said aggressively.

He wore a black T-shirt and black jeans, a stocky man with dark hair gelled and combed straight back, flicking up a little at his neck. His brown eyes held anger and, Sam thought, a measure of real pain.

'What the fuck,' his wife asked, 'do you think this has to do with me?'

'You hated them.'

Karen Christou's eyes were turquoise – probably, Sam suspected, achieved with tinted lenses – and her ash blonde-streaked hair looked carefully brushed. She'd also taken the time to apply pale lipstick at some stage, but she still wore the long green silk caftan that Peterson said she'd had on when they'd arrived.

'In case you haven't noticed,' she said, 'there are two dead bodies out there.'

'Of course I've fucking noticed,' Anthony said. 'I'm not blind.'

Karen looked up at the detectives. 'And just in case you were wondering who the "them" is my husband said I hated, it was the fish, not those poor people.' Abruptly, she began to cry, tugged a tissue from a box on the table.

Christou dropped into one of the armchairs, a hand over his eyes.

Sam and Martinez shared a glance, a tacit agreement to let these two roll on unhindered for at least a few moments longer.

'You probably think it's weird–' Christou let his hand fall into his lap – 'a man sitting here weeping for fish.'

'Not especially,' Sam said.

'It's just because I've tried so hard to give them a good life.'

'I'm sure,' Martinez said.

'That's why I bought such a big tank,' Christou went on. 'Because I figured if I wanted to indulge myself with their beauty, I owed it to them to give them as much space as I could, and now...'

'He loved them so much he walked out on them.' Karen Christou stubbed out her cigarette.

'I walked out on you,' Anthony said. 'Not my fish.'

'He promised to have the tank moved, but his promises mean zip, you know?' Karen went on.

113

'I've had to feed them every fucking day because he's too busy to come do it himself.'

'I have to work, remember?'

'So you can afford to keep your fish in their fucking heated tank.'

Sam and Martinez exchanged another look.

'OK,' Sam said. 'That's enough.'

'A little respect,' Martinez added.

'And a few questions,' Sam said.

'I'm sorry,' Anthony Christou said. 'Ask your questions.'

'Would you like to sit down?' There was a slight lick of shame in Karen Christou's tone as she lit another Marlboro Light with a plastic lighter. 'I could get you some coffee.'

'We're good,' Sam said. 'But thank you.'

He and Martinez sat in the two empty armchairs.

'Do you have to do that?' Anthony regarded Karen's cigarette.

'What do you think?' she said, then deferred to Sam. 'Do you mind?'

'It's your home,' he said.

'All our lungs, though,' Anthony said.

Karen took a long drag, turned away from him again. 'I told the cops who came first, that I didn't recognize those people.' Her voice was quieter now. 'Not that I saw them close to.' The turquoise eyes widened. 'Please don't make me look at them again.'

'We'll be showing you both some photographs in due course,' Sam said. 'Only of their faces. Just in case.'

'Sure,' Anthony said. 'No problem.' He made

114

the sign of the cross with an abrupt, jerky motion, then shook his head. 'I really am sorry, guys.'

'That's OK, sir,' Sam said.

'It must have been a terrible shock,' Martinez said.

'At least you were warned,' Karen told Anthony. 'Imagine what it did to me.'

'I know,' he said.

'I don't understand,' his wife said. 'Why us?' She drew her robe more tightly around herself as if suddenly cold.

'Why *here*, you mean,' Anthony said. 'It has nothing to do with us.'

'It's your backyard, sir,' Martinez said.

'I don't even live here anymore,' Christou said.

'You're incredible,' Karen said, then caught Sam's expression and shook her head. 'Sorry.'

'You don't really think–' her husband asked the detectives – 'that this *could* have anything to do with us?'

'Can you think of any reason why it should have, sir?' Sam asked.

'Of course not.'

'My husband's in the restaurant business,' Karen said.

Leaving Sam unsure if she meant that might preclude enmity or criminality of any kind – or the opposite.

'You own a restaurant?' Martinez asked, as if it were news to him.

'Three,' Christou said. 'All specializing mainly in fish, cooked Greek style.'

Which ruled out goulash or stroganoff on his

115

menus, Sam supposed, his mind clicking automatically back to the first case.

'That's one of the reasons I liked taking such good care of my beauties here,' Christou went on. 'God knows I'm guilty of having cooked enough of them in my line of business, so I figured it was my way of putting something back, you know?'

'Sure,' Martinez said, poker-faced. 'You do takeout, sir?'

Clearly on the same track as Sam.

'For some customers,' Christou said. 'It's not a big thing for us.'

'I used to work with Anthony in the business,' Karen said. 'Now I just stay home and mind his fucking pets.'

Malice never far below the surface with these two.

'You did a great job,' Christou said sarcastically.

'Fuck off,' she said.

'Nice.' Her husband glanced at the detectives. 'They don't need this, Karen.'

'And we do?' she said.

A moment passed, not exactly of truce, but at least of silence, and then Christou got to his feet. 'I need a drink. Anyone else want something?'

'No, thank you,' Sam said.

'Me neither,' Martinez said.

They waited as the man opened a cabinet and poured two fingers of whisky into a crystal glass, half-expected Christou's wife to object, but the truce held.

'Who would know,' Sam asked, 'about the fish

116

tank? Other than your friends and neighbours?'

'A lot of people know about it.' Christou sat down again, took a drink. 'Our customers, for a start.'

'He has big photos of the tank on the walls of all the restaurants,' Karen said.

'And there was a piece in *Miami Today*,' Christou said.

'And a review in the *Herald* a couple of years ago,' Karen added.

'I don't think the tank got a mention in that.' Christou paused. 'One of the officers told me we're going to have to move out because our home is a crime scene now. Is that true?'

'I'm afraid it is,' Sam said.

'But surely...' New horror appeared to strike Karen Christou. 'You don't think they were actually *killed* here? Surely they were just left here, after...'

'Almost certainly they were just left,' Sam said.

'Thank God.' She thought for a moment. 'So where am I supposed to go?'

Christou said, grudgingly: 'You could come to my place.'

'Can I go to a hotel?' Karen asked, blanking his offer.

'Sure,' Sam said. 'A hotel, family, friends.'

'So long as we know where you're staying,' Martinez said.

Reality kicked in for the couple.

'Oh, my God, Tony,' Karen said, close to tears again.

'Tell me about it,' her husband said.

117

'Quite a pair,' Sam said, outside.

'It's good to be out of there,' Martinez said.

Not that it was possible to feel too much relief when faced with the macabre scene still out in the backyard.

Not just brutal homicide here.

A particular kind of degradation, perpetrated for a second time, making them both sick to their souls.

And then, as always happened in the worst cases, they felt it start to galvanize them, to fill them with a determination to do their jobs to the utmost of their abilities.

And then some.

THIRTY-THREE

They had a small amount of good luck with Karen Christou's neighbours, merely in that they were almost all home when Sam and Martinez came knocking. But that was where the luck ended, because no one was admitting to having seen or heard anything suspicious last evening or night.

Still, at least they were *home*, and could therefore be checked off the ever-growing list of things the squad had to do. All of it painstaking and much of it a grind, the tasks that had to be taken care of more meticulously than ever without a big lead. Not that they bitched about it too much because they all knew it was how the job went, and it was all worth doing, too, so long as they got there in the end. Which didn't make it easy, but it was what they were paid for, and it was what they owed the victims.

Big time.

One good thing about today.

Jessica Kowalski was off duty, and having heard about the new homicides, she'd felt a great urge to take care of her brand-new fiancé and had brought in a picnic basket lunch for him and his partner.

Crusty rolls, Canadian cheddar, cold chicken and bottled water.

'I didn't bring wine,' she said. 'With you guys being on a case.'

'Are you kidding?' Martinez said. 'We eat all this, we'll snooze the rest of the day.'

'It's too much,' Jess said, crestfallen. 'I didn't think.'

'Too much?' Sam said. 'It's the best thing anyone's ever done for us in this place.'

'And it means I get to see you,' Martinez said.

'I hope you realize we could get used to this,' Sam said.

Jess's cheeks grew warm. 'I guess Grace can't do stuff like this, not with her work and the baby to take care of.'

Sam smiled. 'Oh, you'd be surprised at how much Grace can do.'

* * *

119

Not much else that was good about today.

About double homicide.

Quadruple now.

'What defines serial killing?' Jess asked just before she left.

'Not this,' Martinez said, then knocked on his desk. 'We hope.'

'Unlawful homicide of at least two people,' Sam said, 'carried out in a series over a period of time, seems to be the minimal definition. Though cops tend not to think in serial terms without something more conclusive than that.'

'More killings, in other words,' Martinez said.

'God forbid,' Jess said.

Though everyone now involved in the investigation was uncomfortably aware that the staged elements of the slayings made it all too possible that whoever was responsible might just feel like rounding off the 'achievement' with a third pair.

God forbid, as Jess had said.

Suddenly, midway through the afternoon, *something*.

A few grains of sand found in the wheel tracks on the Christou lawn.

On the face of it, not the biggest deal, considering Prairie Avenue was in Miami Beach. Except Crime Scene were saying that this was *not* Miami Beach sand, which was golden and comparatively coarse.

The sand in those tracks was white and finer, more like Gulf Coast sand or even sand up in north-west Florida, which had some of the purest, whitest sand in the state – or it might just be from a bunker on one of the numerous golf courses in the area. And given time, they would probably be able to analyze it further, narrow it down. But for now, all they knew was that it wasn't local beach sand, and no one could guess how that might help nail the killers of the fish tank victims.

But it was, at least, something.

It was too late when Sam got home for the kind of Friday evening that he loved; too late for candle lighting and the family gathering around the Jewish Sabbath table that even Grace, born of Italian Catholic and Swedish Protestant parents, had come to cherish since their marriage – and it was a source of pleasure and amusement for the Beckets, on occasions like Thanksgiving, to list their remarkable multiracial, national and religious legacies, with Sam always claiming, until Joshua's birth, that he had won the melting pot contest as an African-Bahamian-Episcopalian-Jewish-American descendant of a runaway slave.

Late as it was tonight, though his son was sound asleep, Grace was waiting for him with beef and potato soup simmering in a copper pan, a ciabatta loaf ready for slicing, and the remains of the good Chianti they'd shared last night standing on the kitchen table.

Sam kissed his wife, sank on to a chair, fondled Woody's ears as the dog leaned against his right leg.

'My day for being spoiled,' he said.

He'd already told her about Jess bringing in

121

lunch.

'Must mean you deserve it,' Grace said.

'Talk about good enough to eat,' Sam said. 'Look at you.'

Nothing overtly sensuous about what she was wearing – Grace didn't do slinky or black lace – but she could make one of his old white shirts look a damned sight sexier than any GQ spread.

'You look bushed,' she said, ladling soup into a ceramic bowl.

'Truth,' he said. 'I am.'

'Too tired to talk over an idea?' She set down the bowl in front of him, sliced a hunk of bread and poured him a glass of wine.

'Of course not.' He grasped at her hand. 'Thank you, Gracie.'

'You're very welcome,' she said, loving the fact that he still bothered to thank her for small kindnesses.

'And the idea?' He had a spoonful of soup. 'That is *so* good.'

'Do you think Al would mind if we threw him and Jess a party?'

Sam raised both eyebrows in surprise. 'Really?'

She sat down beside him. 'Only I can't picture him arranging that kind of thing, but I think they might like it, so if you think it would be OK, I'd love to do it.'

'You are truly a spectacular woman,' Sam said. 'Is that a yes?'

'Definitely,' he said. 'Except I'm not sure we can invite anyone from the department.'

'So they're really not telling people yet?' She

122

pulled a face. 'I don't know who we could invite then. I've never heard Al talk about friends outside the office.'

'He doesn't really have much of a life outside,' Sam said.

'He didn't,' Grace said, 'but he does now.'

'So maybe we'll just make them a family dinner – our family being his.'

'That's fine with me,' Grace said. 'And should it be a surprise, do you think, or should we consult with them?'

'I think we should tell Al, and if he goes for it, leave it up to him to decide if he wants to tell Jess or not.' Sam didn't think he was up to organizing more than one surprise at a time.

'That leaves the biggest problem,' Grace said. 'Finding a free evening for you guys with this case.'

Sam sighed because that was so true. 'Let's see what the next few days bring.' He picked up his spoon, then set it down again, his appetite gone.

'No ID yet on this couple?'

'We can't even be sure they are a couple.'

'Dear Lord,' Grace said.

THIRTY-FOUR

February 14

Romeo the Fifth was missing in action.

The keeper didn't know whether to be more upset or impressed.

It had been apparent, from the go, that he was a rough one, and now it was clear that he was a tough guy, too, with an independent streak, and face it, the buck would have had to go soon anyway.

Anyway, the good news, as it happened, far outweighed the bad.

Because Isabella the Seventh was expecting.

Well, of *course* she was, fecund little mom that she was.

The keeper wasn't going to bug her with stats this weekend, would allow Isabella to celebrate in peaceful isolation.

And who knew, maybe Romeo would show up again.

Food and sex on offer, after all.

THIRTY-FIVE

The squad had come to the station for a Sunday morning meeting, gathering in their own office rather than in the conference room since most of the other detectives were off duty.

Second Sunday in a row for some of them, and they'd had to work late yesterday evening – not that any of them were too sold on Valentine's, but that wasn't the point; what mattered was that they were tired, and some of them had families, and Sam, like most of them, had this old-fashioned wish to be home with Grace and Joshua, which seemed to happen too damned seldom. Though usually when he was pulling overtime, it was because of overdue paperwork, not the violent crimes themselves.

They worked and lived in a peaceful place, for the most part.

All the more reason for them to protect it as well as they could.

The intention this morning was to brainstorm, as well as pool existing information again, trying their damnedest to refresh their minds and produce something new and useful.

One, two or even more killers remained the unsatisfactory consensus, and there was the strong possibility that they were dealing with a strong, highly organized individual, working alone or hiring help – which was their best hope of a weak link – but Sam had brought a sickening list to the meeting, of past partner or team serial killers in the US and worldwide. Lessons to be learned, maybe, or some ingredient of those cases to help trigger new insight in their own squad.

There were more photographs pinned up on the board than there had been just twenty-four hours earlier. John and Jane Doe joining the Eastermans, and the indignity of nameless victims always made Sam's heart ache.

One question was taxing them all, and Martinez voiced it first:

'I still don't get what the hell kind of message is a goddamned fish tank?'

'And how does it relate to the dome?' Sam added.

'The tank's acrylic,' Riley said.

The notion of a plastics-motivated killer gripped no one.

Exhibition was self-evident, but there was no other link they'd managed to conjure up between the garden of a former gallery and the backyard of an occupied luxury home.

Outdoors probably chosen just because it was easier than breaking in.

'And because the displays were more likely to be found,' Cutter said, 'though that goes more for the Christou house.'

'For the gallery too,' Sam said, 'if they knew the gardener's routine. Which would make the dumping sites highly premeditated.'

'Does that make the victims more or less likely to be randomly chosen?' Riley asked.

The phone rang. Elliot Sanders bringing them up to date.

'I'm putting you on speaker, Doc,' Sam told him.

'Same knife,' the ME said, 'or damned close. And we have stomach contents for you. Beef, egg plant, tomatoes and cheese.'

'Moussaka,' Riley said.

'Christou's Greek,' Martinez said.

'His restaurants serve fish,' Sam said.

'Bet he knows how to cook moussaka,' Martinez persisted.

'Not usually with sedatives, though, I'd imagine,' Sanders's voice said through the speaker. 'Temazepam again. Higher levels in the male, maybe just because he ate more dinner. He may have been unconscious before he died.' He paused. 'More to follow, as always, but I thought you'd want to know.'

'We need to know if the victims liked Greek food,' Sam said.

'I'd settle for their names first,' Beth Riley said.

'Moussaka has to make the Christous more interesting,' Martinez said.

'Except it was goulash with the Eastermans,' Cutter said.

'And fish,' Martinez said.

'We're reaching, guys,' Sam said. 'Unpleasant as the Christous are, I can't see them being crazy enough to have to have killed these people and then displayed them in their own fish tank – not

127

to mention calling 911—'

'Karen made the call,' Martinez pointed out. 'Not Anthony.'

'Maybe their backyard was chosen for more reasons than the fish tank being there,' Sam said.

'Still here,' Sanders jolted them from the speaker on Sam's desk.

'Sorry, Doc,' Sam said.

'The glue was in both their mouths, and plenty of it. But I'd venture to say that the big deal here – maybe the turn on, but that's for you people to establish – was the joining of their *lips*, same way the Eastermans were joined down below.'

'Hips and lips,' Martinez said sourly after the ME had signed off. 'Think we got a poet?'

'It wasn't hips, though, remember,' Sam said.

'Sure I remember.' Martinez shook his head. '*So* sick.'

The missing persons report came through just before lunch.

The stuff of nightmares for two more families, and only the beginning.

'Two lawyers from the same firm,' Sam told Martinez, scanning the printout in his hand. 'Not married or even cohabiting, but definitely a couple.'

Elizabeth Ann Price, aged thirty-three, and André Duprez, a year older, both AWOL from their office on Biscayne Boulevard since Thursday morning, according to their close friend and colleague Michelle Webster, who'd been out that day but had felt something was amiss when neither of them had shown up for work on

128

Friday – and had *known* that something was badly wrong when both had failed to respond either to her texts or calls to their homes, cells or Skype lines.

'Ms Webster said she tried to convince herself that they were just acting against type and taking a couple of unscheduled personal days,' Sam went on reading. 'But then she drove to Ms Price's townhouse in North Miami Beach and saw that Mr Duprez's BMW was parked on the street, and Ms Price's Honda was in the garage.'

Michelle Webster stated, in her report, that she'd held off until Saturday afternoon, telling herself they could have gone out with friends or taken a cab to the airport, gone someplace for the weekend. But none of that rang true, so finally she'd driven to André Duprez's apartment building in Miami Shores, and had talked the super into using his key to see if all was well.

Which it certainly had *seemed* to be. If André had eaten there recently, either alone or with Elizabeth, there was no sign of it; in fact, Michelle had reported that the kitchen was pristine, but looking around with the super, she'd seen that all André's suitcases seemed to be there, right down to his weekend bag.

Sam put down the report.

'No signs of a struggle,' he said, 'so far as she could see.'

'She go inside Ms Price's house?' Martinez asked.

'No key.' Sam paused. 'Elizabeth's father and sister live up in Sarasota, mother deceased. André Duprez is from Quebec City – a snowbird who came down about ten years ago and never went home. Both parents alive and living there.'

The photograph handed over on Saturday by Michelle Webster came through.

Two attractive young people having fun at a party. The woman a brunette, with high cheekbones and a laughing mouth, wearing a simple, classy-looking black dress. The young man in an open-necked white shirt, also sharp-looking, his fair hair buzz-cut, his eyes blue and keen.

No real doubts about their identity.

Elizabeth Price's father, Edward, would be getting a visit from the Sarasota Police Department before the hour was out. Same deal in Quebec City. Arrangements would be made for them to fly to Miami as soon as possible.

Their permission would be requested to enter and search their children's properties, and search warrants would be obtained to help the police try to determine if anything bad had occurred at either address, or if the victims' lifestyles – perhaps even their taste in art – might throw up a link with the Oates Gallery couple.

In the meantime, Sam and Martinez would meet with Michelle Webster and head over to the law offices of Tiller, Valdez, Weinman, where two of the senior partners had agreed to come in to help find some other possible connection between the two couples.

Other than their slaying.

And now at least the new John and Jane Doe had real names.

THIRTY-SIX

They met with Michelle Webster at the Medical Examiner's Office as she emerged from the Family Grieving Room just after three o'clock. The young woman had just identified horrific photographs of two dear friends, and was plainly distraught. She was, she told them, Elizabeth's best friend, but had grown very fond of André too.

'I just can't seem to believe it,' she said. 'I can't take it in.'

She was diminutive, about five-one, Sam thought, with short, raven hair and eyes almost as dark behind oval spectacles, their sides glittery with tiny jewels, though that was all that sparkled about the young woman in black.

Her voice was strained, as if it hurt to talk, words coming in intense bursts, between bouts of weeping. Sam and Martinez doubted that there was anything more of practical use that they would glean from Michelle Webster today.

They were gentle, told her that Edward Price and his younger daughter, Margie, would be arriving at Miami International late that night, and that Gérard and Claudine Duprez were booked on the first flight out of Quebec City in the morning.

131

'Can we drive you home?' Sam offered.

Michelle shook her head. 'I don't think I could bear to go home yet. I'd rather go to the office.' She saw their hesitation. 'I know it's Sunday. I don't plan to work, just to be there. I already called Rachel – that's Rachel Weinman, one of the senior partners.'

'We know,' Sam said. 'In fact, we're heading over there shortly.'

'Was I wrong to tell her?' Behind the spectacles, her eyes looked scared.

'Of course not,' Sam reassured her. 'You need all the support you can get.'

'Just one question for now, ma'am,' Martinez said.

'Michelle,' she said. 'Please. And ask me anything, as many questions as you need to. I want to help so badly.'

'Did your friends like Greek food?'

'Sure,' she said. 'Now and then.' And suddenly she seemed to guess the fact behind the question, and her eyes filled with fresh tears of grief and horror.

'We're very sorry for your loss,' Martinez told her.

Nothing more they could say.

The reception room of Tiller, Valdez, Weinman was sleek, expensive and confidence-inspiring – until, Sam supposed, for some of their clients, it came to fees.

The two partners were waiting, grave-faced. The sight of them started Michelle Webster weeping again, and Rachel Weinman, a sturdy

132

woman with short grey hair, wearing a charcoal pants suit and black blouse, took the younger woman in her arms, while Victor Valdez, tall, slim and elegant in a dark suit, patted Michelle's shoulder and explained to Sam and Martinez that their partner, Stephen Tiller, was presently in Berlin.

'Though he's available, should you need to speak with him,' Weinman said. 'I have numbers for him, or he can call you, as you wish.'

'I imagine what you'll need most at this stage,' Valdez said, 'will be to speak to Elizabeth's and André's colleagues, which won't be easy to arrange until tomorrow.'

'That'll be soon enough,' Sam said.

'In the meantime,' Weinman said, 'I've made copies of their personnel files for you.' She paused. 'André was Canadian, as you may already know, but he was a member of the Florida State Bar.'

'*Was.*' Michelle shuddered.

'It's terrible,' Weinman said.

'Such fine young people.' Valdez shook his head. 'They should have had outstanding careers ahead of them.'

'They should have had *life* ahead of them,' Weinman added.

Tears in her eyes now, too.

They agreed, back in the car, that the lawyers had seemed like decent people. Sam had liked the way they'd worked together, arranging to collect the Prices, both tactful with the bereft young woman, not pushy but getting a tough job

133

done well, making the firm's Aventura apartment ready for Edward and Margie Price in case they'd made no plans.

'So what we got here seems like another real nice, regular young couple,' Martinez said.

No known enemies or angry clients, accordingly to the partners.

'Seems that way,' Sam said.

'Depressing as hell,' Martinez said.

THIRTY-SEVEN

The search warrant obtained, they took a first look at Elizabeth Price's townhouse, moving in simultaneously with Crime Scene.

If the couple had been taken together, then, with both their cars left behind, this was the most likely abduction location, and the techs were paying particular attention to the garage and its access to the house. Evidence collection and photography first, as always, no chemicals being brought into the possible scene, the print techs waiting until after that first close look.

Michelle Webster's prints had been taken for elimination, but no one was holding their breath for anything obvious here – though they did have some hopes that another warrant applied for regarding the recordings of vehicles entering and leaving the gated road might yield something of use.

Moving carefully around the small, attractive house, wearing gloves and shoe covers, touching only when necessary, Sam and Martinez found nothing unexpected. Nice quality furniture and fixtures, no overt extravagances, a great many books, mostly alphabetized on shelves, either read or well thumbed; law volumes, biographies and memoirs, novels ranging from Austen to Kafka to Grisham. Two books – Donald Woods' *Biko* and Barack Obama's *Dreams from My Father* – on a side table near the couch, and Sue Miller's *The Good Mother* on a kitchen counter, leather bookmarks in all three books.

There were photographs in every room, some that might be family, one beautifully framed shot of Elizabeth and André on a sailboat, both looking radiant, but in general there was minimal clutter and few frills. Two closets filled mostly with woman's clothing and shoes, much of it conservative, with a section of men's clothes, presumably André's. A hamper overflowing with items for washing. No diary in immediate evidence, the only visible notes stuck to the refrigerator door and relating to food shopping. Any number of kitchen knives that might, in theory, have been used for bloody murder, then washed and replaced – though there was no one left to tell if one or more was missing.

Nothing of particular interest inside the refrigerator: yoghurt, mineral water, a bottle of Sauvignon blanc, a pack of red apples, four eggs and some salad dressing, but no salad.

'I guess shopping was on her weekend schedule,' Sam said.

135

Feeling sad as hell for her.

And angrier by the second for both of them.

Elizabeth's home office, on the first floor, was organized, everything in its place, though it would soon be taken apart by investigators, the MacBook on the desk removed and examined for clues as to what might have turned this young law associate and her boyfriend into murder victims.

There were no signs anywhere of violence. Everything in the house and on the deck at the rear was well maintained and clean, the king-size bed upstairs neatly made, same as at the Eastermans – and was that the way Elizabeth had always left it, they wondered, or had some-one else made it up, someone as skilled as, say, Mayumi Santos?

'My bed never looks like that,' Martinez re-marked.

'Maybe she had a housekeeper too,' Sam said.

'Maybe Ms Santos was moonlighting,' Martinez said.

'You're reaching again,' Sam said.

'So sue me,' Martinez said.

Almost, but not entirely, the same deal at Dup-rez's third-floor Juniper Terrace condo. No trace of a break-in or violence or even intrusion, but his bed *was* rumpled, his pillows dented, and there were indications that the young Canadian had been working in his sitting room some time prior to his abduction or voluntary departure.

'No dirty dishes here either,' Sam said, in the kitchen, an efficient, basic workspace.

'Not even a coffee cup on the drain board,' Martinez said.

Sam used a gloved index finger to open a drawer. 'Not a lot of sharp knives.'

'How many does a guy need?' Martinez said. 'I got one big, one small.'

Sam's nose wrinkled. 'Can you smell something?'

Martinez sniffed, and his dark eyes sharpened. 'Moussaka?'

'Maybe.' Sam was more cautious.

Martinez opened the refrigerator door. 'Bingo.'

Sam looked over his shoulder, saw one shiny eggplant, a half pack of tomatoes and some grated kefalotiri cheese. 'Left here for us, maybe?'

'You think?' Martinez scratched his head. 'Though if Duprez did do the cooking himself, who the fuck added the sedatives?'

They checked the trash can, found no food remains, shone a flashlight into the waste disposal unit – which the techs would remove later, examining it and the pipes immediately beyond it – but for now it all looked as clean and shiny as the rest of the kitchen.

'I don't buy all this hygiene,' Martinez said. 'The Price house was neat and clean, but this isn't normal.'

They headed into the bathroom, found Bayer aspirin, Tylenol and an out-of-date bottle of cough medication.

'No temazepam,' Martinez said.

'What's that?' Sam pointed to a bottle at the back of the top shelf.

Martinez peered closer. 'Propanolol. Mean anything?'

'Rings some bells.' Sam googled it on his cell. 'It's a beta-blocker...' He scanned the results. 'Hypertension ... anxiety.' He paused. 'No mention of health problems for the Eastermans, but we should check if either of them was taking anything for anxiety, maybe even seeing a counsellor.'

'A shrink in common would be good,' Martinez said.

'Too good to be true,' Sam said. 'We'll get this added to the tox screen.'

They left the apartment, found the elevator to take them down to the parking garage, had to wait while someone got in on the fourth floor and took it up to the sixth.

'At least at the Eastermans, there was Mayumi who could have kept the place like new–' the cleanliness was still bugging Martinez – 'but a guy, a busy lawyer...'

'So what, you think the abduction went down here?' Sam said.

'Except it makes no sense with Duprez's car outside Elizabeth's.'

Now the elevator was being held up on the sixth. Sam rapped on the door.

Martinez's mind was back in the kitchen. 'So if we're meant to *think* he made the moussaka...'

'Maybe the killer doesn't care if we think it or not,' Sam said. 'Maybe those ingredients are just a tease and they know we'll know it.'

'So then we have ourselves a game player, or two,' Martinez said.

Sam didn't answer, remembering the biggest bastard he'd ever encountered, who'd been a player of evil games, responsible by the time of his own passing for the deaths of a number of people.

Cathy his main target.

The elevator arrived and he pushed the past away, got inside.

'No camera,' he said.

'Big fuckin' help,' Martinez said.

And only dummy cameras in the garage, it turned out moments later, perhaps because the residents of Juniper Terrace didn't want the extra costs of the real thing.

Or maybe, living in an area like Miami Shores with its low crime stats, they'd never believed they might really need surveillance.

'So still, all we have for now,' Sam said as they looked at Duprez's parking spot, marked with a white-painted 3B, 'are two attractive couples. Young, affluent, career-driven – Suzy Easterman perhaps a little less competitively so, though we can't be sure of that.'

'But all that goes for a big chunk of the Miami-Dade population,' Martinez said. 'So how come *these* people? Even if they were picked at random, something had to make them the chosen ones.'

'And not just targets,' Sam said. 'Exhibits.'

'Which takes us back to the gallery people.'

'Or maybe that's just another part of the tease,' Sam said.

THIRTY-EIGHT

Late Sunday evening Martinez was at Jess's first-floor studio apartment on NE 167th Street in North Miami Beach.

It was cramped, but all she could afford, and the neighbourhood was nice enough, and she'd made the best of her space, and it had a tiny backyard, which she liked. She grew tomatoes, which she'd screened in because the birds and pests had been helping themselves, and she'd told Martinez she'd had a cat for a time named Violet – because, she'd said, her eyes had looked that colour at twilight, and he'd said he'd never met anyone who used the word 'twilight' before. A neighbour had taken care of Violet while Jess was working, but then the cat had disappeared when the neighbour had moved out, and Jess had vowed never to have another animal until she could be around to take proper care of it.

'I never had an animal in my life,' Martinez had told her, because truth to tell he wasn't sure how he felt about having a cat or dog in his house.

'But you like them, don't you?' Jess had asked. 'We used to have a mongrel my dad called Bones, and I loved him because he used to sleep on my bed and listen to all my secrets.'

'Sure I like animals,' he'd said because he didn't want to disappoint her, and anyway, he liked Woody, the Beckets' dog, well enough. 'I guess I prefer dogs to cats, though, no offence to Violet.'

'None taken,' Jess said. 'Dogs are more loyal.'

Martinez felt a little stifled at her place sometimes because it was *so* small and he greatly preferred his house – especially now that she was there so much – but coming here now and again seemed right, and anyway, there was nothing like seeing someone's personal stuff to learn more about them, and he wanted to know all he could about Jess.

Her photographs – and there were plenty of them – had told him more than anything else. All of them of the Kowalski family and of Bones, and one of the cat. George, her dad (real name Jerzy, but Jess said he'd changed it because Americans had trouble pronouncing it), looked like a nice, open kind of a guy, though Monika, her mom, looked a little strained in some of the pictures; and there was one of Jess aged around seven, sitting on her father's knee with her mother standing awkwardly over to the side, and maybe Monika hadn't liked the person taking the photograph, or maybe she was just one of those people who didn't like having her picture taken.

'Did I ever tell you how I got my name?' Jess asked tonight, as they finished off a dinner of spaghetti and meatballs – about the best he'd ever tasted – and though it wouldn't have mattered to Martinez if she'd been a lousy cook, it sure didn't hurt that she wasn't.

'Because your dad was crazy about Jessica Lange in *King Kong*.'

'Oh, God,' Jess said. 'I'm repeating myself, I hate that.'

'I do it all the time,' Martinez said.

'You don't.'

'It's a cute story,' he said. 'And I guess anything about your dad's important to you, which is fine by me.' He leaned in close, kissed her lips, which tasted of spicy tomato. 'I want to stay here tonight.'

'But you're so much more comfy at home.'

'Nowhere's more comfy than your arms,' Martinez said.

He woke just before midnight, not long after they'd both fallen asleep after making love, which had come after they'd washed up together and necked their way through an episode of *Medium* on her lumpy couch.

Thirsty from the garlic in the spaghetti sauce, he padded barefoot to the bathroom and took a drink from the tap, then went to the garden door and looked up at the moon, thinking of his own late parents, his mom, Alicia, in particular, who'd been the most loving person he'd ever known.

He looked over at Jessie, at her hair spread on the pillow, lips slightly parted, all innocent and sweet as a goddamned angel – though the fact was she knew better than any woman he'd ever met how to make him crazy during lovemaking – and he moved quietly back to the bed and

142

climbed in.

The case wormed into his mind, all the sickoes in the world trying to crawl in with them, but quickly he shoved them out of his head and snuggled back up to the woman who was going to be his wife.

Mrs Alejandro Martinez, for the love of God.

Even the sick fucks couldn't stop how great that made him feel.

THIRTY-NINE

February 16

Busy Monday for Sam and Martinez. A potentially promising start with their first close scrutiny of the recordings of three vehicles of potential interest that had entered Elizabeth Price's road late on Wednesday, February eleventh – during the window of time that seemed the most likely for the abduction.

A silver Lincoln Navigator, a black Hummer pick-up and a Volkswagen van. All three vehicles large enough to carry and conceal two incapacitated or, perhaps, bound and gagged adults – and the VW logged as having passed under the barrier at the gate right behind Elizabeth's Honda.

The van was dark, perhaps grey or dark blue, its licence plate clearly distinguishable, but though Ms Price was easily identifiable on the

143

recording of her car passing the camera, the van's driver was barely visible, which might have been because of some glitch, but might more probably have been because the windshield had been tinted or covered with dark film.

It hadn't taken long to learn that the Lincoln belonged to a fellow resident and the Hummer to a legitimate visitor, but the VW's owner remained unknown and, therefore, highly suspicious.

Which pointed again to Ms Price's house being the point of abduction.

'Unless they were apart at the time, and were taken separately,' Sam said.

'That would mean at least two perps,' Martinez said.

'Maybe even a whole goddamned team,' Sam said.

That was where the progress dried up, however, since there was no record of the van's departure. Nor, in fact, was there a record of Duprez's BMW arriving in Elizabeth's road any time that evening or night, but apparently the surveillance camera had failed repeatedly in the last few months, and had probably done so again on the night in question.

'Unless it was disabled by the killer,' Martinez said.

'Why let it record the van then?' Sam said.

'More game playing?'

Sam shook his head. 'I don't buy that. Too tricky.' He paused. 'Anyway, if the van was used in the crime, it was probably stolen.'

'Fake plates, too, I'll bet,' Martinez said, anything else in such an organized slaying being almost unthinkable.

Not such a promising start, after all.

The rest of the day was tightly planned. Edward and Margie Price were at the law firm's apartment, though the detectives did not plan on meeting with them until early afternoon, soon after which they would speak to Mr Duprez's relatives.

In the meantime, the Oates Gallery gardener, Joseph Mulhoon, had been off his ventilator for forty-eight hours, and his doctor had declared him fit for a brief interview.

In a private room at Miami General, blue-and-white with a print of a South Beach scene facing the bed, the man who might, prior to his heart attack, have been strong and tanned, was pale and gaunt.

'I still see those poor people every time I close my eyes.' Those eyes were red-rimmed and haunted. 'What kind of sick monster could do such a thing?'

'We don't know that yet, sir,' Sam said. 'Which is why we need your help.'

'But I don't know anything.' Mulhoon looked bewildered.

'We understand that,' Martinez said. 'But you were the first person to see them, or at least the first to report it.'

'Which means,' Sam said, 'you just might have noticed something that we could have missed.'

'After all, you know that backyard better than

anyone,' Martinez said.

'True enough.' Mulhoon paused. 'Except now I can't seem to remember anything much except those poor people under that *thing*.' He shook his grey head. 'I'm a down-to-earth man, you know, but if you want to know how it seemed to me at first sight, it looked almost like they'd been left by aliens from outer space.'

'That's one avenue we hadn't considered,' Sam said lightly.

'Matter of fact,' Martinez said, 'I did think of flying saucers myself, but then I figured we had enough wickedness on earth to deal with.'

'True enough,' the gardener said. 'Lord knows.'

In the next twenty minutes, Mulhoon gave them nothing new. He said that he had not called Allison Moore or anyone at Beatty Management when he'd found the bodies. He said that he'd noticed the wheel tracks when he'd entered through the gate – which had been unlocked on his arrival.

'Which told me right off that something wasn't right. But then I saw *them*, and it was as much as I could do to call 911 because my hands were shaking so much, and then the pain started...'

They let him rest for a few moments.

'You OK for a few more questions?' Martinez asked.

Mulhoon nodded. 'As I'll ever be.'

'When you arrived,' Sam asked, 'did you see anyone who might have been leaving, or just hanging around?'

'No, sir.'

'Any cars or vans parked outside or close by?' Martinez asked.

'There's always cars parked everywhere,' Mulhoon said. 'But if you're asking me if I saw anything out of the ordinary, no, sir, I did not.'

'And on any of your previous visits,' Sam continued, 'did you ever notice anyone you felt might have been watching you, maybe checking to see when you came and went?'

'No, sir.' Mulhoon shrugged. 'But I wouldn't have been looking. I just park my truck, take out what I need and do my work.'

Sam had left it as long as possible to show the gardener a photograph of the Eastermans, concerned that the reminder might upset him. Not the Polaroids they'd shown Beatty and Moore, but a happy honeymoon picture.

'Oh, boy.' The old man took it, hand trembling, but managing a smile. 'Tell the truth, I'm glad to be able to see these two as they were before. Never know, maybe now I'll be able to try replacing those other memories with this.'

'That'd be good,' Sam said, gently.

'But if you're asking me if I ever saw them before that morning,' Mulhoon went on, 'the answer is no. Not ever.'

FORTY

Cathy, not due at work until evening, had come to the island to visit with Grace before going for a run.

Her mom was finishing up with a patient in the den, which doubled as a consulting room, so, without Joshua – who was at David's house – to play with, Cathy wandered out to the deck and sat down peacefully with Woody.

That was the way she felt a lot of the time these days. Peaceful.

And grateful.

Setting up house with Saul had been such a good move. For him, too, she was as sure as she could be, though because Sam's brother hated causing hurt, even if he didn't like having her around he'd probably never show it.

Cathy thought she'd know, though. That, she supposed, was one of the few benefits of having gone through so much heartache; she thought she'd learned to read people just a little better, not to take them so exactly at face value, and if she hadn't learned lessons from the stories of her life she'd have to be the biggest idiot alive.

Things really were good now, she figured, fondling Woody's ears. Home life with someone she adored, someone *safe*. The rest of the family practically around the corner. Work she actually loved, and beginning, thanks to Dooley and Simone, to shape into the start of something with real potential.

She heard the den door close inside the house, pictured her mom showing her young patient out, then turning back through the narrow front hallway – and then she saw her coming through the lanai and out on to the deck.

'I'm sorry.' Grace gave her daughter a hug, then sat down beside her.

'It's fine,' Cathy said. 'I've been chilling with Woody.'

'Lunch?'

Cathy shook her head. 'Going for a run.'

'It's lovely to see you,' Grace told her.

'I'm actually here,' Cathy said, 'to issue an invitation.'

'Sounds nice.'

'It's kind of a weird one, but I'm hoping you and Sam'll go for it. Dinner at the café Thursday night, but after closing, if you guys can stand to wait.' Cathy took a breath. 'The deal is I'm going to cook under Dooley's tutelage, and Simone says she wants to serve, but I'm hoping to talk her out of that because it doesn't seem right, especially since the point of my working there is to give her time off to be with her mom.'

'It's incredibly kind of them both,' Grace said.

'Please don't say no,' Cathy said. 'I really want to do this.'

'I'm sure we won't say no, provided—'

'Saul says he'll come here to mind Joshua, and I figure even if Sam's still working flat out, the

149

late night thing'll probably work out fine for him.'

'We'll have to check with him, obviously.'

'But if he says yes, you'll come?'

Grace looked at her daughter's clear, eager eyes.

'We wouldn't miss it for the world,' she said.

FORTY-ONE

Sam and Martinez had been back to the offices of Tiller, Valdez, Weinman.

The business of law continuing, but a sombreness in the air, with everyone who had known the victims patently shocked; and even for those who'd had little contact with either Elizabeth or André, this was still a double homicide much too close for comfort, and Sam for one was glad to hear that Rachel Weinman had arranged trauma counselling for those in need.

Next stop Beatty Management.

Ally Moore's mention of 'weird plastic' in the Easterman homicide was still brewing in the detectives' minds, but more thorough computer checks into Moore had yielded a big fat zero, and their meeting today was with her boss, Larry Beatty; the early stages of the interview bringing nothing of interest until the conversation moved briefly to Mrs Myerson's illness and Beatty's role as attorney-in-fact.

150

'Sad business,' he said. 'I'm grateful not to be the lady's health care surrogate decision-maker.'

'You sound like a lawyer,' Martinez remarked.

'Used to be,' Beatty said. 'I changed direction some time ago.'

'Why was that?' Sam asked. 'If you don't mind my asking.'

'Personal reasons,' Beatty answered.

His office, on the second floor, above a busy front office area, had wood veneer walls, a large mahogany-look desk taking up much of the space, the detectives sitting in two upright and uncomfortable chairs facing the man behind the desk.

'Who did you work for, sir, when you were a lawyer?' Martinez asked. 'Anyone we might know?'

'A few firms,' Beatty said. 'Is it relevant?'

'Not at all,' Martinez said. 'I was just interested. We get to know a lot of law firms in our line of work, as you can imagine.'

'I was corporate, though,' Beatty said. 'Not criminal.'

'OK,' Martinez said easily, and let it drop.

'We do have a small request,' Sam said. 'Would you be willing to provide a voluntary DNA sample?'

'Why?'

If Moore had looked edgy when she was asked, Beatty looked appalled.

'A little physical evidence was found in the old gallery,' Martinez explained.

'Just a few drops of blood,' Sam said.

'Not the victims'?' Beatty asked.

Sam shook his head. 'And almost certainly un-connected with any crime. But just as we asked you to provide fingerprints for elimination, it would be useful if you'd agree to provide a DNA swab.'

'Do you recall cutting or scratching yourself any time there?' Martinez asked.

Beatty shook his head. 'No. Never.'

'Still,' Sam said. 'It would be helpful.'

'No reason to be concerned about it,' Martinez said.

'But it's your right to refuse,' Sam said.

Now there was a flush on Larry Beatty's smooth face. 'The fact is, I've given a sample before, voluntarily.'

'How so?' Martinez asked politely.

The flush deepened. 'I was falsely accused of something. I knew that my DNA would prove my innocence, which it did, and my accuser later withdrew the allegation, but it still left a bad taste.'

'That's understandable,' Sam said. 'As I said, it's your right to refuse this.'

'Except refusal might look strange,' Beatty said. 'Maybe even suspicious.'

'You're not a suspect, sir,' Martinez said.

'I can't imagine why I would be, but I'm glad to hear it.' Beatty paused. 'Was that blood old or recently shed, do you know? Only I'm a little surprised, with the cleaners coming in regularly, that it would be there at all.' He picked up a pen and made a swift note on a pad, then looked up. 'Maybe you should ask them for samples, too.'

'We may do that,' Sam said.

152

FORTY-TWO

A swift new search back at the station brought forth a coincidence.

The last firm Lawrence Beatty had worked at had been Tiller, Valdez, Weinman.

Neither Sam nor Martinez believed in coincidences.

They went back to the law firm and found Michelle Webster in her office, a windowless space, tiny but her own, made friendlier with green plants, a couple of framed photographs and a cross-stitched sampler up on the wall with a Benjamin Franklin quotation.

God works wonders now and then:
Behold! a lawyer, an honest man!

'I'm so glad to see you,' Michelle said.

'That doesn't often happen,' Sam said.

She walked around her desk, pulled out two folding canvas director's chairs from behind a filing cabinet and began to straighten them out.

'Please,' Martinez said. 'Let me do that.'

Michelle stepped away, waited till both men were seated. 'I guess I've been playing at working, but frankly it's all such a struggle. I want to *do* something for Elizabeth and André, and I

153

know I can't, but now here you are.'

Sam wished they'd come with something more than what would, almost certainly, turn out to be innocent coincidence.

'All we have is one question,' he said.

'Please,' she said, back behind her desk, still standing. 'Anything.'

'Did you ever happen to know a guy name of Lawrence Beatty?' Sam asked.

'Larry Beatty?' Michelle looked surprised. 'What does he have to do with Elizabeth and André?'

'Probably nothing at all,' Martinez said.

She sat down. 'He used to work here, but obviously you know that.' She shook her head. 'I didn't really know him personally, and he left soon after I joined TVW, but I do recall there was a little gossip going around when he went.' Michelle hesitated. 'I'm sorry, but I'm actually not sure it's right for me to talk about it.'

'That's fine,' Sam said. 'Don't worry about it.'

'Who do you think might be able to help us?' Martinez asked.

'Human Resources, I guess,' she said.

Martinez smiled. 'I meant with the gossip.'

'I don't really know.' Michelle thought. 'I remember one of the girls talking about him, but she's not here any more either.' Frustrated, she raked a hand through her short hair. 'You ask me one small thing and I can't help you.'

'You have,' Sam said gently.

'Every little bit helps,' Martinez said. 'It's like a jigsaw, you know?'

'I guess it must be,' Michelle said.

They went in search of Victor Valdez, who made himself instantly available.

His corner office, Sam estimated, was about eight times the size of Michelle's, modern with an abundance of oak and steel, and immense windows.

'Please, gentlemen, take a seat.' Valdez gestured at a large leather couch. 'How can I help?'

'Lawrence Beatty,' Martinez said.

Valdez's dark eyes snapped suddenly to black. 'What about him?'

'Can you tell us about him?' Sam asked.

'Is it connected with the homicides?'

'Almost certainly not,' Sam said.

Valdez glanced down at his gold Rolex. 'Then I'm sorry, gentlemen, but I have a meeting.' He rose, played briefly with his left cuff. 'If you need any more information about Beatty, I'll ask Human Resources to make his file available.'

Rachel Weinman was more forthcoming.

Her office was smaller than her partner's and had the feel of a busy, untidy worker, the surface of her desk buried beneath stacks of files. Weinman frowned on hearing Beatty's name, but then she nodded, asked them to sit – her couch, too, smaller than Valdez's – offered them water and then sat down close by.

'I need you to respect that what I tell you is confidential,' she said.

'That shouldn't be a problem,' Sam said. 'Unless it turns out to have some bearing on our investigation.'

'I can't imagine how it would.' Weinman paus-

155

ed. 'Some time ago, a staff member here made a very serious allegation against Mr Beatty, which led to considerable unpleasantness. The allegation was false, as it turned out, and was later withdrawn, but Mr Beatty chose to resign.'

'What was the allegation, ma'am?' Martinez asked.

'The *false* allegation,' Weinman reminded him.

'Understood,' Sam said.

'The young woman claimed that Mr Beatty had raped her. He denied it absolutely and offered – actually, he insisted – on giving a DNA sample to clear himself, which it did.'

'Had the victim gone to the police?' Martinez asked.

'No.'

'And didn't the firm report it?' Sam asked.

'A decision was made to handle the matter quietly in the first instance.' Weinman paused again. 'The DNA sample was sent to a private lab, and I can assure you that had there been any possibility of a case to answer, I would have insisted on it.'

'Why the cover-up in the first place?' Martinez asked.

'No cover-up, Detective,' Weinman said firmly.

'So why the initial decision to keep it quiet?' Sam amended.

'Are these questions absolutely necessary?' Her expression was hard to read.

'We wouldn't be asking them if they weren't, ma'am.'

'The young woman in question was Mr Valdez's niece.'

'I see,' Sam said.

'To be candid,' Weinman went on, 'she already had a history of having a somewhat over-active imagination.'

'So she lied,' Martinez said.

'She certainly exaggerated.'

'Didn't Mr Beatty take any action of his own against his accuser?' Sam asked.

'He did not.'

'Was that his choice,' Martinez asked, 'or was he persuaded not to?'

'The young woman was in a bad emotional state, and Mr Beatty let the matter drop. It was definitely his choice. As was his resignation.'

'Is the woman in question still working here?' Sam asked.

'Not any more,' Weinman said.

'But she stayed on after Beatty quit?' Martinez said.

'For a short while.'

'When you used the word "exaggerated",' Sam said, 'were you implying that there might have been something to the allegation?'

'I wasn't implying anything,' Weinman said. 'I can assure you there was no rape.' She shifted in her chair. 'And that really is all I can say about the matter.'

'Did Elizabeth Price or André Duprez know Beatty?' Sam asked.

'Not that I'm aware of,' Weinman replied. 'It's probable that their paths never crossed. Mr Beatty was in our corporate section, not divorce.

I can ask around, if you'd like.'

'It's probably of no consequence,' Sam said, 'but if you should hear anything, we'd appreciate being kept informed.'

'Of course,' she said. 'I'll be discreet, obviously.'

They all stood up.

'Does the name Allison Moore ring any bells with you?' Martinez asked.

'None,' Weinman said. 'But I can check our files.'

At the door, Sam turned back.

'I don't suppose you happen to recall if Larry Beatty was a golfer?'

'If he was,' Rachel Weinman said, 'I never knew about it.'

FORTY-THREE

Promise went on draining out of Monday with every passing hour.

As keenly as they searched, they found nothing further of note regarding Beatty; nothing from the Florida Bar, no other scandals, no scams, no actions pending against him. Nothing from the FBI's NCIC nor the FCIC.

No gurneys or hoists reported missing from hospitals or nursing homes.

No plastic domes on anyone's missing list either.

No stores or websites admitting to selling unusual quantities of glue.

Neither Suzy or Michael Easterman had, to anyone's knowledge, either sought or been in need of any form of counselling or medication for anxiety – slamming the door on that possible link with André Duprez.

Rachel Weinman called less than two hours after their visit to say that she'd found no mention of Allison Moore on the firm's files.

'I guess sometimes,' Sam said, 'coincidences are just that.'

'Maybe,' Martinez said. 'They're still both of *interest*, though, right? And the rape allegation doesn't hurt.'

Sam made a noncommittal sound.

The information now in on the VW van's licence number was nothing that they had not, pessimistically, anticipated. The licence plate traced to a sedan belonging to a woman over in Naples, her Chrysler reported stolen last November. Which made it no help at all, since the van might well be stolen too – but at least it confirmed that the vehicle was almost certainly suspect, might even have been used in the earlier crime against the Eastermans, probably with another set of phoney plates.

The shots of the windshield had been blown up and closely examined, the consensus of opinion that the film on the glass was so dark that the driver would probably only have used it for that journey, since it would have been hard to see out from the inside, plus it was the kind of stunt that might have gotten the van pulled over by cops in daylight.

'And if, say, the guard at the gate had noticed it,' Sam said, 'the driver could just have turned the van around and vamoosed.'

Bottom line though, meantime: no visual on the driver, and no way of knowing if there had been one or more passengers – or victims – inside the van.

And next on the agenda, more grieving relatives.

Only the gentlest probing possible at this stage.

Both detectives allowing themselves a snatched moment to wish they were home with their own loved ones, away from the ugliness of their work.

That wish still a brand-new luxury for Martinez.

'I thought the day couldn't get any worse,' Sam told Grace on the phone at around six. 'That young woman's father and sister were so dignified, but you could see it devouring them.' He shook his head. 'And then the Duprez parents.'

'Too much,' Grace said gently. 'For you and Al, too.'

'We're nothing,' Sam said. 'Unless we can do the jobs they pay us to do.'

'You're doing all you can,' Grace said. 'No one can ask for more.'

'Four families out there with their worlds crashing down around them,' Sam said. 'They have every right to ask one hell of a lot more.'

Grace hesitated. 'It seems almost wrong for

me to ask this, but are we still going ahead with the dinner for Al and Jess?'

'I don't know.'

'Hasn't your general rule always been that life has to go on? Seems to me our friends might need reminding that this is the happiest time of their lives.'

Sam smiled. 'Is Thursday too soon?'

'Not for me,' Grace said. 'Why don't you see what Al says, and then I can pull the rest together.'

'Late night at the Opera Café tomorrow,' Sam said. 'Engagement party Thursday. All of a sudden, we're such social animals.'

'Maybe we should wait till the weekend,' Grace said.

'No.' Sam was decisive. 'You were right about life going on. And who's to say the weekend's going to be easier?'

FORTY-FOUR

On Monday evenings, Evelyn and Frank Ressler often got takeout for dinner, because most Monday afternoons they went to a tea dance at their temple in Surfside, and neither of them ever ate a lot there because the food, frankly, wasn't up to much, and anyway, they were too busy dancing.

Evelyn was seventy-one and Frank three years

older, but the couple were still in love. Her hair was silver, his almost all gone; they both needed glasses for reading and Frank wore dentures, but they were healthy, bright-minded, and some people grumbled that they only had eyes for each other, but they didn't feel that was true, because they knew they were still interested in others – most especially Barbara, their beloved daughter, and Ariel and Debbie, their grandkids, not forgetting Simon, who was a fine son-in-law – and just because they liked to hold hands when they were out walking...

'Some people get jealous,' Evelyn had told Frank just the other day.

'I know plenty of men who're jealous of me because I have you,' Frank said.

'Flattery will get you everywhere,' Evelyn had said.

'Think I don't know that?' Frank said.

It was a tried and tested formula, but they both enjoyed it, so where was the harm, and Evelyn had kissed him then and he'd kissed her right back.

They still did a lot of kissing.

And they were grateful, every single day, that they still had each other.

FORTY-FIVE

The keeper had all but given up on Romeo the Fifth.

There'd been a few occasional sounds to indicate that the little guy was probably on the loose, very likely having a high old time ingesting whatever building components he'd been able to sink his sharp little teeth into.

Not as beneficial to his health as the feed mix his keeper had been providing for him and his good lady, but there was only so much a person could do.

Isabella the Seventh seemed pretty content on her own so far, enjoying her own space, maybe relieved to be spared the buck's persistent attentions.

Splendid isolation for another few weeks for her, gestation in rats being twenty-one to twenty-three days.

And then the patter of teeny-tiny paws.

Decisions to be made as to which of the pups would be the new Romeo and Isabella.

Who would live and who would die.

Power and glory.

FORTY-SIX

February 17

'Oh my God, oh my God,' Frank Ressler said.

Evelyn knew right away that it was Frank speaking, but it didn't really sound like him because usually Frank's voice was nice and clear, and he never mumbled like so many other people, but now it was slurry and husky and he sounded almost *drunk*.

Matter of fact, she felt that way too.

Drunk and nauseated, too, and maybe it was time she opened her eyes and woke up properly, because obviously Frank was sick and needed her, and anyway, there was something wrong with their bed. It reminded her of the time someone said they should put a board under their mattress because Frank's back had been playing up, but the first time she lay down on the bed she let out a shriek, and there never was a second time because she had it taken out, and Frank's back got better just the same.

'Oh my God,' Frank said again.

'Stop with the "Oh my Godding",' Evelyn told him.

Except her voice sounded strange, too.

Open your eyes, she told herself, but her lids felt too heavy.

And then she managed it.

The fear hit her right away.

Hit her hard as a boulder smashing through her body.

'Oh, my God,' she said.

And the last scrap of humour left in her – the *very* last – told her it must be catching.

FORTY-SEVEN

Ten days had passed since the first couple had been found, four days already since Elizabeth Price and André Duprez had been dumped in the fish tank on Prairie Avenue, and Sam and Martinez and the squad were still no place to speak of, which was getting to every last one of them.

No one in or around La Gorce Drive remembered seeing a VW van with or without a darkened windshield anyplace near the Easterman house.

Mayumi Santos's cousin and friends had checked out.

Nothing new on either killing.

People expected better, and so they ought.

Except that the truth of the matter was that unless the cops caught a lucky break, or unless the killer or killers wanted to be found – which did sometimes happen, either because they wanted to be stopped or because they were too hungry for *glory* to wait for capture – then it was

165

not a whole lot better than looking for proverbial needles in haystacks.

For now, the best they could do was continue getting to know everything possible about all four victims; most of it useless to the investigation, but you just never could tell when finding out that Mike Easterman collected old movie posters might become suddenly pivotal. Likewise that Suzy had occasionally treated herself to a day at the Willow Stream Spa at Turnberry Isle Resort – near Mike's parents' home; or that André Duprez had been about to join a cigar club when Elizabeth Price had prevailed on him to give up smoking; or that Elizabeth had dumped her childhood sweetheart, another lawyer named Jay Miller, within a week of meeting André...

Nothing so far leading to any solid links, but if they kept on brainstorming and hitting every avenue hard, maybe, just maybe, the result might come from one or more of the victims.

If this was random killing, though, or random *selection*, then needles in haystacks might prove to be as easy as falling off logs by comparison.

Sam's greatest fear this Tuesday morning was that there might be more killings to come.

Though that, in a sense, was not his greatest horror.

Which was that another double murder might be just what they needed to bring the lead that had so far eluded them.

FORTY-EIGHT

They were in some kind of a *cage*.

'Is this a dream?' Frank had asked Evelyn a while ago.

'I don't know,' she'd answered him. 'I hope so.'

'One good thing about it,' he'd said.

They were in a cage in a padded room, chained up and naked.

Naked.

'What's that?' she'd asked.

'We're together,' Frank had said.

'A second good thing,' Evelyn had said. 'The light's so lousy you can't see me too well.'

Not all her humour gone, after all.

'You're beautiful to me,' Frank had said. 'You know that.'

She had told him then that she loved him.

They kept on telling each other that, the way they always had, though now the repetition reminded them both of the time they'd thought Frank was going to die from his heart attack, and the speaking and sharing of love had taken on a kind of urgent defiance.

'You know what's strange,' Evelyn said now. 'I can't seem to remember what happened before we got here.'

167

'Me neither,' Frank said.

Both their voices were sounding more normal again now.

Normal.

'We were eating dinner, weren't we?' she said.

'I guess so,' he said. 'I'm not sure.'

Evelyn took a breath. 'I don't think this is a dream, honey.'

'Of course it is,' Frank said. 'It has to be.' He spoke with as much conviction as he could muster, doing it for himself almost as much as for her. 'No one would do this for real to two old people who never hurt anyone.'

'Maybe we did.' Evelyn's mind ransacked back through the years. 'Maybe we did hurt someone.'

'Not badly enough for them to do this,' he said.

'No,' Evelyn said. 'You're right. This is a dream.'

'You know what?' Frank said. 'I think we should close our eyes and think about good things, like the children or dancing the foxtrot, and wait till we wake up.'

'I'd feel so much better,' Evelyn said, 'if we could just touch.'

She was shackled to the bars in one corner, and Frank was shackled in the other corner.

Too far apart to hold hands.

The worst thing of all.

FORTY-NINE

Sam grabbed a moment at what ought to have been lunchtime to ask Martinez about the engagement dinner.

'It'll be just us guys,' he said. 'But at least we can make sure we celebrate regardless of what's going on here.' He smiled. 'Pretty much Grace's idea, by the way. She figures you and Jess need to remind yourselves how happy you are.'

'Man.' Martinez shook his head, almost too touched to articulate. 'Your wife is just the best.' He hesitated. 'Maybe we should do it in a restaurant, though. My treat. It isn't right for Grace to have all the work.'

'She wants to do this for you, Al,' Sam said. 'We both do.'

'That's great.' Martinez felt his eyes smart. 'Just so great.'

'It's our pleasure,' Sam told him.

'I think I will keep it a surprise for Jess, though.' He was still thinkng it through. 'Specially since she's not telling her mom and dad yet, you know?' He shook his head again. 'This is just the best thing.'

'Grace is the best,' Sam admitted.

'Like Jess,' Martinez said.

'Why'd you think I'm so damned happy for you?' Sam said.

169

FIFTY

'Oh, my God,' Frank said again.

Evelyn kept her eyes closed.

She was finding she could stand it just a little better this way, because every time she opened her eyes the first thing she saw in the pool of dim light was her own body, all wrinkled and saggy and *old*, and a little while back it had made her think about pictures from the Holocaust, which had, in turn, made her feel ashamed, because she had been so very lucky, had never known starvation or terrible health or deprivation. Best of all, though, she'd had Frank and had kept him into old age, but it still hurt her to look at him like this, too, because it was so dreadfully humiliating. And she didn't suppose it would be that much better if they were a good-looking young couple – but someone had *done* this to them, someone had undressed them and left them here – wherever 'here' was – maybe to die, maybe worse than that.

And it was not a dream.

Evelyn had known that perfectly well almost from the outset, and she knew it was the same for Frank because he was an intelligent man, had been in the bookselling business for most of his life until his retirement and had read more about all manner of subjects than just about anyone

170

they knew. She knew that Frank had been keeping up the foolishness about the dream for her sake, but before long she'd have to start talking sense to him, because if they were going to die soon, there were things she wanted to say.

'Dear God—' Frank butted into her thoughts, his voice urgent. 'Evelyn, open your eyes.'

So she did, because maybe something *good* was happening.

It was nothing good, not really.

Not exactly bad, though, either, just *bizarre*.

So much so that she felt, for a moment, as if she'd stepped back through her lucidity and was back to believing that maybe, after all, it really still *was* a long, crazy nightmare – because right out of nowhere there was a black-and-white movie playing on a screen on the wall to her left. And what was so impossible was that it was of *them*: of her and Frank, just the two of them, like a stream of stuck-together pictures, really, of them looking happy, holding hands, looking at each other the way she supposed they always had. With love.

If they were home now, safe in their house, and if Barbara and Simon had done this for them, had compiled this for, say, an anniversary, it would probably feel warm and romantic and perhaps a little embarrassing, but wonderful just the same. But here and now, in these unspeakable circumstances, the film, or whatever that thing was playing over and over again on the wall, felt disgusting, like a violation.

That was an over-used word, Evelyn thought.

171

Like 'devastated'. People had a little break-in and a vase was smashed and their TV stolen and they said they felt violated and devastated.

She and Frank had never been that way, had always had their priorities down straight.

Here and now, *violated* was exactly right.

'What does it mean, Evie?' Frank's voice was shaky again.

She realized she hadn't spoken since he'd roused her, had been too busy *thinking*, and he sounded so afraid suddenly that she felt a wave of protectiveness sweep over her, and maybe it was her turn to be the strong one now, and she wished with all her soul that she could spare him this.

'Best not to think what it means, honey,' she told him.

'OK,' Frank said. 'I love you, Evelyn.'

'I love you too, Frank,' she said.

'And I'm so proud of you,' he told her, 'for being so brave.'

'No point screaming and carrying on,' she said. 'Though I wouldn't mind a little scream, to tell the truth.'

'Go right ahead,' he said, 'if you think it'll help you.'

Evelyn shook her head. 'I won't give them the satisfaction.'

'Them?'

'Whoever did this to us,' she said, 'could be watching.'

'Watching us watching us,' Frank said, his voice a little stronger.

'That's good, Frank,' Evelyn said. 'It's all we

172

can do, I think. Be brave, and make the most.'
'Of what, Evie?'
'Of the time we have left,' she said.

FIFTY-ONE

A heads-up, late in the day, on a new missing couple.

Evelyn and Frank Ressler, two Surfside senior citizens, had not been seen by family or friends or neighbours since late Monday afternoon when they had left a tea dance at Temple B'nai Torah on Isaac Singer Boulevard.

Their daughter, Mrs Barbara Herman, had spoken to her mother shortly after they'd gotten home to their house on Bay Drive after the dance, and Evelyn had told her that both she and Barbara's father had enjoyed themselves as always. When Mrs Herman had telephoned this morning, however, there had been no answer, but knowing her dad had a check-up scheduled with his cardiologist at eleven, she'd assumed they'd gone out early and that she'd hear from them later.

The receptionist at the doctor's office had called at noon.

Barbara Herman had begun calling hospitals an hour later and Simon Herman had come home from the office to try to calm his wife.

By three, they'd both known that something

was seriously wrong, and Simon had made the call they'd dreaded.

Every cop in Miami-Dade was on the look-out now.

Nothing yet.

FIFTY-TWO

Dinner at the Opera Café was going beautifully, despite the bad news Sam had received. It had been tough, at first, for him to get his mind off the case – off the elderly Resslers, especially, because just the thought of two old people being abducted, let alone terrorized and murdered, was unbearable. But a whole lot of people went missing all the time, usually for just a short while; things happened that had nothing to do with homicide, things like illness and accidents and, especially with seniors, forgetfulness.

Except that was the kind of thing that tended to happen to individuals out on their own. Not impossible, but far less likely for it to happen to a couple, especially when their daughter insisted that her parents both had all their faculties.

Still, this was Cathy's night and it was important to her, so Sam was doing his damnedest to enjoy himself.

Dooley's choice of music was helping: a little Schubert, a sliver of Verdi and a lot of Puccini, all romantic stuff, to match the candles and

174

sweetheart roses on their table and twined around the café.

Cathy was in the kitchen, Dooley there too, but plainly leaving the real cooking to her, and they could see her chopping, slicing, whirling, moving with apparent confidence between the refrigerator and the stove, and steam was rising and the glass partition was steaming and...

'It's hard not to stare,' Grace said.

'I'm just so damned proud of her,' Sam said.

'And so impressed,' Grace said. 'Just *look* at her.'

The food, when it came, served by Simone – who had clearly prevailed on Cathy – was nothing short of great.

'And all of her own devising,' Dooley had said on their arrival. 'Not a thing from our regular menu.'

'Your menu's terrific,' Sam said.

Dooley smiled. 'I don't think it was meant to be an insult to us,' he said. 'She wanted every ingredient to be a special favourite of yours, and I'll be surprised if you don't both love it.'

It was an eclectic menu, but Dooley had been right. There was a light crabmeat ravioli starter, calves' liver cooked to perfection and served with rösti potatoes and a delicate salad of mixed green leaves with a dressing that Grace just couldn't seem to nail.

'Sorry,' Cathy said, emerging briefly. 'I'm not telling.'

'But I'm your mother,' Grace said. 'I've shared my recipes with you.'

'This is professional.' Cathy grinned. 'One

day. Maybe.'

Dooley, nearby, raised both his hands, surrender-style. 'Nothing to do with me, but I'm hoping it's going on our menu.'

After a dessert of tarte Tatin with homemade vanilla ice cream, Simone, Dooley and Cathy finally agreed to draw up chairs and sit with the guests, and maybe the wines chosen by Matt Dooley had added to the sense of well-being that both Sam and Grace were now experiencing, but they were also aware of being moved both by Cathy's talent, and by Dooley's generosity in teaching her.

'It seems you've opened up a whole new world for her,' Sam said.

'She opened it up for herself,' Dooley said, 'out in California.'

'But you've really let her in,' Grace said, feeling emotional, and Sam reached for her hand and squeezed it, and then they both got up simultaneously to give their daughter a hug, just as quickly letting her go again, because tonight had been about her new professionalism, and neither of them wanted to spoil that for her by embarrassing her.

They all sat down again.

'This is it for me, guys,' Cathy said, frankly. 'This is for keeps.'

'So long as you don't stay here too long,' Dooley told her.

'You want to get rid of me?'

The words were lightly said, but Grace could see the vulnerbility beneath.

176

'On the contrary,' Simone said. 'But I know what Matt means. If this is going to be your life, Cathy, you need to learn what you can, take what you can, from one restaurant, one teacher at a time.'

'I'm no teacher,' Dooley pointed out.

'I'd say you're a great teacher,' Sam said.

Dooley's shrug was modest, but his brown eyes were warm. 'Simone's right, though, Cathy. Learn whatever you think you can from us, then when you're ready, find the next place that's right for you. We'll help you, give you great references, whatever you need.'

'There's no rush,' Simone added. 'We love having you here, God knows. And you'll never know what a difference it's made to me, with my mother being the way she is.'

'I'd be glad to do more shifts,' Cathy said, 'if that might help a little.'

'It might,' Simone said, 'when we reach the next stage. But for now, frankly, having the café to come to keeps me sane.'

'I can certainly understand that,' Grace said.

'This lady–' Dooley looked at Simone – 'is a really special person.'

'Takes one to know one,' Sam said.

FIFTY-THREE

February 18

A bad feeling of tension and growing frustration intensified through Wednesday morning, with everyone on the squad sharing the grimmest of fears that the very worst might already have happened to Evelyn and Frank Ressler. They still didn't know the exact timing in the first two cases, but the probability was that the Eastermans had been taken on the evening or night of Thursday the fifth, turning up in the garden of the old gallery on Saturday morning, and the second couple had almost certainly been abducted some time last Wednesday evening – almost a week ago – and dumped in the Christous' backyard in the early hours of Friday.

If there was a connection or even a pattern, then that meant the Resslers might be found any time soon, yet all the detectives could do this morning was grind their way through the scanty news that Mary Cutter had located a similar-looking domed plastic cover on one of the websites specializing in servicing exhibitors for conventions and smaller exhibitions.

'It's not the same,' Martinez said gloomily.

'I think it is,' Cutter said. 'I checked the measurements with Doc Sanders's office, and he took a look at the website and thought I was right.'

'Do we have a list of purchasers yet?' Sam asked.

'I should have it by this afternoon,' Cutter said.

'That's good,' Sam said.

'We don't know that the Eastermans' perp even bought the damned cover,' Martinez said. 'And if they did, they probably bought it second-hand.'

'Or stole it,' Beth Riley said.

'So you all want me to delete the list when it comes?' Cutter asked acidly.

'Not even in jest.' Sergeant Alvarez had just entered the conference room. 'Nice job, Mary,' he added. 'Less of the negativity, guys.'

Sam waited a second, knowing that his input wasn't going to do much more to boost the team. 'They nailed the glue,' he said. 'It's Hero, one of the most common brands on the market.'

'Which makes it about as helpful as a punch in the gut,' Martinez said.

'What was wrong with you in there?' Sam asked his partner after the meeting, heading back to their desks.

'I don't know,' Martinez said. 'Guilt, maybe.'

'What did you do?'

'Nothing, except I arranged to go to this jeweller over on East Flagler at lunchtime, because I figured it might be nice to give Jess the ring on Thursday, maybe before we leave home or actually during the party.'

'So what's wrong with that?' Sam asked,

179

reading a yellow Post-it sticker on his phone. 'Sounds great.'

'Except with the Resslers,' Martinez said, 'I don't exactly have the heart for it, you know?'

'Sure I know,' Sam said. 'But you have to do this, for Jess and for you.' He checked his watch, saw it was almost ten. 'And maybe we're wrong about the pattern. The other couples were both found early morning, so maybe the Resslers are going to be OK.'

'From your mouth to God's ear,' said Martinez.

'Or maybe they've just been dumped someplace less obvious, someplace no one's going to find them for a while.' Sam paused, the likelihood of that stoking up more dread. 'Or ever.'

'Not if they're the third pair,' Martinez said. 'Exhibition being at least half the point, after all.'

FIFTY-FOUR

John Hercules liked to drink himself to sleep at night.

Red wine, mostly, or sometimes Pastis de Marseille, of which he'd consumed rather too much last evening, because Lise, his girlfriend, had gotten mad at him about something he couldn't even remember now, and he'd told her to take a hike, and she had, after which he thought he'd

180

probably gotten somewhat morose and hit the Ricard.

He couldn't recall much of anything that had happened after he'd opened that good old bottle. Nothing until he'd come groggily to a half-hour back, surviving the grisly morning-after parade of symptoms to pour himself a large mug of strong coffee.

Now he was wandering out into his backyard.

Heading for his studio, not because he planned on working, but because it often comforted him just being out there.

Except something was not quite right.

Something about the kiln.

Something that wasn't supposed to be there.

He moved in a little closer.

The coffee mug fell from his right hand.

'Holy Mary,' he said, very quietly.

It was the first and only time in his life when John Hercules thought he might have preferred to be blind.

Artists needed to see, of course, but as a sculptor, he could have gotten by.

Too late now.

This sight was forever etched into his mind, he knew that already.

Like a gruesome, painful, sickening scar.

Forever.

FIFTY-FIVE

It was out of their jurisdiction, but Elliot Sanders, having had the misfortune of being on call,
had wasted no time getting Sam out of the office
and Martinez the hell out the jeweller's and out
to Coconut Grove to a house on Gifford Lane –
not far, Sam had jarringly noted, by the by, from
where Cathy's *friend*, Kez Flanagan, had lived,
over on Matilda Street.

This was one of the smallest properties in the
lane, a little blue house with a porch, banyan
trees and unkempt grass partially concealing the
dilapidated condition of the place. And yet, Sam
thought, eyeing the whole, it possessed a certain
charm, perhaps because the man who lived there
was a sculptor of moderate repute, a guy who'd
probably never made big bucks from his work,
but who had, according to the search engines
he'd swiftly scanned before heading out, managed to sell pieces on a regular basis.

No acrylic sculptures, so far as he'd been able
to ascertain. John Hercules worked with clay
and metal.

He had not, he'd told the officers first on the
scene, had cause to use his kiln for more than
two weeks, but he was in his studio most days,
and to get there from his house he had to walk

through his backyard with the kiln in his line of sight.

In the sitting room-cum-kitchen of the house, Hercules, a shaven-headed, well-muscled, tattoo-armed man of forty-two, looked traumatized.

'I passed a mirror a while back,' he told Sam and Martinez, 'and I hardly recognized myself. I look like Dorian Gray after he wrecks his fucking portrait. I wonder if I'll ever change back.'

Sam caught Martinez's look.

Self-obsessed individuals not his partner's favourite thing.

Still, Sam thought, the poor guy...

If they'd thought the first two scenes bad, now they seemed almost gentle by comparison.

Same MO, but this somehow the cruellest.

Throats cut again. Terror and suffering unmistakable on the faces of Evelyn and Frank Ressler, though their eyes were not visible. It was, in fact, impossible to tell, for the moment, whether or not their eyes were even in their sockets, because the elderly couple had been positioned face-to-face, and their spectacles had been glued together – and, from what the ME and Crime Scene techs and City of Miami and Miami Beach detectives could see, their spectacles had been glued to their eyes.

Their hands had been stuck together, too. Evelyn's right hand holding her husband's left.

Like the other victims, this couple were naked. In their *seventies*.

Sam could not remember ever having seen

Martinez throw up at a crime scene, but this time he did, and Sam managed to hold back, but he would have liked to have been able to weep, and looking around at the other men and women in the backyard, he saw that he was not alone there.

And then there was the anger.

Burning, boiling, rising fury.

Frustratingly impotent fury for now.

FIFTY-SIX

Everything changed.

This was now a serial situation for sure, and a major one. Time to enter the details into ViCAP, part of the FBI's National Center for the Analysis of Violent Crime. Extra help needed now, every kind available.

A Major Crime Squad was being formed, a situation room being set up for the duration, and an FDLE special agent named Joe Duval was joining the team to lend support, and in some circumstances the new man's presence might have pissed off the detectives, but they'd worked with Duval before – a former Violent Crimes cop first in Chicago, then Miami, with experience in profiling – and knew the lean, middle-aged agent to be a good man to have on side, and anyway, they were in no position to gripe.

Crime Scene had found wheel tracks *again* – a signature now, it seemed, as well as evidence of the method of transporting the victims – and though the kiln had perhaps been a less open location in which to exhibit the bodies, the art connection was there, loud and clear.

Which might have led them directly back to Beatty and Moore, except the lab had already prioritized the case and bypassed its backlog, and Ida Lowenstein in the ME's office had reported no match between either of those people and the blood found in the former gallery.

'Which only means they didn't spill their own fucking blood,' Martinez had said, testily.

Two things, though.

It seemed even less likely now that they were looking for a killer working alone, because it was almost impossible to conceive that an individual, however strong, could have manoeuvred Evelyn and Frank Ressler's bodies, maintaining their face-to-face position, into the kiln.

'Unless Doc Sanders was right about them using a hoist,' Riley said.

Sand had been found again, too, for the second time. In the tracks and on the grass. The same kind of white, fine sand as the last time.

'I'd like to go back over the garden at the gallery,' Sam said.

They were snatching a five o'clock sandwich at Markie's – a Cubano for Martinez, and a rare roast beef on rye for Sam – and Lord help them, but they were hungry despite the horrors of the afternoon.

'Think the guys could have missed sand there?' Martinez was dubious.

'Not likely,' Sam said. 'But it's been dry, so it

185

couldn't hurt to look.'

Clutching at straws, and they both knew it.

'I'd like to go looking for white sand at Beatty's and Moore's homes,' Martinez said. 'Think we got enough for warrants?'

'No way,' Sam said. 'But I'd love to do the same at Anthony Christou's place.'

'Not gonna happen,' Martinez said.

'I know it,' Sam said. 'Being obnoxious isn't enough to cut it with a judge.'

'Not even being obnoxious and having two dead people in his fish tank.' Martinez picked up his paper napkin and wiped his mouth. 'Damn,' he said. 'I lost my appetite again.'

They'd all gone over the Christous ad nauseam, had agreed, yet again, that abducting, killing and dumping two victims in their own backyard before calling the cops, would appear to have been an act way beyond insane.

Still, there was mutual dislike in that marriage, perhaps even true hate, and neither Sam nor Martinez felt ready to let go completely.

'I'm not saying I think Christou or Karen had anything to do with it,' Sam said. 'I'd just be happier if we could rule them both out once and for all.'

'We could go visit him in Boca,' Martinez said.

'Or at least drop by his office,' Sam said.

They'd established that Christou ran his small chain from an office above the first restaurant he'd opened in Aventura six years back, Anthony's Taste of Ionia.

'Maybe he has a central storage place,' Martinez mused. 'Like somewhere big and private enough to stash the victims and do the whole glue thing without anyone noticing.'

'Do you have a hint of a motive for all this?' Sam asked dryly.

'We don't have a motive for the Beatty people either.'

'Tell me about it.' Sam shrugged. 'There's still no reason we can't talk to Christou again, ask how he and Karen are coping with the shock.'

'Just a few friendly questions,' Martinez agreed. 'Like does he take long weekends on the Gulf coast or play golf?'

'Or has their own lousy marriage given him and his wife an obsessive hatred of happy couples?' Sam said.

'See?' Martinez stood up. 'A motive.'

FIFTY-SEVEN

A long-anticipated Damoclean sword fell slowly but painfully on the squad in the closing hours of their official working day.

The media had linked the homicides.

It had, of course, been inevitable, but first the numbers and intensity of calls from press, TV and radio newshounds seemed suddenly to quadruple – and then the barrage swelled into something resembling an incoming cloud of angry hornets.

Only good thing, Sam figured as the situation worsened: the Chief was taking charge and senior minds were deciding which details would be passed across to the public, what to give, what to hold back.

Nothing but negatives *to* hold back.

He didn't envy them.

A press conference had been called for eight thirty next morning.

'How in hell can I even *think* of going on a cruise now?'

Finally, in the men's room, no one else in there but his partner, Sam let out the question that had been choking him.

'That's how I felt this morning about the ring, and you told me to go out and buy it anyway, so I did, and God forgive me, I feel I did good.' Martinez shrugged. 'Anyway, there's a week to go before your cruise. Whole lot can happen in a week.'

'Yeah,' Sam said. 'Like more deaths.'

'Or maybe a breakthrough,' Martinez said. 'Maybe even an arrest.'

'I feel no optimism.' Sam shook his head. 'After what we saw in the sculptor's backyard, I feel pure darkness.'

'You think we should call off tomorrow evening?'

'No way,' Sam said. 'Grace is already cooking.'

'Not pure darkness then, man, right?' Martinez said.

Sam's smile had no humour in it.

FIFTY-EIGHT

Isabella the Seventh and her unborn pups were dead.

The keeper was in mourning. Not just for the doe, but for the next generation, and who was to say if there would ever be a Romeo the Sixth or another Isabella?

The cage was empty now, the cedar shavings and nesting boxes and cans and remnants of food burned.

Isabella too.

The rats had been more than a project, so much more than science.

An exercise in control, of course, the keeper was well aware of that.

But more besides. Not just power.

Love of a kind, too.

FIFTY-NINE

February 19

Thursday morning's press conference, located outside headquarters on Rocky Pomerantz Plaza because of the sheer numbers of bodies expected, most with cameras and boom mikes and other paraphernalia, was as grim and miserable an event as Sam and the squad had known it would be.

The City of Miami detectives in whose jurisdiction the Resslers had been found were present as well as the Miami Beach team and Special Agent Duval, but the Chief and Captain Kennedy were kicking things off, and in other circumstances it might have been Sam's conference to head, but with his leave scheduled so soon, Chief Hernandez felt that if the crimes were not solved prior to that – looking too damned probable – it might backfire on the department if Sam Becket was the focal point today.

That knowledge making Sam feel infinitely worse than a heel.

'Good morning. I'm Chief Hector Hernandez of the Miami Beach Police Department, and I'm joined today by Captain Tom Kennedy and Sergeant Michael Alvarez, lead investigator

Detective Samuel Becket, FDLA Special Agent Joseph Duval and the rest of the squad who have been tackling the homicides that have shocked and saddened our peace-loving citizens over the last two weeks.'

The speaker system whined, and Sam and Martinez exchanged uneasy glances, while Hernandez waited a second, then forged on.

'We also welcome, from the City of Miami...'

The whine rose to a shrill howl and Sam winced – hell, *everybody* winced, but he knew that some of the cameras whirring and clicking were focusing on him at that instant, and if he'd had a farm to lose, he'd have bet it that one of those shots of him looking discomfited would be tied to the Chief's description of him as lead investigator.

Not important, he told himself harshly, turning his full attention back on the boss, getting set to listen intently to the questions that the Captain and Alvarez would soon enough be fielding.

Tom Kennedy was already standing and naming the victims.

'Mrs Susan Easterman. Mr Michael Easterman.' He paused between names, giving just the right amount of emphasis and respect to each. 'Ms Elizabeth Price. Mr André Duprez. Mrs Evelyn Ressler–'

A sound came up from the crowd in the plaza, a strangled female cry, and Sam couldn't see who'd uttered it, but he knew it didn't bode well, and they'd tried hard to shield relatives from this conference, but...

'And Mr Frank Ressler.'

191

Silence fell for one long moment – and then the Captain handed over to Sergeant Alvarez, who commenced a brief, heavily censored account of each crime, with approximate discovery locations, following up with an appeal to the public:

'Anyone with information that might lead to the apprehension of the person or persons guilty of these wicked crimes will be treated in strictest confidence.'

More facts missing than included: no mention of glue, nor of the plastic dome or fish tank or kiln. Deemed wiser for the investigation, and an avoidance of sensationalism, in any case, had been agreed upon, the basic facts being grim and alarming enough.

Alvarez continued with help from Joe Duval's profile.

'It's thought that these were signature killings, couples taken either together or separately, then murdered and, finally, left in locations where they were sure to be found sooner rather than later. There was a sense of "display" in all cases, and the time lapse between disappearance and discovery was also similar in all three cases, indicating a high level of organization and a clear desire to show off.'

In the report itself, Duval had said that though none of the victims had been sexually assaulted, there was nonetheless the strong possibility of a sexual motivation in the crimes, certainly of power issues.

Sam was grateful for Alvarez's sensitivity in leaving that out here and now. Lord knew it was all bad enough, whether or not there were relatives present in the crowd beyond the semicircle of journalists and reporters, but any mention of sexual motivation would have been fodder for lurid headlines.

'Our department's intention until now,' the sergeant went on, 'has been to choke off the publicity oxygen that the killer has very likely been craving, but now that a third couple have suffered such a monstrous, tragic end, it's become clear that while there's no need for mass alarm, there is now, sad to say, a real need for vigilance in the Miami-Dade area.'

The questions began, came thick and fast, sharp, searching questions from *Fox*, *7 News*, *CBS 4* and the other big guns, and Alvarez had left enough unsaid to give him room to answer some, but with so much to be kept under wraps, he was at a major disadvantage.

'That's the third question you've evaded,' Ann Nuñez from the *Miami Daily News* snapped, and a chorus of frustration and hostility rose around her.

Time, Alvarez knew – only a glint of sweat on his forehead betraying his stress – to offer them one hard ingredient, partly to appease, but also because it was the kind of thing that might just draw out a real lead.

'We do have reason to believe that in all three cases the victims were brought to their final destinations on a wheeled cart or trolley, possibly a hospital gurney.'

'But you don't *know* that, do you?' Sandy Reiner from the *Miami Star* called out, his voice hard and clear. 'And you don't have the first clue who you're looking for. Six people already dead, and you don't even know for sure if you're looking for one killer or eight.'

'And we're not going to comment on that today, Sandy–' Alvarez's answer was controlled – 'because it's too close to the investigation, but we'll provide more details—'

'—at a later time,' Reiner finished for him. 'Yeah, yeah.'

A female voice rang out in the plaza.

'How do you explain leaving the people of Miami in the dark, Sergeant?'

There was a stir in the crowd, and then a woman stepped forward through the line of invited journalists, and the news people let her through, sensing a 'moment' and eager for it.

She was a tall, middle-aged brunette in a black linen shift dress, and Sam had not met the Resslers' daughter, but he'd seen a photo of her, and his heart sank.

'You left an elderly couple who lived alone completely vulnerable.'

Barbara Herman's voice trembled, yet it seemed to fill the air, and every lens and mike was now trained on the grieving, patently angry woman.

'My parents never hurt anyone in their lives.' She choked back tears, but she wasn't finished and no one was trying to stop her. 'They didn't have a chance, because they didn't even know their lives were in danger. How do you explain *that*?'

Time to take some heat.

Sam stood and stepped forward.

'Mrs Herman, we're so terribly sorry for your great loss, and if you're ready—'

'Ready for what, Detective Becket?' The bereaved woman's guns were blazing. 'For you to fob me off with excuses about how you couldn't know who was going to be taken next?'

'No excuses—'

'Of *course* you couldn't know that,' Barbara Herman cut back in. 'No one expects miracles, Detective, but they weren't even *warned*.'

The Chief was up again, a clear message for Sam to give way.

'Mrs Herman,' Hernandez said, 'may I take—'

'No, you may not.' She was not done with them yet, and her tears were flowing now, but she was making no move to wipe them away, and Sam knew that the press and media people were loving it.

'Because of your ineptitude, my mother and father died in the most unimaginably horrific way.' Mrs Herman turned to face the assembled gathering, visibly shaking. 'And I'm damned sure these people are not telling you the whole truth about this, because they certainly haven't told us everything yet. But you can bet that as soon as my husband and I find out what happened – and we *will* – we'll be making sure that the people of Miami know it, too.'

At last she stopped and walked back the way she'd come, and a man – her husband, Sam supposed – stepped forward to support her, and the cameras whirred and clicked again.

And not long after that, Captain Kennedy called a halt to the conference.

Damage done. A real body blow to the department.

And Sam Becket, for one, didn't blame that poor distraught woman one bit.

SIXTY

They headed out of the station with Jess before noon for an early lunch break, not because any of them were hungry, but Sam and Martinez both wanted a brief time-out after the new load of guilt that had weighed down on them along with the press conference, and Jess, feeling bad for them both, had asked if she could come along.

'If you don't mind,' she'd said. 'I don't want to intrude if you were going to discuss the case or guy stuff.'

'No *guy* stuff,' Martinez said.

'Hey,' Sam said. 'Maybe you two'd like some time alone?'

'No way,' Jess said. 'Not when I can have the both of you.' She tucked her right arm through her fiancé's, then linked her left arm with Sam's. 'OK?'

'Sure,' Sam said, and was glad all over again for Martinez, though he knew it was going to take more than a sweet-natured half-hour with

Jess to seriously boost either of them.

It was sunny and hot now for February, with record highs forecast, and folk out on Washington seemed to be enjoying it, tourists and workers alike, a bustle in the air which was good news for South Beach, Sam felt, with the economy having ground the place down a little over the past year or so. Like everywhere, he guessed, but he had a particular fondness for this district, had formerly lived in a rooftop apartment in a pink-and-white curvy Art Deco building on Collins, a home he'd negotiated for himself through pure luck. He'd loved that place, had spent whole nights in real hot weather out on the roof itself, and he doubted if anything less forceful than his passion for Grace Lucca would have gotten him out of there.

Not a single regret in the world.

'Hey!'

Jess's cry startled him and Martinez as she let go both their arms and took off ahead of them along Washington...

'Jess!' Martinez yelled.

It took a good two seconds for both men to register what she'd seen, what she was heading toward, and they both took off after her, but it was too late to stop her as she hurled herself at a tall teenaged African-American boy.

'Jess, stop!' Martinez shouted.

She whacked the kid hard with her shoulder bag, and he gave a yelp of pain and dropped a black wallet, and Sam and Martinez were on them just as Jess was about to put the kid into an armlock.

'Jess, hold it!' Sam told her.

'He took her wallet!' Jess was breathless, still excited.

'What are you, *crazy*?' A woman, short, round and outraged, grabbed at the teenager. 'That's my *son*!'

'I saw him take the wallet out of your purse.' Jess was stunned, her face reddening. 'Ma'am, I saw it.'

Sam and Martinez both had their badges out. 'Police, ma'am.'

'He's my son,' the woman said again. 'I *gave* him the wallet.'

'But he ran at you,' Jess protested. 'He grabbed it out of your purse.'

'I sent him to the store and he forgot to take the wallet and came back for it.' The mother was still furious. 'Is there a law against that now?'

'Of course not, ma'am,' Sam told her. 'It was just a mistake.'

'I think the bitch broke my *arm*!' The young man's voice rose on the last word, and people were stopping now, a small audience gathering.

'If you're hurt,' Sam assured the teenager, 'we'll call Fire and Rescue.'

'If she's broken his arm,' the mother said, 'I'll be suing the police department.'

'Which is your right,' Martinez said. 'But it was a misunderstanding, ma'am. This woman believed you were being robbed. She was just trying to help you.'

'I'm so sorry.' Jess's cheeks were scarlet now, her humiliation growing by the second. 'I can't believe what I did. I'm just so sorry.'

'It's OK,' Martinez told her. 'It was an honest mistake.'

Five minutes or so later, the mother had calmed down, her son's arm not yet, at least, showing so much as a bruise, and certainly not seriously injured, but the detectives had offered again to call Fire and Rescue, asking the woman to come in to the station and make a complaint, if she wished, which she had elected not to do. And Sam had suggested that the young man might like to take a patrol car ride some time, and though he'd sneered at the notion at first, his mom had said she thought that might be nice for him.

'The least they can do for you,' she'd said.

And the small crowd, a little disappointed, had moved along.

'All's well,' Sam said. 'Shall we go get our sandwich?'

'I don't think I could eat,' Jess said.

'You should have a little something,' Sam said.

They started walking again, and then suddenly, when they were well out of earshot of the mother and son, Martinez stopped and turned on Jess. 'How in hell could you be so dumb? That's the *last* thing in the world you do – if he'd had a weapon, you could be dead right now, not to mention that you just assaulted a teenager!'

'Hey, man.' Sam saw tears welling in Jess's eyes. 'Take it easy. She thought she was helping.' He put an arm around her shoulders. 'But Al's right, Jess. You're a brave lady, but the kid could have had a knife, and your fiancé wants to

199

keep you around for a long time.'

'I know.' She wiped her eyes, hands shaking. 'I really am sorry.'

Sam removed his arm, and Martinez stepped in, gave her a hug.

'OK,' Sam said. 'That's better.'

'I'm sorry, too.' Martinez kissed her. 'I shouldn't have gotten so mad, but you're precious to me, like Sam said, and you gotta take care of yourself.'

Jess pulled away. 'Not in public, Al. I'm embarrassed enough.'

'Quite something, your fiancée,' Sam said.

And saw her colour again.

SIXTY-ONE

Christou's number one restaurant, Anthony's Taste of Ionia, was closed until five, but a dark-haired young woman in a T-shirt dress and wedge sandals responded to the detectives' knocking after a few moments, not appearing overly surprised by their badges, so, they presumed, well informed of the happenings in her boss's backyard.

'It's just a courtesy call,' Sam told her.

'Mr Christou is out,' the young woman said, 'but I hope he won't be too long, so if you'd like to come in and wait?'

She stepped back to let them into a large,

dimly lit, empty restaurant, tables laid with white cloths and silver cutlery, glasses upside down.

'I'm Effie.' She locked the door, then turned back to them. 'Effie Stephanopoulos, Mr Christou's personal assistant.' She paused. 'This was such a terrible thing.'

'Yes,' Sam said. 'It was.'

She seemed at a loss. 'Could I offer you some coffee while you wait?'

'I'd prefer a glass of water,' Sam said. 'If it's not too much trouble.'

'Couldn't be easier.' Effie walked around the long, old-fashioned bar. 'Same for you?' she asked Martinez. 'Or coffee, or something stronger, perhaps?'

'Just water, ma'am,' Martinez said. 'But might you happen to have a couple of headache tablets?'

'Tylenol OK?' She stooped, opened a low-level refrigerator, took out two small bottles of Evian, straightened up.

'Great,' he said. 'Thank you.'

'You're welcome.' She found a small tray, opened a drawer, shook two caplets from a container, set them down with the water. 'I hope you don't mind,' she said, 'but I do need to go back up to the office.'

'That's fine,' Sam told her.

'Make yourselves comfortable,' Effie said. 'Any table or the bar.'

They watched her leave through a door near the back, heard her tread up the stairs, and then Martinez downed the pills and most of his water.

'Bad headache?' Sam asked.

'Uh-huh.' Martinez coughed. 'I think you gave me your cold.'

'I'm sorry,' Sam said.

'Me too.'

They took a slow walk around, and there were the photographs that Karen Christou had mentioned last Friday: three handsomely framed shots of the fish tank, two with its beaming owner standing before it.

'Hey.' Martinez was at the far end of the long bar. 'This remind you of something?'

Sam looked, saw an empty display stand on the bar that might be used for desserts or maybe cheeses.

It had a domed cover made of glass or plastic.

He shrugged. 'Six feet bigger, and you might have something.' He picked up a menu, studied it. 'But here's a thing. Not just a fish menu. "Anthony's Stifado". Like a beef stew, but with paprika and cream.'

They both fell silent for a moment, considering possible implications.

'But it's still nuts, right?' Martinez said. 'No killer in his right mind calls the cops to show off what he's done in his own backyard.'

'It's only nuts if it's Christou himself,' Sam said.

'Karen, you mean.' Martinez coughed again, drank the rest of his Evian. 'With a lover?'

'At least that would make some vague kind of sense.' Sam shook his head. 'Except why kill the Eastermans first and leave them at the gallery? Just for the hell of it?'

'If she's framing hubby and if she's crazy enough, who the fuck knows how far she'd go?'

They heard footsteps again, coming back down, and Effie reappeared.

'I'm so sorry,' she said, 'but I just heard from Anthony – Mr Christou – who sends his apologies, but he doesn't know when he's going to be back, and he asked if you'd mind very much making an appointment.'

'We don't mind,' Sam said.

Effie pulled a face. 'I should have brought down his calendar.'

'No problem,' Martinez said. 'We'll come up with you.'

They followed her up a linoleum-covered staircase and through a door into the front office. In another room, an old man with shaggy grey hair worked at a desk, and through a second open doorway they saw a larger office, probably Christou's.

'Anthony was very shocked by what happened,' Effie said quietly.

'Who wouldn't be?' Martinez said.

'So is this where all the restaurants are run from?' Sam asked.

'It is.' She smiled up at him. 'Did you ever eat here?'

'Not yet.'

'Me neither,' Martinez said.

'You should try it. They're all very good.'

Sam glanced up, saw certificates, photos, letters and spreadsheet printouts pinned to a cork board above what he took to be Effie's desk.

'Let me just look in his calendar.' She opened

up a page-to-a-day book with a number of entries on both visible pages.

Sam waited for prevarication.

'Are you taking a vacation this year?' Martinez asked Effie.

'I sure hope so,' she said. 'No hard plans yet, though.'

'How about Mr Christou?' Sam asked.

'I think he's going to Corfu in the spring,' Effie said.

'I've never been there,' Martinez said, then coughed again. 'Excuse me.'

'I sometimes wonder why people bother going overseas,' Sam said, 'when we're so spoiled for choice in Florida.'

'I know just what you mean,' Effie said. 'I went across to Fort Myers last year and it was so beautiful.'

'Does the boss like the Gulf coast?' Martinez asked.

'I don't recall him ever going there.' Effie looked back down at the book on her desk. 'How would tomorrow morning be for you gentlemen? Say around ten thirty?'

No prevarication.

'That would be good.' Sam stepped closer to Christou's office, saw another fish tank photo on the facing wall. 'He really did love those fish, didn't he?'

'Crazy for them,' Effie said.

Sam moved into the doorway.

There was a glass case on the other side of the room.

Three small silver trophies inside.

'What are they for?' he asked Effie.

'Golf.' She smiled. 'Another passion.'

'Where does he play, do you know?' Sam asked.

'Why?' Effie asked. 'Do you play too?'

'Just interested,' Sam said.

'Mostly, Anthony plays at the Diplomat,' Effie said. 'In Hallandale.'

'I'll bet it's a nice course,' Sam said.

'He likes it,' Effie said. 'He spends enough time there.'

SIXTY-TWO

The dinner party for Martinez and Jess went well, though Sam was finding it harder than ever to get the victims out of his mind, and the dysfunctional Christous, too – and so the hell *what* if Anthony played golf, because thousands of middle-aged men in Miami-Dade and Broward played the game, and sure they'd go collect a few grains of sand from the bunkers at his golf club, and they'd definitely go on checking on Karen's love life. But the fact was, a Greek dish with paprika and cream on a guy's restaurant menu didn't mean a heck of a lot.

Grace had known he was feeling down the instant he'd come home.

'It's a shame we're doing this tonight,' she'd said. 'You need a long soak and a back rub and some good old-fashioned TLC, and I can't give you any.'

'You're making a party for my best buddy,' Sam had said. 'I'd say that was more than enough.'

She'd made sure the television was turned off some time before the others arrived, but not before Sam had seen and heard a whole lot of criticism of the department. And he did feel so bad about that, felt responsible, and he'd made up his mind on the drive home that he was going to tell Alvarez tomorrow that if they didn't have a major breakthrough in the next few days, he was going to call off the cruise because patently he no longer had any real alternative.

Which made him sad as hell.

Still, it was turning out to be a good party anyway, because Grace was a great hostess at any time, but when it was for people she really cared about, then the small house just seemed to hum with welcome.

'I did it,' Martinez told them when he and Jess arrived. 'She's wearing my ring, guys.'

'Jess, let me see.' Grace drew the younger woman into the doorway of the den so that she could admire it. 'Oh, that is gorgeous.'

Jess held out her fingers, turning her hand so the overhead light caught the stones; and Martinez had chosen blue sapphires, three little precious gems set with tiny diamonds in yellow gold.

'I love it so much,' she told Grace. 'Al said he was stressing in case I'd set my heart on just diamonds, but he said these reminded him of my eyes, and I couldn't wish for anything more beautiful.'

'I can imagine.' Grace squeezed her hand gently, found it cold, realized that she was nervous. 'It really is lovely, Jess. We're so happy for you both.'

'Yours is *really* beautiful.'

Grace caught the younger woman's expression, thought for a second that she saw a touch of envy, and was abruptly mad at herself for wearing her diamond eternity ring in case it made Martinez uncomfortable, though she knew that was probably nonsense.

'Sam bought me this after Joshua was born,' she confided in Jess, hoping it would help. 'I never really had an engagement ring at all.'

And the light of pure pleasure returned to the new fiancée's eyes.

The others arrived, first Saul and Cathy, then David with Mildred, wearing a new black dress, which Grace knew David had encouraged her to buy and had wanted to help pay for, but Mildred had insisted she had enough put by.

'You look wonderful,' Grace told her.

'Hardly,' Mildred said.

'Mildred hates accepting compliments,' David said.

'I hope you have a spare apron,' Mildred said to Grace, ignoring him, 'so I can help you.'

'Not tonight,' Grace told her.

'We'll see,' Mildred said.

'Are you feeling OK, baby?' Jess asked Martinez while they sipped Sam's Bellini cocktails out on the deck, everyone except Grace and Mildred outside enjoying the still-warm evening air.

'I'm great.' He squeezed her hand. 'Never been happier.'

'You don't look so great,' she persisted.

'OK, you got me.' He lowered his voice, not wanting anyone else to hear. 'I'm not feeling too good, but it's nothing, just Sam's head-cold, and I'm not going to let it spoil tonight, right?'

'Sure.' Jess stroked his cheek. 'I just want to take care of you.'

'Tonight,' Martinez said, 'I don't need taking care of.'

He took another sip, and it tasted fine, but he was beginning to wonder if he was maybe getting the flu. Which made him feel guilty because Grace had gone to so much trouble, and the house looked so festive, not to mention Jessie, who looked like a goddamned *angel* again in her pretty summer dress with her hair blowing in the breeze off the water...

'If everyone's ready–' Grace said from the doorway – 'we could eat.'

'I'm always ready for your dinners, Gracie,' David said. 'What Tuscan pleasures await us this evening?'

'We're pretty much American tonight.' Grace spoke more softly as they walked through into the lanai. 'Mildred's insisting on helping me, but I want her to enjoy herself.'

'She enjoys helping, you know that.'

'Are my ears burning?' Mildred came in from

the kitchen.

'Grace and I agree,' David said, taking her arm, 'that you look much too elegant to be getting mussed up in the kitchen.'

'Are you saying I'm mussed up?' Mildred asked, patting her hair.

'Not remotely,' David said. 'You still look beautiful.'

They often had celebratory dinners at the big old kitchen table, even on Thanksgiving and at Christmas, using the lanai as a sitting room, especially on consulting days when the den was out of commission, but this evening she and Sam had moved things around to turn the lanai into a dining room. Grace had wanted Martinez and Jess to feel extra special, had made the whole place sparkle with candles and silverware and snowy napkins, and they were having stone crabs for their appetizer, followed by grilled tenderloin – Martinez's favourite – with Béarnaise sauce, sautéed potatoes and enough variety of vegetables to please everyone. And the only Italian touches were coming with dessert in the form of zabaglione, ice cream and home-baked biscotti di Prato complete with little glasses of *vin santo* in which to dunk the biscuits.

Two-thirds of the way through dinner, while Grace was safely ensconced in the kitchen with Cathy, whisking up the last-minute dessert, Sam drew Saul out on to the deck, away from the others, to tell him about the cruise.

'Though the way things are going down at work,' he said quietly, 'it may not happen at all, but if it does, I'm going to need you and Cathy to help me out.'

He swiftly outlined the rough schedule he had in mind if a miracle happened and he didn't have to cancel.

'You can't,' Saul told him. 'It's such a great idea. You guys have to go.'

'Tell that to the victims' families,' Sam said.

'I know,' Saul said. 'I get how you're feeling, but this is just a few days, and Grace is so amazing, and you both deserve it. I'll take care of telling Cathy, and between us we'll get Grace out of the house when the time comes, and Cathy can do her packing.' His brown eyes were shining. 'And man, you just *can't* cancel this.'

Sam felt lighter after that, and Grace and Cathy brought in the desserts, and he poured the *vin santo*, which made it the right time for more toasts to the happy couple, and then it was all about rave reviews for the zabaglione and the vanilla ice cream that Grace had made the previous day.

'I never had a happier evening in my whole life,' Jess told Sam later out in the hallway, as they were all saying their farewells. 'Except I really think Al's getting sick, though you'd hardly have known it, he's been so brave.'

Sam looked over at Martinez, still thanking Grace, and he thought Jess was right, his friend looked far from well, and it struck him that his partner going down with the flu might be the final nail in the coffin for the cruise.

'And I just wanted to thank you–' Jess was still

210

speaking, and he snapped back to the moment –
'for how you helped me out at lunchtime, and I
still can't believe I did that, and I just feel
dumber than dumb.'

'It was nothing,' Sam told her.

'It was not nothing,' Jess said. 'You were so
kind.'

Cathy, three feet away and overhearing,
glanced across at Mildred and noticed that her
expressive eyebrows were just a little raised, and
a look passed between them: a small tacit agreement that took just a little of the pleasure out of
Cathy's evening.

SIXTY-THREE

February 20

'Man, I feel rough,' Martinez told Sam before
the Friday morning squad meeting. 'I think it's
more than a head cold.'

'You think you have a fever?' Sam asked.

'If I have,' Martinez said darkly, 'I don't want
to know about it.'

The Resslers' deaths had brought them nothing
new except heartache.

Evelyn and Frank's last meal had been white
fish, potatoes, carrots and temazepam – the food
neither Greek nor Hungarian – and Barbara
Herman had told the City of Miami detectives
that they'd probably eaten at home that last

evening – and sometimes her mother cooked on Mondays, but sometimes they got takeout, and she didn't know where from because her parents had taken pride in managing by themselves.

All the distinctive features of the first two killings were there. A spotlessly clean kitchen. Abduction and evidence of shackling, the same drug in their system, fatal wounds to their throats and bizarre displaying of the bodies.

'Pure flaunting,' Sam said now.

'Jesus,' Martinez said weakly.

And collapsed.

SIXTY-FOUR

Not working this morning, Cathy had arrived back at her parents' house early enough to help Grace finish clearing up.

'This really wasn't necessary,' Grace said now, as they worked together, returning the lanai to its usual layout.

'I knew Sam couldn't be here to help, so why should you have to do it all?'

'It's appreciated,' Grace said.

Cathy waited for their coffee break in the kitchen – dunking leftover biscotti into their cappuccinos – to ask the question uppermost in her mind.

'What do you really think of Jess?'

Grace caught the 'really', but answered without questioning it. 'I find her a very sweet-natured person. I still don't feel I know her well, but how could I? I'm certainly truly happy for Al.'

'I'd like to be,' Cathy said.

'But you're not?' Grace was surprised. 'How come?'

'I'm not sure I'm the only one either,' Cathy said. 'I had the feeling Mildred was thinking the same.'

'Which was what?' Grace asked curiously, since though Mildred was certainly possessed of strong opinions, she was also particularly non-judgmental.

'I can't tell you exactly what Mildred was thinking.' Cathy broke off a small piece of biscotti and dropped it for Woody. 'We didn't speak about it last night, obviously, but I caught her eye one time, and there was a real *look* in it.'

'So forgetting Mildred,' Grace said, 'what's your problem with Jess?'

'You're going to laugh at me.'

'Try me.'

'I think she's jealous of you,' Cathy said.

'You're right,' Grace said. 'I am laughing at you.'

'And maybe you're right,' Cathy said. 'It's just a feeling I kept getting, though I know she spent half the evening telling you how great you are.'

'She certainly kept telling me how grateful she was, which I asked her to stop after a while, because you know we were just happy to do it.'

'You did it for Al,' Cathy said.

'That's not entirely true,' Grace said. 'Of

213

course it's Al we're happiest for, but Jess has brought him love.'

'I was watching her watching you,' Cathy went on. 'And I was watching her looking at Sam.' She paused. 'I think she may have a thing for him.'

'That's absurd,' Grace said.

'Why is it?'

'Because she's in love with Martinez.'

'Maybe,' Cathy said.

'Oh, stop,' Grace said, and laughed.

'Crazy thought?' Cathy asked. 'I really want it to be crazy.'

'It is,' Grace said. 'Definitely.'

Not a doubt in her mind.

SIXTY-FIVE

Martinez was in the ER at Miami General, being thoroughly checked out.

He was conscious, had, it seemed, simply fainted, but he had chills and a high fever, muscle and joint pain, and he had vomited a while back, plus his cough and headache had both worsened since yesterday.

'It could be anything,' one of the doctors told Sam.

Tests, in other words. A whole bunch of them.

Martinez looked scared, and Sam could not remember ever seeing him look that way, but

214

then Jess arrived, pale with alarm, and instantly her fiancé seemed a little easier, making Sam more thankful for her than ever.

'You better go, man,' Martinez told Sam. 'Catch the fuckers.'

'Back later,' Sam said.

'No need,' Martinez said. 'I got Jessie here.'

'That's good,' Sam said, and saw the fear bright in Jess's eyes. 'He'll be fine.'

'I know he will,' she said.

But the fear was still there.

Sam drove fast back to the station and went straight to Alvarez, who told him he'd moved Beth Riley off other duties so she could replace Martinez until he was better.

'He looks pretty bad,' Sam said. 'Tell the truth, I'm worried as hell.'

'You need time off to be with him?' Alvarez asked.

'There's no way,' Sam said. 'And believe me, Al wants me on the case.'

'And you're stressing because you booked vacation.'

'If things go on downhill,' Sam said, 'I'm going to cancel.'

Alvarez, behind his desk, looked up at the tall, handsome detective, one of the best he'd worked with but, right now, at his professional bleakest.

'Sit down, Sam,' he told him.

'There's no time,' Sam said.

'Sit,' Alvarez said.

Sam sat.

'I don't think you should cancel,' Alvarez said.

'If there's one thing this job – and even a close friend's illness – should teach us all, it's to make the most of every moment with the people who count.'

The sergeant's predecessor, Kovac, had been the bane of Sam's and Martinez's daily lives, and Sam often felt gratitude for their luck in having landed this man as his successor. Alvarez had come through the ranks, had been a detective for fifteen years before making sergeant, that hard experience respected by all the detectives, as well as his natural empathy.

'I get that,' Sam said. 'But surely that goes for my colleagues too. And for the victims' families.'

'Goes without saying,' Alvarez said, 'but there are plans and then there are *plans*. And I don't want to hear of you cancelling this vacation with Grace unless the sky really starts caving in, OK?'

Sam doubted that Captain Kennedy would be looking at his personal arrangements with such compassion, nor would Sam expect him to, and he wondered abruptly if some upstairs might consider that Michael Alvarez had gone too soft. And just the thought of being the cause of any criticism of this decent man sparked more guilt in Sam.

Guilt, at a time like this, equalled procrastination.

No use to anyone, least of all the victims.

'OK,' he said to his sergeant. 'Thank you.'

And went back to work.

* * *

216

Anthony Christou had called to cancel their appointment, which pissed Sam off a little, but Mary Cutter – having found nothing of interest in the website's list of purchasers of their plastic dome covers – had gone up to Hallandale to collect some sand, and for now Sam and Riley were poring over the exhibition theory again, trying to link up past crimes involving artists or gallery owners or even collectors. Riley had already set up a bunch of meetings with key gallery managers and art schools, because who the hell knew, they might learn something about an artist or sculptor whose work might somehow connect to the killer's warped kind of serial 'art'.

'God knows we need something more solid than just a *possible* hate of happy couples,' Riley said en route to a gallery in Lincoln Road.

Sam had, for no good reason, expected her car to be tidier than his partner's, but Riley's Impala was littered with candy wrappers, and Lord knew how someone with such a sweet tooth could stay as wiry as Riley, but life was unfair.

'Hate, envy, resentment, maybe even screwed up love,' he said, as she drove. 'Or none of the above.' He paused. 'Taking it back to art, I'd lean toward sculpting. I'd guess it helps to be physically strong to be a sculptor, and they're the most likely to use unusual materials.'

'All kinds of artists use glue,' said Riley.

'That's true,' Sam said. 'You heard of Rauschenberg?'

'Collages, right?' Riley caught his nod. 'Plenty of weird art around now.' She saw the De Long-ho Gallery up ahead, pulled over into a parking space. 'How about that Brit who exhibits dead animals?'

'Damien Hirst,' Sam said. 'I think he preserves them in formaldehyde.'

'Nice.' Riley turned off the engine. 'So why not John Hercules?'

'Martinez checked him out.' Sam shook his head. 'No record, no marriages gone sour, no known bad relationships or sociopathic tendencies. His work couldn't relate less – mostly abstracts in metal and clay – besides which, word is he spends most of his working time these days drinking.'

He opened his door, sent a quick thought to Martinez, then shut him out again and walked, with Beth Riley, into the gallery.

It was after three dead-end meetings, when they were back in the office doing yet more cross-checking, that they came across Allison Moore's name again.

As an artist. An exhibitor at the Spring Art Show, an annual North Miami Beach event. Not described as working with unusual materials, nothing of that nature; but according to the catalogue that Riley had unearthed online, Moore's painting displayed a 'dark leaning'.

'It's definitely her, right?' Riley pointed to a photograph.

Sam nodded. 'Time to take Ms Moore apart again.'

And Beatty right alongside.

'Let's see them both on home ground this time,' he said.

'Out of their work environment,' Riley agreed.

'Out of camouflage,' Sam said.

SIXTY-SIX

At around four that afternoon, Cathy and Saul were in his workshop near the apartment, drinking pomegranate smoothies she'd picked up in Publix, sitting on a pair of beanbag cushions, surveying the beech table Saul had just finished and talking about the cruise and how much she agreed with him that Sam and Grace *had* to take it.

'I'm not so sure I can see it happening now though,' Saul said. 'Not with Martinez so sick.'

Grace had called them both a while back with the news, had told them that Sam was obviously deeply worried, and though there was nothing any of them could do for the time being, she knew they'd want to be kept in the loop.

'He is going to be OK, isn't he?' Cathy's face was suddenly anxious.

Too many losses in her lifetime. Alejandro Martinez might not be related, but he was a rock in Sam's life, and that made him almost family.

'I hope,' Saul said. 'I figure we should be optimistic, assume they will go, plan as best as we can.' He paused. 'Sam's going to want you to pack for Grace, by the way.'

Cathy knew a distraction tactic when she heard

one, was glad to go with it. 'So we'll have to get her out of the house on the day.' She thought. 'Is Joshua going with them?'

Saul shook his head. 'He's staying with Dad and Mildred. They're cool about it.'

Cathy smiled. 'They would be.'

'It's funny about Mildred,' Saul said. 'She's only been at Dad's a few months, but it feels kind of like she's always been in our lives.' He hesitated, oddly guilty, though there was no reason, no romance between Mildred Bleeker and his father. 'I mean, obviously I don't mean *always*, like Mom...'

'It's OK to be glad that your dad has a friend,' Cathy said gently.

'I know,' Saul said.

Cathy waited another moment, then hit the other reason she'd dropped by.

'I was talking to Grace about Jess this morning,' she said.

'She's so nice,' Saul said. 'I'm happy for them both – and I hate that he's sick, but at least he has her.'

'I'm not so sure about her,' Cathy said. 'To be honest, she creeps me out a little.'

'Why?' Saul was as surprised as Grace had been.

'Maybe that's a little overstated,' Cathy said. 'But I do find her irritating.'

'Don't you think she's sincere?'

'I don't know,' Cathy said. 'I just have a feeling about her.' She paused. 'I told Grace I think she has a thing for Sam.'

'You're kidding.' Saul looked aghast. 'What

did Grace say?'

'That it's a crazy idea.' Cathy drained the last of her smoothie. 'So what do you think?'

'Same as Grace.' Saul took a breath. 'I also think that the way things are, with Martinez so sick and Sam under so much pressure, you should probably keep that kind of thinking to yourself.'

The closest to harsh Cathy thought she'd ever heard Saul.

'Oh God,' she said. 'I sound like a real bitch.'

'I don't think you have a bitchy bone in your body,' Saul said.

'Everyone does,' Cathy said.

'And you think Jess does,' Saul said.

Cathy shrugged. 'I don't know.'

SIXTY-SEVEN

They tried dropping in on Larry Beatty unannounced just after seven, but the doorman at his high-price building on Collins near 71st, a middle-aged guy with Angelo on his name tag, failed to get a response from 14D.

'I just came on duty an hour ago,' he told them, 'but I haven't seen Mr Beatty all week, which doesn't mean he hasn't been home, because it isn't our job to check up on the residents' comings and goings.'

'His office is close by, isn't it?' Sam asked.

221

'I wouldn't know that,' said Angelo.

'Maybe he's having dinner on his way home,' Riley said. 'Any idea where he likes to go?'

'None,' the doorman said.

And plainly, whether Angelo liked or loathed or was entirely indifferent to Lawrence Beatty, he was not going to share any information with them.

'Would you care to leave a message?' he asked.

'I don't think so,' Sam said. 'We'll catch up with him another time.'

They walked back outside, where Sam's Saab was parked nose to tail with Riley's car, but neither of them moved toward their vehicles, just stood for a moment in the well-lit darkness of a Miami Beach February evening.

'You want to go look for him?' Riley asked.

Sam took off his jacket, shook his head. 'Not quite ready to harass him. Tomorrow's soon enough.'

'You going to the hospital?' Riley said.

Sam had called an hour ago, had learned that Martinez had developed a rash and deteriorated sufficiently to have been admitted to the Critical Care Unit, which had struck all kinds of alarm bells in him.

'Later,' Sam said. 'Cathy's working the evening shift, so I thought I might drop by the café first, see how she's doing.'

They moved to the kerb, and Riley reached out and touched Sam's right forearm. 'Send good thoughts to Al, please.'

'I'll do that,' Sam said.

He knew that detouring to the café was really about putting off the moment of seeing Martinez in that place.

Coward.

'You look like you need pasta,' Dooley told him, coming out of the kitchen to shake his hand. 'Which is no big surprise, given all your daughter says you're going through.'

Sam smiled. 'I didn't realize I was hungry till I came in here.' He looked at Cathy, waiting tables this evening while Simone visited with her mother.

'How's your friend doing?' Dooley asked.

'Not so good,' Sam said.

'So you need to keep up your own strength, right?'

'Sure,' Sam said.

'Sit anywhere,' Dooley said. 'We're quiet tonight.'

Sam picked one of the tables with banquettes, remembering the first time he'd come in and Simone had made him comfortable because he'd looked tired.

Getting to be a habit.

One of the better ones.

Cathy brought him over a menu. 'Dooley says you need penne al'arrabiatta, but I figured you should have a choice.'

'That sounds fine,' Sam said, too weary to think about it.

'Have you been to see Al yet?' Cathy asked softly.

Sam shook his head. 'I'm going from here.' He

223

looked up at her, thought how lovely she looked, even with the anxiety over Martinez clear in her eyes. 'I only came in to see you, to be honest.'

'Any special reason?'

'Very special,' he said. 'You make me feel better.'

Cathy bent and quickly kissed his cheek. 'Ditto.' She straightened up, looked around. 'The pasta won't be long.'

It wasn't long, and it was good, though Sam's appetite wasn't in the best of shape. Still tired after he'd finished eating, he drank a whole bottle of San Pellegrino – and for the first time in almost eighteen months he found himself thinking that an espresso might have done a better job of keeping him alert, and maybe it was true that you did get over most things, given enough time...

'I wish I could come with you,' Cathy said as he got up to leave, 'but...'

'You go.' Dooley had come out of the kitchen again. 'I can take care of things tonight.'

'What if you get a crowd in?'

'I'll manage,' Dooley said. 'In case you never noticed, I can multitask almost as well as most women.'

'I'm in no rush,' Sam said. 'Why don't I wait a while?'

'You're beat,' Dooley told him firmly. 'Take your daughter and go visit with your partner.'

'Goddamn tests,' Martinez said when Sam came in. 'Goddamn barbarians.'

He'd been sufficiently compos mentis on admission to have logged Sam and Grace as 'family', along with Jess, which meant there'd been no problem getting in to see him now, though Cathy had had to wait outside.

Still lucid enough now, thankfully, to curse.

'You look like hell,' Sam told him, 'but you still sound like you.'

'Not doing too well,' Martinez said. 'Sorry.'

'I'm the one who's sorry. I gave you my cold.'

Martinez's half-smile was wry. 'This ain't no cold, man.'

Sam looked down at his friend and knew, without being told, that things were grim, which went without saying since otherwise he wouldn't have landed up here in the CCU, and Sam had seen too much of this lifesaving hellhole in the past, including a bad spell here himself about eighteen months back. The fact was, when it was someone you loved lying there, there was just no getting used to it.

He stayed only ten minutes because a nurse told him Martinez needed all the rest he could get, and he didn't like the way his friend gripped his hand before he left, because Al wouldn't have done that if he hadn't been scared to death.

'Tell Gracie I love her,' Martinez said.

'Tell her yourself,' Sam said.

Jess was out in the corridor, waiting for him, Cathy behind her.

'What do you think?' she asked.

'That he's in the best place,' Sam said.

'They don't even know what's wrong with him,' she said.

'Not yet,' Sam said. 'But they will.'

225

She looked drained, almost as bad, he thought, as her fiancé.

'You need to get some rest,' he told her.

'I'm not leaving him,' she said.

'I'll stay, too,' Sam said. 'Keep you company.'

'No way,' Jess said. 'You know how important your case is to Al, so you have to go home and get some sleep.' She dredged up a small smile. 'I promise to call you if there's any change.'

'Well, she's sure devoted,' Cathy said as they left the hospital.

Sam looked down at her, hearing scepticism. 'You have a problem?'

'I guess not,' she said as they walked toward the parking lot.

'Which means you do,' he said. 'Come on, sweetheart, spill.'

There were spaces available, but the place was still busy, and Sam remembered, walking Cathy to her Mazda, that it was always that way, even late at night. Little rest for relatives and friends of the sick.

'Don't you notice the way Jess looks at you?' Cathy's question came abruptly.

'What do you mean?'

They reached the car that had been Grace's until Sam had bought her a new Toyota, and his own car was of an age now, but he liked it and it still responded when he needed it to.

'I shouldn't be saying this,' Cathy said. 'I told Saul what I thought, and he said I should keep my mouth shut.' She shifted from one foot to the other. 'That isn't exactly what he said, of course, being Saul, but it came to the same thing.'

Sam told her then to just spit it out.

So she did.

'You're growing a vivid imagination,' he said sharply.

'Don't get mad at me,' Cathy said. 'I'm not being a bitch. I thought about it hard, in case I was, but I'm not.'

'You never are,' Sam said. 'But no matter what you think – and by the by, I'm telling you, you're way off-track – but even if you believe it, don't you ever say anything like it in five hundred yards of Al, right?'

'I'd never do that,' Cathy said.

'I should hope not,' Sam said.

He waited until after he and Grace had enjoyed a late-night cuddle with their son, who'd woken up when he came home, for which Sam had thanked Joshua warmly, since at the end of days like these, as he'd told his son, there could be no finer bonus than the warm embraces of both his wife and child.

'I think what Cathy said is balderdash,' he said, unbuckling his belt and dragging off his pants back in their own bedroom, 'but I'd like to hear you say that you think so, too.'

'I've always liked the word "balderdash",' Grace said. 'But I'm afraid I'm not completely sure, Sam. Cathy's no fantasist, as we both know, and we also know she's not a trouble-maker.' She paused. 'And according to her, Mildred may have sensed something too, though they didn't actually get around to discussing it.'

'I'm glad to hear it.' Sam sat down hard on the edge of the bed, unbuttoning his shirt, exhaustion starting to hit home.

'I guess I wouldn't dismiss it out of hand,' Grace said. 'At least, not the possibility that Jess may find you attractive.' She smiled, picked up his pants, folded them. 'Women do, you know.'

'Not newly engaged women young enough to be my daughter,' Sam said. 'Especially not when they're engaged to my partner and best friend.'

'What I did dismiss,' Grace went on, 'was Cathy's notion that Jess might be jealous of me.'

'Is that what she said? I don't think I gave her long enough to tell me that.' Sam felt jarred enough to give it some thought. 'I know Jess admires you, which is rather different.'

'Nothing so much to admire, surely, from her point of view,' Grace said. 'Middle-aged mom and part-time shrink.'

'I'm a middle-aged, low-ranking cop,' Sam said, 'but according to you, women find me attractive.'

'Go figure,' Grace said.

SIXTY-EIGHT

February 21

The news from the hospital when Sam called first thing Saturday was that Martinez's condition had worsened overnight.

'I'll go visit on the way to the station,' Sam said.

Grace read the fear in his eyes. 'I'll come by as soon as Mildred gets here.' She paused. 'I'd come now, but I don't want to bring Joshua.'

'Not to that place,' Sam agreed. 'But it would be good if you could come.'

'Want me to call your dad?'

She'd lost count of the number of times David Becket – notwithstanding his paediatric specialty – had gone in to bat for family or friends over the past few years. Too many.

'It couldn't hurt,' Sam said.

Jess was outside the CCU when Grace arrived, leaning against Sam, weeping.

'What's happened?'

Even in that instant of dread, Grace felt herself check out Jess's tears.

No doubting her sincerity.

Shame on her for the thought.

'Nothing's happened.' Sam drew away from

229

Jess. 'But he's not doing good.'

'I'm so sorry.' Grace hugged him and Jess stepped further away, giving them space. Everything as it ought to be.

Except she ought not to be even *thinking* about such things, and Grace wasn't exactly mad at Cathy, but at that moment she felt disappointment in her daughter for stirring up potentially destructive tensions without good cause.

'What have they said?' She directed the question evenly at them both. 'Do they know what's wrong with him?'

'Not yet,' Sam said.

'They're waiting for results,' Jess said.

'More tests,' Sam told her.

'Poor Al,' Grace said.

'He's pretty out of it,' Sam said.

'Can I sit with him for a while, do you think?'

'I'm sure he'll be glad to see you,' Sam said, 'if he comes to.'

Jess began weeping again, quietly. 'I'm sorry,' she said. 'I can't seem to help it. I was just so sure – I kept on telling myself all last night that he'd be better by dawn, but he wasn't, and I think he's getting worse.'

Grace went to put her arms around her, and Jess hugged her back.

'I have to leave,' Sam told them.

'I know,' Grace said. 'We'll look after him.'

He blew her a kiss and strode off along the corridor toward the staircase.

'OK,' Grace said. 'How about we go sit with your fiancé for a while?'

Jess stepped back, and Grace thought she saw

230

something alter in her eyes, felt, for just an instant, that she saw resentment there.

'Why don't you sit with him?' Jess said. 'I could use some air.'

'Sure,' Grace said. 'A little break'll do you good.'

'What'll do me good,' Jess said, 'is Al getting better.'

It was resentment, Grace decided, then hoped she was imagining it.

Most of all, she hoped and prayed that Martinez would pull through.

Then they could all worry about whether Jessica Kowalski was the right woman for him.

Not that it was their place to do that kind of worrying, Grace reminded herself as Jess walked away, erect as a stiff-necked doll.

Now who's being a bitch, she told herself.

And went into the CCU to sit with her sick friend.

SIXTY-NINE

Reporters had been waiting outside Miami General when Sam had emerged, though he'd made no comment other than to point out that his visit to the hospital was a private matter.

More of them out on the plaza when he reached the station.

They'd begun calling the case the Couples

Slayings, which Sam guessed had been inevitable, and it was clear now that they were gunning for him, which he'd also expected and could live with.

'Do you have time for "private" matters, Detective Becket,' one of the journalists who'd followed him from the hospital called now, 'when the families of six Miami citizens have been shattered forever, and when all decent, loving couples are fearing for their lives?'

The day he did not find some way to make time to go sit with a sick loved one was the day Sam figured he'd seriously consider giving up the job.

But he knew better than to tell them that.

Still nothing in on the Resslers to shed any more light on why they'd been chosen. And the hell of it was that if there was a pattern to the timing of the killings, with six days having passed between the first and second, then five between the second couple and the third, the squad was grimly aware that another couple might already have been taken.

No missing persons reports ringing alarm bells yet.

Cops didn't tend to admit to knocking on wood, not out loud anyway.

Sam, having caught the habit from Grace, was sure as hell silently doing that very thing.

'Effie Stephanopoulos called,' Riley told Sam at nine thirty. 'She said it'd be real hard for Mr Christou to make himself available today, because Saturdays are crazy all day for them, but if it's important, he says he'll do his best.'

'Big of him,' Sam said.

'So do we want to see him?' Riley asked.

'Not today,' Sam said.

Not with nothing solid to hang an interview on yet – if ever.

'Effie said Mrs Christou's gone out of town to stay with friends, but she gave me a number for her if we need it. I said we'd appreciate the name and address of the *friends*–' Riley loaded the word – 'and Effie's going to call back with those.' She took a breath. 'And Cutter's still working on Mrs C.'

Ransacking databases for anything of interest on Karen Christou, but nothing new yet. Maiden name Carlsen. Danish-born father, American mother, married to Anthony for nearly eleven years. Two complaints from neighbours on Prairie Avenue about noise from domestic disputes. Nothing since the couple separated two years ago, not even a gripe over the fish tank.

Larry Beatty was home this morning.

Apartment 14D was more tasteful than his office. A modern Miami Beach easy-living residence, with tile floors and a couple of blue rugs and toning lounging furniture, glass units on the walls and broad floor-to-ceiling windows. It looked well maintained and comfortable, but gave no cymbal crash clues about its occupant.

'I'm a little surprised you've come here,' he said after Sam had introduced Beth Riley.

'You don't work weekends,' Sam said. 'I hope

it isn't inconvenient.'

'Even if it was, as I've told you, I want to do anything I can to help.'

He offered them coffee and mineral water, which they declined, and they all sat down, Riley and Sam on the sofa, Beatty in an armchair.

'Is Detective Martinez taking the weekend off too?' he asked.

'He's sick,' Sam said.

'I'm sorry to hear that.'

Sam thanked him, and went directly to it.

'Can you tell us about your relationship with Allison Moore?'

'Relationship?' Beatty's fair eyebrows rose. 'We're colleagues, as you know. She works for me.'

'Would you say you were friends?' Riley asked.

'I'd like to think all my close colleagues are friends.'

'Outside the office,' Sam said. 'Are you friends there too?'

'We've had the occasional drink and a couple of lunches.' Beatty shrugged. 'Another form of meeting, really.'

'What can you tell us about Ms Moore?' Riley asked.

Beatty sat forward. 'Am I allowed to ask you a question?'

'Certainly, sir,' Riley said.

'Is she under suspicion of something?'

'Should she be?' Sam asked.

'Of course not.' Beatty shook his head.

'Though how would I know?'

'You asked the question, sir,' Riley said.

Sam smiled. 'Shall we start again?'

'OK,' Beatty said easily.

'We're interested in learning a little more about everyone we've encountered during these investigations.' Sam paused. 'I'm sure you've heard about the other killings.'

'Hard not to,' Beatty said. 'It's getting scary out there.'

'Mostly for couples,' Riley said.

'You don't have a partner, do you?' Sam asked.

'Not at present,' Beatty said. 'Maybe I should be glad it's only me.' He paused. 'So are you asking Ally the same kind of questions about me? Is that how you work?'

'Ms Moore's an artist, isn't she?' Sam said.

'An amateur artist, yes, I believe so.'

'Have you seen her work?' Sam asked.

'I think I saw one of her paintings one time.'

'You think?' Riley said.

Beatty's headshake betrayed slight irritation. 'I did see one. There was an exhibition, and one of her paintings was included and a few people from the office went along to be supportive.'

'What did you think of it?' Riley asked.

'Of the painting?'

'Did you feel she's a talented artist?' Sam asked.

'To be honest, I'm not sure I even remember it.' Beatty shrugged again. 'I'm no judge, Detective.'

'You managed the Oates Gallery,' Riley said.

'Only from the property standpoint,' Beatty said.

'Has Ms Moore ever shown you her studio?' Sam asked.

'No,' Beatty said. 'I don't know if she has one.'

'According to the catalogue of the exhibition in which her painting was shown,' Sam said, 'her work has a dark quality.'

Something happened in Beatty's hazel eyes for an instant, just a small flutter of *something*, quickly covered, then gone.

'Maybe,' he said. 'As I said, I hardly remember it.'

'Do you know if Ms Moore has a partner?' Sam changed tack.

'I don't know,' Beatty said. 'She isn't married.'

'Does she live alone?' asked Riley.

'I've never heard her mention anyone special,' Beatty said. 'Surely you don't need me to answer something like that?'

'We're just interested,' Sam said.

'I'm sorry,' Beatty said, 'but I just don't have any more to tell you about Ally. If I did, I would.' His smile was strained. 'How about some questions about me? At least that's something I'd be equipped to answer.'

'Not today,' Sam said.

'Some other time perhaps,' Riley added.

Beatty laughed. 'You sound as if you're about to tell me not to leave town.'

'Why would we do that?' Sam asked.

'No reason I know.' The humour was gone.

'OK,' Sam said. 'Two questions about you, Mr Beatty.'

The other man waited.

'When did you last take a vacation?'

'In October.' Now he looked mystified. 'I went to New York City.'

'No weekends away since?' Riley asked.

Beatty shook his head.

'Last question, sir,' Sam said.

'OK.'

'Are you a golfer?'

Beatty smiled again, wryly this time. 'A very poor one.'

'Do you belong to a club?' asked Riley.

'No.' Beatty paused. 'Why?'

'Where do you usually play?' Sam asked.

'Wherever I'm invited.' He thought. 'Last round I had was at one of the Doral courses. Why?'

'Just interested,' Sam said again.

SEVENTY

Cathy called Sam just as he was walking into the hospital at lunchtime.

'I want to say I'm sorry for what I said about Jess.'

Sam stepped back out into the sunlight, away from the sliding doors and the people heading in and out. 'That's OK, sweetheart,' he told her.

'You were saying what you felt.'

'I know, but I've been unloading a little to Simone – nothing specific,' she added hastily. 'And definitely not saying who I was talking about, obviously. But she said that sometimes it's better to keep your opinions to yourself rather than risk causing people hurt, and that struck a chord.'

'You haven't said anything to Martinez or Jess,' Sam said. 'So no one's hurt.'

'But surely if anyone ought to know the harm of gossip or even just plain thoughtlessness, it's me, don't you think?'

Sam smiled. 'Clearly, you do know it, which is what counts.'

'Still, I should have thought before speaking.'

'Stop giving yourself such a hard time,' Sam told her.

'I love you, Sam,' Cathy said.

'I love you too, sweetheart.'

Martinez was no worse, but no better.

Still no diagnosis.

David had just been in to see the patient when Sam arrived, and father and son took a moment to hug.

'I was about to call you,' David said. 'One of the docs was asking if I knew if Al might have been in contact with rats.'

'Are they thinking Weil's disease?'

'More likely rat bite fever or hantavirus,' David said. 'I said I'd pass on the question to you.'

'Not that I know of,' Sam said. 'How im-

238

portant could it be?'

'Could be crucial.' His father's craggy face was calm but intent.

'I'll visit a few minutes, then get over to his place, take a look around.'

'Do you know what rat droppings look like, son?'

'Bigger than mouse droppings,' Sam said.

'Much bigger. Capsule-shaped.'

'Good,' Sam said. 'Thanks, Dad.'

'Don't wait too long,' David told him.

'You bet,' Sam said.

He was at Martinez's house within the hour, let himself in with the keys his partner had given him when he'd moved in, having had no one else back then to name as spare keyholder.

The place looked different to the last time Sam had been here.

Not quite a bachelor pad any more. A softer edge to it all, somehow, even though Jess didn't seem to have pushed flowers or any other overtly feminine touches on to her mostly macho guy.

Right now, what it felt more than anything was *empty*. The kind of empty that ground at Sam's stomach.

He found a flashlight in the cupboard under the kitchen sink and started to check around, began in there, then moved through the rest of the first floor before heading upstairs, checking inside closets and behind drawers, feeling intrusive at the start, but quickly dismissing that, because the way things were going at the hospital this might just be life or death.

Nothing here. No signs of vermin of any kind.
Clean as the proverbial whistle.

That was probably down to Jess, too, since
Martinez hadn't always bothered that much
about domestic stuff; though on the other hand,
he might be taking more trouble because he
wanted the place to be nice for her.

Sam thought back to Cathy's call, was glad
she'd made it.

It made him feel better about Jess, too.

He replaced the flashlight, spent a few minutes
checking around to make sure Martinez had
turned everything off when he'd left the house
yesterday morning, and then he locked up carefully, and keyed his father's speed dial number
as he got into the Saab.

'No sign of rats at his house.' He kept it short.
'I figured it might be better if you called the
hospital, Dad, if you wouldn't mind.'

'I'll do it right now,' David said. 'Try not to
worry too much.'

'Sure,' Sam said.

SEVENTY-ONE

Allison Moore's apartment was on NW 122nd
Street not far from Oleander Park, in a building
that looked fit to be knocked down.

Sam and Riley went in as pre-agreed: one set
of questions only for her today, all relating to her

art and nothing else, unless Moore's responses took them someplace else interesting. Keeping it friendly, assuring her that everyone in the case was of interest to them – same opening spiel as with Beatty, but with no questions about him.

'Any way I can help,' she told them.

Same reaction as Beatty. Surprised to find them at her front door, but not overly fazed, and though she asked, as her boss had, about Martinez's absence and then wished him well, both Sam and Riley felt Beatty had alerted her to the possibility of their dropping by; not in itself an unlikely thing for one colleague to do for another.

'That's great,' Sam said.

She looked pretty, he thought, wearing blue dungarees with a white T-shirt with cut-off sleeves. Her freckles appeared more striking than when they'd previously met, but that was only because in the office she'd worn light make-up, and off-duty she clearly preferred the natural look.

'There's nothing for you to be worried about,' Riley told her.

'I'm not worried,' Moore said, her grey eyes calm.

Her place was small but clean, though there was, Sam noticed as she invited them to sit on her rattan couch, a smell of damp, the kind it was hard to eradicate. She appeared to favour wicker and cane and boldly printed fabrics. There were a number of framed fine art posters on the walls in her tiny hallway and living room, one or two familiar to Sam.

'We'd like to ask you some questions about your other life,' he said.

'Other life?' She looked puzzled.

'We gather you're an artist,' Riley said.

'Oh, that,' Moore said.

'What else might we have meant?' Sam asked.

'Beats me.' She smiled. 'I'm strictly amateur.' She seemed pleased to be asked about it, the way amateurs or small-time professional artists often were. 'I never went to art school. I took a few classes, but that was all.'

'But you've exhibited,' Riley said. 'Which is more than most.'

'If you're talking about the Spring Art Show, that wasn't a big deal,' Moore said. 'I just got lucky, though I guess I was pretty excited at the time.' She paused. 'I've been shown a few times over the years, but I've never sold a work.'

'Why do you think that might be?' asked Sam.

A fly launched itself from a green plant behind her cane chair and flew close to her right ear, and she lifted a hand to swat at it. 'I guess my style's a little unusual for most people's tastes,' she answered.

'The painting in the North Miami Beach show was called *Erebus*,' Riley said.

'Was that Erebus as in the son of Chaos?' Sam asked. 'Or as in the location of Hades?'

'Or the mountain in Antarctica?' Riley added.

'I'm impressed,' Moore said. 'You guys know your stuff.'

'That's our job,' Sam said. 'So which Erebus was it?'

242

'Couldn't you tell from the painting?' Her challenge was light-hearted.

'We haven't actually seen the painting,' Riley told her. 'Though we'd like to.'

'That's no problem,' Moore said. 'If you don't mind seeing a photograph.'

'That would be fine,' Sam said.

Moore stood, crossed the room to a small maple desk, a closed laptop on its surface, and took a black felt-covered album from the bottom drawer, turning pages until she'd found what she was looking for. 'Here,' she said.

Sam took it from her. 'Definitely Hades.'

'Like it or hate it?' Moore asked.

'I think I like it,' Sam said. 'It's intriguing.' He passed the album to Riley, who looked at the photograph in question, then started flipping through.

'I don't usually show people the others,' Moore said.

'Why's that?' Riley asked and went on looking.

'Please,' Moore said, and put out her hands.

'Of course.' Riley gave it back. 'I'm sorry. I didn't mean to intrude.'

'That's OK,' Moore said, though plainly it was not.

Sam waited as she moved back to the desk, returning the album to the drawer, observed the differences in the two women's red hair, Moore's a softly curling auburn, Riley's a brighter, almost violent shade, sharply cut.

'Do you have a studio?' he asked Moore as she sat down again.

'I wish,' Moore said. 'I work out of my spare room.'

'Could we see that?' asked Riley.

'There's nothing to see right now,' Moore said. 'I haven't worked lately, and most of my work's in storage.'

'That must be pricey,' Sam said.

'Not for me,' Moore said. 'A friend lets me use her garage.'

'Good friend,' Riley said.

'She doesn't have a car.' Moore paused. 'To be honest, I don't get why you're so interested in my art.' The edginess that had shown over a week before when they'd requested a DNA swab was coming through again. 'I mean, I'm guessing this must have some connection to the Oates Gallery, but I was never exhibited there, obviously.'

'You're too modest,' Riley said.

Uncertain if the female detective was being wry or not, Moore shrugged.

'We would still like to see the room where you work,' Sam said.

There was bewilderment now too. 'OK,' she said. 'Though there's really nothing worth seeing.'

She took them back through the hallway, opened a door into a small room with an easel near the window. A table held jars of brushes and charcoal, a closed sketchpad that looked new, a fax-phone and an adjustable desk lamp. There was no sign of recent work, and the smells of paint and turpentine were not fresh.

'I told you,' she said.

They thanked her and moved back out into the hall.

'You look a little tired, Ms Moore,' Sam said. 'When did you last take a vacation?'

'The holidays,' she said. 'Same as most people.'

'Go anyplace special?' asked Riley.

'I went to visit a friend down in Key West.' Moore paused. 'Is there anything else?' The grey eyes were quite sharp now, their pupils darker. 'I really mean it about wanting to help, but I just can't see how these questions connect with your case.'

'Nothing more today,' Sam said, then changed his mind. 'Is art your only hobby?'

'Pretty much,' she said.

'No sports?' Riley asked.

'I used to run,' she said. 'Why do you ask?'

'Just interested,' said Sam.

'You're right about those two,' Riley said as they came away from the run-down building and walked back to the Saab. 'I don't like Beatty any more than Martinez did, and I don't like her any better.'

'I just wish we had something more so we could jerk them both in for questioning.' Sam unlocked the doors, newly frustrated. 'Still nothing but gut feelings.'

Riley got in the passenger side. 'Pity State Attorneys and judges don't go with those.'

Sam started the engine and edged out of the space. 'What was the rest of her work like?'

'Weird,' Riley said. 'Some guy who looked

245

like he might have been Lucifer – I'm not big on that kind of thing. A bunch of black-and-white stuff that might have been ghostly – and there was definitely a dragon.' She paused. 'I was trying to get a close look at the posters on her walls. I'm not sure, but I think at least one of them might have had a witchcraft theme.'

'Check out Goya's work,' Sam said.

'Will do.' Riley made a note.

'Can you see that theme having anything to do with the killings?'

'Nothing other than Moore maybe being a little weird.' Riley paused. 'There was one thing.'

He glanced at her. 'Any time today would be good.'

She grinned. 'One of the photos in the album was of a sketch of a naked man. Very dark, hard to make out, so I might be wrong, but I thought the guy might have been Beatty.'

'So they have been involved,' Sam said. 'Or still are.'

'If it was him in the sketch.'

'Still not incriminating.' Sam made a left at the next intersection. 'Just two colleagues reluctant to admit to an affair. Happens all the time.'

'I guess,' Riley said.

'But?'

'Just another feeling,' she said. 'And Moore's art is definitely spooky.'

Sam took a look around, then made a right on to North Miami Boulevard, and he'd be passing home soon, felt a surge of yearning to stop there and stay, to be like a regular guy getting home a little early to his wife and son, just shutting the door and forgetting about his day at the office...

'Earth to Becket,' Riley said.

'Sorry,' Sam said and got a grip, because there was no excuse for any kind of drifting right now. 'Alibis,' he said. 'For Moore and Beatty.'

'Except we don't have exact times of abductions, let alone times of death.'

'Doesn't stop us getting a full picture of their movements on all the days and nights in question.'

Martinez was critical but stable when he got back to Miami General that evening.

Jess was still there.

'I don't know what I'll do if he...' She broke off, her eyes filling.

'He's going to make it,' Sam told her. 'He's strong.'

'Not so strong,' Jess said. 'He's a pussycat.'

'I know it,' Sam said.

They were in the unit, watching Martinez lying there, tubes in him.

'Would you mind,' Jess asked, 'if I leaned on you a moment?'

Not a whole lot he could say except yes.

'Sure,' he said.

Wishing like hell that Cathy hadn't said what she had.

Those kinds of words, even when withdrawn, still pricked pins in you.

And Martinez was too out of it to know that he and Jess were even there.

Sam longed again to get home to Grace.

The sooner the better.

SEVENTY-TWO

February 22

Another Sunday, and they were all waiting for the other shoe to drop.

It had been four days now since the Resslers had been found. The good news was that there were still no missing persons reports to spark a new scare, but everyone on the squad felt that they were scurrying around in barely widening, still aimless circles.

And then, out of nowhere, a possible lead made their hearts leap.

A man named Ludo Birkin, who'd been out of town since Thursday the twelfth, but who lived in Juniper Terrace, had phoned in to say that he had seen André Duprez's BMW exiting their building's underground garage at around eleven o'clock the night before his own departure.

Wednesday, February eleventh.

The night in question.

'Did he say Duprez was driving?' Sam asked Cutter, who'd brought the news.

'Not conclusive, apparently,' she said.

If it did turn out to be so, it would simply help continue with the piecing together of the time-line in the second crime; it would indicate either that Duprez had been heading off to spend the night at Elizabeth's house, or that he had possibly been responding to a cry for help from her. It might also suggest that at that time, Duprez had either not yet ingested the temazepam later found in his system, or that it had not yet had time to work on him. Case-building details for eventual use in a trial, God willing, but nothing of more immediate use.

If, however, this guy thought it might *not* have been Duprez, then that made him a potentially crucial witness.

And with no chance, anyway, of their going into Beatty Management today to try ascertaining Moore's and Beatty's whereabouts on all the relevant dates, Ludo Birkin was numero uno on their agenda for this particular Sunday.

And just for the heck of it, Sam was going armed with three photographs: one of Beatty, one of Moore, and one of Anthony and Karen Christou.

Lord knew they were due a lucky break.

SEVENTY-THREE

With Sam working again, Grace had left Joshua with Mildred and come to sit with Martinez and try to support Jess.

Sam had told her last night that the young woman seemed to have convinced herself that Martinez was not going to make it. And Grace disliked herself for what she was thinking – knew she probably would never have entertained such thoughts had it not been for Cathy – but it had occurred to her that Jess might perhaps be something of an attention seeker.

And one even uglier thought: that her fiancé's illness might even be feeding the kind of attention that she craved – perhaps most of all from Sam.

Unworthy, mean-spirited thoughts, reminding her of a time, a couple of years back, when she'd harboured wholly unjustified suspicions of another young woman.

'Have you called your parents, Jess?' Grace asked now.

'No way.'

'Why not? Wouldn't it help you to talk to them?'

'I don't think so,' Jess said, 'because I'd end up comforting them, and I don't have time or energy for that because I want to give Al one thousand per cent.' She paused. 'Truthfully, Grace, the only people who do seem to understand what I'm going through are you and Sam – well, obviously Sam more than anyone, since he's closest to Al.'

'Obviously,' Grace said.

Disliking herself all over again.

SEVENTY-FOUR

Ludo Birkin was mid-thirties, overweight and spongy-faced with wispy gingery hair. Courteous and almost certainly well-meaning, he had, however, no more to give them than he'd first stated in his phone call.

'I assumed at the time that the driver was André Duprez,' he told Sam and Riley in his sitting room, 'but it was dark, and I had no reason to look closely.' He spoke with regret, his voice croaky from a bout of tonsillitis. 'Though I suppose I might possibly have noticed if, say, a woman had been at the wheel, but I'm afraid I'd be a liar if I said I could rule out even that much for sure.'

Birkin's apartment was of a similar shape and size to Duprez's, but his tastes – if he had furnished and decorated himself – appeared more flamboyant, with wildly coloured textured fabrics and oddly shaped armchairs that felt, to Sam, as uncomfortable as sitting on rubber-covered steel.

'You said you saw the car at "around" eleven o'clock,' Sam said. 'Could you be any more specific about time?'

Now Birkin looked downright uncomfortable. 'I did say that, yes, but the more I come to see

251

how crucial this could be to your investigation, the less positive I feel about that, too.'

'So are you thinking it might have been earlier, sir?' Riley asked. 'Or later?'

'I think it might have been a little later, maybe half past or so.' Birkin paused. 'If I were a TV viewer, I might be able to remember if I'd been watching some movie or the news, something like that, but I hardly ever put the damned thing on.' His lips, already narrow in the round face, compressed further so that they were hardly visible. 'I feel so bad for poor Mr Duprez and his girlfriend.'

'Did you know Elizabeth Price?' Sam asked.

Birkin shook his head. 'I didn't really know him either, except to say good morning or talk about the weather in the elevator, you know, that kind of thing. But I did see him with Ms Price a few times. She was quite beautiful, I thought.' He cleared his throat, then lapsed into silence.

Sam waited a moment.

'Might there have been anyone else in the car?'

'That's hard to say, too,' Birkin answered. 'I thought at the time that he – the driver – was alone, but I wouldn't want to swear to it because of the dark.' He shrugged. 'For all I know, someone could have been in the back, say, hunched down.'

'Was there anyone else around at the time?' Riley asked.

'Not that I saw. The parking garage barrier works on a card system going in and it's automatic going out. There's no guard.'

And no working camera, as they already knew.

Sam took out the photographs, showed them to Birkin.

'Do you recognize any of these people?'

Birkin took his time. 'No.' He paused. 'Are you asking if one of them might have been the driver?'

'Do you think they might?' asked Sam.

'I can't say if they were or were not, any more than I can say, for sure, that it was Mr Duprez.' Birkin shook his head again. 'I do so wish I could be more help.'

They thanked him, told him they appreciated his coming forward, said that what little he knew had been useful, and then they left.

Their hoped-for lucky break shot to pieces.

'It may help with the jigsaw,' Sam said, back in the car.

'Gets us nowhere now, though, does it?' Riley said.

'Nowhere at all,' Sam agreed.

Not even lunchtime yet, still early in the day, only one thing clear.

He was running out of time.

SEVENTY-FIVE

Grace had stayed at the hospital, not liking the way Martinez was looking, nor the expressions on the faces of two of the nurses.

She called Sam on his cell just after two.

'I need to go home pretty soon so Mildred can leave.' She spoke gently. 'But if you can, I think you should get over here.'

Riley saw Sam's face as he ended the call.

'Martinez?'

He nodded. 'Grace thinks he's worse.'

'You go,' she told him. 'I'm going to focus on Moore a while longer, suck up every little thing I can find, if that's OK.'

'Sure.' Sam rose, stood motionless for a moment, feeling oddly vulnerable, uncertain what to do next.

Riley seemed to understand.

'Jacket,' she said, easily. 'Phone. Keys.'

Sam picked them up.

'Just go, Sam,' Riley told him.

Things had changed again since Grace's call.

David had arrived ten minutes before Sam, had been talking to colleagues.

'He has a better chance now,' he told his son outside the CCU. 'They're certain now that it's

254

rat bite fever.'

'How in hell?' asked Sam.

'For now it doesn't matter how,' David said. 'They've been chasing their tails, leaning toward hantavirus or even Rocky Mountain spotted fever, which is very rare in this state – and we know Martinez hasn't travelled for years. But then they got lucky because the culture for *Streptobacillus moniliformis* – rat bite fever – grew faster than it might have, so now they're sure.'

'And it's treatable, right?' Sam said.

'With penicillin.' David paused. 'According to his file, he has no allergies.'

Sam nodded. 'I know he took it for a bad tooth last year with no problems.'

'Good.' David paused. 'Jess could use some encouragement.'

'She still in bad shape?'

'Poor kid,' David said.

'Anyone ask her about rats in her building?' Sam asked.

Right on cue, Jess came out of the unit. 'Did your dad tell you?' Her eyes looked hollow with strain. 'What if there are rats in my place? What if I did this to him, Sam?'

'I guess you'd know,' Sam said. 'Noises, droppings.'

'There's been nothing like that,' she said. 'Anyway, I'd know if Al had been bitten.'

'I'm afraid it's a bit of a misnomer,' David told her. 'Bites are the most common cause, but you can get infected from contaminated milk or water.'

255

Sam saw her horror grow, felt a rush of pity for her. 'If that was the case, Jess, chances are you'd both have gotten sick by now.'

'And we don't spend that much time at my place,' she said, 'because Al has so much more space, and he never says so, but I know he prefers being home.'

They all turned, hearing the familiar sound of wheels on linoleum. A gurney being pushed out of an elevator with a new patient for the unit, and Sam's mind flew momentarily to the homicides, then back to Jess.

'If you like,' Sam told Jess, 'I could do what I did at Al's house. Go take a look around for any signs.' He paused. 'Though I don't want to leave yet.'

'Me neither,' Jess said.

'Anyway,' David said, 'you'd be locking the stable door, so to speak.'

'We still need to check,' Jess said.

'And you will,' David told her gently, 'once your fiancé's out of danger.'

'I thought, now they know...' Sam felt a new punch of fear, hearing that word.

'Now they know, son,' David said, 'his chances are better.'

They were all still for a moment.

'Sam, will you sit with Al for a little while?' Jess asked. 'I'd like to go to the chapel.'

'That's a fine idea,' David said. 'Would you like some company?'

She shook her head. 'In there, I don't seem to need it.'

They watched her move away, heading for the

elevators.

'She's a good kid,' David said.

'Yeah,' Sam said. 'I think she is.'

They drifted in and out of the hospital for the rest of the day. Cathy and Saul came and sat with Martinez for a while. David and Mildred minded Joshua so that Grace could come back and be with Sam. Beth Riley and Mary Cutter came together a little after five, and Mike Alvarez came by around six.

The homicides never far from his or the other detectives' minds.

The other shoe yet to drop.

Still no reports of any missing couples.

'Maybe it's over,' Sam said to Alvarez.

'Or maybe there's been another abduction, but there's no one to make a report,' the sergeant said.

'Or maybe,' Sam said, 'there is no pattern.'

SEVENTY-SIX

February 23

Monday morning started out a whole lot better than Sunday evening.

Martinez was doing better, though not yet pronounced out of the woods. Jess seemed a little less wild-eyed and needy when Sam visited, and he didn't like to admit to himself how glad he was of that, would rather have forgotten such thoughts, but they were still sticking firm.

All that mattered for now was that Martinez pulled through.

Sam spoke to one of the doctors, a pretty woman in her thirties named Dana Friedman who said she'd known his father a long time and held him in high esteem.

'Recovery from this disease can take a while,' she told Sam. 'If your friend gets over the worst, he'll probably need help for some time.' She looked through the window into the unit and smiled. 'His fiancée is very devoted, which is going to be great for Alejandro.'

Sam liked the way she used his first name, the way it seemed to resonate with care and respect, made Martinez more of an individual than just another case.

'He has a lot of people in his corner,' he told the doctor.

'We've noticed,' Dr Friedman said.

'Whatever he needs,' Sam said.

'Let's get him through first,' the doc said, and went on her way.

'No match on the Hallandale sand,' Riley told him an hour later.

Which shifted both the Christous down the list and pushed Moore to the very top – which, to Sam's mind, did not say much for their list.

'I've located one of her art teachers,' Riley said, 'who keeps photographic records of her students' more significant works. She's already sent me over a copy of the painting Moore exhibited at the Spring Show.'

'I thought we saw that one.' Sam sat down at his desk, wishing he felt less tired. *'Erebus,* right?'

'We did.' Riley looked fresh-faced. 'I was about to check with the FBI field office, ask if they could have someone look at it, but now I'm thinking maybe Grace might be willing to bring her psychologist's eye to it.'

'I'm sure she'd be willing,' Sam said, 'but she's no art psychologist.'

'I'll bet she sometimes looks at kids' paintings with a view to analysis.' Riley wasn't giving up on the idea.

'It isn't one of her diagnostic tools, so far as I know,' Sam said, 'but I've heard her say it's an important form of expression.' He shrugged. 'Presumably that goes for adults as well as children and adolescents.'

'So you'll ask her?'

'Sure,' he said. 'This evening OK?'

Riley grinned. 'I also nailed one of Moore's posters – you were right about it being by Goya. It's called *Witches in the Air.'*

Maybe it was Riley's energy, but something was starting to bring Sam back up too. 'You're thinking that sketch of Beatty – if it was him – was about something maybe darker than sex.'

'I don't know much about it,' Riley said, 'but I gather there's a lot of sex stuff in witchcraft rituals.'

Sam thought some more about the young woman he and Martinez had first encountered on day one of the investigation: efficient, pleasant, compassionate about the victims.

But she'd shown that *edgier* quality a few times since.

And she'd known about the domed plastic cover, had almost certainly lied about having heard one of the techs talking about it.

'When Al and I first met her,' he said now, 'she said she'd always found the old gallery "spooky".'

'And now "spooky" seems to be exactly what she thrives on,' Riley said.

'We need to get going on those alibi checks,' Sam said.

Mildred had been at the house since eight, doing an hour's work in Grace's office before minding Joshua while Grace saw her two morning patients, then offering to stay with him while his mom did some essential shopping.

'Are you really sure this is OK?' Grace double-checked before leaving.

'No place I'd rather be,' Mildred said. 'No child I'd rather mind.'

Still out in the Toyota an hour later, her shopping all on board, Grace dropped in at the Opera Café with a bunch of flowers to say another thank-you for last week's dinner. Cathy had just come in to work the lunch shift, and Simone was getting ready to leave for her mother's nursing home, looking tired and drained though the day was still young.

'Could I offer you a ride?' Grace asked.

'It's kind of you,' Simone said, 'but there's no need.'

'Isn't your car still at the workshop?' Cathy butted in, then added to Grace: 'Simone's been walking or taking buses, and I know she has a migraine starting, so of course she'd like a ride.'

'It's out of your mother's way,' Simone scolded.

'You told me it's just off Indian Creek Drive,' Cathy told Grace. 'Only a few blocks south.'

'Your daughter,' Simone said, 'is getting very pushy.'

Grace smiled. 'Will you please let me drive you there? It would be my pleasure, and quite frankly, it's the least I can do.'

At the James L. Burridge Care Home on 33rd Street, Grace insisted on walking Simone through the Spanish-tiled lobby to the reception desk, to be sure that a cab could be arranged for her after her visit, since otherwise she would wait.

'It's unnecessary,' Simone protested.

'More to pacify Cathy than me,' Grace told her.

'It'll be my pleasure to help Ms Regan,' the woman at the desk, name-tagged Alice, told Grace. 'She's one of our special ladies.'

'Oh, Alice,' Simone said.

The older woman went on regardless. 'Always spending time with her mother when many daughters would have stopped bothering long ago because, sad as it is to say, it can be very unrewarding.'

'I don't think it is.' Simone cast a weary glance at Grace.

261

'But that's because your visits really do make a difference to your mom,' the woman said, 'even if it is just for a moment or two. And you recognize that, hon, which is why I say you're special.'

'I wish you'd stop that, Alice.' Simone managed a smile. 'You're embarrassing me.'

'You need to learn to take praise, my dear,' the older woman told her.

Her cab ride home assured, Simone walked Grace back to the entrance. 'You're a lucky woman, you know, Grace, having a daughter like Cathy.'

'I know it,' Grace said.

'I want you to know that Matt and I meant what we said the other night about Cathy moving on. I can tell she's the kind of young person who might let loyalty get in her way. She needs to feel free to find her path, not bother about us.'

Grace glanced back at the desk. 'Alice is right about you being special, Simone. And Matt, too, of course.'

Simone's green eyes were softer than ever. 'The truth is I think we'll miss her terribly when she does leave, and I doubt we'll ever find another Cathy, but we will find someone to help – and to be honest, when my mother does go, I figure I'm going to need my work at the café to lean on.'

SEVENTY-SEVEN

Early afternoon, Sam and Riley were back in Larry Beatty's office.

'This is just routine,' Sam had told him right away.

Beatty had managed a smile. 'More routine.'

'It goes on and on,' Sam said. 'We're running checks now on the whereabouts of everyone with connections to any of the homicides, and we'd appreciate as much chapter and verse as you can give us regarding all your movements on the possible days and nights concerned.'

'More elimination,' Beatty said.

'That's right, sir,' Riley said.

He offered them seats and refreshments, poured himself a Diet Coke from a small refrigerator near his desk, then settled down in his chair.

'Last time we met, you seemed more interested in Allison than me, but right this minute I have to say I'm beginning to feel just a little persecuted.' His tone and expression remained light. 'Should I be?'

'Absolutely not,' Riley told him.

'If you have your calendar to hand,' Sam said, 'that should help.'

'Of course,' he said.

They got to work, one time frame to the next, covering the periods during which it seemed likely the Eastermans had been taken, held, killed and dumped, then going through the same process for the two young lawyers and, finally, the Resslers. Beatty had plenty of appointments and meetings logged to account for his working days, but less information for evenings and weekends.

'Do you have a personal calendar, sir?' Riley asked when they'd been at it for the best part of an hour.

'I'm afraid I don't have that hectic a social life,' Beatty said affably.

'Then you should be able to remember the highlights,' Riley said.

'Not many of those, detective,' he said.

Affability wearing just a little thinner, Sam thought.

'Perhaps if we take it a day at a time,' he said.

'Fine,' Beatty said with a sigh. 'Though I have to say I'm starting to feel uncomfortable again.'

'Why's that?' Sam asked.

'I'd think that was obvious,' Beatty said. 'You're making me feel like a suspect.'

'Everyone feels that way, sir,' Riley said. 'You have plenty of company.'

They went back to the beginning, to the evening of the first Thursday of the month, the day on which Mayumi Santos had last seen her employers alive.

'I can't remember,' Beatty said.

'You have no idea what you were doing that

evening?' Sam asked.

The other man shook his head.

'What do you usually do on Thursdays after work?' Riley asked.

'I don't have regular arrangements,' Beatty said. 'I'm not the kind of guy who has a weekly card game or goes to visit his sister.'

'Do you have family in Miami, sir?' Sam asked.

'My family are all in South Carolina,' Beatty said. 'Which I imagine you already know.'

They went on to Friday the fifth, which Beatty thought might possibly have been the night he rented a movie from Blockbuster.

'Which branch?' Riley asked.

'The one on Collins and 65th,' Beatty said. 'It was a French movie. One of those big eighties hits – *Jean de Florette*. I rented that one, and its sequel too.'

Sam couldn't fault his taste in movies.

'Did you watch them both?'

'I did,' Beatty said. 'Though I'd seen them before.'

Sam watched Riley make a note to check out the rental – though she knew as well as he did that unless the Blockbuster branch had been over on the West Coast, Beatty having taken out two movies meant zilch so far as his having been available to abduct and murder the Eastermans was concerned.

'It might have been that Friday,' Beatty said, 'or maybe the one after. One week seems to blur into the next, don't you think?'

Sam didn't answer.

265

'Let's go back to Saturday the sixth,' he said.

They waited until Beatty had given them all he seemed likely to remember – or choose to remember – and then they changed tack again.

'You told us,' Sam said, 'that your only relationship with Allison Moore is as a business colleague.'

'Except for an occasional drink or lunch,' Riley added. 'And you said that was just another form of meeting.'

'That's right,' Beatty said.

'You said you like to think all your close colleagues are friends,' Sam said.

'I do,' Beatty said. 'Absolutely.' His jaw tensed. 'If this is about—'

'Have you ever posed as a subject for Ms Moore?' asked Sam.

'No, I have not.' He looked astonished.

'Are you aware,' Sam said, 'that she has painted, or rather drawn, at least one picture of you?'

'No,' Beatty said. 'I'm not aware of that.'

'Then you're not aware either that it's a nude sketch,' Riley said.

'God.' Beatty looked appalled. 'No.'

Sam and Riley exchanged looks.

'No.' A protest. 'I mean it.' Beatty stared at them. 'For God's sakes, I told you myself about what happened at TVW, but I guess—'

'This has nothing do with the past,' Sam stopped him.

'We're just asking you about Ms Moore's sketch,' Riley said. 'That's all.'

266

Beatty took a moment to compose himself again. 'I guess anything's possible,' he said. 'Artists do that kind of thing, don't they – paint people without their knowing.' He shook his head. 'It certainly doesn't mean I posed for her, because I did not.'

'OK,' Riley said, easily.

'How did I look?' It was an effort for him to appear relaxed.

'Naked.' Riley smiled at him. 'And a little devilish, I thought. Didn't you think that, Detective Becket?'

'Maybe, just a little,' Sam said. 'Though maybe that's just Ms Moore's style, don't you think, Mr Beatty?'

'I wouldn't know,' Beatty said.

Sam held up a hand. 'I forgot, I'm sorry. You don't really know her work.'

'That's right.'

'You don't even remember the painting of hers that was exhibited last year.'

'Even though you went to the exhibition,' Riley said, harder now.

They both saw it again. It was the second time they'd observed that flutter of something in Beatty's eyes when they'd addressed the dark quality of Moore's art – almost a flicker of panic this time.

'OK,' Sam said, and stood up.

'Thank you, Mr Beatty.' Riley was up too.

He looked uncertain. 'I don't know what to tell you.'

'You've been very helpful,' Sam said.

'That's it?' Beatty said.

'Absolutely,' Sam said.

'For now,' Riley added.

'Something there for sure,' Riley said out on the street.

Beatty had told them Moore was out checking a property over on Byron Avenue, and without a warrant they knew they couldn't go looking through her calendar.

'I wonder how much of that he'll be telling her,' Sam said.

'Depends on what the relationship really is now,' Riley said.

'You're right though,' Sam said. 'We got something with these two.'

Though whether or not it had anything to do with the slayings was still impossible to say.

SEVENTY-EIGHT

'They've taken him off the critical list!'

Jess saw Sam coming down the hallway and ran to him, throwing her arms around him. 'He's going to be OK!'

'Thank God!' Sam returned her hug, relief flowing through him.

'I've been so scared.'

'I know you have, Jess.'

It happened so damned fast. He'd just started to pull away from her, but Jess was on tiptoe, and suddenly her hands fastened around the back of his head, tugging him down, and then she was kissing him on the mouth...

'Hey!' He yanked away from her. 'What the *hell*?!'

'Oh, my God!' Jess's cheeks were flaming. 'Oh, my God, Sam, I'm so sorry.'

'What did you think you were doing?' Sam was trying to keep his voice low, but he was too shocked, too mad at her. 'Your fiancé – my partner, my best friend – is lying in there sick.'

'It was just the relief.' Tears sprang into her eyes. 'It was only meant to be a hug. Please forgive me, please, Sam.'

'That was a whole lot more than a hug.' He was shaken, appalled.

'But I didn't mean it to happen. I love Al, truly. I'd never do anything to hurt him – I swear I didn't mean that, I *swear* it.'

'OK.' Sam was still reeling. 'OK, forget it.'

'But you're going to hate me now,' Jess said. 'I can see it in your face. You're going to tell Al, and you're going to tell Grace, and you're all going to hate me.'

'No one's going to hate you, Jess.' Sam looked back and forth along the hallway, knew there'd been no one in earshot and was glad of that much. 'And I'm certainly not going to tell Al anything – though I hope that if there's anything that does need telling, you'll be the one to do it.' He shook his head, grim-faced. 'But not while he's sick, right?'

'Not ever, Sam,' Jess said.

'That's between you and Al,' Sam said. 'But if

you cause him any more pain while he's in bad shape, you will have me to answer to.'

'All right.' Her voice was hushed, small.

'Then we can forget this,' Sam said.

'What about Grace? Will you tell her?'

'I tell Grace everything.'

'But she'll—'

'She won't mention it to anyone,' Sam cut her off. 'Like I said, we can forget this happened.'

'Thank you.' She was white-faced again now, just two spots of high colour remaining like smears over her cheekbones. 'I can't tell you how sorry I am.'

'Forget it,' he said, not harsh, but firm. 'Just forget about it.'

Except he knew he would not be able to do that. And he hated what had just happened. Hated that it meant that Cathy had been right in her suspicions, hated that he was not, for a very long time – if ever – going to feel easy in Jess's company, and worse, that he was going to have to lie to his friend.

Most of all, he hated its implications for Martinez and the happiness he'd only just found.

Hated it.

More on his mind than Jess Kowalski or even Martinez by the end of that long day of mixed blessings. Tomorrow he and Riley planned to go on cross-checking alibis, would pay a visit to Moore at Beatty Management, dig their heels in if necessary until they got to see her; but they still had nothing good enough to bring in either her or Beatty, still had nothing good enough *period.*

And meantime there might still be some new innocent couple out there in the gravest possible danger.

He went to see Mike Alvarez again before he left.

'In the circumstances—' he hit the point without preamble – 'I really feel I have to cancel my leave.'

'Quit right there, Sam,' Alvarez said, 'and sit down.'

He waited a moment.

'I thought we had this conversation already. I told you I didn't want to hear of you cancelling this—'

'Unless the sky really started caving in,' Sam said.

'You know something I don't?' Alvarez asked.

'No, I don't,' Sam said. 'Which is the whole point.'

The other man leaned forward. 'I get how bad you're feeling, Sam. But this is a cruise, bought and paid for, plus I can't recall the last time you and Grace took a vacation.'

Now Sam was almost thrown, because this kind of thing just did not happen. Senior officers did *not* take this benevolent an attitude with a serial killer on the loose in their jurisdiction, and maybe Michael Alvarez *was* going soft...

'We had a few days in Chicago last year,' he said.

'To close up her sick father's house, hardly a vacation for Grace.'

'We stayed in a nice hotel.'

'Whoop-de-doo,' Alvarez came back, dryly, leaning back again. 'I happen to think your wife's a very special lady.'

'Join the club,' Sam said.

Starting to wonder now if something else was going on here: if maybe Agent Duval or the Captain or even the Chief had been questioning his performance, and maybe this was Alvarez's way of getting him off the scene for a few days, and maybe when he got back, the shit would really start hitting...

'This is Grace's birthday coming up, right?' Alvarez said. 'And it's a surprise.'

'Which is why it won't matter to her if I cancel.'

'And you'll get your money back?'

'No,' Sam admitted.

'Then it just might matter one heck of a lot if she wants you to take a vacation later this year and you can't afford it.'

'But with Martinez off sick, and with this case still—'

'We have a Major Crime Squad working this now,' Alvarez reminded him crisply. 'I hate to break this to you, Sam, but you are expendable.'

Sam considered briefly asking the sergeant if that *was* what was happening here, if he was actually on the brink of being kicked off the case, but then he reminded himself that this was not about *him*, this was about the victims.

'Riley and I are working a possible lead,' he said.

'I know,' Alvarez said. 'And Beatty and Moore may have something weird going, but as yet it isn't what I'd call a lead.' He shrugged. 'Though you still have two clear days to pull something out of the hat.'

'Do you think the killing has stopped?' Sam asked.

'Five days between disappearances instead of four?' Alvarez spread his hands. 'Personally, I don't think it means as much as we'd all like, though maybe three's a charm and that's going to be the end of it.'

'Unholy trinity,' Sam said.

Which seemed to take him right back to Moore and Beatty again.

'Go home, Sam,' Alvarez told him. 'Start again in the morning.'

'OK,' Sam said.

'And no sitting up all night googling satanism or whatever, right?'

Sam got up, relieved to stretch his legs.

'As if,' he said.

SEVENTY-NINE

He'd poured them both a glass of wine and told Grace about the Jess hospital incident within a half-hour of getting home.

'That's not good,' she said. 'How worried are you for Al?'

'If she breaks his heart...' Sam shook his head. 'Who am I kidding? Not a whole lot I can do if she does.'

'You can help mend him,' Grace said.

They looked at each other and then, no words necessary, they did what they always did when they felt especially good, bad or sad. They went upstairs and into their son's room for a while, watched him sleep, whispered love messages to him.

Later, back in the den, Woody between them on the couch, Sam showed her the photograph he'd brought home.

'Beth wondered if you might cast your psychologist's eye over this.'

Grace surveyed it. 'Not painted by a child. Nor a teen.'

Sam shook his head. 'By a person of interest.'

Grace frowned. 'You have experts to do that.'

'And they are,' Sam said. 'But Beth thought it wouldn't hurt to show you.'

'All right. So long as we all remember this is not my field.'

'Goes without saying. We'd still value your opinion.'

She looked at it again, saw what appeared to be a dark, jagged landscape with no redeeming light from above, the only glow emanating from below, and that menacingly flickering rather than consoling. Peering more closely, she thought she saw creatures within the darkness that might have been snakes or worms...

'Take your time,' Sam said.

'I am,' she said, taking a Jungian slant, as she was sure they were hoping she would, trying to psychoanalyze through this single and, therefore, far too limited example of this artist's work. 'But I'm getting nowhere, because there's simply so little to go with, which means there's a risk of over-reacting to what we do have.'

'We've seen more,' Sam said. 'Which—'

'Don't tell me,' Grace said. 'Not yet, at least.' She took a few more moments.

'I can only say that if this were an adolescent's work – imagining a less proficiently painted version of the same – I would probably have some concerns about the child in question.' She shook her head. 'Which is a very far cry from daring to suggest that the artist here might have any connection with violent death. Which I presume is what you and Beth are asking.'

'It's called *"Erebus"*,' Sam said. 'As in Hades's location.'

'How old is the artist?'

'She's twenty-seven.'

'She,' Grace repeated.

'Does that make a difference?'

'Not really.' She went on studying the photograph. 'Many young people have become fascinated by satanic or demonic issues mostly because they're fed so much through TV and computer games.' She shook her head. 'Mind, I'm way out of touch these days.'

'This is an adult,' Sam told her.

'Quite.' Grace paused. 'Are we talking about the woman from the gallery?'

Sam had told her a little about Moore and Beatty, though the way she'd read it, she'd believed it was Beatty he had issues with.

'We are,' Sam said. 'And she has at least one

witchcraft-related painting on her wall at home. By Goya – *Witches In the Air*.'

'That's a wonderful painting,' Grace said. 'I'd have it on my wall.' She paused. 'So Allison Moore's an artist.'

'Riley thinks her work is very dark,' Sam said.

Grace thought about it. 'So supposing she is into some kind of dark arts thing – even supposing she's all the way down into satanism. Does that connect with these homicides in any way?'

'Not on any obvious level,' Sam said.

'Have I helped at all?'

'You always help,' he said.

'Not to nail this killer,' Grace said.

'Not tonight,' Sam said.

EIGHTY

February 24
At eight thirty Tuesday morning they were back at Beatty Management.

Moore was in her office on the first floor, behind the reception area, her calendar ready and waiting for them.

'Mr Beatty told me you'd be wanting this,' she said after inviting them to sit.

Her space was small, plain, well organized, the chairs not matching, as if she'd borrowed them for her visitors. Sam found himself wishing, as

276

he sat on yet another too small, uncomfortable chair, that the day might come when someone more considerate of tall humans, maybe someone like Saul, might be commissioned to redesign office furniture.

'*Mr* Beatty?' Riley raised an eyebrow. 'Very formal.'

'He's my boss.'

'And a little more besides,' Sam said.

'The sketch,' Moore said flatly.

'He told you about that, too,' Riley said.

'Why wouldn't he?' Moore said. 'Those questions seemed so odd to him.'

'Especially as he's never posed for you,' Riley said. 'According to him.'

'He hasn't,' Moore said.

'But the sketch was of Lawrence Beatty?' Sam asked.

Moore hesitated before answering. 'I don't understand why this is important.' She shook her head. 'I mean, I've told you I really want to cooperate, but this stuff seems private to me.'

'And we regret asking you questions about private matters,' Sam said. 'But it's in the nature of homicide investigations to have to work through layers. If the surface doesn't yield much, we start digging a little deeper.'

'So you're digging around everyone connected, however tenuously, to all these killings?' Moore asked.

'Sure,' Riley said. 'Though your connection isn't as *tenuous* as some, given that you were the person who most frequently visited the location where the Eastermans were left.'

'Surely that makes me more of a potential witness than a suspect.'

'No one's referred to you as a suspect, Ms Moore,' Riley said.

'Unless Mr Beatty gave you that impression,' Sam said.

Riley was glancing around. 'Is this your office?'

'It is,' Moore said. 'Why?'

'No posters,' Riley said. 'Nothing art-related.'

'It's my workplace.'

'Was that sketch of Lawrence Beatty?' Sam asked again.

Moore exhaled a swift, irritated breath. 'OK,' she said. 'I sketched him. One time. He was unaware, and the nude aspect was purely imaginary.'

'Do you remember when you sketched him?' Riley asked.

'No,' Moore said. 'Or not exactly. It was over time. It's how I work sometimes, go back and forth with a piece.'

'OK,' Sam said. 'Thank you.'

They continued the interview with what they'd officially come for: the checking of her calendars, both business and personal, the results as inconclusive as Beatty's; though if the shadow of suspicion did begin to broaden over both or either of them, their alibis, such as they were, would be quadruple-checked.

'You look tired, Ms Moore,' Riley said when they were through.

'More troubled than tired.' Her telephone rang. 'It's all right,' she said. 'It'll go to voicemail.' It stopped after four more rings.

'Troubled by our questions?' Sam asked.

'By the dreadfulness of these killings,' Moore said, 'and the fact that I should be deemed to have involvement at any level.' She moved restlessly in her chair. 'I'm sorry. It's a strain.'

'It's a dreadful time,' Sam said.

'Especially for the families,' Riley said.

'Do you imagine I don't know that?' Moore said.

She seemed suddenly close to tears, and Sam's instant gut reaction was to believe her. And then his mind drifted briefly to Jess Kowalski, and it occurred to him, worried him somewhat, that he might, for all his years of experience, be a sucker for women's tears.

He told her they were done, but as Moore was accompanying them out into the reception area, Riley paused.

'I'd like to see that sketch again.'

'Why?' Moore's voice rose with frustration. 'For God's sake.'

'I only saw it briefly,' Riley said, 'and Detective Becket never saw it at all.'

'Do you have a particular objection to showing it to us?' Sam asked.

'No, of course not – but like I said before, it's private.' She looked around, lowered her voice again. 'And frankly, it's embarrassing as hell.'

'Which seemed, I thought when I looked at your work,' Riley said, 'to be an interest of yours. Hell, I mean.'

'Might we come to your home again–' Sam had noted her flush, had gone right on – 'after work today?'

'Just to look at the sketch,' Riley said.

Moore shook her head, visibly sagging. 'What can I say?'

'You can refuse,' Sam said.

'I don't refuse,' Moore said.

'Six o'clock?' Riley asked.

'I'll be there,' Moore said.

Sam and Riley walked out on to Collins, the traffic slow.

'Why did you ask to see it again?' Sam asked.

'A sudden feeling,' Riley said.

'I'm all for those,' Sam said.

They headed for the Saab.

'It's not the subject,' Riley said. 'More the background.'

'Good,' Sam said.

The afternoon meeting in the situation room yielded no positive progress.

Negatives on all Cutter's remaining checks on the Christous. Anthony had called the office again this morning to make himself available and to ask if Karen might move back into the house on Prairie Avenue. And maybe they might turn out to be the craziest, boldest serial killers imaginable, but no one believed that.

Beatty and Moore seemed like the only glimmer of hope, though both were still being regarded as persons of interest rather than full-blown suspects.

Negativity all over. The great hope continuing that these *had* been pattern killings and that the spree would end at three. Six victims.

'I'm not convinced there is a pattern,' Sam said. 'Not to the timing, at least.'

'You have an alternative?' Joe Duval asked.

'One I hope to be wrong about.' He looked around, saw the team waiting, wished he had something worth sharing with them. 'Just the feeling we're being played with. That our frustration, maybe even our ineptitude, is being relished every bit as much as the victims' suffering.'

'You think they're enjoying making us wait for more,' Duval said.

Sam was grim-faced. 'We all know how addictive that kind of evil pleasure seems to be.'

'Too addictive to give up,' Riley said bleakly.

'Someone please tell me I'm wrong,' Sam said to the group.

No one could.

EIGHTY-ONE

At six on the nose, Sam and Riley were back at Moore's apartment.

She did not invite them to sit this time, simply handed the photograph of the sketch to Riley.

'You took it out of the album,' Sam said.

'I'm sorry,' Moore said, 'but wasn't this the sketch you wanted to see again?'

Her belligerence was starting to show, Sam noted. Moving further away from the gentle,

281

straightforward young woman she'd first displayed herself to be.

'It is,' Riley said. 'Thank you.'

She moved beneath the overhead lamp – two screw-in bulbs connected to a ceiling fan – took a long look, then handed it to Sam.

Who saw it too.

'All right?' Moore asked.

'We're interested in the background,' Sam said.

'Background?'

Sam brought the photo back to her, keeping hold of it. 'The subject, Mr Beatty, is in the foreground. There's a column in the background.'

'Yes,' she said, her colour heightening.

'It looks familiar to us,' Sam said.

'It's just a column,' Moore said. 'It doesn't mean anything. It isn't a real place.'

'Oh, that's right,' Riley said. 'Because Mr Beatty didn't pose for you. This was just a work of imagination.'

'Yes,' Moore said again. 'It was.'

'Yet Mr Beatty is a real person,' Sam said. 'So chances are, same goes for the background.'

'That column sure does look familiar,' Riley said.

'You said,' Moore said.

Sam and Riley exchanged looks.

Time marching on, time they could ill afford.

'Looks like one of the columns in the Oates Gallery to me,' Sam said.

'Just like,' Riley said.

Moore shrugged. 'I guess that place might have influenced me.'

282

'Because you spent so much time there,' Sam said.

'Not so much,' she said, 'but enough, I guess.'

'Do you have a photocopier here, Ms Moore?' asked Riley.

'No,' she said. 'Sorry.'

'I thought,' Sam said, 'I saw a fax machine in your studio last time we came.'

'Oh,' she said. 'Yes.'

'Would you have any objection to our taking a copy of your photograph, ma'am?' Riley asked.

'I'm not sure if the photo would fit in the machine,' Moore said.

'I think it would,' Sam said.

Moore smiled. 'I don't suppose it would sit well if I did object.'

'It's your right to refuse,' Sam said.

'At this time,' Riley added.

Allison Moore dipped her head, resentment and resignation about equal.

'Be my guests,' she said.

EIGHTY-TWO

Saul and Cathy were in their kitchen at the apartment, heating up pizza and planning their strategy for the surprise.

'Mildred says she only has one patient Thursday morning,' Saul said. 'Nine thirty. So as long as Grace doesn't make any more appointments,

283

we can get her out of the house by eleven so you can pack.'

'How am I going to know what to pack?' Cathy opened the refrigerator, pulled out a bag of romaine lettuce and some cherry tomatoes.

'You're a woman,' Saul said. 'You'll work it out.'

'Don't be sexist,' Cathy said. 'I'm a waitress and an amateur runner. Grace is a sophisticated psychologist and a beautiful woman. Not all women are the same, Saul, in case you hadn't noticed.'

'We all know what she likes wearing,' Saul said, sticking to the point. 'Just pack everything you see that you think she might need. And don't forget stuff like make-up and perfume and jewellery.'

'You don't say,' Cathy said. 'What if she does schedule more appointments?'

'Mildred's going to do her best to make sure that doesn't happen.' Saul opened the oven door, took a look at the pizza, the aroma of day-old pepperoni and onion flowing into the kitchen. 'My job's the tough part – getting Grace out of the house.'

'You'll have to have an emergency.' Cathy ran the tomatoes under the faucet, then dried them with a piece of paper towel.

'It'll have to be something that only Grace could fix.'

'She's hardly Mrs Fix-it,' Cathy said. 'All she really knows how to fix is people.'

'Oh, man,' Saul said.

EIGHTY-THREE

'What do they do at witches' covens?' Sam asked Riley back in the office just before seven.

'How the hell should I know?'

'You're the one who brought up witches,' he said. 'I'm thinking about the blood in the gallery. And the cocaine. Do witches do drugs, do we know?'

'I'll call Joe Duval,' Riley said. 'See if he can ask his office to locate any covens in Miami-Dade.'

'Tell him not to bother with the official Wiccan churches,' Sam said. 'They seem pretty respectable.'

'Jesus,' Riley said. 'Less than a week ago I'm not sure I'd even heard of Wicca.'

'Tell Duval we need an ear to the ground,' Sam said, 'listening out for something a little smaller, more secretive.'

'And maybe a whole lot nastier,' Riley said.

Sam listened to his messages, smiled.

'What's up?' Riley asked.

'Martinez is out of the CCU,' Sam said.

'Thank God,' Riley said.

'Yeah,' Sam said, abruptly drained by relief.

She picked up her phone. 'I'll call Duval. You go see Martinez.'

'I can see him later.'

'If we get anything fast,' Riley said, 'you can come back.'

'You sure?' Sam said.

'It'll do you good to see him out of that place,' Riley said.

Sam wasn't arguing. 'I'll call you from there.'

Martinez was in a regular room four floors up from the CCU, a pretty room with blue drapes at the window and a framed print of a South Beach scene that Sam thought was probably identical to the one they'd seen in the gardener's room eight days earlier.

Jess was sitting in the armchair as Sam came in.

'Hi,' she said, flushing, looking embarrassed as hell.

As she ought, Sam thought, then pulled his mind sharply off the incident.

In the past, he hoped, his friend's recovery all that mattered now.

For now.

'Hey,' he said to Martinez. 'Look at you.'

'Hey,' Martinez said back. 'So how's it going?'

It was the first time Sam had heard Martinez speak coherently in days, though his voice was weak.

'We're all good.' Sam held his friend's hand for a moment, almost hoping he would object, be fully himself again, but instead, Martinez shut his eyes for an instant, and Sam knew he'd been aware of his own mortality. 'All missing you,' he added.

'I'm talking about the case,' Martinez said.

'Not my popularity.'

Sam felt warm relief. 'You really are feeling better.'

'Come on, man,' his friend said. 'I need detail.'

'You need rest,' Sam told him.

'Are you retiring me?' Martinez said.

'You'll outwork me,' Sam said.

'You're just out of the CCU, Al,' Jess said.

'I know where I've been,' he told her, a little abruptly.

'I know you do,' she said. 'I'm sorry.'

Martinez shook his head, his dark hair sleek against his head from days and nights of fever and no showers. 'No, I'm sorry, Jessie,' he said. 'I just want to feel normal again, like *me*, you know?'

'Of course she knows,' Sam said. 'We all do.'

'So give me something, man.'

'I wish I had something to give,' Sam said.

'Nothing?' Martinez looked incredulous, as if he'd been in bed for a year rather than four days. 'No arrests? No suspects?'

'None worth talking about.'

Jess got up. 'It's because I'm here.'

Sam shook his head. 'It's because I don't have anything worth telling, and because this guy has to get well, which means he has to rest like any other patient who nearly died from rat bite fever.'

'I kept telling them,' Martinez said, 'I never got bitten by any rat.'

'They told you it doesn't have to get you like that,' Jess reminded him.

Martinez shuddered. 'Makes me nauseous just

thinking about it. I hate fucking rats.'

'Then don't think about it,' Jess told him.

'Listen to your fiancée,' Sam said.

Martinez shut his eyes again. 'Jeez, I'm tired.'

'So get some sleep,' Sam said. 'I'm going home.'

His partner opened his eyes again. 'Grace doin' OK?'

'She's doing great,' Sam told him. 'And it looks like we're going to make the trip.'

'That's good.' Martinez mustered a smile.

'Alvarez won't let me call it off,' Sam said. 'Can you believe that guy?'

'What's this trip?' Jess asked.

'It's a surprise for Grace,' Martinez told her sleepily. 'For her birthday.'

'That's so nice,' Jess said.

Sam looked at her, saw apparent sincerity.

'He's taking her on a cruise,' Martinez told her.

Sam wished instantly that he had not.

'Oh, I'm so jealous,' Jess said, then flushed again. 'I mean, it's something I'd love for us to do someday, Al.'

'Maybe we will, baby,' he said.

He shut his eyes again, and this time he slept.

Sam called Riley from the car, told her about Martinez, then asked if she'd gotten anything usable from Duval's office.

'Nothing yet,' she said. 'But he's on it.'

A surge of impatience swept through Sam. 'We have to bring in Beatty and Moore. At the very least, I'm betting they were there, in that house, some time close to what went down –

288

maybe even that night.'

'We have no proof of that,' Riley said.

'I know it,' Sam said. 'But if there's even a chance I'm right, we can't afford to waste another minute.'

'So just questioning, right?' Riley said. 'If they agree to come in.'

'We don't want to arrest them, that's for sure,' Sam said.

'I'm up for it,' she said, 'if the Captain agrees.'

'I'm hoping Alvarez will be on side.' Sam pulled out of the parking lot on to Biscayne Boulevard.

'So Martinez is really on the up?' Riley asked.

'Knock on wood,' Sam said.

'No big plans on my birthday this year, please,' Grace said later, in bed. 'You have enough pressure on you, and I don't need anything but you.' She stroked his cheek, kissed his temple. 'I mean it, Sam. You don't have time.'

'I always have time for you, Gracie,' he said.

'You always *want* to have time for me,' she said. 'That's different. Better.'

'We'll see,' Sam said.

'Just please don't start feeling you need to organize anything,' she persisted. 'I'll tell the others not to expect even a dinner, unless it's a last-minute sit around the kitchen table.'

'OK.' Sam kissed her on the mouth. 'You're amazing.'

'I just hope I have my priorities straight,' Grace said. 'No big deal.'

'You're the biggest deal I know,' he said.

EIGHTY-FOUR

February 25

With no more than the usual cautions from Tom Kennedy, Sam and Riley issued separate 'invitations' to Beatty and Moore to come in to answer a few questions.

'What is this?' Beatty asked. 'Am I under arrest? Should I call a lawyer?'

'You're certainly not under arrest,' Sam said. 'And if you'd prefer it, we would come to your office again, but I figured you'd rather we didn't keep on doing that.'

Moore, even more audibly jarred, also asked Riley if she needed an attorney.

'It's entirely your right,' Riley said.

'Am I a suspect?' Moore asked.

'Not at present,' Riley said.

Noon the agreed time for Moore.

A half-hour later for Beatty.

EIGHTY-FIVE

Cathy had come to see Martinez.

'You look so much better,' she told him.

He looked a million miles from great, but it was true to say that he looked about a hundred times better than he had last time she'd seen him.

Which was more, she felt, than could be said for Jess.

'You look tired,' Cathy told her, kindly, she hoped.

'I am,' Jess said.

'That's because she's been here forever,' Martinez said. 'Best medicine, isn't that what they say about love?'

Cathy thought it was laughter, not love, but kept that to herself.

'I can't believe the change in a few days,' she said. 'David and Sam told me, but I needed to see for myself.'

'You don't need to keep on coming,' Martinez told her. 'You got a busy life.' He grinned. 'Not that it doesn't do me good to see all the pretty girls I can.'

'This guy,' Cathy said to Jess, and shook her head.

'All guys,' Jess said, a little smile on her lips.

291

Not in her eyes, though, Cathy thought.

She got up to leave about twenty minutes later, feeling that Martinez looked weary, bent to kiss his cheek, squeezed his hand, felt him squeeze back.

'You be good now,' she told him.

'Always,' he said.

Jess got up too. 'I'll come out with you.'

'You don't need to,' Cathy said.

'I'd like to stretch my legs,' Jess said.

They walked past the nurses' station toward the elevators.

'Something up?' Cathy asked.

'You could say that,' Jess said.

Cathy stopped, turned to face her, saw that the other woman's eyes looked weird, angry and distressed. 'Tell me,' she said. 'You look upset.'

'You won't want to hear this,' Jess said.

'Try me.'

'You probably won't even believe me.'

'We'll never know unless you tell me.'

Jess looked around, making sure no one was close enough to hear.

'Your dad made a pass at me,' she said.

'And the Pope's a rabbi,' Cathy said.

Her anger already heating up, stoking nicely.

'I said you wouldn't believe me,' Jess said.

'And you were right,' Cathy said, and then – no more screwing around – she went straight on. 'I've had your number since the party at my parents',' she said. 'I don't trust you, I'm not one hundred per cent sure now that you even know what the truth is, but I don't believe one word that comes out of your mouth.'

'Thank you,' Jess said quietly.

Tears in her eyes.

'You seem pretty good at that, too,' Cathy said, harshly.

'Sam made a pass at me the night before last.' Jess kept it soft and low, but every word seemed strung out, elongated. 'I've been struggling with what to do ever since.'

'Well, you go right on struggling,' Cathy told her. 'I can promise you that you won't be able to hurt Sam or Grace with this kind of crap. But if Martinez gets one bit more hurt than he absolutely needs to when you tell him goodbye, then you're going to have a whole lot of people sitting right on your spiteful little back.'

A nurse walked by, and Cathy saw from her expression that she'd heard at least the end of that, and she felt shaken by her own anger, hated the feel of it, the way it clenched up her stomach, made her heart race.

'You're mad at me,' Jess said, 'and I can understand that.'

Cathy didn't trust herself to say any more.

'But you'll come to realize I'm telling the truth,' Jess went on, 'and that your dad is not quite the superhero you'd like him to be.'

'You–' no *way* was she going to let that go – 'are a lying little bitch.'

'It's OK,' Jess said. 'I understand.'

'Oh, fuck off,' Cathy said, and turned on her heel.

She was still trembling with rage when she reached the first floor, hated what she had to do now, and Christ knew the timing could not have been much worse – and she wondered if Jess knew about the surprise cruise, guessed that Martinez had probably shared that with her.

Bitch.

She thought about doing nothing, about trying to keep that nasty encounter to herself, but she was all too sure that Jessica Kowalski did not intend for that to happen.

'Bitch,' she said out loud.

And headed for the Mazda.

EIGHTY-SIX

'This feels like the last-chance saloon,' Sam told Martinez on the phone at eleven thirty, having decided that his partner was probably right, that keeping him in the loop might do more good than harm at this point. 'One of my hunches.'

Besides, keeping Martinez's mind on work might be the best plan in more ways than one.

'I've always trusted your hunches,' his partner said now.

His voice was still weak and a little unfamiliar, but at least he was there to talk to, and that felt great to Sam.

'I just hope it isn't an over-reaction because I'm almost out of time.' He paused. 'Or because I have another goddamned hunch that I may find myself taken off the case altogether when I get back. Maybe this is an ego thing.'

'Do you really believe that, man?' Martinez asked.

'Not really,' Sam said. 'But it is more a case that Beatty and Moore are still all we have.'

Cathy had called just after ten thirty and told Sam about her encounter with Jess.

'I'm not sure I wasn't meaner than I should have been,' she'd said.

'Can't say I blame you,' Sam had said.

'I'm just so worried about Martinez,' Cathy said.

'I know,' Sam said. 'Me too.'

'Can you call Grace?' she said. 'Warn her, just in case Jess tries to get to her. Or do you want me to go tell her?'

'You're due at the café soon,' Sam said. 'I'll call Grace.'

'I'm so sorry,' Cathy said. 'I just thought I had to tell you.'

'You were right, sweetheart, and it isn't you who needs to be sorry.'

'This timing's all such a bitch for you,' Cathy had said.

And that was without his best friend's so-called fiancée.

His call to Grace had been of necessity short and less than sweet.

'This is beginning to feel a little surreal,' he'd said after passing on Cathy's distasteful alert.

'I'm so sorry,' Grace had said, 'for you, but especially for Al.'

295

'I love you,' Sam said.

'Me too,' his wife had told him. 'More than ever.'

It had only come to him after the call that neither of them had felt even the slightest tug of need to affirm that Jess was lying.

It didn't come sweeter than that.

He'd made another call that morning, to Elliot Sanders, who'd been out on a case.

Sam had tried his cell, which had gone to voicemail.

'I need a word, Doc,' Sam had said. 'It's pretty urgent.'

All part of the same hunch.

But nothing ventured and all that jazz.

EIGHTY-SEVEN

Allison Moore had come to the station without an attorney, but her frame of mind was plainly hostile.

'I don't mind telling you I'm getting a little sick of this.'

They were in an interview room, everything simple, stark, designed to concentrate the conversation on what counted. Sam and Riley on one side of the table, Moore on the other, having given permission, after a few minutes of irritable resistance, for the interview to be recorded.

'It's as much for your protection as anything else,' Sam had told her. 'It'll save you from having to repeat stuff yet again.'

'That's assuming I have anything more *to* tell you.'

'Of course,' Sam had said.

She'd shaken her head, then sighed. 'Oh, what the hell,' she said.

'We're very grateful for your cooperation,' Sam had told her.

'We just need a little more,' Riley had said.

Moore had shrugged, said nothing.

Sam had started the machine, noted date, time and those present, and waited a count of two.

'On the night of Friday, February the sixth to Saturday, February the seventh,' he began, 'were you inside the former Oates Gallery?'

Moore stared at Sam. 'Of course not.'

Only a split second's hesitation, but it had been there.

'We have reason to believe,' Riley said, 'that you may have been in the house either alone or with one or more others.'

Moore took a deep breath, seeming to compose herself.

'No,' she said.

Sam smiled. 'Would you like some coffee now, Ms Moore?'

She'd refused their first offer, had said she'd rather start and finish as swiftly as possible.

'No,' she said again now. 'No coffee.'

'Only we need to ask you to wait just a few minutes,' Sam said.

'What for?'

'While we do a little checking,' he said.

'What kind of checking?'

'Nothing for you to worry about,' Riley told her.

'Please don't patronize me,' Moore said.

'I wasn't meaning to,' Riley said.

'Detective Riley was merely reassuring you,' Sam said, stopped the recording and stood up.

Beatty was in another room, had also come without legal representation, had also granted permission for the interview to be recorded, but Sam and Riley had known right away that this was going to be a whole different ball game.

He seemed like a man who couldn't take any more.

Ready to talk.

'OK,' he said, within seconds of their first question about the Oates Gallery. 'I have to tell you something, but I need you to promise me you'll keep it confidential.'

'That depends,' Sam said.

'On what?' Beatty asked. 'Because I'm telling you, it has nothing – *I* had nothing – to do with any killings. Lord God, I'll swear that on all my family's lives.'

'Not on the Bible,' Riley said, then twisted her mouth a little. 'I guess not.'

'Oh, Christ,' Beatty said. 'You know.'

'What do we know?' Sam was quite gentle.

'Please, Detective Becket.' Beatty's pleading was more intense, his eyes flicking back and forth between the recording machine and the detectives' faces. 'I need to know this isn't going to go public.'

'Like the man said,' Riley said, 'that depends on what you have to tell us.'

He took another moment, then made up his mind, and once he began, it was the way it sometimes went with people who'd stepped into something way too deep for them. A torrent of words with no order, powered by fear.

'I only went this one time,' he said, 'because I was a little intrigued, I guess, and because of Ally. Not that there's anything really going on with us, it's just that she's pretty and – you know, you've seen her. But once, when we'd gone out for drinks after work, she started talking about her *group* and at first I thought, hey, that's disgusting, how can this nice young woman spend time with people like that? But then it seemed to prey on my mind, and she talked about how everyone in the group had to provide a location for a meeting at least once every few months.'

'OK.' Sam hated to interrupt the flow, but he needed clarification for the record. 'When you say her "group", and when you say "meeting", can you be more specific?'

Beatty stared at him, his hazel eyes swimming someplace between defiance and horror, and then he gave it up and visibly sagged.

'Coven is what I mean when I say group,' he said. 'Coven, as in a gathering of witches.' He shook his head. 'I can hardly believe those words are coming out of my mouth, it's so crazy, so idiotic, and I don't know how I could have been so stupid. God knows I've made mistakes

299

before, but I'm not a stupid man.'

'I'm sure you're not,' Sam said. 'Go on, please, Mr Beatty.'

'So she said she wanted to use the old gallery this one night, and I said no, it was out of the question. But she said it was so perfect, and it wasn't as if anyone could ever find out, because the only people who ever went in to check the place out were her and the cleaners, and they – the group – always cleaned up after themselves. And no damage would be done, she said, because the meetings weren't like that, and anyway, there was nothing in the house to damage.'

'So what are these meetings like, Mr Beatty?' asked Riley.

'I can only tell you about that one meeting,' Beatty said. 'That one night.'

'That's OK,' Sam said.

'It was a ceremony.' Beatty paused. 'An initiation ceremony. That's what I'm so damned ashamed of, you have to believe me. As I said, I was intrigued, but when it came to it, I was repulsed by the whole thing, and if people find out, I will never live it down, the shame of it.'

'What happened?' Sam asked, keeping his manner easy, interested.

'Sex,' Beatty said frankly. 'That's what it came right down to, at least that was what it looked like to me. All kinds of weird stuff, some of it almost funny because it was so bizarre – but what it was really about was sex. Not full-on intercourse, but real sick stuff.' He shrugged, relaxing just a little. 'At least, to my point of view.'

'So were you the one being initiated, Mr Beatty?' Sam asked.

'No *way*,' Beatty said. 'It was a young woman.' He shut his eyes briefly, the small respite gone, gritted his teeth, then went on. 'Ally told me just before it began that the initiate is supposed to study and prepare for the ceremony for a year – a year and a *day*, was what she said.' He shook his head. 'Everyone in the coven votes before the new person can go through this garbage.'

'So were you a member of the coven?' Riley asked.

'No, of course not, I told you.'

'Then how come you were allowed to be there?' Riley asked. 'Sounds like quite a tight circle to me.'

'Ally swung it for me,' Beatty said. 'I wish she hadn't.'

'But she swung it for you because you were intrigued.' Sam grew a little sharper. 'Seems a little strange to me that one minute you're *intrigued* enough to ask your colleague to get you into this ceremony, and then the next you're so disgusted. You must have known at least a little of what would happen.'

'Not till just before, like I told you.' Beatty's eyes fixed on Sam momentarily, hoping to rekindle his kinder side, but then he gave it up. 'And then it all started happening and I was right in the middle of it, and there didn't seem to be anything I could do except go with the flow.'

'Couldn't you have left?' Riley asked.

'I didn't like to,' Beatty said. 'Because of

where it was.'

'You mean, on premises for which you're responsible,' Sam said.

'Yes.'

'Couldn't you have told them to leave?' Sam asked.

'I thought about it,' Beatty said. 'But I figured it might get nasty.' He twitched his mouth. 'I mean, witches...'

Sam and Riley were both aware of time passing, of Moore waiting in the other interview room, aware that she still had the right to leave at any time.

'So what time did this ceremony start and finish?' Sam asked.

'We got there at eleven,' Beatty said.

'Eleven p.m.,' Riley clarified.

Beatty nodded. 'And I guess it was over by one thirty, or maybe two a.m.'

'That's when you all left?' Sam said.

'The coven left then,' Beatty said. 'Ally and I stayed behind to clear up.'

'What did you need to clear up?' Sam asked.

'Candle wax, mostly, and chalk – they'd marked out this circle–' Beatty drew it with his hands – 'and lit four candles – I can't remember why. There was water on the floor, too. They'd brought in a tub that they bathed the woman – the initiate – in before they dried her off and...' His voice shook a little and he cleared his throat. 'Do you need all the details, because I'd just as soon forget it.'

'What else did you have to clean up?' Sam asked.

'They'd pricked her finger as part of the *thing*, so I thought there might be some blood on the floor.' He winced. 'Clearly we missed that.'

'Anything else?' Riley asked.

'Not that I can think of,' he said.

'So what happened after you'd finished cleaning up?' Sam asked.

Beatty didn't answer right away.

'Mr Beatty, we're nearly done here,' Sam said. 'It would help if you'd answer.'

'Ally and I made love,' he said.

'And then?' Riley asked.

'And then I went home,' Beatty said.

'What time was that?' Riley asked.

'Around three thirty, I guess.'

'Did you both leave together?' asked Sam.

'No,' Beatty said. 'Ally stayed behind to lock up.'

'Why didn't you wait for her?' Riley asked. 'I thought you came together.'

'We came in separate cars. And to be honest, I just wanted to get the hell out of there, but she was still in this weird *mood* – she wanted to stay. She said she loved the feeling left behind after the ceremony.'

'Afterglow,' Riley said.

'That makes it sound as if she made a habit of staying behind afterward,' Sam said. 'But the venues weren't always arranged by her, were they?'

'I don't know.' Beatty looked at his watch. 'Are we done?'

'Almost.' Sam paused. 'Mr Beatty, were you still at the house when the bodies of Michael and

303

Susan Easterman were dumped in the garden outside?'

'No,' Beatty said. 'I was not.' He hesitated. 'At least, not so I was aware.'

'And was Allison Moore still on the premises when the bodies were brought into the garden?' Sam asked.

'You'd have to ask her,' Beatty said. 'If she was, she never told me.'

'Might the bodies have been in the garden before you arrived?' Riley asked.

'No.'

'How can you be sure?' Sam asked.

'We opened the shutters for a while because the moon was so bright, and I looked out for a few minutes. Then we closed them again because we didn't want anyone seeing the candle-light and reporting it.'

'And you had a clear view of the whole garden during those minutes?' Sam asked.

'I believe I did,' Beatty said. 'I saw nothing that ought not to have been there.'

'Then thank you for your cooperation,' Sam said.

'Is that it?' Hope sprang into his eyes.

'Aside from asking you for the names of those others present on the night in question,' Riley said.

'I don't know their names. Not their real names, at least.'

'What does that mean?' Riley asked.

'They used their coven names,' Beatty said. 'And I only remember a couple of them.'

'Such as?' Riley asked.

'Willow,' Beatty said. 'And I think one of the women was called something like Silver Moon.' He rolled his eyes. 'Like something out of one of those trashy teen magic dramas.'

'You watch a lot of those?' Riley again.

'So Ms Moore aside,' Sam said, 'you don't know the real identities of any of the people who were in the house with you.'

'No,' Beatty said. 'I don't. I'm sorry.' He paused. 'Did I mention that they were masked?'

'No,' Riley said.

'Did you wear a mask?' Sam asked.

'Yes. Just a plain black eye mask with slits in it, like Zorro.'

'You weren't masked in Ms Moore's sketch,' Sam said.

'Are we back to that again?' Beatty sighed. 'I told you, I didn't know she did that.'

'One more thing,' Riley said. 'Did you or anyone else use cocaine that night?'

'I didn't,' Beatty said. 'If the others did, I was not aware of it.'

'I have one more too,' Sam said.

'OK.'

'Did they use a kind of dagger or sword during the ceremony?'

'Yes,' Beatty said. 'I guess it was a kind of a sword, not a dagger. The guy they called the High Priest waved it around a few times.'

'Is that all he did with it?' Sam asked.

Beatty's face flushed darkly. 'The initiate was wearing a gown when she came in, and they used the sword to cut it off her.' He paused, had to lick his lips, swallow. 'There was some cord around her wrists, too, and the High Priest cut that.'

'Anything else?' Sam asked.

'They never cut her with it, if that's what you're asking.' Beatty's eyes were suddenly appalled. 'Are you telling me that sword was used to kill those people?'

'Have you any reason for thinking it might have been?' Sam asked.

'No, of course not,' Beatty said.

Sam got to his feet. 'Then once again, we thank you. You've been very patient.'

'Has any of it helped?' Beatty asked.

'Every piece of information helps at least a little,' Sam told him.

Elliot Sanders had called fifteen minutes before, and Sam took a moment between interviews to check back with him.

'Have you heard of an athamé?' Sam asked.

'I have,' the ME said. 'It's a ceremonial knife, a kind of double-edged dagger.'

The number of things Sanders knew about never ceased to impress Sam.

'Or sword?' Sam asked.

'Maybe. I only know of it as a dagger.'

'Any chance an athamé was used to cut the throats of the couples?' Sam asked, even though Beatty had talked about a sword.

'Not impossible,' Sanders said. 'Though from the wounds, I couldn't tell if the blade was single or double-edged.'

Sam winced. 'Inconclusive, then?'

'Sorry, Sam,' Sanders said.

306

EIGHTY-EIGHT

'Your friend, or rather your boss,' Riley told Moore after they'd restarted the interview, 'has been very helpful.'

'Good for him,' she said.

'He doesn't seem to have enjoyed his night at the gallery too much,' Sam said.

Moore said nothing.

'Maybe the last part,' Riley said, with a small smile.

'According to Mr Beatty,' Sam went on, his tone formal, 'you and he attended an initiation ceremony of a witches' coven at the former Oates Gallery on the night of the sixth to the seventh of February.'

Moore tightened her lips, shook her head, eyed the recording machine, then, finally, shrugged. 'What do you want to know?'

'The truth,' Sam said.

'I was there,' she said.

'That's a start,' Riley said.

'No law against it,' Moore said, 'so far as I know.'

'That depends on what went on,' Sam said.

'Trespass comes to mind,' Riley said. 'Not to mention that traces of blood were later found on the premises.'

'And cocaine,' Sam added.

'Nothing to do with me,' Moore said.

Neither detective spoke.

Moore was silent again for another moment. 'Should I get a lawyer?'

'Entirely your decision,' Sam said. 'As we told you earlier.'

'Maybe if I just come clean,' she said, 'about what "went on", as you put it.'

'We'd be glad to hear that,' Riley said.

'I'll bet you would,' Moore said acidly.

'In your own time,' Sam said.

She talked for a long while, and there was no noticeable shame in her, more of a matter-of-fact approach to the way in which she described the night in question. She told them about the High Priest who'd run the show, about the female – Moore used the word 'candidate' rather than 'initiate' – whose clothing had been sliced away with a sword, about the rituals that had included the young woman being blindfolded and led naked to a bathtub.

'The water ought to be heated by fire,' Moore said, 'but I felt that wasn't safe in the gallery, so it must have been damned cold for her, but she put up with it.'

'Marks in her favour,' Riley said.

Sam gave her a look.

Moore went on, told them that the candidate had been dried off, then carried into a chalk circle where the High Priest and every member of the coven had kissed her before going on with a ritual which had included something Moore

308

called a 'five fold kiss', bestowed with blessings, on her feet, knees, womb, breasts and lips.

And more besides, bizarre rituals, including
the blood pricking that Beatty had referred to,
and a litany of stuff that made Sam and Riley
want to leave the goddamned room and take a
shower.

None of it, so far as they could see – including
the sword – connected to the killings.

Which they got back to as swiftly as they
could.

'According to Mr Beatty,' Sam said, 'you stayed behind to lock up.'

'That's true,' Moore said, then took a deep
breath before adding: 'I didn't see the bodies
being dumped in the backyard.'

'Maybe you were one of the ones who did the
dumping?' Sam said.

'No way,' Moore said. 'No *way*.'

It was, by far, the most agitated they had seen
her.

'Come on, Ally,' Sam said. 'Tell us what happened. What you saw.'

'You knew about the plastic dome,' Riley said.
'And not because you'd overheard anyone
speaking about it.'

'No,' she said. 'I'm sorry about that.'

'That's "no" to which part of Detective Riley's
statement?' Sam asked, for clarification.

'I knew about it,' Moore said softly, 'because
I'd seen it.'

'What did you see, Ms Moore?' Sam leaned
forward.

'I saw the bodies.' Her face was paler, the

freckles standing out, her expression strained. 'After Larry left, I went on checking around, making sure there were no traces left. And then I felt very drained – it was late, and it had been quite a night, and I was tired. So I lay down for a rest, and I fell asleep. And when I woke up – I don't know if there was any noise, I wasn't aware of any, but something woke me – and I went over and opened one of the shutters, and I looked out and the dawn was rising, and I saw them.'

'Them?' Sam echoed, hope stirring faintly.

'Not who brought them there,' Moore said. 'I'm sorry.' She rubbed her right temple with her fist, a turquoise gemstone on a ring leaving a slight indentation. 'I'd like to believe that if I'd seen that, I'd have told you right away, but I didn't, so there was no point. All I'd seen was those poor people, and at first I thought they might be mannequins or something, but then I could see that they weren't, and they were so obviously dead, I knew I couldn't help them. All I could do was get out of there.'

'You didn't go out into the garden?' asked Sam.

She shook her head. 'I knew Mr Mulhoon would be arriving pretty early, so I knew they'd be found. And it just seemed to me that the only thing I was going to achieve was big trouble for myself if anyone knew I'd been there, let alone...'

'Let alone arranging a coven initiation,' Riley said.

'You can understand why I didn't say anything, can't you?' Moore asked them both, appealing.

'You're a material witness,' Sam told her. 'You failed to report a grievous crime, and you lied when asked about it.'

'What now?' Her voice was down to a whisper.

'We need names and addresses,' Riley said, 'of your fellow coven members.'

'I can't give you those,' Moore said. 'It's secret. Anyway, I don't know their real names. We use special names.'

'Weren't any of your friends there?' Sam asked. 'Maybe the one who lets you store your paintings in her garage? Or the one you visited last Christmas in Key West?'

'They weren't there,' Moore said. 'They know nothing about it.'

'What's your *special* name?' Riley asked.

'Fawn,' Moore said, and flushed.

'Who keeps the sword?' Sam asked.

'I'm not sure. The High Priest, I guess. I don't know his real name.'

'How do you get in touch with each other to arrange meetings?' Riley asked.

'Email,' Moore said.

'We'll need your computers,' Sam told her. 'Work and home.'

'I don't use the one at work for personal stuff.'

Riley made a soft, snorting sound.

'We'll still need both,' Sam said. 'We'll be obtaining search warrants, and meantime, someone will wait in your office and outside your apartment to ensure that you don't touch the equipment.'

'But you don't have a warrant yet, do you?' Moore asked.

'Are you refusing to cooperate?' Sam asked.

'No,' Moore said. 'Of course not.'

'Good,' Sam said.

EIGHTY-NINE

So much to do in so little time.

Apply for search warrants for Beatty's office and computers as well as Moore's.

Learn as much as possible about witchcraft and how it might or might not relate to the homicides.

Find the High Priest and every other damned member of the coven, not to mention the initiate so they could confirm her blood match. Because whether or not they had just pranced around and kissed and touched and stroked and pushed that poor, idiotic young woman down on to the floor, or whether they'd all screwed their brains out, all or any one of them might also be material witnesses, and Sam and Riley and the squad needed them.

But Sam was taking his wife on a surprise birthday cruise *tomorrow.*

So Sam was just about out of time.

And it hurt him that something intended to be so happy should presently be giving him an almost physical pain because of what he saw as a dereliction of duty and a betrayal of all the victims.

Suzy and Michael Easterman. Elizabeth Price and André Duprez. Evelyn and Frank Ressler. And all their loved ones.

'You'll only be gone five days,' Alvarez said when Sam came in just before six.

'Five of the most critical days since this began,' Sam pointed out.

'They're all critical,' Alvarez said, 'but if it helps you come to terms, I'm planning to work the case with Riley till you get back.'

Startled, Sam nodded. 'It helps a heck of a lot.'

Which might not have been the case with any number of sergeants he'd known, but Mike Alvarez had all those years of experience as a homicide detective under his belt, was one of *them*, and suddenly, for the first time in days, Sam could picture getting Grace on board that ship after all.

'So now would be the right time for you to pass on any ideas you think the rest of us might not be coming up with,' Alvarez said.

'A lunar calendar,' Sam said. 'I've already downloaded one.'

'In case there's any kind of link-up between the witchcraft thing and the other killings,' Alvarez said.

'The moon wasn't full on the night of the fourth, but it seems that witches or Wiccans get together at new moons, too, and they have festivals called sabbats.' Sam was speeding up.

313

'I've downloaded what they call the Wheel of the Year, too, which is kind of a witch's calendar – I'll get a copy right to you.'

'Worth looking at,' Alvarez agreed.

'Only one of the festivals fits the bill for this month,' Sam said. 'It's known by a bunch of names, but the one we'd recognize most easily is Candlemas.'

'I thought that was a Christian festival.'

'Also a pretty major thing for witches, apparently, which might have connected time-wise to the first two killings, but not the last.'

'Unless maybe it was a spark that lit a longer fuse,' Alvarez said.

'More likely, this whole witch angle is going to mean nothing more than our best shot at finding witnesses,' Sam said. 'But we need to sit hard on Beatty and Moore. We need them to tell us exactly where they and their *group* were every second of all those days and nights, and if their alibis aren't diamond solid...'

'I said anything we might not be coming up with,' Alvarez said dryly.

'Then one last thing about the Wiccan wheel,' Sam said. 'If this is a link, and if the killing has stopped, it might just start again next month. Spring equinox is another big deal for them, a regaining of strength being one of the notions I read up on.'

'Let's hope we get lucky before then,' Alvarez said.

'God, yes,' Sam said.

'Go clear your desk,' the sergeant told him. 'Give everything to Riley, copies to me, then go see Martinez, make sure he's under control. I don't want to have to worry about any crazy grandstanding by him when they let him out of the hospital.'

'I doubt he'll have the strength,' Sam said.

'Then get yourself home.'

'I can't go home early,' Sam said, 'without making Grace suspicious, so I'd like to keep on working the case for another hour or so. And since I'll have to leave home as usual in the morning, I might as well come to the office.'

'If you come here tomorrow,' Alvarez told him, 'there's a pile of outstanding paperwork with your name on it. If you're not here, that's OK, too. You're officially on vacation, just try and remember that.' He smiled. 'And give my love to Grace.'

NINETY

February 26

No setbacks on Thursday morning.

David had come over earlier with Mildred and taken Joshua out to the beach, leaving Mildred in the office to man the phones and do a little filing while Grace saw her patient, an eight-year-old still severely traumatized by her older brother's accidental death a year ago.

Saul was nervous as hell, waiting to play his part; definitely, he figured, the toughest job of

315

this day. Not a natural actor, he also felt genuine repugnance for what he was about to do; trivializing something that he personally knew to be all-consumingly painful.

Still, all in a fine cause, and as he and Cathy had agreed, nothing much else would persuade Grace to drop everything and get over to their place.

He waited till ten forty-five, checked his watch for the umpteenth time and made the call.

Mildred, sitting at the small pine desk that had first been used by Dora Rabinovitch, then by Lucia Busseto – her memory the source of more horrors for the Beckets – answered. 'Good morning, Saul.'

'You sound calm,' he said.

'And why wouldn't I be?' she said. 'Is it me you're after?'

'Is Grace still with her patient?'

'No, she's free to speak with you.'

Mildred asked him to hold on, passed the phone to Grace, now at her desk, completing her notes.

'Hi, Saul,' Grace said. 'How're you doing?'

'I'm good.' He hesitated, then bit the bullet. 'Grace, I hate to ask this, but I think I could really use your help.'

'Sure,' she said. 'What do you need?'

'You,' he said. 'To talk to.'

Grace sat back in her chair. 'You got me.' She glanced at her watch. 'You want to come over now?'

'Would it be a great imposition–' Saul was wincing – 'to ask you to come here?'

'Are you OK?'

He heard the concern in her voice, had to toughen up. 'I'm not sure.'

Tension hit Grace in the pit of her stomach. 'I'll be right over.'

'Grace, there's no need to rush,' Saul said swiftly. 'Drive safely.'

'Don't you worry about me,' she told him.

Cathy watched the blue Toyota cross the causeway and disappear from sight, and then she drove the Mazda around the bend and parked outside the house.

Mildred was at the door, waiting. 'All clear.'

Cathy kissed her, bent to greet Woody. 'Thank you so much.'

'No trouble to me,' Mildred said.

'I've still no idea what to pack,' Cathy said, already halfway up the stairs.

'Don't ask my advice,' Mildred called after her. 'I used to be a bag lady, remember?'

'You're a woman of great style,' Cathy told her.

'Just get up there,' Mildred said, 'and start packing.'

'How's Joshua doing?' Cathy called from the bedroom door.

'He's with his grandpa, so he's doing just fine. Now you stop procrastinating and *move* it.'

Cathy came back to the top of the staircase. 'What if Grace comes back?'

'She won't,' Mildred said, 'and if she does, I'll let you know and you can climb out of the window or hide under the bed or whatever you damned well decide.'

'You're a big help.'

Mildred grinned. 'I aim to please.'

'I should never have got you over here,' Saul said. 'Talk about an over-reaction.'

'To what?' Grace asked.

'Would you like some coffee?'

'If you're having some, sure.'

She had liked the feel of his kitchen right away when he'd first shown it to her and Sam, liked it even more since Cathy had come to share with him. It might be small and modern, but the atmosphere was just fine.

Good people made good atmospheres, stood to reason.

'Are you in a hurry?' Saul asked.

'Not at all,' she said. 'Your dad has Joshua, and he's going to pick up Mildred in a while, and they both told me they have plenty of time today, so you can take as long as you need.'

'As a matter of fact,' Saul said, 'I feel better already.'

'Good,' Grace said.

She waited while he made coffee, always mindful of the therapeutic benefits for troubled people of *doing* – something that became reversed, of course, in their sessions with their psychologists. Nothing to do then but talk.

Saul, thank God, was not her patient.

She watched him, though, as he fussed uncharacteristically over making fresh coffee, taking down their better cups, finding cookies, making inconsequential chatter until he sat down at the small table opposite her.

'Do you have plans?' she asked him.

'No. Why?'

'You keep checking the time,' Grace said. 'You seem very wound up.'

'Only because I made you come here,' Saul said. 'You have enough to deal with, and I took you away from it.'

'Right this minute, I have my best beloved brother-in-law to deal with,' Grace told him warmly. 'Or at least to listen to. If he wants to talk to me.'

'OK.' Saul managed a smile. 'Thanks.'

'So?'

'I've been feeling a little down.'

Grace waited. She had grown to feel that waiting had become one of her greatest accomplishments. Knowing when people were ready to unload or, as was so often the case, not ready or even willing.

'Not about anything specific,' Saul said. 'A little of everything, I guess.'

Grace stirred her coffee, went on waiting.

'I miss Teté,' he said.

That, at least, was the truth. He was getting better, had begun healing properly a while back, but he did still miss Teri Suarez, his lost love, every single day of his life.

'Of course you do,' Grace said.

'And I'd be a liar if I said I missed studying or medicine,' Saul said. 'But that still troubles me now and then. The fact that I wasted people's time, took up space that someone better than me, more committed than me, could have used.' He paused, painfully aware, suddenly, that none of this was a lie. 'And I know that if all that hadn't happened to me, if I hadn't been attacked that way, I might just have gone on at UM, but I never really believed I was cut out to be a good doctor, not like Dad.'

None of this was new to Grace, but it had been a long while since Saul had spoken to her about it, and if he had not been talking to anyone else either, then maybe it was just time to let it spill out again.

Unless there was something new behind it, something worse.

'Has this been building up again for a while?' she asked.

Saul shook his head. 'Not really,' he said. 'Or not that I've been aware.' His smile was tinged with guilt. 'I've been feeling pretty happy, in fact. Especially since Cathy moved in.'

'I know she feels that way,' Grace said.

'So what do I expect?' Saul stood up, finding the deception even harder sitting there face to face with her. 'No one feels happy all the time. I have so much. The best family anyone could wish for. A nice home. Work I really love.'

'And yet?' Grace said into the pause.

Saul fought against checking the time again, but it was impossible not to, and it was almost noon now, which meant that soon he'd be able to suggest making lunch for them both, and then he'd already decided he'd take Grace to the workshop to show her his new project, and then it wouldn't be too long before Sam arrived.

Come early, Sam.

320

They had talked, he and his brother, about Saul being the one to drive Grace to the port, but they'd realized there was no getting around her bringing her own car here, so short of arranging for someone to come and let down her tires, they'd run out of ideas; and anyway, the final part of this deal ought to be down to Sam.

Sam the man.

Best big brother in the world.

Pretty damn good husband, too, from where Saul was sitting.

If he ever found another woman to love and be loved by, he hoped he could be half as good as Sam, or as their father, come to that.

'Saul?'

Grace was looking at him quizzically.

He told himself to get a grip.

'I'm sorry,' Saul said. 'I was a long way off.'

He took a deep breath, and went on.

NINETY-ONE

Sam was carrying flowers when he arrived.

Nothing too fancy, just a bunch of pretty pink-and-white early spring flowers that had caught his eye.

There would be red roses in their stateroom on her birthday.

'What's going on?' Grace said when she saw him coming into Saul's hallway.

'Plenty,' Sam said, gave her the little bouquet and a kiss on the lips.

'I knew it,' she said.

'What did you know?' Sam challenged.

'That something was fishy.' She looked at Saul. 'Are you going to tell me?'

'Absolutely not,' Saul said. 'Do you hate me?'

'Not in this or any future lifetime,' Grace told him.

'I knew it was a shameful ruse,' Saul said, 'but it was good to talk to you.'

'I'm glad.'

'So, are you ready?' Sam asked.

'For what?'

'That would be telling,' Sam said.

'And judging by the naughtiness in those eyes of yours,' Grace said, 'you're not about to do that, apparently.'

'Are my eyes naughty?' He felt happy already.

'Wicked,' she said.

'All will become clear,' Sam said.

They both gave Saul a hug and went down on to the street.

Grace saw the Saab. 'I brought my car.'

'It won't come to any harm here,' Sam said. 'This is a nice neighbourhood.'

'My goodness,' Grace said. 'I'm feeling very confused. I haven't lost track of days, have I? It isn't my birthday yet, is it?'

'Not yet,' Sam said, and opened the passenger door.

'No clues?'

'Not one.'

'Ah well.' Grace shrugged and got into the car,

her flowers in her lap. 'I guess I'd better just stop asking questions then and enjoy myself.'

'I guess you had.'

Everyone was at Port Everglades in Fort Lauderdale when they arrived, all standing around outside First International's utilitarian, rather than beautiful, terminal building; but there was no overlooking the vast, snowy white *Stardust* rising up behind the terminal, and seeing David and Joshua and Mildred and Cathy – and Saul arriving just behind them in his own car – Grace was stunned and deeply moved.

'But why?' she asked Sam, bewildered. 'I'm not forty till next year.'

'Because you deserve it,' he told her. 'Because I want to whisk you away right now.'

'Happy pre-birthday,' Cathy said, and gave her a bunch of pink roses.

'You'd better hold these for her, Samuel,' Mildred said, handing him her tied bouquet of delicate bluish-purple flowers, before giving Grace a hug. 'Enjoy every minute, both of you.'

'And you'd both better have a good hug from this little man.' David put Joshua into his father's arms.

'Dada,' the small boy said, staring wide-eyed at the bustle and flow of vehicles and people and baggage.

Sam held his son close, kissed his head, inhaled the smell of his hair, and turned to Grace, saw that she was close to tears.

'He'll be fine,' he told her softly. 'He couldn't be in better hands, Gracie.'

'I know that,' she said, 'and dear God, I love you all.' She stroked Joshua's soft cheek, swallowed hard, worried about upsetting him. 'And I'm the luckiest woman in the world to have you to take care of him, but we're going out on the ocean, and what if something happens, what if Joshua needs us and we can't get back quickly enough?'

'Nothing's going to happen,' David told her.

'You can't know that,' Grace said.

'You're scaring me now,' Sam said.

'It's the twenty-first century,' Cathy pointed out. 'Communications are pretty good these days – haven't you heard of satellites?'

'And you're not even going far,' Saul added.

'And if you're anxious about these people not being careful enough,' Mildred said, 'remember they'll have me to reckon with.'

Grace laughed, and commonsense returned, and then suddenly it was farewells and thanks all around, especially to Cathy for her packing.

'I've probably left out something really important,' Cathy said.

'I don't care if you have,' Grace told her. 'I don't care if I only have one dress and nothing else, because I have the best husband and children and family–' she smiled at Mildred, hoping she knew she was included – 'and nothing else matters.'

'You wanted a dress?' Cathy said.

They went inside the terminal, still laughing, to begin check-in.

And Sam only realized much later, as they entered their lovely stateroom on the tenth deck, complete with its own balcony, that he had not so much as thought about the homicides, or Riley and Alvarez as a team, or even about Martinez, since he'd collected Grace from Saul's apartment.

Not until now, at least.

And then he saw the beautiful king-size bed.

And forgot all over again.

NINETY-TWO

March 1

Grace's thirty-ninth birthday dawned after two days of bliss, the first on calm open seas followed by a formal dinner – for which Cathy had packed a perfect black cocktail-style dress for her – which had been a delight, with two other couples at their table, both full of fun, one pair from North Carolina, the other from New York City. And yesterday, the *Stardust* had been in port at the Mexican island of Cozumel and most people had gone ashore on excursions, but when Sam had asked Grace which of those she'd like to choose, she'd remembered their friends, Jay and Annie Hoffman, saying that one of their favourite things on cruises was staying on board when so many passengers disembarked.

'That sounds like heaven to me,' Grace had said. 'Or am I being antisocial?'

'A little unadventurous, maybe,' Sam had said.

'But I'm all for it.'

So they'd left the exploring to the majority and made the most of peace and quiet, sunbathing on deck, playing a little table tennis, swimming and, it seemed to them, endlessly eating.

Cozumel was in the past now, and it was already the third day, the last full day of the cruise, and it was seven thirty and they were still in bed, snuggling close with breakfast on their balcony not due till eight, and anticipating a long, happy day.

'When did we last get time like this?' Sam asked her now, lazily.

Grace kissed his chest, traced with her lips one of the narrow scars that were a legacy of the Cal the Hater case, and there were more scars on this man, including a vicious reminder of John Broderick, Cathy's biological father, and she had a reminder of her own on her left shoulder from that same terrible night...

Long time ago.

'There is one thing I'd love to do,' she said now, 'if you don't mind, and that's phone home later on and make sure everything's fine.'

'You want to speak to our son on your birthday,' Sam said amiably against her left breast. 'Seems perfectly reasonable to me.'

'Expensive, though.'

'To hell with expense,' Sam said.

They made the call after Grace had opened all the gifts and cards that Sam had smuggled on board, and David managed to reassure them both that Joshua was in great shape, not missing them at all, after which their son had come to the phone and chattered happily for a few moments. And then Sam had called Martinez, who was out of the hospital and home and sounding bushed but much better, and Jess was with him, taking good care of him, according to Martinez, and Sam decided to believe that, at least for now.

All was right with their world.

'This is something almost worth starting a journal for,' Grace told Sam as they strolled on deck after lunch in the Andromeda Café, where they'd sat at one of the vast windows, feeling lulled as they'd eaten crab salad and roast beef.

'You don't like journals,' Sam said.

'True,' Grace agreed. 'I just feel I'd like to really *capture* all this, but I guess it'll all stay locked up in here.' She tapped her head. 'So we can take it out and look at it when we're old and feeble.'

'You'll never be feeble,' Sam told her.

'I won't mind too much,' Grace said, 'so long as we can be feeble together.'

A lot of love flowing back and forth between them, and it was, they supposed, always like that with them, except that back in the real world, they seldom had this kind of time or peace.

'I never knew till now,' Sam told Grace softly, holding her hand as they walked, 'that ships make me horny.'

'Me too,' she said. 'Who knew?'

And they turned about, without another word, and went back to their stateroom.

NINETY-THREE

Everything changed at five minutes after eleven that night.

Peace of mind blown clean away.

Being the last night, discipline had come briefly back into their lives, with instructions to pack all but their overnight needs and have baggage ready for collection before midnight, and Sam and Grace had, like most passengers, taken care of business before dinner to free them for the evening.

Everyone seemed to be making the most of that freedom, as they'd seen while dining on prime rib and lobster in the Stardust Grill, filled to capacity, and even now, sitting at a corner table in the Aurora Bar sipping cognac, there were people milling around in fancy dress, someone throwing a private party someplace on the ship, and Sam had just told Grace that he was going to have to go on a diet when they got back – when his gaze fell on a character about twenty feet away, at the far end of the bar...

A man all done up in silver, from head to toe.

A ghost from the past.

'Dear God.' Sam felt shock, like icy claws, crawl up his spine. 'Cooper.'

Jerome Cooper, Grace's stepbrother, aka Cal

the Hater. Multiple killer and the man who had almost destroyed their family less than a year ago.

Sam had never seen Cooper dressed up that way, all shimmering in silver, but Mildred certainly had, more than once, and had almost paid for the privilege with her life.

Grace turned in her seat, eyes torn wide, saw him too.

'It can't be him,' she said. 'It can't, Sam.'

Because Jerome Cooper was dead.

Presumed dead. His body never retrieved from the ocean.

The silver man was moving, was already out of the Aurora Bar, heading toward the centre of the ship.

'I'm sorry.' Sam got to his feet. 'I need to be sure.'

He was gone before Grace could speak again, and intense fear clutched at her suddenly, and she was up, too, going after him. And she saw the silver figure way up ahead, moving quickly toward the Star Theater, Sam catching up to him – and Grace wanted to scream, but instead she kept on walking, not running but moving fast, her heart pounding in her chest because there was something *terrible* about to happen here, something that felt inexorable to her – and this was her birthday, this was one of the best days of her life...

Flashes of the way it might happen scalded her eyes, her mind.

Not might. Happening *now*.

Sam had caught up with him, and it looked as

if they were speaking, and then Sam took a backward step, and for in instant Grace thought it had *happened*, the worst thing imaginable, and now she did start to run...

'It wasn't him.'

Sam speaking.

To her. Right in front of her, alive and un-harmed – and the silver man had gone, vanished, but Sam was smiling, and the worst had not happened.

'I thought...' Grace flew at him, held him, began to weep.

'Oh, God, Gracie, I'm so sorry.' Sam kissed the top of her head, stroking her hair. 'What a mistake to make, and spoiling your special evening this way.'

'It wasn't him?' She drew back, wiping away her tears. 'Are you sure?'

'Hundred per cent,' Sam said. 'I spoke to him. Not Cooper. Just a guy in fancy dress.'

'Thank God,' Grace said.

'Amen to that,' Sam said.

NINETY-FOUR

March 2

A little after two a.m. on Monday, when Sam was sound asleep, Grace, still restlessly awake, felt a sudden need for air and exercise, and maybe it was a reaction to the loveliness of the day or to the brief, but shocking, fears that had assailed her a few hours ago, but whichever, she needed soothing, and a little walk, ocean air and starlight seemed just what the doctor might have ordered.

She left a note on the pillow in case Sam woke.

Couldn't sleep. Gone for a stroll. I'm fine and very happy, so don't worry. Back soon. Thank you for the best day ever. G.

In the long narrow corridor outside their stateroom it was hushed, all baggage gone now – vanished as completely as their Jerome hallucination.

Grace shook off the thought, the *man*, and headed toward midships, taking the staircase down three flights, remembering that Deck Seven was one of those where the doors were kept open for late-night strollers.

There were still people around, most younger, still in party mood, some just emerging from the casino, a few romantic couples – one pair who looked to Grace like honeymooners – and a few solitary, like herself.

Outside on deck it was just the way she'd hoped, breezy and cool, but more exhilarating than chilling.

A few minutes of this, and she knew she'd be ready to go back to sleep.

She didn't see anything.

But she *heard* him.

His voice, unmistakable, coming out of the dark.

'Hello, Grace.'

It was true what they said about blood seeming to freeze in the veins.

'Here I am again. Roxy's boy, back from the deep.'

'Jerome?' She spun around, thought for an instant that she saw the shadow of a figure near one of the doorways, looming eerily against the white paintwork, and then it was gone again, back into the dark.

'Can't keep a good sailor down,' the voice said. 'Nice boat, though I preferred my *Baby*.' There was a pause. 'How is your little one, by the by?'

Grace turned and ran.

Running for her life.

Sam was awake when she got back inside the stateroom, sitting with his feet up on the small couch as she came in, springing up as he saw her face.

'What the hell happened?'

She barely made it into the bathroom, on to her knees, to throw up.

'Gracie, sweetheart.' Sam was beside her, a towel in his hand, helping her.

'Jerome,' she said. 'He's on the ship. He was talking to me out on deck.'

She was still shaking, perspiring, and Sam eased her up off the floor, gave her water, helped her out of the bathroom to the bed, sat her down, then crouched, staring into her face. 'What happened? Did he hurt you?'

'He didn't touch me,' Grace said, a sense of

unreality overcoming her. 'He just talked to me, said something about his boat, the *Baby*...' Her eyes were huge with fear. 'And then he asked about Joshua.'

'What did he say?' Sam was taut, old rage returning, new fury erupting.

'He just said: "How is your little one, by the by?" And then I ran.'

'But you saw him, before you ran?'

'Just a shape in the dark – I couldn't be sure,' Grace said. 'But it was definitely his voice.'

Sam's mind was racing, trying to keep control. 'Might it have been a recording of his voice?'

'I guess it's possible.' She took a deep breath, steadying herself. 'Though even if it was, it still means Jerome's alive and playing tricks, doesn't it?'

'I can't think of a better explanation,' Sam said grimly.

He straightened up, heading for the phone.

'How would he have known I was going to go for a walk?' Grace said.

'I don't know,' Sam said.

'He must have been waiting, watching,' she said, feeling sick again. 'He's probably been watching us the whole trip.'

Sam picked up the phone, pushed the key for Guest Relations, waited.

'I need to see the captain,' he said.

NINETY-FIVE

The captain was unavailable and not, in any case, Sam was informed, the right person to talk to.

The ship's security chief, a man of around fifty named Arlo Larsen, was lanky and bespectacled, putting Grace in mind of James Stewart, perhaps too affable and laid-back, she and Sam both felt at the outset, to be as effective as they needed him to be. Especially as Mr Larsen was probably more accustomed to dealing with complaints of theft or gambling-related frauds than with inconclusive sightings of presumed-dead psychopaths.

'If this man was on board at two a.m.,' Larsen told them in his office in the Passenger Relations department on Deck Five, 'then he'll still be on the *Stardust* now, which means there's every chance we'll be able to find him before he disembarks.'

A photograph of Jerome Cooper lay on his desk, faxed to the ship by one of the night shift back at South Beach after an urgent satellite call from Sam to Mike Alvarez at home, and the sergeant himself had spoken to Larsen to confirm the Beckets' credentials and the seriousness of the old case.

'You have to remember we're talking about a full-blown psycho killer and child kidnapper,' Sam reminded him now.

'I understand that, Detective Becket,' Larsen said. 'And I also understand that even if the voice you heard—' he looked at Grace – 'does turn out to have been a recording of some kind, it makes it no less sinister.'

'You have to search the ship,' Sam said. 'Whether it's for Cooper or a recording machine.'

'The ship will be thoroughly checked after debarkation,' Larsen said.

'And meantime, what?' Frustration fed Sam's anger. 'You let him stroll off?'

'Of course not,' Larsen said, 'but you know better than most, Detective, that we can't conduct any personal or property searches without a warrant.'

'If it was a tape,' Grace said, 'it's probably been thrown overboard.'

'I agree.' Behind the spectacles, Larsen's narrow blue eyes were couched in wrinkles. 'But so far as the man goes, or perhaps his accomplice, in my experience people who want to go on living tend not to jump off moving cruise ships out at sea. If this was your man, he sounds more like a survivor than a suicide.'

'Jerome Cooper blew up a cruiser while he was still on board,' Sam said.

'Then we'd have to say that if he jumped tonight, he's gone,' Larsen said. 'But since I seriously doubt that, we'll proceed as if there's a good chance he's still with us, presumably under an alias.'

'So if you can't search,' Sam asked, 'what do you plan to do?'

'Everything possible,' Larsen said, 'without causing alarm to our other passengers, especially since there's no proof of any threat to them—'

'If this is Cooper,' Sam said, 'you can't assume that.'

'Of course not,' Larsen said. 'But the fact seems to be that if it was Cooper who spoke to you, Mrs Becket, he made no overt threat.'

'It certainly felt threatening to me,' she said.

'I'm sure it did,' Larsen said gravely. 'For now, I'd like the three of us to take a walk around Deck Seven with a couple of flashlights, see if this man left any trace behind.'

'Good.' Sam stood up. 'I've noticed you have CCTV.'

Larsen nodded. 'Cameras on all decks, and my people are already checking the time in question.' He paused. 'The most time-consuming task will be checking Cooper's photograph against our passenger and crew photos. With the best will in the world, I'd say there's zero chance of completing that before we disembark.' He opened the door for them. 'But we'll do our very best.'

They found nothing out on deck, and though Larsen's team were able to track Grace at two points on her walk, there was not a single figure on the CCTV footage even remotely fitting Cooper's description.

'My best advice to you,' the security chief told them at four a.m., 'is to get yourselves some rest, since we'll be docking in about an hour and a half.'

'Nice idea,' Sam said, 'but with debarkation starting at around eight—'

'Eight thru ten,' Larsen confirmed.

The *Stardust* had a disembarkation schedule similar to that of most large cruise ships, organizing passengers into manageable groups to stagger the customs and immigration process, departure itself via two main gangways.

'We're scheduled for eight thirty,' Sam said, 'but I'd appreciate our being allowed to stay on board until the last group.'

'You have in mind, I daresay,' Larsen said, 'being in a position to view passengers as they leave.' He took off his glasses, rubbed his eyes, put them back on. 'If none of the officials raise any objection, I think we'll find a way to arrange that.'

'We'd be very grateful,' Grace said.

The security chief threw her a sympathetic glance. 'Not the finale to your cruise you had in mind, Mrs Becket.'

'Not exactly,' she agreed.

Neither the Fort Lauderdale police, nor the customs and immigration officers who came on board the *Stardust*, objected to their scrutinizing passengers as they left the ship, and Arlo Larsen told Sam and Grace that the job of checking passenger photographs against Cooper's shot would continue till completion.

337

'If that man is or has been on the *Stardust*,' Larsen assured Sam, 'then unless he's altered his appearance considerably...'

'Which is possible,' Sam said.

'But if he has not,' Larsen went on, 'we should at least find out if he was on board.'

Watching from two separate vantage points was arduous and dispiriting, their eyes burning as they struggled to concentrate on one face after another, and Sam and Grace both knew before they'd gotten halfway through that it was hopeless.

Not going to happen.

And definitely not, as Arlo Larsen had said, the way they'd have chosen to end a beautiful trip.

More than anything, it was frustrating as hell.

No sign of Cooper anyplace they looked.

Cal the Hater was gone again.

NINETY-SIX

Martinez was more than glad to be home.

But he was not a happy man.

He had known, ever since he'd been back to being coherent, that something was up with Jess, that the sparkle in those pretty eyes when she looked at him had gone. She'd still been kind and attentive, hell, she'd been sweet as ever – yet something about her had been *off*.

And she'd been hiding something from him too, though he hadn't been able to figure out what it might be, and it had been bugging him.

Driving him nuts, to be honest.

If not for that, he didn't think he'd have stooped so low as to do what he had yesterday.

He'd waited until she was taking a shower, and then he'd taken a look in the canvas shoulder bag she carried with her everywhere.

He wasn't sure why he'd done that, didn't think he'd been expecting to find anything significant, had felt lousy even as he'd opened it, a real fink, as a matter of fact, but something had kept pushing him, goading him on.

He'd found more than he'd bargained for, that was for sure.

A small bound notebook, not much bigger than a wallet, stuffed inside a zipped compartment in the bag; the book filled with tidy notations, with reports and statistics and conclusions.

About rats.

About goddamned, frigging *rats*.

So he'd had it out with her.

'Are you crazy or something?' he'd asked her straight out of the shower, one of the new white towels he'd bought for her still wrapped around her wet body. 'Are you a secret scientist or just a whack job?'

Not the gentlest way to talk to his fiancée.

But after what he'd just been through...

'I could have died,' he reminded her.

'You think I don't know that?' Jess said.

Her face was very pale again, the way it had

looked when he'd been in the hospital, while she'd seemed so scared for him.

'But they were asking if I'd been in contact with rats anyplace,' Martinez said, 'and Sam came here to check it out, and his dad told me you were horrified and saying what if you had rats at your place and you didn't know it, then that would mean you'd done that to me.' He was shaking suddenly, trembling with exhaustion, and Dr Friedman had said he'd need time to get over this, that he had to take things easy and avoid stress, but he couldn't help himself. 'And all that time you were keeping fucking rats and you didn't *tell* them?'

'I'm sorry,' Jess said.

'You're *sorry*.' He had taken a moment, trying to calm himself down. 'Why the hell did you want to keep them in the first place?'

'I like them,' she told him, a touch of defiance in the statement. 'I like them, and they never judged me, and I guess I liked being in charge of them, learning about them, having control over them – over *something*, I guess – and I looked after them well. I was calm and efficient around them and I made sure they all had good lives until it was their time. Except one of them escaped and I guess, maybe, he was sick.'

'You guess *he* was sick,' Martinez said. 'Oh, poor Ratty.'

'Romeo,' she said. 'His name was Romeo the Fifth, because he was the fifth buck – the fifth male – I'd kept.'

'Jesus,' Martinez said, and sank down on his bed. 'Jesus F. Christ, I've been engaged to a total fruitcake.'

'Thank you,' Jess said.

'Can you blame me?'

'I guess not.' She half smiled. 'But it reminds me why I prefer rats to men.'

Martinez looked up at her and saw in her eyes that it was true.

He stood up with an effort. 'Get out.'

'You don't mean that, Al.'

'Get the hell out of my house.'

Jess nodded slowly. 'OK.'

'Now,' Martinez said, quietly. 'I want you gone.'

'Can I get my things first, please?' Jess asked.

'Get them,' he said, trying to control the trembling inside him. 'And go.'

She had come to him just before she left, had handed him back the ring.

Martinez had looked down at the little sapphires and tiny diamonds in his hand, and it was all sparkling because she'd polished it every day.

'You don't have to,' he said.

'Sure I do,' she said.

Looking at the ring made him sad, made their ending real.

'I think you should know,' Jess said, 'about your good friend, Sam.'

'What about him?'

'Only that he came on to me,' she said. 'A couple of times.'

'Liar,' Martinez said. 'You lousy little liar.'

He ground the ring hard into the palm of his

341

hand and then threw it with as much strength as he could muster at the wall, where it struck an old painting of a young Cuban boy which had been one of his mother's favourite possessions.

'Cathy didn't believe me either,' Jess said.

'You told her that?' He was incredulous. 'You total bitch.'

'Am I?' Jess's voice was suddenly smaller. 'I've always tried not to be. I've tried to be good to people.'

Martinez thought abruptly back to all the *good* things she was always doing for other people, the kindnesses and favours and overtime to help colleagues out. Never wanting praise for it, but still making sure everyone knew about it. And then he thought about the way she was so often there when things went wrong for other people, like the woman at the office with a busted ankle who Jess did everything for...

It made him wonder.

And then that made him feel even more tired.

'You'd better go, Jessie,' he'd told her.

His anger was all gone again now, only the sadness remaining.

'Will you miss me at all?' she asked him.

'I'll miss the woman I thought you were,' he said.

'But not really me,' she said.

'I don't know,' he said, and shook his head.

'I'm going to miss you, Al,' she said.

Martinez shrugged. 'You can always get yourself some more rats.'

'No.' Jess shook her head. 'That's all finished now.'

'Because they made me sick?' A small spike of hope rose up in him.

'Sure,' she said. 'And anyway, it's all spoiled now. It wouldn't be the same.'

'Why did you bring the notebook here?' One last piece of curiosity striking him. 'Why didn't you leave it at your place? I'd never have known.'

'I thought Sam or the public health people might go to my place.' She paused. 'And I didn't think you were the type to go through my things, Al. I thought you were a gentleman.'

'Guess you were wrong about that,' he said.

'Maybe you're wrong too,' she said, 'about Sam.'

'Get out,' he told her again, feeling nauseous.

'Goodbye, Al,' she said.

And went.

All alone again now in his bachelor pad.

He'd taken a closer look at his mother's old painting after she'd gone, had seen that one of the little stones in the engagement ring had torn a small rip in the canvas, and that had triggered some tears, but they hadn't lasted long, and he was composed again.

Sam and Grace would be back soon, so he guessed they'd come visiting.

He didn't have a shred, not so much as a fragment of doubt over what Jess had said about Sam.

Martinez knew Sam would never have done that in a thousand years.

But what did it say about him, he wondered,

343

that he'd been so much faster to believe in his friend than in his fiancée?

More to the point, what did it say about his relationship with her?

Not a whole lot, that was for sure.

NINETY-SEVEN

By the time Sam got home, most of the day had gone.

Which was not the way he'd planned their homecoming.

First, he and Grace had gone together to the station, partly so that Sam could catch up on the investigation – nothing new, Alvarez had said, had told him to finish up and get home while he could – but mostly because they'd needed to make an official report of Cooper's survival and possible presence, the previous night, on the *Stardust*.

Then they'd driven up to Golden Beach to see David and Mildred and bring Joshua and Woody home. After which, concerned by the way Martinez had sounded on the phone when he'd called, Sam had gone to visit his partner.

He listened, feeling anger at Jessica Kowalski, then a little compassion for one screwed up young woman.

What he felt most was sorrow for Martinez.

'I'm real glad to see you, man,' he'd told Sam.

344

'Even if my ex-fiancée does claim you made a pass at her.'

Sam had a moment of real loathing for Jess then – until he saw the expression in his friend's dark brown eyes and saw humour there along with the sadness.

'Not for a single second, man,' Martinez said.

'Thank Christ for that,' Sam said.

'I was going to say she had better taste,' Martinez added, 'but then I remembered she prefers rats.'

NINETY-EIGHT

'Cathy called,' Grace told him when he got back to the island. 'She's getting us some takeout, said there's no way I should be allowed to cook tonight.'

'It's a shame.' Sam sank on to a kitchen chair. 'We shouldn't be feeling like this today.'

'We wouldn't be,' Grace said, 'if it weren't for Jerome.'

'I need to tell you about Martinez,' Sam said. 'But first, I need a drink.'

'Let's both do that,' Grace said. 'Joshua's sound asleep, Woody's fed and watered. Let's open a bottle, wait for our dinner to arrive and pretend we're still on the ship.'

They were in the den, napping on the couch,

when they woke to hear the car and familiar voices.

Then the front door.

Not just Cathy.

'Special treat,' she told them as Dooley and Simone came in behind her, carrying insulated food containers into the hallway. 'I brought your car home, by the way,' she told Grace.

'Thank you, sweetheart,' Grace said, and went to kiss her.

'Guys,' Sam said. 'You shouldn't have done this for us.'

'You never do takeout,' Grace said.

'Cathy bent our ears a little,' Simone said, 'so we stole these from the Italian down the street, and here we are.'

'Kitchen, please?' Dooley said.

'Down here.' Sam led the way.

'Wow,' Grace said. 'This is just amazing.'

'What about the café?' Sam asked.

'Closed for a couple of hours,' Dooley said. 'We're never busy Monday evenings.'

'I'll bet that's not true,' Grace said.

'You two look so tired,' Cathy said. 'It's such a shame about Cooper.'

'We are pretty bushed,' Sam admitted.

'Would you rather not eat?' Dooley asked. 'We won't be offended.'

'Are you kidding?' Sam said.

'Then you both go sit down while we dish up in here,' Simone told them.

'What have you made?' Sam asked.

'Comfort food,' Dooley said. 'You'll see.'

'Go rest while we take care of this,' Simone

said.

'And then we're all leaving,' Cathy said. 'Simone and Matt will give me a ride home.'

'You have to stay and eat with us,' Grace said.

'Stop being polite,' Cathy told her. 'One night only, you do as you're told.'

'You eat, then you go to bed,' Dooley said. 'No worries about washing up either. We'll pick up the dishes tomorrow, put them in the machine at the café.'

'I'm sure I can manage a little clearing up,' Grace said.

'No need,' Simone said. 'All part of the service.'

'How much do we owe you?' Sam asked.

'It's our gift,' Dooley said.

'But that—' Sam caught Grace's eye, stopped. 'It's very generous.'

'Much too generous,' Grace said.

'We're very grateful,' Sam said.

And kissed his daughter, then Simone, then shook Dooley's hand.

NINETY-NINE

'This is so good,' Grace said, about an hour-and-a-half later, at the kitchen table. 'And so kind of them.'

'Matt was right about comfort food,' Sam said. They'd eaten chicken braised in wine with

347

mushrooms, served with mashed potatoes and assorted vegetables, all of it delectable, and now they were looking at a good old apple pie topped with meringue.

'Except I'm too tired to eat any more,' Grace said.

'Me too,' Sam said, sleepily. 'But is our daughter a sweetheart or what?'

'The best,' Grace said.

'I love you,' Sam told her. 'I'm so sorry your birthday was spoiled.'

'Only the very end of it,' Grace said. 'Everything else was perfect.'

'Like you,' Sam said.

'You look tired enough to fall asleep at the table,' Grace said.

'You too,' Sam said, fuzzily.

It started to come to him then.

Mashed potatoes...

'Oh, Christ,' he said.

'Mm?' Grace said.

Sam tried to get up, his fogging mind fighting to put the truth together.

His knees buckled.

'Gracie,' he said.

She didn't answer.

And he was already sliding.

Going down.

ONE HUNDRED

When Cathy called to say goodnight, there was no answer from her parents' house, just the machine kicking in.

Only ten o'clock, and they never got to sleep this early.

Though they sure had looked beat.

At least this way, they'd both be back on form in the morning, and then she looked forward to hearing every last romantic detail of the cruise – romantic, she guessed, until that bastard had done his best to wreck it.

More good people in the world than bad, Cathy reminded herself.

She smiled, winged silent renewed thanks to Dooley and Simone.

Whatever became of her new career, she'd always be grateful for them.

The fact was, the more knocks you took in your life, the greater your appreciation for the good guys.

She doubted they came better than Matt Dooley and Simone Regan.

ONE HUNDRED AND ONE

March 3

Sam knew almost as soon as he came to.

Felt instant despair at his own sheer, breath-taking *stupidity*.

'Grace,' he said.

His voice sounded thick, unclear.

He tried to move, to get up, but his head was muzzy, his left leg seemed heavy, pinned down, and his vision was fuzzy.

Grace.

He struggled to a sitting position, looked to his left, saw her on the ground eight or nine feet away, still sleeping, still out of it.

She was naked and chained, by a shackle around her right ankle, to a run of iron bars behind her – and he was naked and shackled too, but seeing Grace that way drove something sharp right through his heart.

'Grace,' he said. 'Grace, sweetheart, talk to me.'

She stirred, but did not respond.

Terror, sour and violent, filled him. He pulled at the chain, and the shackle bit his ankle, but nothing gave. *'Grace.'*

She gave a small moan, started to come to.

'Thank God,' Sam said. 'Grace, don't be

scared.'

If he'd ever said anything more foolish, he could not recall it.

They were in some kind of a cage measuring about fourteen feet by ten. Steel bars behind and in front of them, a steel gate in the middle.

Locked, he presumed. Not that he could get to it to find out.

The only light came from a single overhead low-wattage bulb.

Impenetrable darkness beyond the bars ahead of them.

Shackled and naked in a cage.

Naked.

The latest couple.

Matt Dooley's and Simone Regan's.

Never, since this had all begun, had they even entered his radar.

'Sam?' Grace's voice was hushed, frightened. 'Sam, what's happened?'

'Dooley and Simone,' he said. 'They put drugs in our food.'

Temazepam, same as the others, maybe a bigger dose.

The truth hit Grace, hard as a wall.

'My God, Joshua.' She sat up. 'Where's Joshua?'

'Not here,' Sam said. 'They won't have touched him.'

'What about Cathy?'

'Not her either.' Sam paused. 'They only take couples, remember?'

'Yes,' Grace said. 'Loving couples.'

They both looked around, but there was little

to see, just something that resembled a coiled snake over by the wall eight or nine feet away from him. The visible walls, beyond the bars behind them and to both sides, were padded, probably soundproofed, and a semi-transparent screen ran a foot or so across the front of the left-hand wall, just beyond Grace.

Like a lanai screen, maybe, Sam thought, processing facts despite the thick fuzz in his head, because only one thing mattered now, and that was getting them out of here, before...

He suppressed a shudder, went on looking, wondered if the walls behind the padding were concrete or cinder block or brick, scanned the cage for anything he might use as a tool if he managed to free them of the shackles.

Nothing.

The floor beneath them was concrete and cold, and the place smelt of damp.

Of something else, too.

Glue.

'Sam,' Grace said softly. 'I am scared.'

'Me too, Gracie.'

The snake was a hosepipe.

He didn't want to contemplate what that had been used for, but his cop's eyes were already roaming the floor and walls – for here, finally, was their crime scene – for telltale bloodstains or anything that would ultimately help build the case against these bastards.

'You think we can get out of here?' Grace said.

'Damned straight we can,' he said, and Lord knew he didn't have the smallest idea how, but he meant it.

Grace fought against the urge to weep, did as he had, tried to yank the chain from the bars, gave a small cry of pain and frustration, then saw Sam's face.

'I'm OK,' she said, and took a deep breath. 'If we turn ourselves around and stretch our free legs as far as we can, maybe we could touch.'

They tried it, touched toes.

It was uncomfortable, but it felt like an achievement, something almost auspicious.

'That's better,' Sam said.

He wondered abruptly if *they* were watching, if that was part of the reason they'd left a light on, though maybe they had night vision goggles, or maybe they were not watching at all. But they must have debated whether the terror of total darkness would be as satisfying to them as having their victims *seeing* the hopelessness of their predicaments.

'They took my watch,' Grace said.

'Mine too,' Sam said.

He looked at his left hand, said nothing.

'And our wedding bands,' she said softly.

'I know.'

'I think,' Grace said, 'I could stand this more if we weren't naked.'

'You'll stand it because we're together,' Sam said. 'And because we are going to get out of here.'

She was silent for a moment.

'What if Joshua wakes,' she said, 'and we're not there for him?'

Sam pictured their son awake and clutching the side rails on his crib and calling for them, maybe scared by now and screaming.

He wanted to kill Dooley and Simone.

'He'll be OK, sweetheart,' he told her.

'What if Simone's there with him?' she said, and began to cry. 'What if *no one's* there with him?'

'Don't cry, Gracie,' Sam said, and stroked her toes with his own.

'I'm all right.' She willed herself to cut out the tears. 'Except how will anyone know that he's all alone or where we are, when we don't know ourselves?'

'We have clever, caring people in our lives,' Sam said. 'They'll work it out.'

'I hope so,' Grace said.

She waited another long moment before asking her next question, uncertain she was ready for the answer.

'I know the others were naked, too,' she said. 'But you've never said, and the reports never mentioned...' She stopped.

'There was no rape,' Sam said. 'Look at me, Grace.'

She looked into his eyes.

'I don't believe that any of this is about sex,' he said.

About gratification of a different kind, he thought, but chose not to say.

'So it's power.' She paused. 'I think I can fight that a little more easily.'

'We can fight it,' Sam said.

ONE HUNDRED AND TWO

Mildred arrived at the house on the island at eight fifteen Tuesday morning.

The blue Toyota and Samuel's car were both there, parked outside, which was unusual in two ways, Mildred thought, since Samuel generally went to work much earlier, and when he was home he parked his car in the garage.

Though by the sounds of it, they'd had themselves quite a time yesterday.

Which had taken a little of the stuffing and a lot of the ease out of her too.

Hearing that *he* was still alive.

The one who'd nearly ended her life, and taken Joshua, and killed at least three people.

She thought of pushing the doorbell, then decided to use her key, because maybe they'd had a bad night, same as she had, and maybe they were sleeping late.

She knew, as soon as she was inside, that something was wrong.

Very wrong.

Joshua was crying and Woody was barking from someplace in the house, when by rights he ought to be skittering around her in the hallway.

Other than that, there was silence.

The wrong kind of silence, Mildred thought.
'Grace?' she called.
Received no reply.
'Samuel?'
Nothing.
Something *wrong* here.
Joshua's crying was coming from above.

Mildred moved quietly but quickly up the staircase, her heart thumping uncomfortably, her palms sticky, not letting herself think, first step only to get to that little boy.

He was alone in his nursery, standing up inside his crib, holding on to the rails, all damp and upset, his beautiful dark eyes drowning in tears.

'Sweet child,' Mildred said and plucked him up in her arms.

He was hot from distress, his diaper wet and soiled, his wailing turning to screaming as he tried to express his fearful isolation to her, and she held him close and did what she could to soothe him.

'There, there,' she told him softly, crooning against his warm ear. 'I've got you now, I've got you.'

She steeled herself.

Went to the next room, knocked on the door and then, readying herself to spin the little boy right around if something *terrible* was in there, she opened it.

Nothing terrible, except that the Beckets' bed had not been slept in.

'There, there,' she said again to Joshua.

She hugged him close as she took a swift tour of the rest of the small house, checking the bathroom and the bedroom that had been Cathy's, then heading back downstairs again, going out to the deck, then looking in at the den and the spotless kitchen and the lanai.

Woody was in Grace's office, shut in, and he was mightily upset too, had wet the rug in there, and his noises were shrill and strange, as if he was trying to tell her something.

'Oh, my,' Mildred said.

And went to the telephone to raise the alarm.

ONE HUNDRED AND THREE

Sam had been putting it all together, in his mind for the most part, not so much to spare Grace as to keep his thought processes from *them* if they were listening, and he'd told her that much, because what difference could that possibly make to their situation?

'I'm trying to work out some stuff, Gracie,' he'd said a while ago, 'but I'm not saying it out loud.'

'Fine with me,' she'd said, understanding.

He reached down to the shackle on his ankle, tried again to see any way of releasing it, knew it was hopeless, gave another hard yank on the chain, then another mightier one and gave it up again.

'Gotta keep trying.' He smiled at her, shifted and stretched out his free leg again, pressed his toes against hers.

'I'm OK, you know,' she said. 'You go on thinking, and I'll just watch you.'

'Not looking my best right now,' Sam said.

No matter what he'd said about their nakedness, he found that he hated it almost more than anything, and Grace was being brave, and she was strong, but seeing her this way, supposing that their intent was to humiliate, to debase, he knew that if Dooley were in his grasp right now, he might not be able to stop himself from killing him.

Though it was hard to fathom which of them was more wicked: the man with a prison record, who'd been so open about that, so fucking *benevolent* to Cathy; or the bitch with her migraines and sick mother.

'You're always the best sight in the world to my eyes,' Grace told him.

'Joshua aside,' Sam said.

'About equal,' she said.

'Mind if I sit up again,' he asked her, because it was good to touch, but it was uncomfortable, and it was easier for him to think properly when he was sitting, knees bent, hunched over a little.

'No problem,' Grace said, and withdrew her foot, sat up the same way.

Some things were becoming clearer to Sam. The domed plastic dish could have been what Martinez had hit on when they'd been in Christou's restaurant, a monster version of the kind of thing sometimes used to display desserts or cheeses. Large tanks were often used in upscale seafood restaurants to let customers choose their own dinner. And even if the Resslers' dumping ground had been a sculptor's kiln, that was still a goddamned oven, if you wanted to look at it that way.

All restaurant-related, at a stretch. Part of their game – they'd been right about that much, at least. The Christous and their fish tank probably chosen with as much care as any of the victims. The art connections just more game-playing.

So what did they have in mind for the Beckets?

'They're going to think this is Jerome, aren't they?' Grace said abruptly.

Sam knew she was right, that the squad might still be heading in pointless directions, wasting valuable time – and *time* was something he'd lost track of, and it had to be Tuesday, though how far into the day he couldn't guess.

'They won't think it once Cathy tells them about the dinner,' he said.

If Cathy was free to tell them.

He did not say that, knew Grace had to be thinking it anyway.

He tried controlling his thoughts again, wondered when *they* would come here, if there might be some way to persuade them to make do with him, to let Grace go for the sake of their son or even Cathy. None of the other couples had had dependent children, and maybe, if even a fraction of the kindness that Dooley and Simone had seemed to show Cathy over the months had been genuine, then maybe he could find a way to spare Grace.

He knew how improbable that was.

He also knew that he and Grace were not the only ones now who would ultimately be able to identify the killers.

If Cathy didn't know yet that they'd been taken, if she had not been able to let Alvarez and Riley know about last night's dinner, if she was not already under protection, then their daughter was in such danger again, and it was too much.

He looked at his wife, saw pain in her eyes, tautness in her jaw, knew she was thinking about Cathy too.

'She'll be OK,' he told her, his voice husky.

'Keep telling me that,' she said.

ONE HUNDRED AND FOUR

Within an hour of Mildred having called David, everyone was on it. The Couples squad, the whole unit.

'Is this Cooper?' Alvarez was the first to voice it. 'Could this all have been down to him? All the homicides?'

It was a crazy thought, yet suddenly it seemed the most obvious proposition of all. Cal the Hater had survived the Atlantic and had crept back into Miami Beach to play a weird and inexplicable new killing game.

'I don't buy it,' Riley said. 'Cooper's big thing was race hate.'

They'd all learned a lot about the man from his

writings. *The Epistle of Cal the Hater*, a long series of ramblings in a number of exercise books found in Cooper's last hiding place, had been read by everyone involved in the case and was likely to become study material, long-term, for student profilers.

'He hated Sam and Grace, too,' Mary Cutter pointed out.

'So what?' Riley said, sceptically. 'One happy couple turned him into the Couples Slayer?'

'I've heard wilder theories,' Alvarez said.

And it was, right this minute, the best and only one that did make sense.

Jerome Cooper was wanted all over again, this time as prime suspect in the killings of six people.

And for the suspected abduction of Sam and Grace Becket.

ONE HUNDRED AND FIVE

David thought he might lose his mind.

This time, he might *really* lose it.

He'd managed the first call, the crucial one, to Sergeant Alvarez, because Sam had told him the sergeant was working the case with Riley in his absence, and because he knew Sam thought Alvarez was a good man and a fine cop.

And Alvarez had taken the information on board: that Sam and Grace were missing and had left their beloved eighteen-month-old son alone in the house, which he knew, almost as well as Sam's father and Mildred Bleeker, they would never, under any circumstances, have done.

Unless something very bad had happened.

Unless someone had forced them to.

And the Beckets were a happy couple.

Perhaps in the mind of this killer, *the* couple.

So Alvarez had taken David seriously, had asked if he or any of the family had seen Sam or Grace since their return, and David said that the last he and Mildred had seen of them was when they'd picked up Joshua and Woody yesterday, and he knew that after that, Sam had gone to visit Martinez, but then they'd all agreed to leave them to rest after the traumatic final hours of their cruise.

'Do you know what they did for dinner last night?' Alvarez had asked.

Asking it casually, but thinking of the other couples.

'I have no idea,' David had told him. 'Probably something simple. We'd shopped for a few basics, put them in their refrigerator.'

Alvarez had offered to send someone over for support.

'No, thank you, Sergeant,' David had told him. 'I'm not alone, and I'd sooner you didn't waste manpower babysitting me.'

Alvarez had told him to stay put in Golden Beach with Joshua and Mildred, had told him that as of now Sam and Grace's house was a crime scene, so there was no point any of the family going over there.

'You have to leave this to us,' Alvarez had said. 'I know how incredibly tough that's going to be, Dr Becket, but we're going to get them back, believe me.'

'So you really think this is Cooper again?' David had said.

'I think it's too big a coincidence for him not to be involved,' the sergeant had said. 'We'll be looking at every option, but Cooper's our prime suspect.'

David wasn't sure how he'd managed not to cry out with pain before and after he'd put the phone down, but his little grandson was in the house, poor child who'd suffered at Jerome Cooper's hands once before. Bad enough that he'd been alone and frightened for heaven knew how many hours before Mildred had found him this morning – David was not going to do anything more to distress Joshua, so he kept his pain locked down.

But if anything happened to Sam and Grace...

It was Mildred who made him call Saul.

He'd been putting it off, hoping to be able to spare both his younger son and poor Cathy more suffering, praying that this would turn out to be some impossible mistake, that they'd return any minute, guilt-wracked for leaving Joshua, but unharmed.

Impossible was the word for it. He knew that all too well.

'If you don't call Saul,' Mildred said to him at ten thirty-five, 'I will.'

'You will not do any such thing,' David said.

'And you can put on your fierce old man snarl and speak to me any way you want,' Mildred said, 'but Saul and Cathy have the right to know, besides which it'll help you to have them close by.'

'I'm doing all right,' he said. 'I have you here.'

They seldom touched – these two 'elderly housemates', as Mildred had once described them to Grace – but now she came and sat beside the doctor on the beaten-up sofa that had been there for over thirty-five years, and put her arm around him.

'I am so sorry for your pain,' she said.

'Don't,' David said. 'Don't start me off, please.'

'Please call Saul,' she said. 'If he finds out another way, he'll be mad, and worse, he'll be hurt.'

So David made the call.

'I don't want you to panic,' he said.

'Dad, what's wrong?'

David filled him in, heard his son's struggle for composure.

'Did you talk to them last night?' he asked.

'No,' Saul said, 'but Cathy saw them.'

He told his father about the dinner that Dooley and Simone had made for Sam and Grace, about how kind they'd been when Cathy had told them about the lousy end of the cruise and about how exhausted her parents were.

Something triggered in David's mind.

Something that Sam had told him about the homicides.

'Dad? Tell me what you're thinking.'

'I need to speak to Cathy,' David said.

'She isn't here,' Saul said.

New fear stabbed at David. 'Have you seen her this morning?'

'I saw her,' Saul said. 'She was fine, you don't have to worry about her. She went running.'

'She didn't go to work?'

Mildred had left the room, but now she was back in the doorway, alarmed by the expression on his face, the intensity of his eyes, the hawk nose seeming to jut more sharply as he listened.

'No,' Saul said, 'but she said she'd be going in to thank the guys for what they did last night.'

'Oh, dear God,' David said.

'What?' Saul paused. 'Dad, *what*?'

'OK,' David said. 'Son, I want you to stay home and call Cathy and tell her she is *not* to go to the café.'

'Why not?' Saul was bewildered.

'Just *tell* her she must not go near those people.' David was sharp, clear. 'I have to make a call. You stay there, try to reach Cathy, tell her to phone Sergeant Alvarez at the station right away.'

He cut off his son, his hands trembling as he made the new call, and he looked across at Mildred, grateful for her silence, for her realization that he needed to act first, fall apart later.

Alvarez took his call swiftly, listened, absorbed.

'Jesus,' he said after a moment, softly.

'Oh, my God,' David said. 'You think I'm right.'

'I guess I do,' Alvarez said. 'You said Saul is

365

trying to reach Cathy?'

'As we speak.'

'Hold on, please.'

David waited.

'OK, Dr Becket.' Alvarez was back. 'Cathy's already on the phone, she's OK, and we're bringing her in to the station.'

'Thank God,' David said, relieved.

And then he remembered that Sam and Grace were still missing.

ONE HUNDRED AND SIX

'Oh my God, Sam,' Grace said. 'Look at the wall.'

He followed her gaze to the wall to her left, the one with the screen.

Took it in for a moment, and then, in his flat-test deadpan, said:

'Whaddya know, dinner *and* the movies.'

'It's us in the café, isn't it?' Grace said.

She knew that because she was wearing the blouse she'd only ever worn once previously, a silky ice-blue in reality, distinctive even in black-and-white.

And anyway, it made sense to her now.

She felt sick, felt like screaming, but she wouldn't do that to Sam.

Wouldn't do it for *them*.

Sam stood up, trying to spot anything he might

366

have missed embedded in the padding on the wall to his right, maybe something as tiny as one of those new pico projectors he'd read about, and he wouldn't have picked Dooley as a hi-tech man, but then he hadn't picked him as a god-damned monster either, and he'd always been highly organized at the café.

He could hear a low hum, but there was nothing visible.

The series of clips played over and over in a loop: the two of them enjoying the 'special' evening that Dooley and Simone had helped Cathy set up. The hidden camera – and now Sam wondered where the hell that had been – zooming in on their closeness, the moments when their eyes met and when they touched, and though neither of them were big on public displays, they did like to hold hands, to lean close and, now and then, to brush cheeks.

It was all there now on the screen on the wall, real up-close-and-personal, silently repeating, and Sam imagined this was what the other couples had endured, tried to analyze, rather than watch, and was it that, was it the closeness that *they* hated about couples? Though he'd seen tenderness between Dooley and Simone; they'd appeared to have feelings for each other, had not seemed obviously emotionally stunted. So what *was* their particular shtick, their problem with happy couples?

If this had turned out to be a solo killer, they might have been examining the triad theory – neurological problems, perhaps caused by disease or injury, paranoid thinking and a history

367

of abuse; nature, nurture, neurology – but with a *pair* of monsters like these...

He tried thinking back to other 'team' killers, but the list he'd brought to the squad meeting two Sundays ago had been so long that now it felt like a jumble of horror in his head. There were files and books crammed with homicidal histories of friends, married couples, mothers and sons, siblings, strangers thrown together, all kinds of killing partnerships fed by drugs or greed or lust or mutual insanity, or sheer, unadulterated evil.

'Sam?'

Grace's voice was soft, gentle, as if she realized that his thoughts were too much for him, as if she wanted to stop them for a little while, to heal him.

'Yes,' he said.

'Let's talk for a bit, about good times, while we still can. Is that OK?'

He felt something in his chest, a sensation like a fiery ball of love, so real and solid and hot that he thought it might be able to squeeze out everything else for a little while.

So he let it, sat down again.

'That's more than OK, Gracie,' he said.

'We could start with the cruise,' she said, 'and work back.'

'The cruise *until* the last night,' Sam said.

Because if they were going to play this game, then he'd be damned if Jerome Cooper was going to destroy that too – though how in hell could he have insinuated himself into their vacation right before *this*? Or could it be that

Dooley and Simone were behind that, too? Might they have known that even the most inconclusive evidence of Cal the Hater's survival would have been like a direct hit to their Achilles heels?

'Come on, Sam,' Grace said.

'Yes,' he said. 'I'm with you.'

'It was the best present anyone could have been given,' she said.

'Not nearly as much as you deserve,' Sam told her.

'I don't need anything except you,' she said. 'And our family.'

'I'm sorry,' he said, not able to shift the thought. 'I have to ask you. Do you think they could have been behind what happened on the ship?'

'It comes to mind,' Grace said. 'But I don't see how.'

Sam wondered if they'd ever find out.

'Hey,' she said, gently. 'Look at the movie. That's a nice memory, in spite of them.' She paused. 'I'll bet they don't want us to enjoy looking at it.'

'They can go to hell,' Sam said.

'I expect they will,' Grace said.

ONE HUNDRED AND SEVEN

'Just to let you know,' Mary Cutter told David on the phone, 'that Cathy's safe here with us, talking to Beth Riley and Sergeant Alvarez.'

'Is she OK?' David asked.

'She's very shocked,' Cutter said, 'but she's holding up well.'

That sounded like Cathy, he thought, except at what point did a young person reach the end of their rope? When did too much finally become just that?

'Has she been able to help?' he asked.

'Right now,' Cutter said, 'every single thing she can share with us is bound to help, Dr Becket.'

David steeled himself.

'Do you have any idea where they are yet?' He paused. 'Truth, please.'

'Not yet,' Mary Cutter replied. 'But I'm sure we will.'

'I'd like to come down there,' David said.

'Best to stay home, Dr Becket,' the detective said. 'When Cathy's done here, we'll give her a ride either back home or to your house, as she chooses – so long as she's not alone.'

'Please tell her to come here,' David said.

'Will do,' Cutter said.

They'd caught a small break shortly before Cathy's arrival at the station from one of the witches, dragged unwillingly from anonymity by Beth Riley's ongoing and unrelenting pursuit of Allison Moore.

The witch in question, a twenty-eight-year-old sales assistant named Marcia Keaton, small, round-cheeked and bright-eyed, a physical model of wholesomeness, had told Riley and Alvarez that as she and her pals had been leaving the old gallery, they'd noticed a dark blue van with two people in it – possibly a man and a woman, though she said she couldn't be certain – waiting near the corner of 81st Street and Collins.

'It freaked me out,' Keaton had told them, 'because I thought they might be watching us, and it was still dark, but the licence plate was under a street light, and I don't know why I wrote it down, but—'

'You have it with you?' Riley had jumped on it, though she knew the plates were probably stolen, same as those on the van recorded in Elizabeth Price's road.

'I kept it in my wallet.' Marcia Keaton had paused. 'Is it going to make this trespass crap go away?'

'If you don't give us the number,' Alvarez had told her, 'you'll have a whole lot worse than trespass charges to worry about.'

The details were being put through the database now.

ONE HUNDRED AND EIGHT

The movie on the wall was still playing when they heard sounds.

Weird sounds.

Creaking, rolling.

Wheels, Sam thought, and realized that any second now he'd know if the killers had used a gurney or a dolly, and he wondered if he'd ever be able to tell Martinez or Riley...

More sounds. Keys jangling. One being inserted into a lock someplace in the darkness beyond the cage.

'Gracie,' he said softly. 'Stay strong.'

'I love you,' she said.

The key turned in the lock.

'I love you too,' Sam told her. 'We'll get through this.'

Light penetrated, shaped like a sliver of cake expanding to a wedge, partially blotted by someone entering, then shrinking back on itself again as the door closed.

Dark again.

The killers in here now, with them, the gurney still outside.

The voice came out of the darkness.

'We might have known.'

Dooley's voice.

'You two. Making the most of every moment.'

'Every *last* moment.'

Simone Regan's voice.

'Another perfect couple,' she added.

'*The* couple,' Dooley said.

ONE HUNDRED AND NINE

'So Cathy doesn't know where they live?' Martinez said. 'No addresses, so far as I know,' Saul said. 'Anyway, everything they've told her has probably been lies.'

Right after Saul had reached Cathy and told her to call Sergeant Alvarez, he'd called Beth Riley direct to find out all he could. She'd shared only the bare minimum, as he'd known she would, and he had made his next decision based on nothing more than instinct.

Martinez had to know.

Not that that had been Saul's only reason for coming to the house on Alton. For one thing, Saul had known he would not be able to take sitting around with his dad and Mildred and the baby, being told to wait and do nothing.

'We have to do something,' he said.

The real reason he'd come.

'Damned straight we do,' Martinez said.

'Riley says they're getting a warrant to search the café.'

'I'm not waiting for any search warrant,'

Martinez said.

Saul knew he'd come to the right man.

'So what, are we breaking in?' he asked.

'Not you,' Martinez said. 'Just me.'

'But you're still sick,' Saul said.

'You never heard of adrenalin?' Martinez said.

ONE HUNDRED AND TEN

The address at which the van seen by Marcia Keaton was registered was a fake.

At least, it was a real address, but the present occupants – who had never had a vehicle stolen – had lived there for over eighteen months. And the mail that had kept on coming for the previous residents after they'd moved in had been addressed to some other name which they could not now recall.

Except it had been Hispanic, they thought.

Nothing like Dooley or Regan.

No help at all, just distraction and a waste of time and manpower at a moment when one of their own and his wife were in mortal danger.

The BOLO – Be On the Lookout For – was still active for Jerome Cooper.

But the biggest hunt now going on in Miami Beach and beyond was for Matthew Dooley and Simone Regan – and their presumed captives, Samuel Lincoln Becket and Grace Lucca Becket.

ONE HUNDRED AND ELEVEN

'Why don't you come out and show your-selves?'

Sam's voice was loud and clear, and it was almost a relief to stop speaking softly, to let it rip – *almost* a relief, too, that the waiting was over.

He got to his feet again, tested the shackle on his ankle, but it and the chain held fast, and for an instant his mind went to his great-grand-father's great-grandfather, a slave who'd escap-ed from Georgia in the 1830s and made it to the Bahamas, and in memory of him, Sam stood a little straighter.

Their steps were rubber-soled, their breathing audible, and then their shapes loomed out of the blackness into the semi-light just outside the cage bars.

Both wore black tracksuits, their hands dark-gloved.

'I hope,' Dooley said, 'you're not too uncom-fortable.'

'No, we're just peachy,' Sam said.

Grace, who'd chosen not to stand, moved closer to the bars and wrapped her arms around her knees to limit her exposure, depriving them as well as she could of the satisfaction of seeing her nudity, but holding her head high.

'Could you please at least get something to cover my wife with?'

'We could,' Simone said.

'But we won't,' Dooley said.

Rage rose in Sam, but it was impotent and he knew it, so he took a breath, brought himself back under control. 'Why not?' he asked.

'Because it would spoil things,' Dooley said.

'Simone?' Grace said.

'I wouldn't bother trying to appeal to Simone,' Dooley told her. 'This is her fantasy, not mine.'

Grace felt bile rise, fought to master it, then asked the question uppermost in her mind, the one that mattered most.

'Are our children all right?'

'Of course they are,' Simone said. 'That's not what this is about, Grace.'

'We suppose,' Dooley said, 'you'd both like to understand.'

'A cop and a shrink,' Simone said. 'Stands to reason.'

'If you can spare the time,' Sam said.

'I wouldn't bother with sarcasm either,' Dooley told him.

'I'd very much like to understand,' Grace said. 'I'm very confused.'

'I expect you are,' Simone said.

'I thought...' Grace stopped.

'What?' Simone said. 'That I liked you?'

'Yes,' Grace said. 'You said as much, so I believed you.'

'I guess that makes me a liar.'

Grace was staring at her, struggling to reconcile this person with the capable, kindly woman in the Opera Café, with the weary daughter she'd taken to visit her sick mother. And she realized abruptly that she didn't even know the nature of her mother's illness, had assumed it was either a form of dementia or perhaps stroke, had not felt it her place to ask.

'What happened to you, Simone?' she asked now.

Psychologists seldom asked questions like that of their patients, but this was no consultation, and Grace found that she wanted, needed, to know, and maybe, in any case, dialogue might buy them a little more time.

'To make me do things like this?' Simone shrugged. 'I like it. It makes me feel alive.'

'Don't tell her anything you don't want to,' Dooley said.

Still protecting her, Sam registered. Not quite everything a lie then.

'I don't mind,' Simone said. 'After all, we know it's going to be over after this.'

'For them,' Dooley said. 'Not us.'

'Over for us too,' she said. 'At least for now.'

ONE HUNDRED AND TWELVE

Martinez and Saul were at the café.

Too late to break in.

Black-and-whites everywhere.

'Damn it,' Martinez said. 'Drive on.'

He was pissed as hell on one hand that the guys had beaten him to it, had thought they might focus on the Becket house first, but he had no business being surprised, and he guessed it proved the doc's point, proved that even mentally he was unfit for work – and it was fine that Sam and Grace's abduction had brought all hands on deck. Except Martinez badly needed to help, to do something.

Not here.

He was glad now that Saul had insisted on driving, and Martinez had griped when he'd seen the old Dodge pick-up Saul was using for business, but now he figured that at least the guys were less likely to spot him than in his own car.

The last thing he wanted was to be stopped, ordered to go home.

'So what do we do now?' Saul asked.

'Just drive,' Martinez said. 'Give me time to think.'

Except his brain was still mush, home probably the only place he was fit for.

Not going there yet, no way.

Over his dead body.

ONE HUNDRED AND THIRTEEN

'How long have you been together?' Sam asked.

'A long time now,' Dooley said.

Over on the screen on the wall, the silent movie still played, casting shadows over the cage, and Sam had sat down again because it was less confrontational plus he was closer to Grace, and she'd gotten a dialogue going with them, and this was the right way, the only way to go.

'Where did you meet?' Grace asked.

It was hard for her to believe she could go on formulating questions and controlling responses even now, yet if the nakedness was about power, then continuing this was more than just a means to gain information or even of delaying tactics.

It was a measure of defiance, for now all they had.

And it seemed, at least for the time being, that the killers wanted to talk.

'We both worked in a restaurant over in Naples,' Dooley answered. 'I found Simone in a storeroom late one night after everyone else had gone home. She was hurting herself. Cutting herself with a knife.' He paused. 'That's what they'd done to her.'

'Who?' Grace asked, and it seemed that Dooley, more than Simone, was the one choosing to talk, either because he wanted to unload or just because it suited him. 'That's what *who* did to her?'

'The perfect couple,' Dooley answered. 'Celine and Dougie Regan. Her wonderful parents.'

'They were very gifted,' Simone said. 'They ran their own restaurant in Sarasota. Everyone thought they were the most talented, charming couple, and they loved each other and they were beautiful too.'

'So beautiful they used to torture their kid,' Dooley said.

'Torture,' Simone said, 'is a strong word.'

'They used to scald her, burn her,' Dooley said. 'Sometimes they just hit her with pots or pans. They always did it together.'

'They hit me so hard once,' Simone said, 'I was in the hospital for a while.'

'Weren't they prosecuted?' Sam tried not to let cynicism leak into the words, though everything that came out of these two felt like lies to him now, and he wondered how far Alvarez and Riley and the squad had come, and so long as Cathy was OK and able to tell them, they'd know by now who had taken them.

'I didn't tell anyone they'd done it,' Simone said. 'No one would have believed me.'

'Why not?' Grace asked. 'I believe you.'

Simone made a scornful sound. 'I ran away instead. Took the bus to Naples and learnt to get by.'

'On work and dreams,' Dooley said, then looked at Grace. 'I expect you'd like to know what kind of dreams.'

'Only if Simone wants to tell me,' Grace said.

Sam knew she was playing their game with them, was aware she was being toyed with, and yet she was moving steadily on with it, and he was, as he'd so often been, filled with admiration for her.

'My, what a tactful shrink,' Dooley said. 'They're not all as patient as you.'

'I'd like to hear about Simone's dreams,' Sam said.

'She didn't want to tell me about them in the beginning,' Dooley said, 'but I was gentle with her, and she began opening up. She said if I really knew her thoughts I'd run, think she was crazy, but I told her that I had "thoughts" too – which was true, by the way, just in case you think I was using her – and I'd never found anyone I could talk to like I could to her.'

'He said we were meant to be,' Simone said.

'And wasn't I ever right?' Dooley said.

'You always are,' she said.

That tenderness again, perhaps for real, Sam acknowledged, yet now every to-and-fro between them made his flesh creep.

He faked a cough, used the small convulsive jolt of his body to take another yank at the chain.

'You pull away, big guy,' Dooley said. 'But I bought the strongest.'

'Can't blame a man for trying,' Sam said.

'Were you bored?' Simone asked suddenly, a

new sharpness to her tone. 'Were we boring you with my story?'

'I think you're right,' Dooley said to her.

He took two steps closer to the outer bars and Grace experienced a new rush of terror, felt he was going to do something now, enter the cage and punish Sam.

'I'm sorry,' she said.

'Wasn't you who faked the cough,' Dooley said.

Sam looked through the bars down at the other man's sneakers and found himself suddenly *willing* him to come inside, because if the sonofabitch came close enough for him to make a grab, he could maybe tackle him, bring him down.

'I wouldn't even think about it if I were you,' Simone said.

Neither Sam nor Grace spoke.

Dooley stayed right where he was, smiling.

'You need to take this woman seriously, guys,' he said.

Sam looked up at him, unblinking.

'Oh, we do,' he said.

ONE HUNDRED AND FOURTEEN

Martinez and Saul sat in the pick-up outside Saul's apartment building.

'What do we do now?' Saul asked.

He could feel the cracks beginning to show.

The agony of what had already happened.

What still might. What might be happening even as they sat here.

Useless.

The loss of Teté came back again.

He'd loved her, and he loved Grace, but his big brother was the lion of his life.

'What do we *do*?' he asked again.

'I do the only thing I can,' Martinez said, feeling the young man's pain. 'Go join the squad, make damned sure we find them fast.'

'What if they won't let you?' Saul said.

'They'll let me,' Martinez said.

Saul looked at him and believed him.

'You doing OK?' he asked.

'I'll only be doing OK,' Martinez said, 'when we get Sam and Grace back home where they belong.'

ONE HUNDRED AND FIFTEEN

'Simone's mother's in a nursing home,' Cathy said suddenly. She was still with Beth Riley in the Violent Crimes office.

Everyone else out on the streets looking, without a clue where *to* look, and Riley was itching to be out there too, but Alvarez had ordered her to stick with Cathy in case there was one still-buried piece of information left to drain from the young woman.

And now, abruptly, here it was.

Might be, Riley told herself.

'Grace drove her there only last...' Cathy shut her eyes, fought to remember, dug it up. 'Last Monday,' she said. 'Simone was having one of her migraines.'

'She gets bad migraines?' Riley made a note.

Cathy nodded. 'Or she says she does.' She put one hand over her eyes for a moment, trying to drag up details. 'Grace came to the café Monday afternoon – she'd brought flowers to thank them for this dinner they'd helped me make for them a few days before, and I told Grace that Simone's car was in the workshop—'

'What car does she drive?'

'I don't remember, I hardly ever saw it.' Cathy shook her head, mad at herself. 'It was red, I know that, and small.' She shut her eyes again. 'Two doors. I can't tell you the make, I'm sorry.'

'You know which workshop she used?' Riley asked.

'No.' Cathy clenched her right hand, pounded it suddenly on her thigh. 'God, I'm worse than useless.'

'You're doing great,' Riley told her. 'Go on about that afternoon.'

Cathy took a breath, got back on track. 'Grace told me later that the home seemed nice, that a woman at reception said Simone was a wonderful daughter.' Her mouth compressed bitterly. 'Wonderful.'

'Did Grace tell you the name of the home?'

'No, but Simone told me it was off Indian Creek Drive, just a few blocks south from the café.'

'But she never told you the name?'

'Not that I remember.' Cathy paused. 'Grace might have told Mildred, though, because she was minding Joshua that day, so she'd have been home when Grace got back.'

Riley was already keying in David Becket's number.

She had the name less than three minutes later.

'It was the James L. Burridge Care Home,' Mildred said. 'I asked Grace for the name because it sounded like a nice place, and you never know when you might hear of someone in need.'

'Burridge,' Riley said. 'You're sure, Ms Bleeker?'

'I'm sure,' Mildred said. 'I hope it helps.'

Alvarez came in as Riley was printing out the details.

'Cathy's given us something,' she told him, grabbing the printout from the machine. 'Regan's mother's nursing home.'

'Let's go,' he said.

Cathy was on her feet. 'Can I come along?'

'Afraid not,' Alvarez said.

'We'll get you taken to Dr Becket's,' Riley said.

'That's just going to be a waste of your time,' Cathy said, 'and anyway, I don't want to sit at David's pretending not to be going crazy.'

'I'm sure he could use your company,' Riley said.

They were out of the office, already on the stairs, Alvarez ahead and moving fast.

'He has Mildred and Saul and Joshua,' Cathy

said. 'And you never know, I might remember something else.'

'OK,' Alvarez said, 'you can come, but I need your word you'll keep your mouth shut at the nursing home, or we'll lock you in the car.'

'That'd be against the law,' Cathy said.

'So sue us,' Riley said.

ONE HUNDRED AND SIXTEEN

Grace was shivering, mad at herself for showing weakness, but finding it beyond her control.

'Please.' Sam tried again. 'Grace is really cold. Couldn't you please just find something to cover her with?'

'If you're concerned about her catching a chill,' Simone said, 'I wouldn't be.'

'Oh, what the hell,' Dooley said.

A wisp of humanity left in him, Sam wondered, maybe even of shame.

And *maybe*, with that, a scrap of hope for them.

Dooley stepped away back into the dark beyond the scope of the light bulb, came back holding something.

He took a key from a pocket in his tracksuit.

'Are you sure?' Simone asked.

'Won't make any difference to us now,' Dooley said.

Sam saw her shrug, and maybe Regan did

defer to him, even if Dooley had said this was her 'fantasy', and Sam logged that mentally, getting down every tiny detail that might possibly help them get out of this mess alive.

The cage gate opened and Dooley stepped inside.

The thing in his left hand was a filthy white towel.

He turned to Simone, nodded to her, and she followed him through.

'You give it to her,' Dooley said, and passed her the towel.

And was there a little propriety in that, Sam wondered, and might their 'friendship', monstrous sham as it was, nonetheless be making this a little less easy for Dooley? Maybe, despite himself, the man felt some respect for Grace, or maybe some of his fondness for Cathy had been real. And Sam was trying not to think about Cathy and what this was going to do to her, though it was *he* who'd brought these people into their lives, not her...

Simone threw the towel on to Grace's knees, stepped quickly back.

More nervy now, Sam thought, than she had been outside the cage, and the soft green of her eyes looked opaque now.

'Thank you.' Grace covered her breasts with the towel, tucked it beneath her armpits like a bath towel, told herself not to think what it might have wiped up before, maybe blood or...

Stop.

'Thank you,' Sam said too.

'What happened to your father?' Grace asked

Simone. 'If you don't mind talking about him.'

'He died.'

Sam wanted to know how, wondered if the pair had maybe murdered the bastard, knew better than to ask, though clearly they had not done the obvious, had not made Regan's parents their first 'couple'.

'Is that when your mother came down to Miami?' Grace asked.

'Oh yes,' Simone said. 'When she needed looking after.'

'And you've done that for her,' Grace said, keeping her tone neutral.

'More than the bitch deserved,' Dooley said.

'What happened to her?' Grace asked.

'She has vascular dementia,' Simone said.

Grace waited a moment.

'I'd like,' she said, carefully, 'to hear about your dreams.'

Still holding on to the small truce, Sam realized, then saw Regan glance at Dooley, clearly deferring to him now.

'Simone's dreams,' Dooley said, 'were all about punishing her parents.'

'And did you,' Sam asked Simone, 'punish them?'

Better for the question to come from him, safer for Grace, he hoped.

Simone said nothing, leaned back against the outer bars of the cage.

'She never had the chance,' Dooley answered for her. 'The old man was dead and then Celine got sick, so Simone had to *adapt*.'

'There were so many perfect couples,' Simone

said. 'I hated them all.'

'The trouble was,' Dooley took over again, 'she hated herself too for feeling that way, felt she had to be bad to want to harm them, which was why she'd been self-harming instead.'

Classic stuff, Sam thought, maybe just a little too textbook, and he risked a glance at Grace and felt that she *was* buying it, and if it was good enough for her...

Besides, it was all they had.

'And you helped her move on?' Grace asked Dooley.

'Matt made me see that making my dreams happen for *real* was the only way I was ever going to break free,' Simone said.

'And was he right?' Grace asked. 'Has it helped you?'

'Matt helped me see it was what I was meant to do.' Simone denied her a direct answer. 'He told me I wasn't a bad person at all, because he hated those kinds of people too, hated their self-righteousness, their vanity.'

Sociopaths, in other words, Sam thought. A pair of goddamned sociopaths stumbling across one another, feeding off each other. Regan in part a victim, first of her parents, then of Dooley's delight in finding someone he could control, someone so needy, and Sam had come upon those types before, had read volumes about them.

And the game that these two had been playing must have been challenging, and maybe Dooley thrived on that, too, maybe that was why they'd conducted their terror campaign in such a

389

bizarre way – and game-playing had formed a basic part of the MO of so many serial killers.

'I get the display choices now,' Sam said.

'Bully for you,' Dooley said.

'Very smart,' Sam said. 'The restaurant stuff laid down with the false art trail.'

'We liked it,' Simone said.

'But *why* the display?' Grace asked.

'Because there's no point making any kind of protest,' Dooley said, 'unless people are going to know about it. No point killing people and just digging a hole.' He smiled at Grace. 'No point unless someone *gets* it, right?'

'And the glue?' Sam asked, and he thought he knew the answer, but the longer they were prepared to go on talking, the better.

'Together forever,' Simone answered.

'Like the song,' Dooley said.

'Those touchy-feely, happy, smug couples. We talked about it, and we figured it ought to be just the way they'd like to end their days.'

Grace felt sick again.

She wondered just how they would be joined together if no one came in time.

Skin, presumably. Brown to white.

And maybe Simone wasn't altogether wrong in what she had just said, because she would rather be holding Sam's hand forever than live without him.

Except what about Joshua?

She swallowed down the agony, mustered a smile for Sam, then realized it might be held against them.

Careful.

390

ONE HUNDRED AND SEVENTEEN

Celine Regan was in no condition to be interviewed.

Norman Gardner, the manager of the home, had told Alvarez as much right away, but had, after some persuasion, allowed Beth Riley to see for herself.

She came downstairs after less than ten minutes.

'Hopeless,' she said.

Gardner had also handed over the two contact phone numbers that Simone Regan had entrusted to them. One the number of the Opera Café. The other her cell phone.

No reply on that, nor voicemail, and pinpointing current locations of cells was, in reality, nowhere near as miraculously rapid as it appeared to be in movies. All kinds of hoops to be jumped through first, court orders to allow cell trackers being even slower to obtain than search warrants.

Besides which, no one was betting on Simone using that phone right now.

Cathy, silent until now, asked the next question before Alvarez or Riley.

'Where did Mrs Regan live before she came here?'

'I don't have that information to hand,' Norman Gardner told her, then turned to Alvarez. 'And even if I did, it would be a huge breach of confidentiality for me to give it to you.'

'What about her doctor?' Riley asked. 'He might have it.'

'Not necessarily,' Gardner said, 'since the lady's been here a long time.' He paused. 'And he'll very likely have the same issues.'

'We'll try him anyway,' Alvarez said.

'Quickly,' Cathy said. 'Please.'

'I'll get you the number,' Gardner said.

ONE HUNDRED AND EIGHTEEN

Coming to the end of question time, Sam suspected.

Simone was still leaning against the bars, but Dooley had started moving around just inside the cage. No perceptible impatience in him yet, but Sam knew there had to be a limit on how much *conversation* these two would permit.

He doubted if the Eastermans or the others had been granted these 'privileges' before dying, and he only hoped it had been quick for them, had a better understanding than before of the terror they must have endured.

'What about the couples you chose?' he asked.

'Customers,' Simone answered simply.

'So what, just happy people who came in to

the café?' It was hard for Grace not to load that question with the loathing she felt, almost impossible to grasp such random cruelty.

'That's about it,' Dooley said. 'I let Simone do the choosing.'

Jess Kowalski came into Sam's mind, what Martinez had said about her liking the fact that she had control over her rats.

This was another control thing, all the way down the chain. Dooley in charge of Simone, giving her his blessing, letting her choose their prey, then the pair of them exerting ultimate power over the victims.

Us now.

'It had to be customers who came when Cathy wasn't working,' Sam said, knowing that had to be true since otherwise she'd have seen their photographs in the media and been one of the first to put it together.

Putting herself in even greater danger than she had already, unwittingly, been in.

'Except in our case,' Grace said.

Dooley nodded. 'Different in your case.'

'Not so different,' Simone said. 'We heard more from Cathy about Grace and Sam, the greatest couple in the world, than we ever heard about any of the others.'

'And I was working the case,' Sam said.

'Sure,' Dooley said. 'Which made you the most likely person to track us down, given enough time.' He shrugged. 'Not that you were doing so great.'

'But Matt said it made you the obvious final choice for Miami,' Simone said.

'Are you planning to move on?' Sam asked.

'Don't suppose we'll have much choice,' Dooley said. 'After you guys.'

ONE HUNDRED AND NINETEEN

Celine Regan's personal physician, Dr Richard Massey, was in bed with the flu, according to his housekeeper, Maria Rodriguez, who was refusing to wake him because she said he needed his rest.

Alvarez wasted no more time, called Tom Kennedy, who got right on the phone to Rodriguez.

'Either you get Dr Massey on the line right now, ma'am,' the Captain told her, 'or we'll hit the doc *and* you with a subpoena, and what that means, in case you don't understand me, is if you don't do as you're told you could go to jail.' He paused. *'Prisión. La cárcel.'*

'For me?' Maria Rodriguez was aghast.

'Get the doctor *now*, ma'am.'

Less than three minutes later, the physician was on the phone, apologetic and plainly pissed with his housekeeper for making the police wait.

'I know I have that address on file,' Massey told Kennedy, 'though Mrs Regan's been at the Burridge for a while, so her house could have been sold or rented.' He hesitated. 'I remember she did go walkabout though a few months back,

394

and I don't know where she went to hole up.'

'Would she still have remembered back then where she'd lived before?' Kennedy asked.

'She might have,' Massey said.

'Did she come back of her own accord?'

'Her daughter brought her back. I'm afraid Mrs Regan was never the same again after that. I had to come in to see her several times during that period to calm her down, and she was ex-remely confused.'

'In what sense?' Kennedy asked.

'She seemed obsessed about being locked in a cage,' Massey said. 'She said her daughter kept her locked up when she was bad, which we knew was the dementia talking, because Simone was highly thought of at the Burridge.'

'We need that address,' Tom Kennedy said.

'It's in my office,' the doctor said. 'I'd need to—'

'We need that *now*, please,' Kennedy told him. 'The lives of two fine people are depending on you, Dr Massey.'

Not the Captain for nothing.

ONE HUNDRED AND TWENTY

Grace was shivering again.

She hated herself for it, but it was a reaction she could do nothing about, and she needed to pee, too, but for now she thought she'd die before she'd do that in front of them.

And maybe she would.

At least Joshua would still have their wonderful family, and he was young enough to grow up scarcely aware of missing them.

But not Cathy.

Like Sam, Grace could not bear to think about what this would do to her.

There had been no peace in that young woman's life, no real peace for any length of time since childhood, and thinking about her, Grace knew that she would, given the chance, claw these people's eyes out with her bare hands if it helped.

'My wife's still cold,' Sam said.

'I'm sorry about that,' Dooley said.

His right hand moved to his back pocket.

Drew out a medium-sized knife sheathed in leather.

Not a goddamned sword or athamé, Sam registered, though he couldn't see the blade – didn't *want* to see it – but the cop in him was remembering the time-wasting diversion that Beatty and Moore and their sick witches crap had lured him and Riley into.

Though it wasn't their fault he hadn't seen what had been under his nose all the time. *His* fault, as a detective and as a father and husband, for taking these bastards at face value, and if anyone ought to have known better...

He stared at the sheathed knife, thought of the other victims and their wounds. Looked at Grace and knew that he could not bear it, not for her.

'For the love of God,' he said to Dooley.

'God doesn't love us,' Simone said.

'Where do you plan to leave us?' Grace's voice was husky, her mouth and throat dry. 'You must have worked it out.'

'Of course,' Dooley said.

'I'm trying to think what's left,' Sam said. 'I don't think they make cooking pots our size, even as exhibits, though maybe you could have found a couple of old movie props.'

'Much simpler,' Dooley said. 'Our solution.'

'And not too far away,' Simone added.

Running out of time.

'I have a couple more questions,' Sam said. 'I mean, what difference to you if this is almost finished?'

'Try us,' Dooley said.

'How did you work it with the second couple? I get that you delivered dinner to Duprez's apartment, but then what?'

'Good question.' Dooley seemed satisfied. 'I like that you haven't worked it all out. Means we did a good job.' He shrugged. 'We'd expected

Price to stay the night, of course, but we had a back-up plan in case she left before she fell asleep.'

'I followed her home in the van.' Simone was beginning to show signs of impatience, a wish to be done with them. 'It wasn't hard because she was out on her feet, so I took her in her garage, got her inside the house and waited.'

'And you waited for Duprez to fall asleep...' Sam looked at Dooley. 'Or maybe you told him you'd come back to collect your dishes and he let you in.'

'He sure did, and I told him to take it easy while I cleaned up, and he offered me a tip and told me I was a nice guy, even apologized for falling asleep.'

'And when you'd done?' Sam was feeding the other man's vanity now – anything for more time, and besides, the cop in him still wanted the facts. 'You got him down to the garage, into his car.'

Dooley nodded. 'That guy saw me driving out, right? But I'm guessing he didn't give you a description.'

'Afraid not,' Sam said.

'It's time,' Simone said to Dooley.

Sam's pulse kicked up a gear. 'Just a little more,' he said. 'Call it a courtesy, guys.' He paused. 'Was Duprez in the passenger seat, or did you stash him in the trunk?'

'In the trunk,' Dooley said. 'No one was in the garage, which made it easier, though if someone had seen us I'd just have said the poor bastard was sick.'

'So you drove over to Elizabeth's house,' Sam said.

'We moved her car out of her garage,' Simone came in briskly. 'Put the van in there instead, backed the BMW into the driveway, got Duprez out of the trunk into the van, finished the clean-up inside, got her into the van, drove her car back into the garage, end of story.'

'The rest all happened here,' Dooley said.

He stroked the knife handle.

Running out of time *fast*.

'What about the sand?' Sam asked, changing tack.

Dooley looked gratified again. 'I didn't get the idea till number two, but I'll bet it had your people going.'

'Sure did,' Sam said. 'One more question.'

'No more questions,' Dooley said.

'Is it a hospital gurney you use, or a dolly or what?'

'A gurney,' Dooley said. 'Would you like to see it?'

'I would,' Sam said.

'Too bad,' Simone said.

She nodded at Dooley.

Who unsheathed the knife.

ONE HUNDRED AND TWENTY-ONE

They were on the move.

Cathy left behind, placed almost forcibly in a black-and-white and dispatched – 'like a parcel', she'd complained vehemently – to Golden Beach to sit it out with David and the rest.

Not that she did not understand the necessity.

What mattered to her was that they *were* on their way at last.

Every available unit, along with a SWAT team, was now heading toward an address on East Meridian Avenue in North Miami, where it was strongly believed that a Miami Beach Police Department detective and his psychologist wife were being held against their will, and were at imminent risk of being murdered by the two prime suspects in the so-called 'Couples' case.

Extreme caution was being used.

ONE HUNDRED AND TWENTY-TWO

Martinez was on his way to East Meridian too.

He'd never intended to go to the station – that had just been a ploy to get Saul off his back – because he'd known full well no one would have let a sick man rejoin the squad.

So instead he'd been sitting in his own car listening in on the radio and devising a kind of a plan. And he knew that physically he was barely up to sitting in his backyard, let alone digging out the old SWAT black BDUs he'd gotten himself the one time he'd ever agreed to go to a costume party. Let *alone* strapping on his Glock and driving himself to a major crime scene. But Sam and Grace were in the greatest imaginable danger, and Alejandro Martinez's adrenalin was pumping harder than ever.

Saul had wanted to come to the station.

'If you come, too, they sure as hell won't let me work the case,' Martinez had told the younger man.

'And you think I'd get in the way,' Saul had said.

A realist, like his father, gone north now to Golden Beach, like Cathy. To wait with their family and maybe say a few prayers.

Martinez wasn't sure what exactly he was on

his way to, or what the hell he was going to do when he got there.

Watch and wait while the *real* cops did their stuff and got it right, he hoped with all his soul.

But if they did not, and if there was one more step that could be taken, if there was any damned thing he could do, he was going to *do* it.

And nothing much less than a bullet was going to stop him.

ONE HUNDRED AND TWENTY-THREE

Sam could see the blade of the knife now.

Single-edged, not double. Probably a cook's knife from the café.

Like it made a goddamned difference.

He looked at Grace, wanting, more than anything, to hold her, saw in her beautiful blue eyes the same desperate need reflected back at him.

And then he turned back to Dooley.

'You never answered the question about what you're planning to do with us.'

'Give it up,' Dooley said.

'Refrigerator,' Grace said suddenly.

Like it was a quiz show.

'Close,' Simone said.

'Freezer?' Sam said.

'Give the man a prize,' Dooley said.

'One more,' Sam said. 'Last one.'

'No more,' Dooley said.

The knife blade glinted dully in the light from above.

'It's OK, Matt,' Simone said. 'I'd like to hear it.'

Sam looked at Grace again, praying for her continued strength. Loving her more than ever, which he would have thought impossible. Seeing the love returned, and he supposed it ought to be enough, that he ought to be grateful for all that he'd had, and he *was*, but he was human and he was greedy.

And he wanted more.

'"Together forever", you said.' His gut was clenched with tension. 'About the glue.'

'He wants to know which part of them we're going to join,' Simone said.

She was enjoying the moment, plain to see.

'Easy enough to guess,' Dooley said, 'in your case.'

Grace knew she'd been right.

'Skin,' she said.

'And a prize for the lady,' Dooley said.

'How about one last request?' Sam tried.

'Depends what it is,' Dooley said.

'I'd like to hold my wife one last time.'

'Sure you would,' Dooley said.

'Except we'd have to unshackle you,' Simone said, 'and then you'd jump us like the big macho cop you are, and then things would get ugly.'

'Sorry,' Dooley said. 'Simone always gets the last word.'

'Thank you,' Simone said.

ONE HUNDRED AND TWENTY-FOUR

Everyone was in position, including marksmen and spotters on the neighbouring roofs on both sides of the house in question.

Most of the street's residents had been moved out, but not before a woman from the house to the left of the Regan home, one Miriam Guam, had swiftly and competently helped give the squad a reasonable picture of where they now believed the killers were probably holding the Beckets.

Five houses in a row on the street had screened in lanai enclosures, all constructed at the same time, except that work had been carried out about eighteen months ago on the Regan property, erecting white-painted cinder block walls around their lanai.

Miriam Guam had been shown photographs of Simone and Dooley.

'He's one of the builders,' she'd said right away. 'And she's the daughter.'

One of the squad's problems, so far as they'd been able to ascertain, was that the enclosure's door was the only potentially 'clean' entry point, and they were going to have to reach that point via the backyard, securing the house itself before they made their move.

The likelihood was that they were either too late, or almost out of time.

Final orders were being given by SWAT commander Thomas G. Grove.

There was no possibility of a clear shot from outside.

So they were going to have to go in fast.

Now.

ONE HUNDRED AND TWENTY-FIVE

'Police! Put down your weapons *now*!'

The SWAT team, having made it through the empty house into the backyard unopposed and in almost perfect silence, stormed the door to the enclosure and pounded through, yelling and dazzling those inside with ultra-bright tactical lights.

Clear shots now at both the male and female suspect.

'Don't shoot!' Sam, half-blind, bellowed through the noise.

Because he'd seen Dooley drag Grace up on her feet, and now he had her pinned against his chest, holding the knife blade to her throat.

Blood already trickling from a wound.

'Do not shoot!' Sam yelled again. 'He has my *wife*!'

Grace stood motionless against Dooley, her ankle still shackled to the bars, her right hand still clutching the filthy towel against herself.

Sam's heart felt like it was almost out of his body.

Simone had fallen on her knees, her eyes fixed on Dooley's face.

Dooley's back was to the screen wall.

The movie still playing endlessly on it.

No one in the SWAT team looking at it, their eyes focused on their targets.

'You shoot Simone,' Dooley told them, 'and I cut this woman's throat for sure.'

'This is finished, Matt,' Sam said. 'You know it.'

'It isn't finished till I say so,' Dooley said, 'because I'm covered by this very nice, kind, almost-naked woman, and if anyone screws up and makes me kill her now, I'd guess her handsome buck-naked husband is going to make their life a living hell till the end of his days.'

'They can wait,' Sam said.

'For me to get tired, right?' Dooley shook his head. 'When I get tired, Simone can take over, and we can play this game for a long time yet.'

'What's the point?' Sam asked. 'It's going to end the same way.'

'The point,' Dooley said, 'is that it's our game, not yours.'

'For God's sake,' Sam said.

Trying with all his strength of will *not* to look at the screen behind the killer.

He'd seen the shadow move a few seconds ago, and he didn't know who the hell it was behind there, but instinct told him that whoever it was, they were Grace's best chance.

So long as they shot Dooley right through his goddamned head.

The shot sent blast ricochets through Sam's panicked brain.

Dooley stood still for one endless second.

The knife fell from his hand first.

And then he went down, Grace falling with him, but *alive.*

'Matt!' Simone flung herself at him, reached for the knife. *'Matt*!'

Sam couldn't count how many bullets hit her at the same instant.

He praised every last one of them.

ONE HUNDRED AND TWENTY-SIX

Between the cinder blocks and the old lanai screen wall, Alejandro Martinez – wearing the counterfeit SWAT battle dress uniform that had been good enough to get him through into the backyard with the rest of the pack, and was probably going to get him arrested before the day was through – was trembling more violently than when he'd still had the chills in Miami General.

Pure gut instinct had made him separate from the pack as they'd launched themselves straight ahead through the door of the enclosure, and no one had stopped him slipping into the narrow gap he'd spotted, with weird, flash-like clarity, to their right.

Miracle or all-time horror.

And if he didn't find out in the next two seconds if Sam and Grace were alive, he was going to puke, and then, maybe, shoot himself.

Two men were coming at him *now*: the real SWAT deal.

Martinez laid down his gun.

'Detective Martinez,' he identified himself. 'Miami Beach PD.'

'Holy Jesus,' Beth Riley's voice said from somewhere.

He squinted, thought he saw her shape a few feet behind the men.

'He's one of ours,' he heard Riley confirm.

'Did I do it?' His voice shook with the rest of him. 'Or did I screw it up?'

The guys backed away and Riley came to him, put her arms around him.

'Oh, dear God,' Martinez said, and began to weep.

'You did it, Al,' Riley told him. 'You saved them both.'

And Martinez turned from her just in time, puked against the wall, and passed out.

ONE HUNDRED AND TWENTY-SEVEN

March 6

Martinez, still off duty on sick leave and waiting for news of disciplinary action against him, called Sam at the office on Friday morning, his first full day back.

'I just got bad news,' he said. 'Jess is dead.'

'My God,' Sam said. 'What happened?'

Suicide in his mind before he could stop the thought.

'It was a fire,' Martinez told him. 'At her house.'

'Jesus,' Sam said. 'Al, I'm so sorry. Poor Jess.'

'I just came from talking with Fire and Rescue,' Martinez went on. 'They don't know for sure, but they think it might have been the fucking rats, snacking on wires, stripping the plastic coating, shorting it out. Little bastards electrocute themselves all the time, they told me.'

His friend sounded OK, but Sam knew better.

'Al, sit tight and I'll be there soon as I can.'

'Later,' Martinez told him. 'After work is soon enough.'

'You want me to bring beer or whiskey or both?' Sam asked.

'I already bought,' Martinez said.

He took a big slug of whiskey before he made his next call.

To Jess's parents in Cleveland.

Monika Kowalski answered, but handed the phone straight to her husband.

George Kowalski, the father who'd named his daughter after the movie star, was polite to Martinez, told him, in strongly accented English, that he was going to be coming to Miami to fly Jess's body home.

'Did you work with Jessica, Mr Martinez?' Kowalski asked.

'We were friends, sir,' Martinez said.

Because if Jess hadn't even mentioned his existence, he couldn't see any point telling the poor guy they'd been engaged to be married.

'I'm sorry not to know that,' George Kowalski said.

'It's not a problem, sir,' Martinez said. 'If there's anything I can do to help you with the arrangements, I hope you'll let me know.'

'The truth is,' Jessica's father went on, 'her mother and I hadn't heard from our daughter in over a year, and that was just a Christmas card.'

Martinez thought about all her stories of home, the tales of Thanksgiving and Christmas visits, the photos in which her mother had looked strained, but which had been the only hint that life back home hadn't always been straight out of a Frank Capra movie.

Except, of course, for the oddness of not wanting to share their happy news.

'You probably think we're bad parents,'

410

Kowalski said now.

'Why would I think such a thing?' Martinez said.

'Life with Jessica wasn't always easy,' the other man said. 'She was a needy child, but sometimes very hard to help or even to understand. But we loved her, and at least I can do this much for her.'

'A lot of people here werc very fond of Jess,' Martinez told him. 'She was a very good person, always helping others.'

'It's nice of you to say so,' Kowalski said.

The pause that followed felt awkward.

Martinez figured it was time to tell the poor guy goodbye.

And then Kowalski said: 'We always knew it would be too much for her.'

'What exactly, sir?' Martinez asked.

'Life,' Jess's father answered.

And put down the phone.

Sam and Grace came together at the end of the day.

'I hope you don't mind my coming along,' Grace said.

'Are you kidding me?' he said.

It was the first time Martinez had seen her since the abduction, and he noticed that she looked thinner than he'd ever seen her.

Sam, too, matter of fact.

'How are you guys holding up?' he asked.

'Pretty well,' Sam said. 'Glad to be alive.'

He winced soon as the word was out of his mouth.

411

Martinez grinned wryly. 'If I hadn't figured you would be glad, maybe I wouldn't have gone to the trouble of shooting the sonofabitch.'

They went out into the backyard with some beers and the extra large pizza – a Mediterranean from Master's, one of Martinez's favourites – that they'd picked up on the way.

They talked about the case for a while, about all the blind alleys and wasted lives, and Sam spoke a little about his own burden of guilt for not having glimpsed even a trace of the evil in Dooley and Regan, and then he stopped going down that route because it seemed to him an indulgence.

And anyway, they were here for Martinez and because of Jess.

He told them about his conversation with George Kowalski.

'I wanted to know what he meant by that last thing he said – about life being too much for her, but I figured it would have been like prying.' His eyes were filled with sorrow. 'I think I gave up the right to understand her when I told her to get lost.'

'I'm not sure that's true,' Grace said, gently.

'Me neither,' Sam said.

Martinez gave a sad, wry smile. 'It's how I feel. And I think Jess might prefer me to remember her the way she wanted me to. Before, you know?'

'Sure we do,' Sam said.

Martinez raised his bottle of Bud.

'To Jessie,' he said.

Sam raised his beer too. 'To Jess.'

412

'Sleep peacefully,' Grace said.

Martinez tilted his bottle, drank, wiped his mouth with his free hand.

His dark brown eyes were wet.

'Sleep sweet, pretty girl,' he said.

ONE HUNDRED AND TWENTY-EIGHT

March 14

Sam, taking the whole weekend off work, found the small padded package in their mailbox eight days later, on Saturday morning.

The handwriting on the white label was vaguely familiar.

No postmark.

It was addressed to 'Detective Samuel L. Becket'.

Sam lifted it higher in the sunlight, not exactly looking for wires, but finding that he had a *hunch* about the package, perhaps because he seldom received mail at home addressing him as 'detective'; and then he tore open a corner, saw that it was harmless, shook his head, smiling at his paranoia, and took it into the house.

Woody wagged his tail, hopeful of a walk.

'Soon,' Sam told him.

Grace was at the kitchen table, Joshua in his high chair.

'Anything good?' she asked.

'I don't know yet.'

413

Sam kissed the top of his son's head, then sat down at the table and opened the envelope fully, saw there was a CD inside, and withdrew it. Grace leaned across to look at it, saw that it was a recording of two ancient Beatles hits: *Love Me Do* and *PS I Love You.*

'Did you order that?' she asked.

And then she saw what Sam was looking at.

The words 'Love' had both been crossed through, and 'Hate' had been inserted, in the same handwriting as on the label, in the spaces above both titles.

Sam looked inside the envelope, saw a folded piece of paper.

He took it out carefully, unfolded it, held it by one corner.

They read it together.

Dear Sam,

It was good seeing you and Grace again.

Good to be back on the ocean too.

I guess you think that what happened to Ms Kowalski was an accident.

Think again.

I imagine you're asking yourself right now how I could have known about your partner's girlfriend before, and I guess you'll conclude that I could not. That there's no way I could have been following your lives so closely, that probably I just read about her dying in the local newspaper. And maybe that's so, and maybe it isn't.

But you'll never know for sure, will you?

Fire is an ugly way to go.

You may be surprised to know that I was happy to hear that you and Grace survived the 'Couples' killers.

I guess there are just some pleasures I'd rather keep for myself.

Yours ever,

Cal.